THE JHELUM BETRAYAL

SHAHJAHAN

Book Two

THE JHELUM BETRAYAL

NNIRAJ SRIVASTAVA

NU VOICE PRESS

First published by NU VOICE PRESS 2025
An imprint of Hubhawks Pvt. Ltd
www.nuvoicepress.com

This is a work of fiction. Space and time have been rearranged to suit the convenience of the book. Except for public figures, hotels, and institution names, any resemblance to persons living or dead or the real events are purely coincidental. The opinions expressed in the book are those of the characters, and should not be confused with that of the Author.

ISBN: 978-81-988726-0-9

Illustrations by Smita Niraj Srivastava

Typeset by Ashwani K. Sinha

Printed at Thomson Press (India) Ltd.

Published by Nu Voice Press

Dedicated to my darling wife, Smita ...

Our souls have travelled together through
Boundless Ages,
And Time, faithful as ever,
Shall keep us bound together, forever,
Joyfully blessed and entwined!

November 30th, 2023.

HINDUKUSH
KABUL
KASHMIR
INDEPENDENT TRIBES
QANDAHAR
SULAIMAN RANGE
MULTAN
LAHORE
PANIPAT
DELHI
HIMALAYAS
AJMER
ARAVALLI HILLS
AGRA
GWALIOR
OUDH
BIHAR
PATNA
ALLAHABAD
MALWA
PATAN
AHMADABAD
VINDHYA RANGE
KALANJAR
BENGAL
KHANDESH
Burhanpur
BERAR
GONDWANA
ORISSA
AHMADNAGAR
BIDAR
GOLCONDA
BIJAPUR
WESTERN GHATS
Indus R.
Ganges R.
Narmada R.
Tapti R.
Godavari R.
Krishna R.
Kaveri R.
Mahanadi
THE MUGHAL EMPIRE
1605

Family Tree

- Taimur the lame
  - Babur 1483-1530 r 1526-1530
    - Humayun 1508-1556 r 1530-1556
      - Akbar 1542-1605 r 1556-1605
        - Jahangir (Salim) 1569-1627 r 1605-1627
          - Khusrau
          - Parviz
          - Khurram (Shah Jahan) 1592-1666 1627-1658
            - Jahanara
            - Dara Shikoh
            - Shah Shuja
            - Roshanara
            - Aurangzeb Alamgir 1618-1707 r 1658-1707
              - Bahadur Shah 1643-1712 r 1707-1712
            - Murad
            - Gauharara
          - Shahrayar
          - Jahandar
        - Murad
        - Daniyal
      - Hakim

DRAMATIS PERSONAE

From the lost pages of history

Emperors:

Jalal-ud-Din Mohammed Akbar – 3rd Mughal Emperor; father of Prince Salim (Jahangir). The first of the Grand Moghuls.

Nur-ud-Din Mohammed Jahangir Padshah Ghazi – 4th Mughal Emperor. Salim Jahangir. Eldest son of Akbar. Father of Princes Khusrau, Pervez, Khurram, Jahandar and Shehrayar.

Shahab-ud-Din Mohammed Shahjahan Padshah Ghazi – Succeeded Emperor Jahangir. Favourite grandson of Emperor Akbar, famously christened 'Khurram' or 'Joy' by him. Builder of the Taj Mahal. Known as the Magnificent Mughal. Father of princes Dara Shikoh, Shah Shuja, Aurangzeb, and prince Murad.

Royal family:

Manmati Bai aka Jagat Gosain aka Taj Bibi Bilqis Makani – Rajput queen of emperor Jahangir. Daughter of Raja Uday Singh (Mota Raja) of Jodhpur. Commonly referred to as Jodh Bai- sister from Jodhpur. Mother of prince Khurram (Shahjahan).

Empress Nurjahan – Daughter of Ghiyas Ud Din Itmaduddaulah; widow of Sher Afghan; 25th wife of emperor Jahangir. One of the most influential royals of the Mughal empire.

Anarkali alias Zehrunnisa Begum urf Nadira – Kashmeri dancer; concubine in prince Salim's harem. Mysterious and enigmatic historical figure. She did exist!

Arjumand Bano, famously known as Mumtaz Mahal – The third, but the most beloved queen of prince Khurram (Shahjahan). The Taj Mahal is a monument dedicated to her.

Princess Purhunar Begum – Eldest daughter of emperor Shahjahan. born of Kandahari Begum. Lost in history

Princess Jahanara – The eldest child of emperor Shahjahan andempress Mumtaz Mahal. Loved and respected by all. Very influential in the Mughal empire.

Dara Shukoh – Eldest son and second child of emperor Shahjahan and Mumtaz Mahal. Sufi inclinations, open to all religions. Shahjahan's favourite child along with princess Jahanara.

Shah Shuja – Second son and third surviving child of Shahjahan and Mumtaz. Raised mostly by emperor Jahangir and empress Nurjahan.

Roshanara – Second daughter and fourth surviving child of Shahjahan and Mumtaz.

Aurangzeb – Third son and fifth surviving child of emperor Shahjahan and Mumtaz. Zealot, bigoted. The Mughal empire started disintegrating in his later years.

Murad Baksh – Fourth son and sixth surviving child of Shahjahan and Mumtaz. Brave, but foolish. Given to wine and women.

Gauharara – Third daughter and seventh surviving child of Shahjahan and Mumtaz. Mumtaz Mahal died giving birth to her. She was reviled by Shahjahan and relegated to the interiors of the Mughal seraglio. She was hardly ever presented before Shahjahan.

Royal Courtiers and Generals:

Mirza Raja Man Singh – Rajah Of Amber (Jaipur). Trusted general of emperor Akbar and one of his nine 'Navratnas.' Brother of prince Salim's Chief Queen Man Bai, and maternal uncle to prince Khusrau. One of the bulwarks of the Mughal empire.

Zamana Beg aka Mahabat Khan – Born Sagar Singh, son of Raja Uday Singh of Mewar. Close cohort and trusted general of prince Salim. Fearless warlord

Khubu Chishti alias Qutubuddin Koka – Grandson of Hazrat Salim Chishti. Foster brother and childhood friend of prince Salim. Trusted confidante.

AUTHOR'S NOTE & GRATITUDE

This sequel took me almost six years to finish—a lifetime for an author! In any relay race, the second and third legs are very important as they blend the beginning and a victorious end—so it is with *The Jhelum Betrayal* and the forthcoming *Emperor By Deceit,* trying to sew the past and the present together.

I am the unseen Khufiya Navees, hidden in the shrouds of centuries past. What you will read, is what I have seen and heard with my own senses. Who knows when my time will come, thus, the hurry to chronicle all that I know.

You may choose to believe what you may choose to believe, but remember, History does not beggar your beliefs. It is there, and will remain so, unchanged and hidden, till some storyteller comes along and shakes off the dust.

Each word that I have written is embedded in stone. Every word—true! You just have to scrape off the fossilized dust and blood from these gnarled, silent stones to verify my words.

This journey of a hundred and forty-six thousand days (four centuries!) would not have been possible were it not for the supportive hand of my wife, Smita, and my children—Devesh and Riticka. This story is as much theirs as mine!

I am grateful to the many Mughal emperors, courtiers, queens and concubines who entered my Soul to tell their stories. I have listened to them and narrated their tales to you, intrigued reader.

My journey is not yet complete—I must hurry, for the Mir Manzil waits for me at the next Dak Chowki.

Manzil Mubarak!

Nniraj Srivastava

Khufiya Navees

1200 Zat/ 300 Sowars

Cell: 76170-55999

Email: niraj.adelphi@gmail.com.

BAYAAN – i – MIR TOZAK

'Khushamdeed!' indeed to my pilgrimage through the tattered pages of lost and hidden history, through the lurking shadows of romance, lust and gore ...

I am not just the author, but an itinerant Mughal, swapped in Time! The words are mine—the characters and events, long gone, buried and forgotten ...

Smirk not at the seemingly fictional parts; History has a way of hiding between half- truths and stark facts.

Tarry not—the mighty Mughals have chosen you to witness their affairs.

Nniraj Srivastava
Itinerant~Waqia Navees
1200 Zat / 300 Sowars

18th September 2025 (22 Safar 1444 AH)

Dak Chowki: niraj.adelphi@gmail.com

THE STORY THUS FAR

Book 1: ***Daggers Of Treason***

Exactly one thousand years from the birth of Islam is born prince Khurram (05th January, 1592), grandson of Padshah Ghazi Akbar and son of Salim Jahangir.

Just two days later, in prince Jahangir's harem is born Firdaus to a Kashmiri concubine, Zehrunnisa, bearing an uncanny resemblance to the new born prince Khurram.

Akbar, to forestall harem intrigue and poisoning of a royal prince, banishes Zehrunnisa to the northernmost fringes of the empire with her infant son, Firdaus. Her name is changed to Anarkali ...

Prince Salim, devastated at this separation prepares to rebel, but is held back by the tethered might of the enormous Mughal army and the lascivious comfort of women and wine.

Prince Khurram becomes the adored grandson of Akbar, in whom the ageing emperor sees the resurrection and sustenance of a mighty Mughal empire.

A few years later, one of the adherents of prince Salim espies Anarkali in one of the Lahore bazaars, and the legendary romance is ignited once again. The turrets and sinister chambers of mammoth gateways become the rendezvous for this cursed pair of lovers. Moti, a gnarled old guard apprises the emperor of the romantic escapades, and Misery follows Death.

Akbar has Anarkali bricked alive, and her six-year-old son, Firdaus Salim Sultan, cut into pieces.

An embittered prince Salim embarks upon a warpath of rebellion and revenge, setting up a phony Court at Illahabas (Allahabad) and striking coins in his name as the new emperor.

Prince Khurram watches in disgust as his father rebels against his revered Shah Baba, who exercises utmost restraint in quelling his errant son's revolt. This rebellion by Salim Jahangir lays the foundation for future revolts as a matter of family recipe, and no future generation of Mughals will escape this curse.

Poisoned by his own, emperor Akbar dies, and the empire passes on to his famously debauch and opium infested son, Padshah Ghazi Nuruddin Mohammed Salim Jahangir.

History continues to write itself...

CHAPTER 1

PROLOGUE
DASTAAN- e -LAHORE
(THE LAHORE CHRONICLES)

Anarkali's Tomb,
Civil Secretariat Compound,
Lower Mall, Lahore.
17 January 2015.
11.00 a.m.

I stand staring at the beautiful sarcophagus of pure white marble.

A great one for crying, my eyes are easily swimming in tears as I gaze at the white marble slab, with exquisite etchings on its top and sides. I gaze too long and too hard, and it suddenly seems as if I can see the beautiful Anarkali with her large grey eyes lying stretched inside the sarcophagus.

I shake my head and look at Aamir, a school friend of my wife and my main contact in Pakistan. He seems to have read my mind, and quietly says, 'This is just her gravestone, displaced many years ago when this was converted into a church.' He turns around and points to a place in the absolute centre of the octagonal room, 'She lies there. Five feet under.'

I move to the spot, which is marked by plain brickwork. I cannot bring myself to step onto that three feet by six feet area in sheer deference to the lady underneath—she *was* the celestial love of Mirza Nur Ud Din Baig Mohammed Khan Salim Jahangir Padshah Ghazi, and finally rests here in eternal solitude.

Solitude? Maybe.

A government clerk, reeking of *attar*, hurries in with a few fat folders tucked under his arms. Ferreting a bunch of keys from his *achkan* he quickly deposits the folders in a small steel almirah and glares at us.

'*Mian*, don't keep standing there. She will not get up to welcome you.' The junior government officer remarks rudely.

'Wise guy,' mutters Aamir as we walk out into the cold bracing air of a winter morning.

We stop by a tea vendor, and I ask casually, 'Aamir, is it really Anarkali's tomb? Did she ever even live?'

The tea vendor squirts a generous amount of lemon juice, and putting his kettle down, loosens his woollen muffler and addresses me, 'Saheb ji, you have come to the right place. Anarkali does lie here ever since she was bricked in a wall by Badshah Akbar's orders.'

'You know, our taxi driver referred to this place as *Bhoot Bangla* while he was driving us over. Any idea, why?' I cannot help but ask.

There is a tender look in the old man's eyes as he answers, 'Anarkali was too sweet a person to become a ghoul and wander around this God-forsaken place. The only ghosts I have seen are the ones who haunt the main civil secretariat building looking for their lost pension files!'

He smiles at our laughter and suddenly draws my attention to a set of two dark grey pigeons sitting on a raised rim midway on the central dome.

'You see them? They are *Shehzade* Salim and his eternal consort, Anarkali. They are inseparable and you will always find them sitting here and cooing. At dusk, they will fly inside the central hall and spend the night there. She might rest within her grave with Salim, or he might travel to his own tomb in Shahdara, not so far away.'

I look at him speculatively and he beckons me towards the sepulchre once again. As we walk inside, he places a glass of tea in front of the rude clerk who grunts his annoyance.

He takes me close to the beautiful white marble gravestone, and explains, 'You see the fine engravings on the top and sides? These are the ninety names of Allah or His attributes engraved in Persian. And here, see here, is the couplet in Persian inscribed by a lovelorn Shehzade!'

'What does it say?'

He recites from his memory. 'It says, *"If I could behold the face of my beloved once more, I would thank Allah until the Day of Resurrection."*'

He bends down and points towards a squiggle which seems to be a signature in Persian. 'See Saheb! It is signed as *Majnun Salim Akbar*, meaning *'The Profoundly Enamoured, Salim, son of Akbar.'*

I shiver involuntarily, imagining the two pigeons coming in to roost here, and then slowly transforming into the star-crossed figures of prince Salim and Anarkali to find their resting place in this white gravestone.

I ask out of curiosity, 'When was this made?'

He points to some fine etchings on the marble, '1008 Hijri and 1024 Hijri.'

It corresponds. 1008 Hijri would mean 1599 AD, the year in which Anarkali was bricked alive, and 1024 Hijri would mean 1615 AD.

But why 1615 AD?

I turn to Niyamat, the tea seller, and ask him, 'Niyamat Saheb, why is the date mentioned to be 1615 AD? Do you think it would have taken prince Salim sixteen years to build a modest mausoleum like this? The Mughals were prolific builders, and honestly, this is not even close to their other creations in terms of finishing or beauty. They were fond of red sandstone and marble—this is just a brick, lime, and mortar edifice with a thick limestone coat.'

He answers petulantly, much to Aamir's amusement, 'Listen, *Janab*, till 1605 Badshah Akbar did not allow him to build anything. Prince Salim ordered the commencement in 1607, and then got infatuated with Nur Jahan who came into the royal court upon her husband Sher Afghan's murder. He lost interest in Anarkali and forgot about her tomb. Money was sparse in coming from the royal treasury, and the master craftsmen slowly sought other cities and jobs.'

'Then who finished this?' I can feel the beginning of an enchanting tale now.

Niyamat pointed to a huge banyan tree in the distance, under which an old bearded gentleman was sitting with an ancient typewriter supported by wooden blocks and wads of paper.

'You see the old man sitting with the typewriter? His typewriter doesn't work, but he comes here every day, lugging it. His name is Sharafat Ali and he was the government pleader until he retired, and now comes here to spend his remaining years in the place which he loves. He told me this story. It so happened that after four years of infatuated courtship, Salim, now Emperor Jahangir, married Nur Jahan in 1611. During one of their sexual sessions, Jahangir in his opium induced state called out the name of Anarkali. Empress Nur Jahan, though miffed beyond words, suffered the indignity of being equated with a dead dancing girl, and waited for the right opportunity. The palace became rife with rumours.'

'Anyway,' he continued, 'when the rumours became frequent, she took the help of Prince Khurram, later Shahjahan, to have the mausoleum completed and quell this foolish rumour once and for all. Khurram had just been engaged to her niece, Arjumand Bano, and was in the good books of the empress. He was entrusted with the task of having it completed, which he did, out of his own funds!'

'Emperor Jahangir was not a miser,' I mused. 'And, he was not in Lahore during 1615 AD. He was, in fact, encamped at the shrine of Hazrat Moin Ud Din Chishti at Ajmer from November 1613 to October 1616. Hence, he obviously could not have dedicated this mausoleum in the year stated.' The historian in me was coming to the fore.

'True, Janab! It is a fact that after laying eyes on Nur Jahan, the emperor was so besotted by her, that he forgot all about Anarkali and his earlier proclamations of inexhaustible love.' He chuckled as he picked up his kettle once again.

Aamir and I walk towards the old man under the banyan tree. As we draw close, Aamir wishes him and introduces me. Sharafat Ali Saheb turns his rheumy eyes on us and looks at me with interest.

He shifts a little on the stony platform and waves at us to sit, asking in a dignified mellow tone, 'What can I do for you, my friend and brother?'

Smitten, I reply, '*Hazrat*, I am researching Prince Khurram, and Emperor Jahangir and Empress Nur Jahan play a very important role in his early career. And, Sir, the story of Anarkali is inseparable from *Jannat Makani* Jahangir. Thus, here I am!'

'Yes, inseparable.' His quiet words carry heavy import.

Turning to me, he suddenly points towards the Bus Stand and Main gate of the Civil Secretariat and exclaims, 'You will find nothing here. This is just the burial place of a Kashmeri dancing girl—enwalled by an emperor, loved by his son, ridiculed by society and preserved by an anxious history.'

I am numbed by the force and eloquence of his words.

He touches my hand and softly instructs, 'Lahore is a city full of history. Kings, queens, and maidens of centuries gone by still breathe and walk the streets of the Old City. Ancient walls, frayed with algae and moss are suddenly wiped clean, as a royal spirit passing that way puts his spectral attendants to work. From dilapidated and abandoned havelis come the sounds of music and the beat of a *Tawaif*'s feet as she sets the cadence for her long dead admirer. On moonless nights, or winter nights when the bitter cold hangs heavy, the sounds of marching feet and clattering hooves can be heard, especially near the Lahori and Dilli Darwaza.'

Touching the few A4 size papers lying by his side, he continues to spin his magic, 'The Anarkali that you seek cannot be found in this bedlam of governmental activity. Go to the Old City, the *Androoni Sheher* as it is called by the knowledgeable, and there you shall find Anarkali in the abandoned shrines, towers, and derelict alleys. Her spirit walks in quest of Salim. Forever.'

Again, I can feel a shiver run down my spine.

I cannot resist the temptation to ask, 'Hazrat, what about the two pigeons there? If Jahangir had forgotten about Anarkali then how do you explain the two resident pigeons?"

'Nur Jahan was an interlude. Salim and Anarkali are eternal.'

***

Invited for dinner at Aamir's place, I am introduced to a rich assemblage of Lahore's cultural aristocracy spanning several fields and generations. It is difficult to imagine a more varied congregation of liberated women, orthodox purists, media gurus, and the social glitterati.

As is so common these days, I am forced to speak on my research and dark secrets of the Mughals. Nothing binds an assembly more than scandalous gossip and sizzling details of sexual liaisons and macabre plots!

Immersed in my recall of great secrets buried in Lahore's own belly at Bhairon Ka Sthan, Ichhra, and within its Shahi Qila—I see an aged gentleman, noble in his bearing with a very fair countenance, broad forehead and gentle blue eyes—discomfited by my cavalier unravelling of Mughal lores.

Too much of a gentleman, he does not interrupt me, but accosts me in a corner over dinner.

'Nniraj Saheb, the Mughals cannot be interpreted by visiting a few ruins or reading dusty books,' his voice is gently reproachful. 'You would have had to live in that era to even come close to imagining their magnificence or depths of cruelty. It is my sincere advice that you do not stray from recorded history—it is not wise to dig skeletons which have lain buried for centuries!' He smoothly glides away.

My appetite has simply disappeared at the subtle, implied threat.

I corner Aamir. 'Who is that gentleman in the turquoise sherwani?'

'Oh, him! He is Mirza Anwar Baig, a direct descendant of Mirza Shamsuddin Atgha—the foster parents of emperor Akbar. Have you heard of Akbar's famous remark "I am bound by a river of milk?"'

'Yes.'

'Well, he is bound to the Mughal dynasty through the same river of milk. He is a *farzand*, a son of the Mughals!'

***

Mirza Anwar Baig Fateh Jung Khan Bahadur Atgha walked into the central corridor of his haveli which was lined with beautiful paintings and portraits of his ancestors and the Grand Mughals. He stopped at a miniature painting of Empress Nur Jahan with gilt edges and stood gazing for a long while, a troubled look on his face.

Would the secret stay safe? A secret so implausible, that it may defy acceptance even when unveiled!

***

Bhairon Ka Sthan
Ichhra, suburb of Lahore
19 January 2015

I now understand what the freezing north western winds must have done to the Mughals as they traversed these mountainous regions south of the Hindu Kush.

Having spent the better part of yesterday in organising my collective information, I made a quick visit to the *Shahi Qila* at Lahore which was a cradle to so many events of rejoicing, betrayals, and death. Though the fort is huge and cannot be covered in a single day, I concentrate on the four subterranean floors which housed the dungeons, execution cells and the gallows, aptly termed 'The Well of Death'. Though most of the secret passages have been barred by iron gates and the subterranean chambers sealed, still, there are enough rooms, alleys, and shifty passages to recreate the aura of terror, misery, and death which resided in these hidden chambers.

My visit was propitious as I saw the secret tunnel from under the royal *hamam* which led to the *Morchi Darwaza* and was used by Prince Salim to rendezvous with his ethereal love, Anarkali.

My seven-day visa will expire the day after, and I must visit the shrine which launched me on this wild journey across hostile borders. My thoughts go back to the ancient manuscript, and words from my previous book, 'Daggers of Treason' come rushing forth.

"I mull over the ramifications, and wonder what secrets are hidden in those old walls of a Hindu temple.

Will they ever talk?

I need to go to Lahore... The words of Shakespeare come unbidden, 'There is a tide in the affairs of men, which, when taken at the flood, leads on to fortune. Omitted, all the voyage of their life, is bound in shallows and in miseries.'

I must go.

History calls. The walls shall speak."

***

Lahore. Present Day.

The loud *'thwack'* of a tennis ball on my shin brings me out of my reverie. I send the ball sizzling back into the cupped hands of a young cricketer. Street cricket in Lahore!

I walk inside an arched gate which is high and wide enough for an elephant to pass through. It is not just a gate, but a covered alley which runs for almost ninety feet, and then opens into a forecourt with a cluster of small residential houses around it. Diagonally to my left, is the conspicuous conical dome of a Hindu temple and the lower walls of the sanctum sanctorum. There is a flag mast on the dome but no Hindu religious pennant flies from it. On my right are parked a few cycles and a green coloured auto rickshaw. Some quilts and mattresses have been dragged into the forecourt to soak in the warm winter sun.

I enquire about the presiding priest, and am directed to a low roofed dwelling.

I climb the few steps to the veranda and peek into the darkened room. An old man with a long flowing beard sits cross legged on a string charpoy with prayer beads in his hands. He tries to focus on me with his timeworn eyes.

'*Aadaab,* Hazrat!' I say, and wait at the threshold.

'Aadaab, Mian!' He squints a little more at me, and then beckons me to enter.

His voice is now strangely gentle as he speaks to me. 'Forgive me, son. I do not recognize you.'

'You would not, Hazrat. I have come from Allahabad, India, and this is my first visit to Lahore.'

His old, wizened face lights up. 'Illahabas! You come from Illahabas, the *Suba* of prince Salim and Padshah Akbar. *Khush amdeed, Khush amdeed!*'

His eyes are lost in the memories of ages gone by.

'I have been to India only once. Long before partition. I was about twelve years old then, and visited with my parents, my siblings, and my grandfather. I remember it well.'

'Sir, did you visit Allahabad too?'

'Yes, my son. We visited Dilli, Agra, Illahabas, and Kashi.'

'Why Kashi, Hazrat?' My interruption seems to annoy him.

'Call me Hazrat Rehmat Shah,' he commands, while adjusting his large green turban with a red feathered plume stuck in its fold. A pause, and then he answers my question, 'We went to Kashi because a very old family friend of my ancestors shifted there long back. Many centuries ago. Anyway, what brings you here, my son?'

'Hazrat Rehmat Shah, I am researching the life and times of Emperor Shahjahan, and I was intrigued to learn of a Hindu shrine at Lahore, dating from the Mughal era. Even more interesting is the fact that it stands even today, when most of the temples have been destroyed.' I indicate the adjacent shrine.

'It is a protected shrine, son. From times immemorial it has stood here, revered and unmolested. Furthermore, it was given *Shahi* protection under the reign of Emperor Jahangir.'

'You mean there was an imperial order issued by the emperor?'

'Yes, there was a *Shahi Farmaan* issued by the Badshah. Even now, by the Grace of Allah, *Bhairon Nath* stands in His celestial majesty.' He nods his head in the shrine's direction.

'May I see the Shahi Farmaan, Sir?'

'I am sorry, son, I do not have a copy. It was taken by the family of Hindu priests when they left Lahore for good.'

'You mean the family of Pundit Ramadeen?' My words come tumbling out.

He is stunned. 'What do you know of Pundit Ramadeen?'

'I know, Sir, that he was the chief priest at this temple during the last years of Akbar's reign.' I will only divulge what is necessary.

He guardedly asks, 'And what else do you know?'

I decide there is no harm in telling him the truth. 'Well, Hazrat, I also know that Nadira Begum urf Anarkali was sheltered here after she was turned out from Lahore fort with her newborn son, Firdaus Salim Sultan.'

'Bakwaas, sub bakwaas!' he denies vehemently.

'What about Chooza Mastan, Hazrat Rehmat Shah? Is he a part of this myth too?' There is an underlying spite in my words.

Rehmat Shah suddenly seems to suddenly shrink. He turns his cataract filled eyes to me, and whispers. 'No, my son, Hazrat Chooza was my ancestor and a *Qalandar* in his own right. He lived here, and died here.'

'But where is the tree under which he stayed?' I am tingling all over with the anticipation of being so close to a hidden part of Mughal history.

'How do you know so much, Son? These are not chronicled anywhere.' There is puzzlement in his voice.

'Hazrat, I found a manuscript near Chunar Fort while researching my project. It records the life of emperor Shahjahan, and carries such details as is impossible to believe. A book was written by me on a part of the manuscript contents, titled 'Daggers of Treason', and it is available in the market. Wait. I have a Hindi translation in the car.' I return a few minutes later and he eagerly grasps the book, turning it over and over again. I hold his wrinkled hands and say, 'That is how I know so much, Hazrat.'

'*Allahu Akbar!* You are truly blessed, *Farzand!* Such divine revelations are made only by the Will of Allah. Come, I will show you the tree under which Chooza Mastan sat.' He touches my arm and walks past the shrine.

I follow him as he hobbles towards an ancient tamarind tree with huge gnarled roots and a forest of branches overhead. A few motorcycles and a push cart are parked underneath. There is a smell of smoke in the air with a peculiar sweet smell to it. I sniff around.

Baba Rehmat Shah smiles. 'The sweet smoky smell is that of *hashish.* Since the time of Shah Chooza Mastan, we have been daily smoking *chillum* beneath this tree. It is so suffused with hashish over five centuries that even the tamarind fruit of this tree can intoxicate you.'

I smile at his words, and seek permission to offer my prayers at the shrine. He nods in acquiescence.

I remember just in time. Turning, I hasten to ask, 'Hazrat, what happened to the family of Pundit Ramadeen?'

'Remember I mentioned our trip to Kashi with my grandfather? Well, his descendants settled there. Near one of the burning ghats,' he replied.

'Manikarnika Ghat,' I venture. He nods his assent.

I climb the four shallow steps to the shrine and rest my forehead on the threshold. As I step into the darkness of the sanctum, I see a *diya* flickering at the feet of the deity. I move closer and find a few fresh roses kept reverentially at the deity's feet.

I look at the statue of Shree Batuk Bhairav—the child manifestation of Lord Shiva in a ferocious form. It is a jet-black statue in stone, unadorned, save for the few roses at the Feet. His eyes are stern as he sits astride a dog, his celestial vehicle, and gazes at me with a mesmeric glint. A Bhairav devotee through many lives, I lower my eyes.

I do not wish to disturb his silent repose of several centuries, and hence, curb my wish to take a photograph. Bowing my head at his Feet again, I move out.

I feel a sudden tug on my pullover, and freeze. I turn around carefully, my spine tingling, and can see the eyes of Shree Bhairav radiating with the orange glow of the earthen lamp. Is it a long farewell?

A gentle waft of a strong rose fragrance envelops me as I retrace my steps.

As I thank the old *Mastan,* Rehmat Shah, for looking after Bhairavji and believing in His sanctity, he simply says, 'Allah is in every name and every form. It is we who discriminate. Take this, Farzand. It shall remind you of our meeting,' and he puts a small piece of paper in my hand.

I quickly open the paper, and look at the few Urdu words scribbled in haste. I look at him inquiringly.

His eyes are watery with accumulated tears, as he hoarsely whispers 'It says *'Aqeeda hai to patthar mein Khuda hai'*. We shall not meet again, *Farzand*. Go and prosper by the Might of Allah!'

My cheeks wet with tears. I bend to kiss his hands and turn towards the main gate.

I must rush back and write all that has happened.

Happened, but hidden, in the dusty covers of wandering centuries and silenced voices.

***

THE VARANASI INTERLUDE

By lanes of Manikarnika Ghat,
Varanasi/ Kashi
10th February 2015,
10.30 a.m.

I had spent the major part of an hour searching for Pundit Ramadeen's house, narrowing my search parameters using two key factors—(a) priest for Shree Bhairav, and (b) having migrated from Lahore many centuries ago.

I was directed to visit the Chief Priest of Manikarnika Ghat, as he would have the Family Tree and antecedents of everyone in that area. And even beyond.

Half an hour later, I was standing in front of a narrow double storied house, festooned with open electricity wires and TV cables.

Presently, I was led into a dark semicircular room, where surrounded by parchments and horoscopes, sat an elderly gentleman with the symbolic three sandalwood marks on his forehead.

He listened intently to my narrative, including my visit to Bhairon Ka Sthan at Ichhra, Lahore, and my research on the life and reign of emperor Khurram Shahjahan.

It took him many nail-biting minutes to open up. 'Nniraj ji, your research is fascinating, and yes, Pundit Ramadeen was our ancestor. My name is Pundit Lallan Pandey.'

Unable to restrain my curiosity, I blurted 'What happened to Pundit Ramadeen and when did he leave Lahore?'

He thought for a while, before replying 'I think he left Lahore immediately after emperor Shahjahan was imprisoned by his son Aurangzeb. See, what I am telling you is what we have heard from our ancestors as part of family lore.'

'Can you please provide more details? It is a very crucial factor in my research.'

'He left Bhairon Ka Sthan in early 1659 just as Aurangzeb embarked on his bigoted and tyrannical crusade against Hindu temples and religion. He was afraid that the *Shahi Farmaan* issued by emperor Jahangir on his deathbed for the protection of this shrine, and honoured by Shahjahan throughout his reign, would not be enough to protect it from Aurangzeb's destructive wrath. He could not bear to see Bhairav Baba's shrine desecrated, and thus, decided to leave, forever.'

'Was it not plain cowardice on his part to desert his deity, fearing reprisals from a tyrannical monarch?' I asked derisively.

The rebuttal was quick and vicious. 'He was no coward! He left the shrine in the hands of his friend and fellow mystic, Chooza Mastan, who was a Sufi *Qalandar* of the highest order. He knew that the empire would not destroy a shrine tended to by Islamic clerics.'

I leant forward and took his hand, 'I know, Sire, what you say is correct. Just a fortnight back, I had visited the shrine, and Hazrat Rehmat Shah, a descendant of Chooza Mastan, was maintaining his silent vigil over the shrine. I was delighted to see roses kept at Shree Bhairavjee's Feet! Such reverence, such love for the Almighty!'

Hoping against hope, I ask 'Punditji, do you have the *Shahi Farmaan* with you? I was told by Rehmat Shah that the royal decree was taken by Pundit Ramadeen when he left Lahore.'

He delves into a small bundle tied in a mustard cloth.

My heart sinks as a parchment in tatters, ridden with holes is offered to me. The only thing of interest seems to be the gilt-edged border and the mark of a huge seal towards the right bottom. I look gloomily at the illegible Persian script left unscathed in some places.

'Mice and time have eaten parts of the decree,' he looks ruefully at me and then rummages for a few more documents.

My eyes are caught by several pages in a beautiful cursive script. The edges are again in gold and green, though the design is coarser and more unrefined. I pick them up.

He dismisses them with a cursory glance. 'Oh, these are nothing but the scrawls of a daughter of Pundit Ramadeen. Apparently, she had an artistic streak in her and was said to copy all that she found beautiful. She copied this from a letter purportedly written by empress Nurjahan.'

'It is very well preserved, considering the others,' I observe.

'Yes. It is rumoured that Pundit Ramadeen had instructed that the original sheaf of papers be burnt along with him on his funeral pyre. Must be something very inauspicious.'

I wave the bunch of papers at him, 'Then these copies must be inauspicious too? Can I take these?'

He doesn't even blink an eyelid, 'You sure can. It is useless for us. Just don't blame us for any evil which may befall you!'

I request for a photocopy of the tattered royal decree and depart with my sheaf of Persian scripted pages and a blurred photocopy.

Besieged by trepidation at the warnings received, I shove the sheaf of scrawled pages into a corner of my car's backseat. A charcoal sketch of two women tumbles out from the pages. I give it a cursory glance—an old woman in a simple saree is sitting demurely next to a beautiful woman in a bejewelled dress, smiling in regal splendour.

Who was to know that these 'evil' pages were to unleash a secret so incredible that it would astound the world and turn recorded history on its head!

* * *

CHAPTER 2

PARANDEGAN SAKT BODAND

(Silent Were the Birds)

Babur's Baoli
Shahi Qila, Agra.
30 October 1605.

Khurram's chronicle cannot give all the details as I can, for I am Fatima Bano Begum, the dead child of Akbar and a free spirit in this world. And beyond.

I travelled with my father's bier from the Diwan-e-Khas through the main avenues of Agra into my father's chosen resting place here, at Bihishtabad. I flitted near the grieving form of Prince Khurram and desperately wanted to comfort him. At the same time, I wanted to strangle the scheming Prince Salim (who will shortly proclaim himself as Padshah Ghazi Nuruddin Jahangir) for having conspired to poison our father.

I saw the desperate desire of Khurram to walk a few more miles with his adoring Shah Baba's coffin resting on his left shoulder, but alas, Salim in his wasted, intoxicated form could accompany his father no further than half a kos on his final journey.

But it did not matter. The bravest and the most loyal generals of Al-Hind carried my father's body—as they had carried his dreams, hopes, and visions on their untiring shoulders during his lifetime. Shortly, my younger brothers, Hasan and Hussain, arrived from their spectral abode at Fatehpur Sikri and walked along with me. Sometimes, we flew, and at times we walked, formless. The three of us cried too, and our tears, falling on the uncovered heads of the court grandees, were dismissed as errant raindrops.

And the grief of a kingdom walked with us.

26th October had been Deepawali, the Hindu festival of lights, but it had dawned in darkness, as the greatest of monarchs, Zille Ilahi, God's Own Shadow on Earth, had passed into the Realm beyond. There were no lights, no sweets, no rejoicing, just the overwhelming shadow of gloom. Even the birds were silent.

We escorted our father through the small arched gate, on which he had inscribed 'These are the Gardens of Eden. Enter them, to live forever!'

And forever he shall reside.

* * *

The Tomb Complex
Bihishtabad (Sikandra)
Past midnight
03/04 November 1605

The imperial guards were huddled over a small fire of dried leaves and twigs, as the slaves and labourers slept amongst the mounds of limestone and crushed rocks. A few stray dogs, excited by the recent activity over the last ten days, had decided to share the dead emperor's final resting place and had formed a motley group of keen sentries.

In the dense undergrowth towards the western side, a Moslem faqir sat upon a fallen log. He paid scant attention to the soldiers who traipsed by holding flickering *mashals,* but gazed steadily at the dark silhouette of the half-risen mausoleum. His thoughts went back to that night in the Three Domed Mosque at Kalanaur when Anarkali had bid him farewell.

His eyes scoured the heavens for tattling stars and the Moon, which always cribbed. He felt the night breeze traversing gently with no signs of lament or recrimination, and knew that the protective shroud of oaths given to Anarkali that fateful night eight years ago, could not have been so easily dispelled.

His fingers sped busily over his rosary, as unbidden, a shout escaped his lips and shattered the stillness of the night. 'Your time has come, Anarkali!'

Immediately a soldier wrapped in coarse rags, rushed in and said hoarsely, 'Begone, old man. Do you not see the dead rest here?'

The faqir slowly gathered his blanket and *himyan*. The soldier scowled as the ascetic said turning away, 'Just wait. The fun is about to begin.'

* * *

Prince Salim's Palace,
Jumna riverfront, Agra,
04 November 1605
04.30 a.m.

'Raise the Royal Ensign! His Majesty boards!' The boatswain's cry rang loud and clear.

Prince Salim, resplendent in his *qaba* of gold woven muslin with a gold sequined Portuguese short cloak in scarlet touched the hilt of his broadsword as if to reassure himself. His turban in orange silk sparkled with the string of diamonds entwined around the thick heron plume.

He stopped a few yards before the gangplank as *Mir Bahri* Mustaid Khan Turrani performed the kornish. The royal musicians on an accompanying boat struck up the valorous tune of *'Fateh Jung Ilahi'*, and in the manner of his ancestors, Ruknuddin Rohilla, a liege in Prince Salim's army, struck his sword against his shield in a slow cadence. Immediately, the assembled nobles, *Ahadis,* regular troops, and the *panjaris* on the barges and river boats, took up the cadence with their swords and shields.

The scarlet main sail of the royal barge billowed and strained against the restraining halyard as prince Salim stepped on board to a deafening blare of trumpets and the beat of *naqqaras.* The panjari crouched in the crow's nest atop the main mast showered tiny flakes of silver and gold on the turbaned head of the prince, as he took his place on the raised platform with a small silver throne under a gilded awning. In a few moments, the sails billowed and the royal barge surged forward.

As the royal barge neared the special pier of Khijri Gate, it slid to port and the panjaris prepared to throw down the mooring lines. The battlements and ramparts of Agra Fort were aglow with thousands of diyas as the entire harem and the palace attendants lined the walls holding flickering earthen and silver lamps.

The red sandstone of the thick fort walls, rising almost seventy feet in the air, were resplendent in the golden glow which seemed to fringe the walls and ramparts.

Navroz, the royal barge, bumped gently against the pier and the royal musicians struck up the auspicious notes on *shehnai* and conch shells. Naqqaras placed on the fort battlements and the *naubatkhana* played a prolonged celebratory roll as Prince Salim stepped on to the stony path.

* * *

Agra Fort,
04 November 1605
Sunrise.

Welcome to the Ascension ceremony at the Diwan-e-Aam! I am the spirit of Babur, the first of the Mughals. I am buried the farthest from Agra, my capital city from where I ruled for a few short years. I detest the dust and the hot weather of Hindoostan, and the impoverished, dark-skinned people who inhabit this country. But, for over seventy-five years

now, Humayun and Akbar, especially Akbar, have extended the fruits of my blood and toil to cover almost all of the northern fiefs.

Let me confess now, as I may not get a chance to address you again—I have dearly loved my son, Humayun. For despite all his losses of dominion and kingship, he has honoured my word and not harmed his erring brothers, Kamran, Hindal, and Askari, even when they raised the banner of rebellion against him. Only my youngest, Mirza Khalil, sided with the righteous Humayun, proving that my blood flowed more freely in his veins than in those of his villainous brothers.

I have not forgiven that blackguard Sher Shah Sur for having desecrated the half-finished tomb of Khalil, as he pursued Humayun across the rivulet Karam-Nasa. That river between the Subas of Rohtas and Illahabas is actually a 'destiny destroyer', as its name suggests!

I was vexed and frustrated when Humayun was forced to leave a fourteen-month old Akbar in the wilderness of Kandahar mountains with just Jouhar Khan, Maham Anga, Jiji Anga and a few faithful followers. I walked unobserved, and cried in silence by Humayun's side, as he and the Illustrious Hamida Bano Begum grieved through the snow-clad passes for their toddler son. December had never been colder and darker.

It was Allah's Merciful Will which brought my other rebellious son, Mirza Askari to the infant prince's camp, and blessed by Allah's Compassionate Hand, nurtured Akbar as a father would. His wife, Sultanum Begum too considered Akbar as one born from her womb and lavished all the care and affection due for a Timurid prince.

Enough of the past! Let the present prevail.

There! I see my great grandson, Salim, walking in procession with the bravest of the brave escorting him to the Diwan-e-Aam for his coronation.

'Salamati Barshumabad!' cries a chorus of children's voices.

'Niz Barshumabad!' I answer instinctively. And I turn.

Oh! My long dead great grandchildren are here! Hassan, Hussain, and little Fatima Bano are there. I knew that the spirit of Fatima resided in Agra Fort, but it is really nice of Hassan and Hussain to come all the way from Fatehpur Sikri to visit their great grandfather. I gather them in my arms, and as the sun breaks into a golden glow, I put little Fatima and a lean Hassan in the crook of my left elbow and armpit, and the stouter Hussain under the other, and run across the fort ramparts. It was one of my favourite pastimes in my younger days—I regularly exercised by tucking a soldier under each of my armpits and running across the battlements of the forts at Samarkand and Kabul, much to the delight of my nobles.

Hark! Mir Tozak calls for the Court to pay obeisance... The emperor approaches.

Before I inspect the state of the 'Baolis' built by me in the western complex of suites and palaces, I must watch the coronation ceremony of my great grandson. And, if I get a chance, I will whisper in his ears to renounce his addiction

to wine and opium, as I had done seventy- eight winters ago, just before the Battle of Khanwa.

Now, to the Emperor's lair...

***

Diwan-e-Aam,
Agra Fort,
04 November 1605.
06.20 a.m.

Prince Salim walked slowly past the marbled colonnades of Macchhi Bhawan preceded by a squadron of twelve *Ahadis* carrying the royal standard on silver poles encrusted with a medley of jade, emerald, and spinel beads. The trumpeters and naqqaras stationed along the ramparts of the *Daftarkhana* and the *Toshkhana* on the opposite sides of the Macchhi Bhawan suddenly erupted in a raucous call to attention as the ascending emperor was first sighted through the open arches.

Salim cast his eyes over the assembled nobles; almost all the titled *mansabdars* were in attendance, and the concourse was full with the bejewelled dresses and turbans from across the empire. His eyes rested on the group of nobles who stood closest to the throne. It was a testimony to their loyalty, and it was time to reward them.

Sa'id Khan Chugatai, the Mir Tozak, called the Court to order and bowed in the prince's direction. At Salim's nod, he announced, *'Ba-adab, Ba-mulaizah, Hoshiyaar!'*

Sheikh Hussain Jami, a slender man with a trimmed beard and earrings in fashion of the Chishtiya sect stepped forward and faced the prince. Immediately, the senior *ulema*, Sheikh Abu

Farid turned towards Mecca and gave the azaan, calling the faithful to pray. As the last notes died, Sheikh Hussain climbed onto a small square slab of marble which had been kept to the right of the imperial balcony, and in his sonorous voice commenced the auspicious invocation.
'Assalamu 'alaikum wa rahmatullah wa barakatahu!

Al hamdu Lillaahi nahmaduhu wa nasta 'eenahu wa nastaghfiruhu, wan a 'oodhu billahi min shuroori anfusinaa wa min sayi aati a 'maalinaa...

(Praise be to Allah, we seek His help and His forgiveness. We seek refuge with Allah from the evil of our own souls and from our bad deeds. Whomsoever Allah guides will never be led astray, and whomsoever Allah leaves astray, no one can guide. I bear witness that there is no God but Allah, the One, having no partner. And I bear witness that Muhammed is His slave and Messenger....)

Yuslih Lakum A'malukam wa yaghfir lakum dhunabakum wa mayin yuti Illaha wa rasulahu faqad faza fauzan adheema. Amma Ba'ad!

Rubbana athina fiddunya hasanah wa fil akhirati hasanah wa kina azabannar...

(Our Lord! Grant us good in this world and good in the hereafter, and save us from the punishment of the Fire.)

Wa aqimissalah!

As Sheikh Jami withdrew from the marble slab paying obeisance at every step, Emperor Nur Ud Din Khan Mohammed Salim Jahangir Padshah Ghazi leaned forward and put the ancestral crown of the Timurids being proffered by his chief eunuch *Khoja* Qaid Akram, on his head with his own hands.

There were immediate shouts of *'Padshah Salamat'* from the assembled nobles and the royal ladies as showers of tiny gold and silver flowers flew through the air. Naqqaras and trumpets erupted in a wild paroxysm of celebration and martial music.

Emperor Salim Jahangir raised his hand for silence.

'Alhamdilullah wa Salatu Wassalamu 'ala Rasulullah! It is not easy for me to sit here today, a throne made sacred by the grace and valour of my revered father, *Arsh Ashiyani* Jalal Ud Din Mohammed Akbar. His shadow is too long and my credentials too small to ever bring the same dignity and majesty to this royal throne.'

'I am not unjust,' he paused for effect, 'nor am I burdened by the slights, insults, or favours of the past. To those who opposed me by their words or deeds, I bear no malice; to those who stood by me in troubled times, I expect the same allegiance from you. The favours and posts granted by my Most revered father shall continue as before. No grants will be withdrawn or lands reclaimed, as long as you are true to the sword you gave your allegiance to.'

'There are twelve royal proclamations which shall come in force from today. But, before that, I bestow one hundred gold *mohurs* on Sheikh Hussain Jami, who exactly one hundred days back prophesied that I shall be enthroned on the 04th of November. And so, I have! None other, but the great moslem mystic Khwaja Baha 'Uddin had come to him in a dream and had presaged this day. Step up, Sheikh!' Picking a heavy velvet bag decorated with golden brocade, he leant forward over the gold inlaid railing and dropped it into the hands of Mir Tozak.

As Sheikh Jami retreated with his purse, a senior noble from Persia, Shah Beg Khan Arghon stepped forward from behind the second railing and performed the *kornish*. Sa'id Khan Chugatai who was closer to Shah Beg could make out that his eyes were bloodshot and fists clenched, as he stood waiting for permission to speak.

Before Mir Tozak could admonish him for this breach of royal protocol, Emperor Jahangir spoke up, 'Shah Beg Arghon, what ails you, that you stand unsteady and suffused with the colour of blood on your face and temple?'

Shah Beg swayed unsteadily on his feet and in a voice loud enough to be heard by the assembly, called out, 'Your Majesty! I am just a small mansabdar of your empire, but it pains me to tell you this—In the Court of your revered father there were many nobles to whom I, Shah Beg, was not even worth a pubic hair. Here, today, in this Court I see none who can compare to my pubic hair. That is all that I have to say, Your Majesty.'

There was pin drop silence. Emperor Jahangir gestured for the ahadis to move back as he saw them advancing with raised swords and lances towards Shah Beg Khan.

Jahangir dismissed him with an exasperated wave of his hand. 'Shah Beg, this mixture of cannabis, opium, *poshtu*, and wine shall be a cause of your death someday. Go home and rest. And then, within this fortnight, depart for the fort at Qandahar. It shall cure you of your illness. No wonder people call you *Shah Beg Khor Chaar Lagbrez!* Now, begone!'

Shah Beg Khor Chaar Lagbrez, happy in his inebriated state, retreated with much aplomb, performing obeisance at every step.

***

The past two hours had been spent in receiving the gifts and presents to waves of great rejoicing, and the aisles along the walls were stacked with mounds of rich brocades and golden cloth. Trays of sparkling rubies, emeralds and diamonds rested alongside heaps of gold mohurs and diamond encrusted swords presented as *nazrana* by the Court Grandees.

Thirty-three elephants from the royal *Fil Khana* with caparisons of gold and silver were brought before Emperor Salim Jahangir fitted with the *gajnal and hathnal* pieces of light artillery. In addition to the two *sowars* responsible for unloading and firing these swivel guns, the elephants carried two archers each. At a command from the *Qurbegi,* the archers stood up in the *howdahs* and shot blunt arrows into the sky. Each arrow carried a long tail of gold *mohurs*, and fell harmlessly into the joyous, celebrating populace outside the fort walls, initiating a minor stampede as people struggled to lay their hands on the *mohurs*.

Emperor Jahangir longed for his two cups of opium mixed with wine; these court proceedings had gone on long enough, and he was tired of the repetitive formalities. The succour of the seraglio with its bevy of beautiful begums, concubines, and the intoxicating opium mixed in wine beckoned the new emperor with tantalizing urgency.

He looked towards Mir Tozak, who immediately recognized the signs of a restless emperor.

Padshah Ghazi Nuruddin Mohammed Salim Jahangir proclaimed loudly 'The Mughal Sultanate felicitates the brave and faithful nobles of this Court. My revered father, *Arsh Ashiyani* Jalal Ud Din Mohammed Akbar, had spread the glitter of His majesty far and wide. It is now for us to carry it even further and add to the majesty of his legacy.'

'We, Timurids, never forget—those who stood by the Realm shall be rewarded; and those, who faltered in their path and took to shame and treachery, shall be punished.'

Let the courtiers quail overnight, thought Jahangir, as he departed for the imperial harem. It never struck him that he was countermanding his own assurances of a few minutes ago.

* * *

CHAPTER 3

FARMAN SIZADEHAM

(The 13th Decree)

Diwan-e-Aam
Agra Fort
25 November 1605
10.30 a.m.

Emperor Nuruddin Salim Jahangir settled himself on the gold upholstered bolsters of the royal throne amidst the roll of royal drummers and the resounding blare of trumpets. The forty hangmen in their leather smocks, pickaxe and symbolic noose took their places near the far pillars of the hall. The *Shahi Qur* bearing the arms and insignia of the emperor ranged themselves near the small doorway which led to the entrance passage of *Machhi Mahal*.

It was time to reward the faithful.

'Farzand Shareif Khan, step forward now, and in the everlasting shade of the Reigning Hand, be appointed to the state of *Vizier-i-Mulk!'* The rich baritone of the Mir Tozak rang out.

Shareif Khan dressed in the emperor's favourite colour of sparkling green prostrated himself and placed his black turban on the marbled floor.

Emperor Jahangir spoke softly, 'Rise, Farzand. You have been true to my soul, and I command your loyalty to my Hand.'

'Allah be my witness. My soul is yours!' Shareif Khan trembled with loyal fervour.

The voice of Mir Tozak rang out again as Shareif Khan moved back, performing the *taslim* at every step. 'In this auspicious hour of the Sovereign, Zamana Beg Kabuli, erstwhile Sagar Singh, scion of the House of Mewar and brother of Maharana Pratap, now stands ennobled as Mahabat Khan with a mansab of one thousand five hundred horses.'

Zamana Beg, colourful in the fiery red of his rajput ancestors, stepped forward seven paces and extended his bejeweled sword to the emperor.

The emperor leant forward, and said 'Much have we shared, Zamana Beg, and many arrows of Fate have we survived. Your unwavering fortitude is your greatest strength, and henceforth, you shall be known as *Mahabat Khan!* I also appoint you *Bakshi Shagird Pisha* as a mark of special favour to you.'

The hall resonated with the cry of the Mir Tozak once more, 'From the state of Orchha, Datia, and Panna comes the Bundela chief, Bir Singh Deo, to seek the favours and auspicious glance of the Shahenshah-i-Hind, Padshah Ghazi Nuruddin Mohammed Salim Jahangir, and to kiss the threshold of the Supreme Sovereign now presiding in Court.'

As Bir Singh stepped forward from the third row behind the silver railing with his mace held across his chest, the enraged prince Khurram stepped forward and commanded, 'Drop your mace, Bundela. You cannot carry a mace in the presence of the Sovereign.'

Bir Singh Deo, his dark face creased with the weary lines drawn by the arid wastelands of Central India, replied sourly, 'I am the Bundela chief, prince, and I carry the weapon I deem fit.'

Like lightning, prince Khurram's narrow bladed rapier was against Bir Singh's throat, and in a voice laced with pure venom, he spat, 'I will not caution thee again, Bundela. Yield, or I shall have thy head on my sword!'

The emperor watched silently as several Rajput and *Akbarshahi* nobles drew their swords and moved towards the silver railing. The small clutch of Bundela warriors who had accompanied Bir Singh had already been surrounded by the Ahadis and the Afghan soldiers who were on royal duty today. The treacherous conduct of Bir Singh with the late emperor's most trusted general, friend and Vizier, Sheikh Abu'l Fazl, had not been forgotten.

Bir Singh took a step back, and raising his eyes towards the emperor, implored 'Your Majesty, I have served your call much before the glory of the Mughal throne adorned your silver feet, and in the killing of Sheikh Abu'l Fazl at your behest, I suffered the calamitous debacle of losing my lands, forts, treasury and clansmen to the imperial fury and might of your illustrious father. Back then, none of these who stand with their swords drawn today were a spectre in your distant land of Allahabad. I slew for you and invited the Demon of Perdition upon my dynasty!'

The emperor remained silent.

Stepping forward, prince Khurram lanced the heavy gold chain festooned around Bir Singh's neck, and with a flick of his rapier point, sent it flying across the hall.

The stern voice of Sher Khan Fauladi, a trusted noble from Emperor Akbar's reign came from behind, 'Yield to the prince's sword, Bir Singh. You are a vassal of the Realm and shall abide by the *Dastur-ul-Amal* of the Mughal Court.'

Eyes red with fury, Bir Singh Deo dropped his mace and advanced, performing the obeisance at every step. As he stood with his head bowed before the throne, Jahangir took pity on his discomfiture and announced 'To you, Bir Singh Deo Bundela, we grant the *mansab* of three thousand horses and the throne of Orchha. You shall rule your lands under my hand, and your elder brother and rightful heir to the throne, Ramshah, will be exiled to the jungles of Chhatarpur. For services rendered by thee to this royal court, you shall forever remain a cherished jewel of our empire.'

Performing four taslims, Bir Singh took his appointed place amongst the nobles in the third row.

'Pick up your mace, Bundela chief.' Prince Khurram still had his unsheathed rapier in his hand.

Squirming with humiliation, Bir Singh looked at the surrounding courtiers for some comfort, only to be met with disdainful stares. His steps were heavy as he stepped back with his weapon.

Their eyes met.

Our paths will cross someday, Bir Singh consoled himself.

It sure will, thought prince Khurram. And you will rue that day, he silently promised.

* * *

Imperial Suite,
Agra Fort,
02 December, 1605
11.25 p.m.

Emperor Jahangir's favourite concubine, Fareeda Khanum, a beautiful woman from the Persian plains of Isfahan, gently administered the aphrodisiacal oil on the lower torso and thighs of the reclining emperor.

As the astute fingers of Fareeda touched and flitted from the muscled torso of the emperor, Jahangir felt the first stirrings of desire. He pulled her hand towards his hardening member, but Fareeda, trained for years in the courtesan's art of imparting sexual delight, deliberately stayed away from grasping his swollen penis.

The emperor opened his eyes to see a smiling Fareeda leisurely drape her shapely thighs over his groin. As her full, soft thighs gently pressed and rolled against his erection, he wrapped an arm around her waist and pulled her on top. Her perfumed tresses fell around his face as she straddled his groin and slowly descended on him. She leaned over and gently raked his armpits with her fingers, while her extended thumb played with his erect nipple.

Jahangir groaned in pleasure. These past six years had lain heavy on him, and the memories of Nadira Anarkali had refused to fade, even as he cursed his father, fate, and time. Regrettably, Time had not proved to be the proverbial healer, and the wounds still hurt with cruel mirth.

He cupped her buttocks as she rode him with the delicate passion of a royal concubine. Fareeda had the same luscious softness in her figure and face, so reminiscent of Anarkali, and had inadvertently imbued her spirit of lovemaking too, which absolutely delighted Jahangir. He moved his right hand and teased her engorged nipples as she swayed over him.

As her fair thighs clamped around the emperor, she flung herself forward, and entwining her palms in his, stretched it behind his head. Jahangir felt her breasts hard against his chest as she rhythmically moved her pelvis against his, and shifting a little, pressed her nails into his nipples. Jahangir, galvanised by the searing sensation, thrust upwards and closed his eyes as waves of orgasmic rapture swept over him.

His lips curled, and then let forth a low moan. Despite all the pleasure enveloping him, the beautiful, pleading face of Anarkali flashed before him yet again, bringing forth those painful memories of a past long buried.

Pain could be sedated, but never forgotten.

He was the emperor, and Justice must be done.

The *Zanzeer-i-Adil* would toll for the emperor now!

***

The next day,
Early morning hours,
Diwan-e-Khas

Emperor Salim Jahangir's voice was cold, as he tersely said, 'Mir Bakshi, you are well aware of the persons responsible for *Sahiba e Jannat* Anarkali's murderous enwalling. I want all the troop commanders, especially Hamid Gul Afghani, and Mubarak Sarwani who were responsible for her capture and death, to be exterminated. Limb by limb.'

Sheikh Farid Bokhari bowed in assent, and slowly moved backwards.

The emperor's voice halted his steps. 'The Twelve Decrees were for the people and the kingdom. This, the 13th Decree, is for me. Fail me not, Sheikh Farid.'

* * *

There was just a faint ripple in the golden tapestry behind the emperor, as an ewer bearer rapidly carried the news to the soldiery in the *Fil Khana.*

CHAPTER 4

NISHAN SHROOR VAZIR:

(The Vizier's Villainous Nishan)

Imperial Dak Chowki,
Main Gate, Agra Fort,
The same evening.

The set of eighteen relay horses, nine on either side of the main ramp closest to the main Delhi Gate, swished their tails and leisurely dipped their heads into the coarse bag of oats hung around their necks. Their riders sat on the low stone platform with their short whips curled in their hands. A big trough full of fruits stood on both platforms, as also a huge copper vessel filled with water.

The riders stiffened as they heard the signature cry of a royal runner from the palace precincts. In a moment the royal runner emerged with his leather pouch slung across his shoulders and carrying the light spear hung with several small bells, running swiftly across the open promenade. In a flash, several riders had unhitched their horses and were wheeling them. The runner swerved left, and in one fluid motion had uncoiled the leather belt and pouch from across his neck and handed it over to the nearest rider.

The rider dug his heels, and the horse broke into a furious gallop, scattering small stones and pebbles in his wake.

Along with royal mail and Hakim Gilani's potions for an ailing Khane Azam Mirza Aziz Koka, the swift horse also carried to Lahore, a secret message sewn into the leather strap of the mail pouch. The arrest warrants for Hamid Gul Afghani, Mubarak Sarwani, and a few others, lay safely within the leather strap.

The revenge of Anarkali rode in sinister bursts of speed, covering the distance of roughly two hundred *kos* in nine days.

***

The Guslkhana,
Jahangir's Palace,
Agra Fort.
8.30 p.m.
07 December 1605.

The voice of Prince Khurram was subdued. 'Majesty, ever since the demise of Shah Baba, there pervades a morbidity in the fort. Each hour hangs heavy on us, and the walls seem to have lost their strength. The halls so full of merriment and grace, now accuse silently.'

Emperor Jahangir took Khurram by the hand, and bade him sit. 'We all miss him terribly, Khurram, and in our own ways we lament his loss.'

Tears glistened, as Khurram bravely tried to hold them back. 'Your Majesty, Prince Khusrau lives in misery and with each passing day, he seems to move further and further apart from us. As his younger brother, and in the name of Shah Baba, may I request you to find favour in your heart and forgive him?'

Khurram was astonished to see a pool of tears in the emperor's eyes. 'I know. Khusrau has grown his beard and dresses in the robes of a faqir. Do you, or anybody else feels that I derive pleasure from his arraignment? I am an emperor, true; but I am a father first. He is my first born, Khurram, and I see my future in him. But, what does he see? He sees his own father as a rival, an enemy, and wants to bring about my ruin.'

The emperor wept.

'I forbade his coming to the Court and confined him to his quarters, only because his melancholic presence had a debilitating effect on the energy and majesty of the Royal Court. And frankly, Khurram, every time I saw him standing there in front of me with his dour expression, I beheld treachery.'

Khurram clung silently to his father's hand as his tears moistened the gold embroidered sleeve of the emperor's coat.

The emperor wiped his tears away. 'Do not grieve, Khurram. Prince Khusrau will be given his freedom today. Now, go and give the good tidings in the harem. Your grandmother and the begums would be delighted.'

A wan smile flashed over Khurram's face as he performed thc kornish and left. The Night Commander, Sunder Singh Rathore, stood aside for the young prince to pass by, and then addressed the emperor, 'Your Majesty, there is a person held outside, who says he has urgent business with you.'

'Is he a royal envoy?'

'No, Your Majesty.' The night commander's voice was troubled. 'He is wearing the tattered robes of a mendicant, and claims that he is the spirit of Raja Birbal.'

'Fool! Do you think I am here to listen to the rubbish of every demented person who lives in my kingdom?' He took a quick gulp from his wine cup. 'You should know better than this, Rathore.'

'Your Royal Highness. He carries the *nishan* of the late Vizier, Sheikh Abu'l Fazl Allami.'

Blood drained from Jahangir's face.

***

Jahangir's Palace,
Agra Fort.
9.10 p.m.
07 December 1605

Jahangir stared moodily at the flickering candle nearest to him. Its soft glow and warmth refused to enthuse the flagging spirits of the monarch, and the nip in the cold December night further settled around Jahangir as an unwelcome shroud. The emperor's constitution, weakened by consumption of wine mixed with opium, had made him susceptible to bouts of morbid melancholy and extreme anger.

The sudden exposure to two names from the past had unnerved him. Though Raja Birbal and Sheikh Abu'l Fazl had never been cordial to each other, yet their names invoked an unease in the emperor's mind. He motioned for a refill of his large wine cup.

Loud voices could be heard in the echoes of the long colonnaded path to the inner room. Jahangir lazily plucked a tender piece of roast mutton from the gold salver and looked up as there was a rustle of curtains and Sunder Singh Rathore, the *Yatish Begi,* pushed a frail old man inside the room.

Emperor Salim Jahangir saw a dark withered face, with a mop of untidy silver hair trying its best to escape from under the small dirty turban. The long cloak was coarse with loose sleeves, and the wrists were made colourful with several strings of beads and threads. The half shoes were held together by strings, and the old man had his hands clutching the folds of his cloak securely.

The captive squinted his eyes to see the emperor properly. His brows furrowed, and the sunken cheeks sucked in a breath at the grandeur of the gilded room glowing with the iridescence of the silver and gold candelabras. His rheumy eyes rested on the emperor as he craned his neck for a better look. The emperor leaned forward and spoke.

'Speak, fellow. Who are you and what do you want?'

The old man shifted on his feet, and exclaimed softly, *'It's true!* You do not resemble your father at all! The contents are true, then...'

The night commander cuffed him across his shoulders. 'Address His Imperial Majesty with due respect, you old heathen, or you will be in irons.'

The frail looking person whipped around and dug his skinny elbow into the ample stomach of the sentry commander and stomped on his toes. For good measure, he lunged and gripped Rathore's testicles, almost mangling them.

Jahangir laughed loudly and slapped his thigh in merriment at the painful amazement on his night commander's face.

Straightening, the decrepit looking man again made towards Rathore, murmuring audible obscenities. As the sentry commander reached for his dagger, the emperor's voice rang out.

'Enough!'

'Ho! Friar. You have not answered my question. Who are you, and what is your business?'

The destitute pulled his cloak closer, and answered with equanimity. 'I am Baiju Mishra from Champaner. Your father, the Illustrious Akbar, knew me as Baiju Bawra.'

'Oh! The famed singer...' Jahangir looked at him with interest.

Baiju continued with a quizzical look in his eyes. 'If I had not seen you with my own eyes, I would not have believed the contents of this nishan.' He waved a sheaf of elegant parchment paper.

'Speak clearly, old man. What contents?' Irritation had crept into Jahangir's voice.

The shrouded figure rolled his eyes, and pointing at the sentry commander, and other slaves within the room, said, 'In privacy, my lord. Your reign is at stake.'

***

Having sent his attendants away, the emperor extended his hand for the sheaf of papers being waved around by the manic visitor.

'Not so quick, O Chief!' he sang. 'First promise me that you will not make a decorative vase of my skull after reading this.'

'And what if I will, friar?'

'Then you will sing like I once sang in your father's court. And.' He stopped and smiled, before continuing, 'And, then the spirit of Mian Tansen will take a kettle drum and beat it on your head, Shehzade.' He squealed with merriment.

'You need to be flogged, old man.' Jahangir called out, 'Sentry!'

The guard commander appeared, 'Yes, Majesty?'

'Throw this maniac into the dungeons, and have him flogged at first light tomorrow.'

Baiju implored as he was being dragged away, 'O, Chief! King of Kings and the Statue of Justice, hear me out. These parchments carry your destiny, infamy, and dishonour! Burn them, and you shall reign forever!'

The emperor waved the sentry away. 'Let him be. *Taqhliya.*' Jahangir could feel the onset of a massive headache.

'Now, friar. Show me what you carry. If it is a pile of rubbish, then you shall be soundly flogged, notwithstanding your old age. If you bring good tidings, you shall be rewarded.'

Baiju Bawra shuffled forward and put the sheaf of parchment papers in the emperor's hands.

Jahangir unrolled the parchment and began to read.

Having read the first few pages, his brows furrowed and he gave a quick glance towards the cloaked figure. Soon, his fingers shook and he staggered to the nearest chair.

Jahangir's eyes were wild with anger, 'Who gave you these papers and who exactly are you?'

'My Lord, I am Baiju the singer, and *Bawra* the person. You will not remember me, for you were but an infant when I sang at the Anup Talao. But the walls of Fatehpur Sikri will remember me. As to who gave me these? The answer is—Sheikh Abu'l Fazl Ibn Mubarak, the Grand Vizier of the Exalted Court!'

Fear was evident in the emperor's eyes and voice. 'Who else has seen this?'

'None, my lord. Have you not read the fine *Naqshbandi* script on the reverse of the last page? The good Sheikh has forbidden its contents to be ever shown to anyone.'

With trembling fingers Jahangir turned the papers over. Yes, there was a note in the fine Persian scribble of the late Vizier, which he recognized so well.

Jahangir drained his wine cup, and haltingly asked, 'Why were these given to you, Master Singer?'

'It is a long story, Chief.'

'We have the whole night ahead. Now, tell me from the beginning.'

'Yes, my lord. May I sit down?' Jahangir nodded.

The withered singer folded his cloak around himself and sat cross legged on the floor. The creases on his forehead became deeper as he burrowed into forgotten chapters of the past.

'Many winters ago, I was again cheated by Destiny.' The voice remained low. 'I came back from a long tour of Khandesh and found that my entire family had deserted me and gone. Vanished. I had no son, but a son—my beloved, Gopal! I had adopted him when he was barely six months old, and raised him as if he was my own seed. I taught him my own skills, and prayed to Shri Krishna to make him a better singer than me. When the time came, I had him married to Prabha who was a favourite disciple of mine. Then came the light of my life, my granddaughter, Meera. Then one day suddenly, everyone was gone. No words, no goodbyes, not even words of hate! Because the miserable *dam* spoke. I later learnt that some Kashmiris had lured my son and his family away by promising one thousand dams per month.' He stopped and shook his head.

'I gave up singing. I became a mendicant and roamed the forests of Khandesh and Bundelkhand in search of God, whom I wanted to punish. I learnt the language of the squirrels and the brown *mynah,* for they were my constant companions. And then one day...' His voice trailed off.

The emperor leaned forward, the papers clutched in his fist.

Collecting his thoughts, the shrivelled old man began again. 'And then one day, in the early part of August when the parched earth of Bundelkhand turns green for a few weeks, there arrived the Grand Vizier enroute from Sironj to Agra with his small escort. I was in the forest tracts near Antara when the Vizier stopped for his prayers and mid-day meal. He could not recognize me, but I definitely did from my days at Fatehpur Sikri.'

Jahangir's gaze was intense, as Baiju started after a brief pause. 'I am not an oracle or a soothsayer, *Jahanpanah,* but seeing him kneel for his prayers in that dusty forest tract that day, I was filled with dread. I could envision the destruction of the pious Sheikh just as clearly as I see you, my lord. I warned him of the ambush ahead, but he paid no heed. Or so I thought. When he was gone, I went near the big stone where he had partaken his lunch in the hope of finding some morsels of fine food. What I found was this!' He gestured to the sheaf of papers in the emperor's hands.

His voice was lost in thoughts of faraway times. 'Placed securely under the stone were these parchments. And the next day was the Sheikh's engagement with Death. With the treacherous Bir Singh Bundela.'

Jahangir flinched as the bard fixed him with a malefic stare.

'Have you read the Sheikh's note on the reverse, Jahanpanah? It is dated the 11th of August, 1602.' There was a biting sarcasm in the singer's voice.

Blinded with pain and disbelief, the emperor read again.

'Most Revered Bard, Baiju Bawra, the chief angel of harmony! Hail, to thee! You thought I had not recognized you? You are celestial and cannot be hidden in the shrouds of a monk. I have very little time, hence, this short note. The four pages of parchment were sent to me by Raja Birbal from Swat Valley, Kashmere, just before his

demise in early 1586. I have kept the contents to myself, as I could not bring myself to inform the Shahenshah-i-Hind of this perfidious missive. I could not destroy it either, as a part of very crucial Mughal history would be lost forever. For over sixteen years I have lived with the venomous contents herein. Now, as I go forward to engage with Death at Prince Salim's behest, yes, my spies have informed of the prince's plan to have me ambushed, I entrust these valuable pages of lost history to your care. Do not, repeat, do not ever approach His Majesty with this missive. The pain for him would be too great to bear; I have only wished peace and happiness for my Sovereign Lord, and in my few remaining hours I can but only pray for one more life to serve him again.

When the Great Sovereign passes into the Realm of Allah, only then may you hand this over directly to Prince Salim. Directly, mind you. It shall be for him to decide whether to proclaim the truth, or promote fallacy. I know I have burdened you with a monumental responsibility, but I have no choice. I just have a few hours left, as YOU know very well.

I wish you well, my friend. Take heart, and sing again.

Sheikh Abu'l Fazl—The Unfortunate One!

***

The old bard's voice pierced the silence. 'Jahanpanah, you are not Akbar's son!'

***

CHAPTER 5

NAMAK POSHIMANI

(The Salt of Remorse)

Guslkhana, Agra Fort,
Early morning hours,
The night of 07 December 1605 (contd.)

Emperor Jahangir had spent the night in anxious turmoil. The Yatish Begi and the personal attendants had stood outside, watching the room dim as the candles wasted themselves into misshapen sculptures of molten wax. The thick cotton wicks had also shrunk, trying to furiously burn themselves at the emperor's vigil. Not that it mattered.

Frightened into reckless action by the bard's proclamation, Jahangir had ordered his immediate arrest and confinement. The long hours of the night had been punctuated by the ululating wail of the recalcitrant bard, and the harsh knock of manacles on the iron doors. The subterranean chambers of Bangali Mahal had echoed with cries of 'You are not Akbar's son!' till the emperor was forced to order his gagging.

Jahangir looked at the burning embers of the poisonous letter spread in an ugly pile at the candle's base, and was repelled by its accursed insinuations. Even the burnt ashes held enough gunpowder to destroy the kingdom with its venom, and herald the end of the Mughal empire.

Jahangir, despite his best efforts, could not banish the hateful words so deeply had they become etched onto his psyche. The words burned their way into his eyes:

'The Mughal Camp,
Burliyas Pass, Kashmere,
29 January 1586
11.30 p.m.

For the eyes of His Lordship, the Sipahsalar, and the emperor's Own Soul!

Sheikh Abu'l Fazl Ibn Mubarak,

Salaam to thee!

I do pray that His Imperial Majesty Zille Illahi reigns in supreme glory, and that your nobility finds itself in the Most Fortunate Shadow of his Grace!

Dear Sheikh, I have been a loyal follower of His Divine Grace, Padshah Ghazi Jalal Ud Din Mohammed Akbar all these years, and have marvelled at the sweet words which flow from your golden quill, and their eternal eloquence. However, I now feel betrayed, and honorific titles are but vacuous sounds to me. Mark my words, Sheikh. History will remember you as the greatest flatterer and sycophant of all times!

Surprised? Do you smell the rancour of jealousy and hatred in my words? Do you feel my words are unkind arrows? So you should!

I have suffered these past three months in the snow-clad wastes of Kashmere, searching for the uncouth band of rogues with whom the empire first cavorts, and when their insidious treachery strikes, then the empire sends Hindu nobles to fight the scourge of these Yusufzais!

Do not even for a moment try to contradict me by pointing to the worthless forms of Hakim Abul Fath and Zain Khan. It would have been better if the emperor could have provided me with two pack mules instead of these stultified bottom peckers. Unfortunately, Sire, these two generals cannot differentiate between the sharp end of an arrow and the smelly backside of a female elephant! Pardon my words, learned Sheikh, for I am not as eloquent as thee.

The Shahenshah-i-Hind sits secure in his fort of red sandstone, while we hunt and pillage for him, so that his treasury may overflow with blood tainted gold. Does it overflow with the screams and cries of orphaned children and widows, too? Do put your ears to the gilded doors of the mint and let His Royal Highness know, Sheikh.'

Jahangir was aghast at the malevolence of Raja Birbal's words. To think that he was one of the Nine Jewels of his father's illustrious court!

'Tell me, Sheikh. What inspired you to volunteer that cold night of October? It was certainly not your valour—perhaps, it was my doom which answered your call? Do you know, Sheikh, that we Hindus believe in the maxim of Karma? I sullied my faith and my Karma the day I succumbed to His Majesty's religious fervour and converted to Din-i-Ilahi. I am ashamed that I was the only Hindu to convert. The emperor's own shadow, Mirza Raja Man Singh, had stood by his faith. I still clearly remember his words to the emperor—" If it is my life you desire, I have already pledged it to you; If it is my faith you want, then take my life instead!" Oh, how valorous were those words!

It is my fickle faith, which changed my Fate on the roll of a dice, that evening. My bad Karma spoke! What if number five or three had turned up instead of four? Would the emperor have sent you to this God forsaken land? No, my friend. The emperor would have used his regal powers to appoint someone else.

In his defence, you will say that he shed tears for me that evening. I agree. He cried, but not for me. He cried at the perfidy of it all and the loss of a companion who had spent more than twenty-four winters with him. My hand shaketh, Ibn Mubarak, for I can hear the bells toll.

The bells toll for me, only because of the greed and deviousness of a monarch. And, do you know, learned Sheikh, the Mughal dynasty will end with the demise of our Grand Emperor? It is not just the lands, or the vassal tributes that will shrink, but the very blood of the great Taimur The Lame and Ghengis Khan will dry up.

You feel that my words are those of a rambling fool? Then read this carefully:

Shahenshah Jalal Ud Din Mohammed Akbar had thrown the yoke of Mirza Bairam Khan's regency in 1561, and had a free reign over his pursuits of mind and body. His promiscuity with the wives of his nobles is well known, though not recorded. Is it not so, Sheikh? His lust differentiated not between married-unmarried, Hindu, Muslim, or Jews; not even if she was a sister! I am sure you know, dear Sheikh, that the emperor's first wife and Chief Consort, Ruqaiah Begum is the daughter of Mirza Hindal, the emperor's own uncle? You would also be knowing, O Great Fountain of Knowledge, that the other senior Queen, Salima Sultana Begum is likewise the daughter Of Begum Gulbadan, the emperor's own paternal aunt? Marrying your own sisters is incest, is it not? And, do not forget that Begum Salima Sultana is the widow of our emperor's

Shah Baba, Bairam Khan, the person singularly responsible for creating and holding an empire for our emperor. And what did Bairam Khan receive? No khillats or jagirs, but the ingratitude of a selfish king who had him exiled and murdered.

Do you remember Abdul Wasi, the Persian noble, my friend? He poisoned himself to death in 1562, just after our emperor forced him to conduct his wife, Bibi Daulat Shad, into the emperor's harem. That was the year I joined the Court of our Exalted Emperor.

Unfortunately, none of his children survived in the early years. You see, Karma is not limited to Hindus only; it afflicts everyone on this planet, and now the Karma of our ungracious king was speaking up. The aggrieved spirit of Waqil Ul Sultanat, Yar Wafadar, Baradur Neku-siyar, Farzand-i-Saadatmand, Nawab Bairam Khan Bahadur Khane Khanan was in appeal at Allah's Court, seeking justice against the humiliation, ingratitude, and murderous action of one who was more of a father to Akbar, than even his own father Humayun was.

And Allah responded.

None of Akbar's children born immediately after Mirza Bairam Khan's treacherous murder survived. The first born, Fatima Bano, died just a few days after Hazrat Bairam Khan's death. Hassan and Hussain, the two twins born to the emperor in 1563, survived but a few months. And then, the walls and precincts of Agra Fort were besieged by the spirits of these unfortunate children as they were chased by the avenging spirit of Bairam Khan. The situation became so desperate that Zille Illahi had to shift his capital from Agra to Fatehpur Sikri to escape the assault of these disturbed spirits. But you surely know all this, learned Sheikh. You are a great chronicler of events, hence, you must record these for posterity.

Harassed, doomed, and dejected, the emperor turned to the mystic Sheikh Salim Chishti for relief. From 1564, just after the death of Hassan and Hussain, his visits to the hamlet of Sikri became very frequent, and a handsome abode was built for the mystic and his extended family.

The emperor persevered in his efforts, and one day the Revered Saint Chishti agreed to pray for the emperor's wish to have a male successor. He retired to his room for forty days and forty nights without food or water, and upon completion emerged as a much-worried man. His prayers and penance had enlightened him to the fact that Emperor Akbar's fate did not permit a child till the age of twenty-eight, which was a good six years away. As an Enlightened Soul, he knew well enough not to meddle in Destiny's course, but to succumb to Allah's Will.

But who could refuse an emperor's will? What Destiny could not provide, Providence could!

The Munnawar blessed our Most Glorious Emperor with three sons. The only condition being that the pregnant queens be sent to Fatehpur Sikri during their pregnancy to be within the grace of the Divine Sufi's protection, and away from the malefic environs of Agra Fort. The emperor readily agreed.

As Providence would have it, Princess Heer Kunwari of Amer became pregnant in late 1568, and was sent to the abode of Hazrat Salim Chishti for necessary care. The Sufi was greatly worried—he had assured the emperor of a legitimate heir, while Destiny indicated otherwise. He knelt to offer prayers and remained like that for the next three days. On the fourth day, a son was born to one of his son's wives who had been pregnant, and was brought to him for benediction.

As soon as the Great Master lovingly touched the head of the new born child, it miraculously opened its eyes, and spoke, 'Do not worry, Shah Baba. I am the answer to your prayers. I shall die now, and be born again, when the time comes.' And saying so, this godly child closed its eyes and passed away into the other Realm.

Eight months later, on 30 August 1569, Begum Heer Kunwari gave birth to a male child. It was stillborn.

In an interior room was born another boy to the wife of Badruddin Chishti, the Sufi's eldest son. It was born healthy.

The name of 'Badruddin' was the only link that the newborn shared with his biological father and the childless emperor.

I hope you have not forgotten the words of Jauhar Khan, Sheikh Allami? Jalal Ud Din Mohammed Akbar was actually born Badruddin Mohammed Akbar, until his father Jannat Ashiyani Nasir Ud Din Mohammed Humayun changed it to Jalal Ud Din for astrological reasons in 1542.

There were tremendous rejoicings in the Imperial harem and the Mughal Kingdom. A prince had been born.

There was quiet rejoicing in Sheikh Salim Chishti's household. A future emperor had been spawned!

Do you now understand, Sheikh Abul Fazl Ibn Mubarak? Does it now strike you why prince Salim is swarthy and corpulent and does not resemble his Timurid ancestors or the Rajputs from his mother's side?

But, do not descend into lamentations—at least the father's name is the same : Badruddin!

When you next visit Fatehpur Sikri, Sheikh, pay special obeisance to the small infant's grave on the right of the saint's grave. This is where the real son of emperor Akbar rests!

Now, I must close. It is past midnight and we have to move camp tomorrow. There is a chill in my bones, Sheikh, and it is not because of the biting cold here.

This is probably my last letter. I have no words left.

Al-Vida, Sheikh!

* * *

Emperor Jahangir sat lost in thought. What monumental mistakes had he made in life—orchestrating the ambush and killing of this kind and affectionate Vizier, who had kept this destructive secret to himself. He could have profited from it, and could have ransomed emperor Akbar for his kingdom and his steed, such was the power of the secret he carried.

His tears, as they rolled, were crusted with the salt of remorse.

* * *

CHAPTER 6

KHANIAGAR KHAMUSH

(The Silenced Minstrel)

Jahangir's Palace, Agra Fort,
15 December 1605
06.40 a.m.

The emperor had not slept properly for almost a week now, and the royal *hakim* had conveyed his anxiety to the Vizier, Shereif Khan, and to the senior royal ladies of the harem.

There was another reason for the hakim's unease; the emperor had started consuming a full bowl of wine mixed with opium, and Begum Jodh Bai had informed the veteran physician of her concern at the emperor's deteriorating health. Of all the emperor's wives, this queen, a princess from the Royal House of Jodhpur, was the third wife of Jahangir and the mother of Prince Khurram, and though not the *Padshah Begum,* she wielded immense influence within the seraglio.

Deep inside the imperial apartments, emperor Jahangir studied the squatting figure of Baiju Bawra, gazing intensely at the gilded carvings on the roof. No words had been spoken since he had been brought forth from the dungeons a few minutes ago.

Jahangir stretched his legs as the wretched effects of opium seemed to drag him down, yet again. 'Tell me, bard, what inspired you to write such spurious tales of malice? You do know that the only punishment for this can be death?'

Baiju replied with a malicious smirk, 'If this be false propaganda, Your Highness, then give me back my parchment and I shall go back to my home in Chanderi, where the spirit of Sheikh Abu'l Fazl waits for me.'

Jahangir's eyes turned red. 'What parchment, bard? That bundle of lies and concocted accusations will fetch you the hangman's noose, and nothing more.'

Baiju Bawra struggled to his feet. 'So be it. My meeting with the Sheikh is predetermined—whether it happens in Chanderi or *jannat*, is entirely at Your Majesty's discretion. And there is nothing, Sire, which you or your minions can do to forbid it.' The fetters rankled.

'You might have been a good singer, minstrel, but you are of unsound mind. *Arsh Ashiyani* judged you correctly for your devious ways and banished you from Sikri so many winters ago. Your presence in this world must come to an end, and with it the venomous lies that you carry.'

'You mean the truth about your birth, Jahangir?' Baiju's words were laced with malice.

'Shut your mouth, mongrel. You deserve to be trampled to death. Sentry!' roared Jahangir.

'Your Majesty?'

'Throw this cur in the dungeons. Gag him, and have him executed by the elephants tomorrow.' Jahangir's eyes were shod with red streaks.

He sank onto the cushioned recliner. The splitting headache again.

***

Agra Fort,
The same day.
11.40 a.m.

Prince Khurram walked in his father's wake, as the emperor retired from the *Diwan-e-Aam* to the imperial harem. The Most Gracious *Mariam Uz Zamani,* the Dowager Empress, had specially invited the emperor and the royal family to her apartment. The forty days ritual mourning for Emperor Akbar had ended just last week, and the palace was again awash with the splendid colours and gaiety that so defined the Mughal court.

The *Gurzbardars* walked a hundred paces ahead of the emperor, twirling their golden maces and proclaiming His Imperial Majesty's arrival.

As they turned left onto the long corridor which led to the royal harem, prince Khurram stumbled and crashed into the unyielding armour of a sentry. The emperor turned around to see several hands reaching out to steady the young prince whose wide-eyed gaze was glued towards the royal garden on the left. The emperor followed his gaze.

Arjumand Bano, wearing a pink and gold dress of gossamer silk, stood watching the regal procession. A beguiling smile lit her face as she saw a stumbling Khurram settle his turban. Their eyes locked.

The emperor sighed wistfully. He could not really blame Khurram for his love-struck wonderment. This girl *was* beautiful; just like Anarkali. Jahangir winced, as a shot of pain ran through his chest.

Mariam Uz Zamani descended the few steps to the colonnade surrounded by the queens and the royal concubines. Cries of *'Padshah Salamat'* went up as the royal ladies showered perfumed rose petals on the emperor. The Dowager Empress embraced her son as Jahangir bowed to kiss her hand.

Khurram shook his head and swung his gaze towards the milling crowd of the royal ladies. His eyes settled on the beautiful girl child as she held the hands of a pretty maiden and recounted something in merry detail. Both the girls laughed, when her eyes again strayed towards Khurram. Her laugh slowly folded itself into an enigmatic smile as she swung her eyes away from the deep probing stare of the young prince, and walked away into the swaying, clapping throng of palace revellers.

His eyes continued to search for her amongst the mass of glittering royals and their invitees, as an attendant bowed proffering a silver tray heaped with finely chiseled pieces of dry roast venison with spiced honey. On the side were small mounds of pickled guavas and spiced cranberries with sour cream. The prince waved her away.

The sun had traversed south and Khurram could feel a welcome warmth on his back, as he cut a long shadow on the marbled walkway in front. His thoughts were cut short as he saw a shimmer of dainty feet encased in gold and silver *juttis* touching the periphery of his shadow and then hastily withdrawing. He looked up.

The beautiful girl of pink gossamer stood on his left wearing a beatific smile and holding a tray heaped with fruits, almonds, and raisins. Mesmerised, Khurram stood up and held the tray. For several seconds, they both stood there looking into each other's eyes, the tray held between them. The girl smiled and dipped her head, dissolving this magic moment.

'Thank you,' murmured the young prince as he gestured to the marble slab for her to sit.

Khurram sat down heavily; his heart was beating too fast. He kept the tray on his knee, and taking a deep breath, asked 'What is your name, Princess?'

The young girl smiled that slow angelic smile of hers, and delicately removed the tray from the prince's knee and kept it between them on the marble slab. 'Arjumand, Your Highness. Arjumand Bano.' Her voice was soft and cultured.

'Well, Arjumand. Why did you wrench your feet away a few moments ago? Were you planning to run away with my tray of dry fruits?'

Arjumand looked up and spoke softly, 'Your Highness, I snatched my feet back as I realised that I was about to step on your royal shadow. It would have been a transgression.'

'Oh, come on, Arjumand, you know that rule applies only to the emperor's shadow, not to princes,' Khurram's voice was cracking with nervousness.

She glanced up, and her words were prophetic, 'You shall be an emperor one day, Your Highness.'

Khurram felt a warm flush coursing through his body as he stared intently at this exquisite apparition in front. He took in the rose and peaches complexion, the hazel eyes with their long eyelashes and a perfectly arched brow, an alluring oval face with a dainty nose, and full ruby lips which seemed to change easily into a charming smile. The hazel eyes were large and swam with the promise of a thousand fairytales.

Too flustered to answer, Khurram just smiled at her. *You shall be my queen one day, Arjumand, come what may,* promised the young prince to himself.

As if reading his thoughts, Arjumand blushed and delicately nudged the tray closer to him.

Khurram wanted to touch her, hold her hand, and kiss her delicate fingers, but all he could manage was a guttural croak, 'Where do you stay, Princess?'

She replied with a smile, 'I am not a princess, Your Highness. I am the granddaughter of Mirza Ghiyas Beg, and have come here with my mother and aunts.'

Khurram nodded and glanced towards the festivities. Several maidens and harem attendants were now watching them closely and nudging each other in jocular appreciation. As if on cue, Queen Jodha Bai rose and turned towards the palace. A fleeting scowl of annoyance crossed her haughty features as she looked at her son engrossed with an apparently beautiful girl. The folly of youth, thought she, as she settled once more into her mask of imperial hauteur.

Arjumand had not missed the questioning look of Queen Manmati, and hastily stood up gathering her skirt. 'I must go, Your Highness.'

'Please don't, fairy. Stay awhile.'

She smiled, 'This is what I was afraid of, Your Highness. You have already forgotten my name!'

Khurram stood up, and in great agitation said, 'I shall never forget your name, Arjumand. But to me, you will always be a fairy.' After a pause, he blurted, 'When will I see you again?'

Arjumand laughed softly, 'Fairies only come in dreams, Highness.'

'Then I shall make you my queen one day. My fairy Queen.'

Arjumand blushed scarlet, and fled.

***

Khwabgah,
Jahangir's Palace, Agra Fort,
Past midnight.

Emperor Jahangir was restive in his sleep, and intermingled sounds of indignation and apology escaped his scarcely moving lips—the visage of a furious emperor Akbar seemed to be admonishing him.

'You are being unjust and tyrannical as always, Sheikhu. What the bard has shown is the truth, Sheikhu, and there is no denying it. You will not have him executed, do you hear?'

'You are not my son, you never were!'

Jahangir screamed and sat bolt upright. The ornamented room was dark, and the soft silk curtains swayed lazily in the night breeze, the silver of the night moon grazing the emperor's pale visage.

The scent of Akbar lingered in the air.

Jahangir shook his head. The vital evidence was irrevocably burnt and cast away.

Truth was buried. Deceit survived.

***

Half an hour later...

The night commander was sent immediately to the dungeons near the gallows.

Baiju Bawra, the demented singer, was not to be executed, but sent to Gwalior Fort under royal command.

***

Cluster of rooms,
NW corner, Agra Fort
20 December 1605
6.30 p.m.

The prince walked slowly across the royal apartments, and passing behind the royal *hammam*, continued towards the northern tower. On an impulse, he stooped and plucked a few red narcissi for his elder brother. Khusrau loved flowers.

Burly Afghans in their green and white turbans stood guard, and the entrance to prince Khusrau's temporary incarceration was through a narrow corridor under the steps leading to the northern tower. The wide colonnaded passage, in front of the suite of rooms, had been recently bricked and was guarded by several eunuchs of the emperor's own harem. Prince Khurram passed the corridor and entered into a wide courtyard, fringed by beds of flowers in winter bloom.

'Come, Khurram, come.' Prince Khusrau stood up from the stone slab, and stepped forward to embrace his half-brother.

Beti Begum, wife of Prince Khusrau and the daughter of the *Khanzada* Mirza Aziz Koka Khan e Azam, smiled prettily as she performed the taslim, and Khurram half bowed in acknowledgement. Khurram sat on the stone bench and studied his hands. Prince Khusrau cast an amused glance at his wife, who gathered her shawl and sat on the perch of a pillar nearby.

'I understand the prince is in love now.' There was mild amusement in her voice, as Khurram's head snapped up.

Colouring, he asked, 'How do you know, *bhabhijaan?*' Khurram looked at his elder brother's wife, 'I have just met her. Once.'

Khusrau and Beti Begum both laughed at the rueful expression on Khurram's face. 'But, prince, why do you grieve? You have promised to make her your queen!' She leant forward and gently lifted Khurram's chin. 'I know she is very beautiful, Khurram. I have seen her many times in the company of her mother, Diwanji Begum, as she frequently visits the royal harem. She is quite a darling in the eyes of both the Queen Mothers, Ruqaiah Sultana Begum and Salima Sultana Begum.'

Khurram's face lit up. He was about to say something when his eyes fell on an archer stationed well above in the tower, and the excitement faded from his voice. He ran his eyes over the several abutments, high windows and wall apertures—there were musketeers and archers spread all around.

Prince Khusrau was calmly looking at him and put a gentle hand on Khurram's shoulder as he saw the evident distaste in his eyes.

'This is the first time, Khurram, that an innocent royal has been imprisoned.' There was deep sadness in his voice. 'Never mind that I am a Timurid prince with the blood of Taimur and Genghis Khan; never mind that I am the grandson of Shah Akbar of Sultanat Mughaliya or with matrilineal lines to the brave Kachhawas of Amber; what is important is that I am innocent with no crimes against the emperor or the State. Yet, I am put under arrest in a secluded corner of this misbegotten fort, and left to live my life as a common criminal. My wife suffers with me.'

Khurram remained silent and watched the glow of the lamps faithfully replace the waning light of the setting sun.

'Sire, let us not dampen Khurram's happy spirit with our sad circumstance. Wait, I shall fetch something hot and sweet for us to drink.'

The young Timurid princes sat in silence, each wrapped in his own thoughts, as the princess appeared with steaming silver glasses of Kashmiri tea. 'Drink this, and wish the sadness away.'

Khurram smiled gratefully, and turned to his brother, 'Your Highness...'

'Oh, come now, Khurram. We are not in the royal court, please.'

'Sire,' both the princes smiled. Formal courtesy was so ingrained in them, that it was difficult to ignore. 'Why don't you seek the emperor's forgiveness, and play to his sense of justice?'

'What sense of justice, Khurram? You don't become an Angel of Justice by hanging the golden *Zanzeer i Adl* to the fort ramparts, do you? It is your actions, Khurram, which speak and define who you are. Remember, in full court, my father proclaimed me as his beloved son and publicly forgave what he construed as my trespasses. And, what was my fault? It was the will of a section of the populace, and of several important court nobles who preferred to see me on the throne. And the reason for that is well known to you, Khurram.' His words became heated.

'A huge majority of the populace and Court Grandees were shamed by the rebellion of our illustrious father, and their sympathies lay with *Arsh Ashiyani Ala Hazrat Akbar Shah,* the forgiving and tolerant father of an errant son. Not once, not twice, but many times did Emperor Salim Jahangir march against His Imperial Majesty, and each time he was forgiven. Where have I erred so grievously that I am made captive in this fort and denied the freedom of a Timurid?'

His voice rose with passion, 'I was promised the grand mansion of Munim Khan and a lakh of rupees in full court, was I not? And see, what have I got? This set of filthy rooms, which were the Ahadi barracks! Our slaves and attendants have been snatched away from us, and these spies substituted in their place.' He swept an arm towards the apartments.

'I am not the son born of a *kenchan,*' he raged. 'I am born of the Shah Begum, the first wife of His Royal Highness, and deserve the privileges of a Timurid prince!' His eyes burned, as he spat, 'And *Insha-Allah,* I shall have them too!'

'We all pray for your safety and wellbeing, brother. There is nary a soul in the harem who does not pray for your safe conduct every day.'

'The sword shall achieve what prayers cannot.' There was an edge to prince Khusrau's words.

Khurram felt uneasy at these words, and tried to fathom the meaning. There was a glint in Khusrau's eyes as they strayed towards the entrance doorway. He stood up.

'I must go, Highness, or I shall be missed. *Khuda hafiz!'* Midway, he turned back, and added, 'Please do not do something foolish, brother. The stars are not in your favour. I implore you.'

Khusrau acknowledged with a wave.

As Khurram entered the narrow corridor underneath the tower steps, his hand flew to his dagger. He caught the form nearest to him.

'Mercy, prince, mercy. I am Husain Beg of Badaksh, and these two are my followers.' There was panic in his voice as Khurram still held the dagger pressed to his throat.

Recognising him as one of prince Khusrau's retainers, he put the dagger away. 'Stay away from the shadows, Husain Beg, or you will come to harm.

'But, of course, prince Khurram.' The shadows retreated performing the taslim.

Khurram turned to look, but the shadows had merged in the wicked plot being hatched at this furthermost corner of Agra fort.

***

The night of 22 December, 1605, was cold and dark, as a few riders on feeble horses left the walls of Agra Fort for the dungeons of Gwalior Qila. Riding between them in the winter haze, was the silenced minstrel, Baiju Bawra.

***

CHAPTER 7

SHAMSHIRAT RA GHLAF NAKAN, KHOSRO!

(Sheath Not Your Sword, Khusrau!)

Inner Apartments, Near Fil khana,
Agra Fort,
24 February 1606.
10.40 p.m.

Prince Khusrau paced the long corridor oblivious to the strong drizzle which slanted its way onto the flag-stoned veranda.

His begum stood just behind the heavy velvet curtain which shielded the royal apartment from unwanted eyes, aware of her husband's suppressed anger and despair at his imprisonment within the palace.

Khusrau saw her beautiful, oval face gazing worriedly at him, and walked slowly over. Extending her delicate hand, she pulled Khusrau inside the room, handing him a small goblet of iced *sherbet.*

'Sire, there is a small package for you, which carries the seal of Mirza Raja Man Singh,' softly did the begum speak, as she watched Khusrau drain the goblet in a single gulp.

Khusrau's head snapped back, 'Who brought it? Where is he?'

'I was in the *zenana khana* this afternoon at the request of Begum Ruqaiah Sultana, when a weaver from Chandausi came in with exquisite bolts of silk, and gold flecked bangles from Bengal.'

The prince looked with suspicion at the mustard-coloured cloth rolled tightly around a small bundle.

'As *A'la Begum* was choosing gold embroidered silk for all of us, this woman picked up some bangles and silver ankle bells, and handed them to me in a small velvet pouch. She refused to take any money, instead she prostrated herself before A'la Begum and begged for the right to gift to "her little princess", as she referred to me. Inside the pouch was this *sanad.*' She indicated the small bundle.

'Another strange thing, my prince. When the tradeswoman and the eunuchs had left, A'la Begum told me to take it safely to you, as it could mean your freedom or kingdom. Seeing the query in my eyes, she just told me to deliver it to you personally, and she had the Chief Eunuch escort me all the way to our apartment here.'

Khusrau nodded as he unrolled the sealed epistle from his maternal uncle, Mirza Raja Man Singh of Amer. His right temple pulsating, he scanned the parchment.

Your Highness Sultan Khusrau Mirza,
Khamaghani!

You may feel surprised upon receiving this missive from me with such subterfuge, but the fabric of our times does not make it easy for those of us who carried the imperial banner of our late Padshah Ghazi Arsh Ashiyani! The empire is rife with rumours and uncertainties, while the Royal Court is darkened by the odious spectre of a virulent, inebriated king.

I reached Murshidabad at the end of November, and have since then not been allotted any quarters commensurate with my imperial post. The provincial revenue, administrative and military commanders have also been steering clear of me, but it really does not matter, prince. I am biding my time!

While the Khufiya navees will be circulating reports to the emperor and that moron, Shareif Khan, about my official isolation, I have not been idle. The Portuguese, who hold the ports of Hooghly, have approached me with an audacious plan to reverse our fortunes. In this regard, several of our Rajput chieftains have also sent their embassies, offering allegiance.

Our clans have not forgotten the demise of my beloved sister (your mother), poisoned by the hands of your father, and we shall avenge the death of our sister!

You were the chosen one for the throne; it was only the illness of Alampanah and the resurgence of the Afghans and Turqis, led by the Sayyids of Barha, which prevented your ascension to the throne. But I have made alternate arrangements...Escape! Escape from the fort and ride North in a feint, then circle back from Palwal and join me at Bengal. In the east, from the fort of Rohtas to the mouth of Hooghly is ours—dominated by the rebel Afghans, vengeful Portuguese, and the Dutch artillery. To the west, from the ramparts of Amer to the desert garrisons of Jaisalmer, will rise the Rajput Kesariya. More than seventy Rajput chieftains have vowed allegiance. Remember Khusrau, that the Rajawats neither forget nor forgive, and our revenge is severe and brutal.

It saddens me to write, but I must bring to your notice, that several of the court sycophants are daily poisoning His Majesty's ears about your perceived threat to the royal throne. I fear for your life, O Prince, and must advise you to be very cautious in your daily routine. The assassins are not far from you, and dwell in close proximity.

Tarry not, but make your arrangements quickly. Perhaps, immediately after Navroz?

I pray to Lord Krishna for your well-being, and for the eternal prosperity of Arsh Ashiyani's fabled kingdom! Do send me your wellbeing per return horse.

In one voice your ancestors call, 'Sheath not your sword, Khusrau! Rise and Reclaim!'

Obedient Mansabdar of the Realm,
Mirza Raja Man Singh of Amer
7000 Zat/ 5000 Sowars

There was deep gloom in Khusrau's eyes as he let the parchment catch fire from a flickering lamp.

***

CHAPTER 08

ZIRA PADSHAII KHISHAVANDI NEMISHENASAD

(For Kingship Knows No Kinship)

Dilli Gate,
Agra Fort,
06 April 1606.
3.40 p.m.

'Prepare to mount', came the hoarse cry of the prince's royal guard.

Prince Khusrau, attired simply in the garb of a devout seeker, cantered his way through the gathered cavalry near the main quadrangle of the western part of the fort. To his side, rode the brave Mirza Hasan in full combat armour, and Caliph Khan, the huge Uzbeg master archer. As usual, his long bow and heavy quiver were slung low by his horse's side, and he wore his plumed helmet with casual disdain.

Khusrau reined his horse into a lazy trot, as the column made its way down the cobbled incline towards the massive arches of the Delhi Gate. A few of his attendants, moved swiftly past, to apprise the sentries of the prince's arrival. The sentry commander stepped forward.

'Who goes there?'

'His Highness Prince Khusrau, Darogha, to offer prayers at Bihishtabad. It is his royal wish to visit *Arsh Ashiyani Jalaluddin Mohammed Akbar's* tomb at Sikandra, and offer the evening prayers. Now, open the gates.'

Eight horsemen of the royal cavalry, riding four abreast, moved forward and shouted, 'Make way for His Majesty, the First Born and Heir to the Throne, Shahzade Mirza Khusrau! Make way, Make way!'

The sentries hastily moved the pulleys, locks, and bolts to open the huge gates, as the prince and his mounted bodyguards rode into view. They drew their spears to the side, and bowed as the prince cantered by.

Moving to close the gate, a guard with a missing thumb, asked the sentry commander, 'Sire, what were those large covered vessels for, tied to the horses of the rear echelons?'

'Food for the poor, you dumb fool! Don't you know that food is distributed to the poor and destitute after a *fateya* has been read?'

The guard looked at his missing thumb. You could never be careful enough, he consoled himself.

The prince's consort, Beti Begum, alone and desolate in her suite of rooms, wiped her tears as the clatter of hooves receded into the distance. She lowered her head and prayed.

The extra weapons concealed inside the huge cauldrons and vessels, clamoured for comfort as the contingent broke into a gallop over the rough cobbled streets, and stretched for Sikandra.

***

Bihishtabad (Sikandra)
6 p.m.

The inner sanctum remained silent, as the young prince knelt in prayer.

Prince Khusrau raised his head, swinging it first to the left and then to the right, and then blew upon his palms, passing them over his closed eyes. Reciting the last few lines of the evening prayer, he slowly opened his eyes and gasped in alarm.

Standing before him, at the head of the tomb, was the all too familiar figure of the dead emperor, Akbar.

Frightened beyond words, Khusrau threw himself forward at the foot of the raised grave and with shaking fingers, clutched the smooth marbled motifs at the edge. The spectre of a dead emperor, unsmiling and gaunt, stared ominously back at the kneeling figure of the young prince.

Trembling, Khusrau raised his face and slowly opened his eyes. The bejeweled, turbaned apparition seemed to slowly dissolve into smoke, until, only the sorrowing decayed face was clearly discernible. Soon, there was just the hint of a familiar perfume left.

Khusrau felt a stabbing pain in his groin, and made an effort to stand up. He looked around, but the sanctum sanctorum was silent and bereft of another soul. The massive circular walls, freshly decorated with delicate threads of beaten gold and encrusted with semi-precious stones shimmered in melancholic seclusion as the huge golden lamp suspended by a narrow chain of gold from the roof of the domed chamber, cast its eerie glow and swayed lightly.

Moving hastily away, Khusrau staggered into the long narrow corridor with a shallow incline. Mirza Hasan and a few of his close attendants were surprised at the wan expression and unsteady gait of the prince, and moved forward to help him. He waved them away.

'Bring my horse,' muttered Khusrau.

Settling unsteadily in the saddle, his eyes went back to the small gateway of red sandstone, and the words seemed to mock him, 'These are the Gardens of Eden; enter them and live forever!' The vision of a forlorn and melancholic emperor continued to haunt prince Khusrau, as he spurred his horse into a gallop, and turned right towards Mathura.

Mirza Hasan, riding just behind the prince, raised his sword and shouted, 'To Freedom; To Victory!' And, so did the 350 horsemen of the Imperial cavalry.

The prince's unfurled flags, streaming towards Mathura and Lahore, heralded a new chapter in royal rebellion.

* * *

Khwabgah, (Imperial Chambers),
Agra Fort
Same evening
One hour to midnight.

There was complete silence in the emperor's bed chamber, as the senior queen Begum Jagat Gosain stood contemplating the inert form of emperor Jahangir. He lay on his side, with one of his arms tucked underneath his head and the other thrown carelessly over the gold sequined bolster. The consumption of wine mixed with opium had effectively put him into a deep inebriated sleep.

'Your Majesty, please wake up,' she said gently and touched the emperor on his arm. Qaid Akram, the emperor's chief eunuch, raised his eyes to the roof and cried loudly, *'Allahu Akbar!'* The emperor stirred slightly and Akram raised the intensity of his chant. Finally, Jahangir opened an opium sodden eye and tried to sit up.

Begum Jagat Gosain touched his shoulder, 'The *Vizier Ul Mulk and Mir* Bakshi are waiting outside, Your Majesty. They send their compliments.'

'What? What brings them here?' His voice slurred, he tried to get off the bed. 'Wait. Tell them to wait.'

The Vizier, Shareif Khan spoke first, 'Your Majesty, please forgive us our trespass, but the news could not wait.' His voice was trembling.

'Speak, Shareif Khan. Is it Deccan, or the Gujarat campaign?'

'I wish it were so, Your Highness.' His trembling voice became lower. *'Rustam i Hind Padshah Ghazi,* The Ray of Imperial Sun, forgive me, please. It is my misfortune to inform you that prince Khusrau escaped from Agra *Qila* this evening.' Shareif Khan hung his head in shame.

Emperor Jahangir swayed slightly and reached for a bedpost to support himself. His voice became hoarse. 'When did this happen? And, *how* did this happen?'

The Vizier and Mir Bakshi looked at each other. Finally, Sheikh Bokhari spoke, 'Majesty, the young prince rode out just before dusk on the pretext of visiting *Arsh Ashiyani's* tomb at Sikandra. A few of his followers and royal troops assigned to guard him, were also with him.'

'How many?'

'Three hundred and fifty riders, Sire.'

'It has taken you two watches to inform me of this... this rebellion?' The emperor's question was more of a shriek, and it petrified the two court grandees. They were well aware of Jahangir's wrath and cruel punishments.

The Vizier, almost in tears, said '*Bandanawaz,* Refuge of the Poor, it was just a few minutes ago that the chiragchi informed me. Your Highness, as the *chiragchi* went around snuffing the primary wall torches, he was concerned by the absolute stillness in the prince's apartment. A few questions later, it dawned that the prince had not returned from Bihishtabad. He came running to me, and I made haste to your imperial presence. I met the *Mir Bakshi* in the royal stables, and we came directly to you, Sire.'

The emperor's temple was throbbing, and his eyes seemed to protrude, as he glared at them. The eunuch, Akram, laid a warm shawl around the emperor's shoulder. Though the marble lattices carried the night breeze from across the Jumna, there were beads of sweat on everyone's forehead. Jahangir willed his voice to normal.

'What do you suggest we do now, Vizier? Wait till morning, or pursue now?'

There was complete silence. He continued, 'Should I ask Khurram to pursue him, or should I ride forth?' He mused aloud, absently stroking his beard, 'He could not have travelled far at night. If he is avoiding the regular roads and the *dak chowkis* and riding cross country, even then he will be lucky to find Mathura before morning'. He seemed to ponder a bit, and then turned his gaze on them, 'This could be a ruse too. Mirza Raja Mansingh is at Bengal, and that is where he will rush. Mir Bokhari, send men in every direction.'

Sheikh Bokhari nudged the Vizier, Shareif Khan. Reluctantly, Shareif Khan offered 'Your Imperial Majesty, it is my negligence which has led to this catastrophe, and I should be permitted to make good the loss. If you will allow me, My Lord, then I shall set out forthwith in pursuit.'

Jahangir's face softened. 'So be it, Shareif Khan. Time is of the essence, and you should delay not. Ride forth, and bring Khusrau back to me.'

Performing the kornish, Shareif Khan and Farid Bokhari slowly moved backwards. The Vizier suddenly asked, 'Majesty, should the prince not see the folly of his ways and raise arms, then what are my orders?'

Jahangir's eyes became bulbous again, as he frostily replied. 'Kingship knows no kinship, Vizier. Treat him as you would a common traitor. The way of the *Chugatais.*'

***

Imperial Chambers, Agra Fort
An hour past midnight.

'Sheikh Bokhari, I am not too comfortable with the idea of Shareif Khan in pursuit of the errant prince, and I wish for you to command this force. You see, the prince stores much hatred for the Vizier, and I do not wish that in the heat of the moment, he should carry the taint of the Vizier's blood on his hands.' Jahangir kept quiet for a few seconds.

Sheikh Bokhari kept his mouth and eyes closed. How quickly does History repeat itself, he thought. Hardly four winters ago, this same emperor as a prince then, had stained his hands and disgraced his name by having his father's Vizier, Sheikh Abu'l Fazl Ibn Mubarak, ambushed and killed in the forests near Gwalior. Now, perhaps, the same fate awaited his Vizier?

'I shall proceed as ordered, Your Majesty.'

'Good. Now, send Muizzulmulk to recall Shareif Khan. For your detachment, use your own troops as well as those who were entrusted with the prince's custody. The main body of the Vizier's force will merge with you enroute, and also have Ibrahim Beg join you with his Afghan archers.'

Sheikh Farid Bokhari bowed in salutation, and turned to go.

The emperor's voice followed him. 'Make haste, Sheikh, for I will be following you. At first light.'

***

Dawn was breaking when the emperor's war drums were beaten and flags unfurled, as the fort garrison along with the emperor's own bodyguards assembled in the huge quadrangle in front of the Hall of Public Audience, and lined the pathways inside and outside the citadel. The emperor, following the family rituals before departing on a war campaign, dipped a fish in curd and touched it to his forehead.

Surrounded by his generals, royal guards and the Shahi Qur, the emperor swung himself up onto his favourite stallion, *Shamsher*, and spurred his horse into a furious gallop. The Ahadis, used to more sedate and ceremonial departures, were nonplussed for a few seconds, before they galloped after the emperor's flag with fearsome cries of *'Ya fateh! Ya jung!'*

Long after they had disappeared from view, the red stone walls of the fort reverberated with the sounds of dynastic calumny.

***

Narela,
Outskirts of Delhi
08 April 1606.
Just before noon.

Prince Khusrau sat up in alarm.

Turning towards the commotion, he saw several of his troops hastily mount their horses, shouting wildly. Khusrau squinted his eyes, and tried to focus on a small dot in the distance, rapidly drawing nearer. Farther away, a small contingent of cavalry seemed to be pursuing the lone traveller, which was drawing closer by the minute.

Rising from the gnarled roots of a huge tamarind tree where he had been resting, Khusrau signalled for his horse, even as Caliph Khan and a few others formed a protective cordon around him. A small squadron of Badakshis and royal troopers had already ridden out to engage the new arrivals, and could be seen waving their swords and shouting in glee, as they surrounded the solitary traveller. In a few moments, the cavalry which was in pursuit, also mingled with the Badakshis amidst great shouts of joy.

As they drew close, Khusrau smiled at the gaily decorated she-camel, *Budhiya Rani,* which was bearing down on them in the very ungainly gait so typical of camels. Though her name suggested an 'aged queen', her speed belied the false insinuations. She was famous for being the fastest camel in the *Shahi Shutr Khana* and was mostly used for transporting royal treasury, and had gained much notoriety for her personal foible of working only after she had properly snorted an opium laden *chillum* for a good five minutes!

Abdul Rahim, the Governor of Lahore and Dilawar Khan the fort commander, raced their horses to the front as their standard bearers galloped by their sides carrying the Mughal flag in green with a golden crouching lion. Alighting, they performed the kornish to the young prince.

'Welcome, Abdul Rahim and Dilawar Khan. It is indeed fortuitous that we meet today.'

'Your Highness,' spoke Dilawar Khan, eyeing the roguish assembly of Badakshis, 'we are on our way to pay obeisance at the royal court.'

'Indeed. This too is a royal court of His Royal Highness Prince Khusrau Mirza.' These words, spoken loudly by Husain Beg, brought an immediate hush upon the gathering.

In the ensuing silence, Abdul Rahim, trusted general over several decades, ventured to ask 'Majesty, have you raised the flag of rebellion against the monarch?'

'I am not in rebellion, *Subedar*. I am in quest for what was rightfully mine, and what was ordained for me by my revered grandfather, may peace be upon His Majesty's soul.'

Dilawar Khan watched the unfolding drama with perturbation. The eight hundred to a thousand strong followers of prince Khusrau seemed firmly entrenched in this treasonable act. Worse, they were spoiling for a fight. His thoughts went back to the royal treasure under his charge.

Abdul Rahim looked uncomfortable at this revelation. He observed, 'Your Highness. The late emperor's fondness for you is well known, but he did assign his sword, realm, and the imperial turban to his eldest son and rightful heir, in the manner of the Chughtais.'

'The Chughtai way, Abdul Rahim, is the rule of the strongest and most capable,' scoffed Khusrau.

Husain Beg Badakshi spurred his steed forward, and thundered, 'Which rightful heir are you talking of, Rahim Khan? The ignoble prince who rebelled against his own father, and set up a parallel, farcical kingdom at Allahabad? Who repaid the bounty and trust of his father by arranging the treacherous murder of his Vizier and closest confidant? Or, are you referring to the inebriated prince who tried to poison his own father in 1591, and was imprisoned at *Bala Qila* in Alwar as a result? Which heir do you speak of now, tell me?' Angry specks of spittle ran down his chin.

Dilawar Khan drew his sword. So did many others. His voice was scathing, 'Watch your tongue, Husain Beg! It is the emperor you talk of, and your words are seditious.' He pointed his sword at the seated Afghan, 'If you utter one more word against the emperor, I shall remove your head with great pleasure.'

With a roar, Husain Beg drew his sword, as did the accompanying Badakshis. Caliph Khan quickly swung his huge horse and his own imposing bulk between the two warriors.

Khusrau, disliking the turn of events, turned to Abdul Rahim. 'What business takes you and Dilawar Khan to Agra? And, who looks after the Shahi Qila at Lahore, while both of you are here?'

'Nuruddin Quli Kotwal is there, with a garrison of about five thousand soldiers, Highness.' Abdul Rahim pointed to the small train of camels, 'We are also carrying a part of the royal treasury from Lahore to Agra.'

Dilawar cast him a warning glance.

There was an immediate ripple of excitement amongst Khusrau's troops, which prompted Dilawar Khan to jump upon his horse, and with a wild roar, gallop away, signalling for his cavalry and camel riders to follow suit. As Abdul Rahim tried to reach for his horse's bridle, the point of Caliph Khan's sword caressed his neck.

Several of Khusrau's men kicked their horses into pursuit, but a stentorian shout from Khusrau stopped them. 'Let them go. We are seeking an empire, not a few camel loads of silver. We must proceed towards Lahore with all haste. And you, Abdul Rahim, what does your heart say?'

Shaken, the weary general stood silent. However, the words were not long in coming.

'Your Majesty, my refuge is in the shadow of the Mughal emperors.' He pointed towards *Budhiya Rani,* which was placidly chewing its cud. 'It is an omen, Sire. Allah has sent you this she-camel as a sign of Divine Grace. Remember the she-camel of Prophet Saleh, Peace Be Upon Him, which Allah bestowed upon the people of Thamud? The same divinity shines upon you, Majesty! The Realm shall be yours.'

'SubhanAllah! SubhanAllah!' rose the raucous cries from the spirited warriors.

'And, Your Majesty, Budhiya carries one lakh rupees in silver from the royal treasury, which is now submitted to you.'

Prince Khusrau could not believe his good fortune. Elated, he leant down to touch the shoulder of Abdul Rahim. Turning his horse around, he announced, 'I raise Abdul Rahim as the *Malikulwazira,* and he shall henceforth be known as Anwar Khan.'

Hamza Beg, an old Badakshi wearing a cape of bear skin even in the heat of April, stood up from the rocks where he was sharpening his sword, and shouted, 'And the same she-camel brought about the utter destruction of the Thamuds, when they desecrated the righteous. The earth heaved, and the infidels were buried and lost forever! Forget not the righteous path, O Prince, as you march for glory.'

***

CHAPTER 9

TAATTUL-e-SHAHI

(The Royal Interlude)

Dera Arjan Dev,
Tarn Taran, Punjab.
14 April 1606.
Just before dawn.

Guru Arjan Dev sat cross legged on the round stony platform encircling the enormous Banyan tree, and absently ran his fingers through the wavy, brown hair on the prince's uncovered head, his lips moving in silent prayer.

He slowly lowered his legs, and holding both of prince Khusrau's hands, pulled him up. Rising, he dipped his thumb into the vermilion paste and drew a long linear mark on the prince's forehead. The prince bowed, and then leant forward to whisper in the Guru's ears. The saint nodded and gestured for an old iron trunk to be brought across. A singularly burly Sikh dragged the half open, ramshackle box and at the Guru's bidding flung it open.

Khusrau was struck by the glitter of silver coins scrupulously bound in banana leaves as the saint gestured for Khusrau to help himself. The prince folded his palms, 'Sire, I am a seeker, not a forager. Please, with your own hands, give what you deem fit.'

The Sikh Guru took off his shawl, and filled it with silver coins. Tying the small mound, he proffered it to Khusrau, who raised it to his forehead, and kissed the saint's hand.

'Go with the Almighty, my son, and seek only what is yours, and ye shall find.'

Kissing the saint's hand once again, Khusrau spoke in a choked voice, 'Sire, you offered me refuge and shelter under your shadow, when even common peasants as well as the royal *karoris, jagirdars and zamindars* closed their doors fearing imperial reprisal. I can never repay you for your kindness, Sire, because silver and gold can never compensate for the goodness of a saintly heart.'

Guru Arjan smiled. 'I am a servant of the Almighty, prince, and my faith decrees that I help everyone in distress. I am not in fear, nor bound by the chains of royal commands. There is just one *Saccha Padshah* for me, and it is His bidding that I do. For Servants of God, there is no emperor, leper, prince, or pauper—just His children, and we serve and protect all. Therefore, young prince, ride forth and seek what is yours, and it shall be thine. Covet, what is not rightfully yours, and the flames of destruction and chastisement shall blind you.'

Guru Arjan Dev raised his hand in benediction, and prince Khusrau stepped back. Refusing to mount his horse in the sage's presence, he walked towards the main gate of the *Dera*, his troops following behind.

Guru Arjan Dev looked pensively at this horde of common peasants, carpenters, ironsmiths, and professional soldiers trailing the young prince in search of a Fate as yet unknown to any of them.

Pain and Death followed faithfully in their wake.

* * *

**Ramparts of Shahi Qila,
Lahore,
16 April 1606
Just after dusk.**

The fort commander, Dilawar Khan, stood on the eastern rampart of the imperial fort, along with Husain Beg *Diwan* and Nuruddin Quli *Kotwal*, watching prince Khusrau's troops pitching and staking their tents in a wide arc. Some parts of the contingent were still trailing in, and Dilawar, a veteran of many campaigns, was struck by the relative lack of supply wagons.

'Kotwal, they hardly have any supply wagons or animals with them. Their siege won't be long,' assessed Dilawar Khan.

Husain Beg, the Diwan, answered crossly, 'What do they need supplies for? They have been plundering and pillaging their way across the kingdom! His Majesty is close on the heels of the rebel prince with a large part of the army, and I understand that he has reached Shahabad. Prince Khusrau shall have the imperial army at his back, with us in front, and a grave beneath his feet.'

Dilawar nodded. 'Look at these men, Husain Beg. They cannot even stake their tents and horses in a straight line. How do you expect them to fight?' The men sneered in derision.

Dilawar Khan turned to his chief cannoneer. 'Shamshad, give them a warm welcome once they have settled in for the night. Cannons and fire tipped arrows.' Facing his garrison colleagues, he said mildly, 'Why put His Majesty to so much trouble? We may be fewer in numbers, but our soldiers are battle hardened and disciplined. And, we have the Sayyids of Barha with us, fearsome fighters as they are. We can rout this rabble in a day.'

***

That night, the silence was torn apart by the thunderous roar of cannons from the fort walls, and the sizzle of fire tipped arrows as they sought the sleeping weary forms of animals and men. The shrieks of men and the terrified neighing of tethered horses rent the tired fabric of this spring night, as hefty cannon balls continued to explode amidst the unnerved camp.

Unable to assess the extent of damage caused by them in the darkness, the fort cannons stopped firing after about an hour.

Next morning, before the sun was up, the rebel camp had commenced pitching at a site much farther back, out of artillery range. The siege was neutralised.

* * *

The Emperor's Camp,
Shahabad,
17 April 1606
7 a.m.

Emperor Salim Jahangir, waiting for his attendants to fasten the buckles of his leather arm guards, turned his attention to the old faithful of his father, Sheikh Nizam Thanesari, 'What brings you here, Sheikh? You voluntarily gave up the *jagir* bestowed upon you by the late emperor, and retired from the Court. Now, what ails you?'

'Your Majesty, just three days ago, I heard that Prince Khusrau was marching towards Lahore bearing the standard of revolt. I could not believe it! So, I made my old bones travel to meet him. Just outside Tarn Taran, I had the good fortune to lay my eyes on the glorious persona of the prince, as he rode out of the Sikh Guru's abode.'

'Which Guru are you talking of?' There was irritation in the emperor's voice.

'Majesty, Guru Arjan Dev of the Sikhs.'

'Are you sure of this, Thanesari?'

The old man shrank at the sight of the emperor's knitted brow. 'Your Highness, I have been ever faithful to your salt, Sire, and I wish you to know, *Huzoor,* that having convinced myself of the prince's evil designs, I tried to evince as much as I could from him, so that I may be able to inform you.'

'Go on,' replied Jahangir coldly.

'Your Majesty,' fawned the Sheikh, 'The Sikh Guru not only gave shelter to the prince, but also anointed him with a Hindu caste mark on his forehead.' He bowed even lower. 'Matter of shame, Your Majesty, but the prince also took five thousand rupees from this sage.'

'What sage?' shouted Jahangir. 'This man is just a shameless imposter, surviving on my grace and bounty. How dare he put the infidel's mark on the prince? Sheikh, are you sure of what you have said? You surely would not like your intestines trampled upon by *Gajraj* in old age?'

The old man sank to his knees, trembling. 'Majesty,' he wailed. 'I saw the caste marks with my own eyes, and the words are from the prince's own lips.'

Jahangir's lips curled in fury. 'The imposter shall be buried. And you, Sheikh Thanesari! You are not faithful; you have betrayed the trust reposed in you by prince Khusrau, and may do the same with the imperial throne tomorrow. Treachery runs in your blood. Proceed to Mecca immediately and atone for your sins.'

Jahangir watched with beady eyes as the old man curled up on the ground, wailing.

* * *

The Plains of Bhaironwal,
24 April 1606
7 a.m.

The soldiers trudged wearily through the rain sodden fields, having spent the night under trees and makeshift shelters, as the late spring rain continued to pour in heavy, unrelenting torrents. Mounted soldiers swayed by as the horses sank almost to their knees in the mushy quagmire, weighed down by their armoured riders.

This was not going to be a pretty battle.

The eight thousand imperial troops under Sheikh Farid Bokhari stood in a loose spear head formation, with the Sayyids of Barha, leading the vanguard as per their traditional rights. The battle plan was fairly simple—make a single, ferocious charge at the centre of the rebel forces, cleave them into two and then decimate them systematically.

On the far side stood the rebels. Prince Khusrau, advised by Abdur Rahim and Husain Beg Badakshi, had arrayed his almost twelve thousand troops in a shallow semi-circular formation. The rebel plan was to allow the Sayyids of Barha to charge at the centre, and then using their numerical superiority, surround them in a pincer movement and annihilate.

The imperial *harawals* led by the fearsome troops of the Sayyids of Barha had cleaved their way through the loosely held formation of ill-equipped foot soldiers and untrained mounted troopers of prince Khusrau's contingent.

Husain Beg Badakshi, leading his command of seven hundred Afghan horses, rode in from the left flank that it was holding, in conformity with the original plan to surround and decimate the imperial troops. Husain Beg, followed by his standard bearer and sizable cavalry, tore into the middle of the emperor's troops with blood curdling cries of *'Ya Allah! Al Madad!'* and for a few minutes it seemed as if the Barhas would scatter under the Badakshi onslaught.

Saif Khan Barha who was leading the central contingent of imperial troops, raised his spear and sent it searing across to dislodge the Badakshi standard bearer from his mount. As the rider fell, and the black and green Badakshi flag was trampled upon by the hurtling hooves, the Barha war cry went up.

The galloping Afghans barely had time to line up their weapons, before they were met by the resolute, battle-hardened troops of the Barhas. Swords flashed and spears gored the warriors of both sides as bodies fell in the dust.

As the frenzied Badakshi's leaned from their horses and cut into the foot soldiers who formed a major part of the Barha troops, their resolve seemed to waver. Battered, maimed, and trampled, the Barha footmen broke ranks and fled in different directions. Hazma Beg Afghan, an able ally of Husain Beg and distantly related, chased the fleeing troops wielding swords in both hands with the reins tied to the saddle horn. Emboldened, a sizable part of the Badakshi horse joined the chase, swiftly killing and maiming the fear-stricken deserters.

From the distance came the sound of war drums being beaten hard in staccato bursts and the rousing cries of a contingent preparing to charge. The Badakshi's, intent upon their relentless assault on the fleeing Barha troops, failed to register the dust rising behind them.

Saif Khan, a young ebullient scion of the Barha clan, snatched the standard from his bearer, and rising in the stirrups, rode in a wide arc shouting the fearsome war cry 'Allahu Akbar'! The disarrayed Barha's, spurred by the sight of the fearless Saif Khan, reined their horses and formed a tight circle. To their left, rode the lone figure of the young Barha, crouched over the horse's neck with the clan's flag fluttering high in his wake.

An angry shout went up from the closely formed Barhas as they saw Saif Khan tumble to the ground with a javelin protruding from his unprotected back. His horse shied in terror, and almost clubbed him to death with its hooves. The surviving Barhas, bellowing in anger, wheeled their horses and tore into the Badakshis and Jats near their fallen hero.

Husain Beg's voice could be heard above the terrible din, 'Tear these Barhas apart! They are just about a hundred and we are four hundred... Send them where they belong... to the burning fires of hell, and let their bodies be smeared with the eternal shame of not being buried in a warrior's shroud!'

Blinded by raging fury, and inured against pain, the valiant Barhas raised their famous battle cry, *'Ya Fateh, Ya Taboot'* as they charged into the rebel troops. The fierce battle seemed deadlocked as none was prepared to give any quarter, and the ground grew slippery with congealed blood. Suddenly, from the rear came blood curdling yells, as Sayyid Kamal Bokhari, nephew of the Mughal general, attacked the Badakshis from the rear.

Prince Khusrau, surrounded by his personal bodyguards, saw the brutal massacre of the Jats and Badakshis, and made a swift decision. Tomorrow was more precious than today.

Surrounded by the proxy of valour, the rebel flag fled towards the safety of Chenab.

***

CHAPTER 10

'TO BAH MAN BADI KARDI, CHENAB!'

('Thou hast wronged me, Chenab!')

Banks of the Chenab,
Shahpur Ferry,
28 April 1606
3.00 p.m.

Prince Khusrau dozed in the shade of a huge tamarind tree. This coastal glade had offered a much needed respite after the military rout at Bhaironwal, hardly seventy-two hours ago. The three hundred odd Badakshis, survivors of the carnage at Bhaironwal, lay staggered around the thick clump of trees, suffused with fatigue and despondency.

Husain Beg Badakshi and Abdur Rahim sat on a coarse mat of large banyan leaves hastily woven together. There was fear and anxiety writ large on the Badakshi chief's face as he whispered tensely, 'It is time we made our move across the Chenab. Dusk is a good three hours away, and we can easily cross to the other side. We shall gain the advantage of a night. I am worried that those Afghans and Hindus who deserted us yesterday may have been captured, or may have surrendered, to the royal forces. If that be the case, our escape would be doomed.'

Abdur Rahim glanced at the dozing prince, before replying testily 'In hindsight, I believe the Afghans and Rajputs had more sense than us! The emperor will gladly forgive them their intransigence and shall induct them into his fold. And here we are, a skeleton force of just three hundred cavalries, lured by your promise of four lacs of rupees at Rohtas Fort. Sheer madness!'

He lapsed into silence as the huge form of Caliph Khan cast a shadow over them.

'Time to cross the river, generals. Riders have just confirmed that Raja Basu, Mahabat Khan and Mirza Ali Akbarshahi have fanned out in pursuit, and are but a few hours away.' Caliph Khan continued with quiet authority, 'Also, there are no boats here, hence, we must immediately move to Sodharah, where boats are reported.'

***

The sun was struggling to stay aloft, as the western horizon seemed to relentlessly swallow the huge orange orb. Prince Khusrau with Caliph Khan and a few of his trusted generals galloped towards the makeshift pier, where two large boats were moored.

'Good. Both the boats are large,' observed prince Khusrau, 'and will serve our purpose well.'

'There are no oarsmen in the second boat,' observed Husain Beg dryly.

Caliph Khan, in his gruff voice addressed the fear stricken boatmen, 'You are in the presence of His Highness, prince Mirza

Khusrau, heir to the throne. We need you to ferry us across. You shall be paid in gold.'

The boatmen prostrated themselves, as a man with a small white turban, spoke 'Sire, I am Sriram, head of this small hamlet. We come under the jagir of Kamal Choudhury, and have been warned not to help the rebel prince, upon pain of death.'

'Fool!' shouted Caliph Khan as his heavy iron shod shoes thudded into the village chief's chest. The man doubled over with pain, retched once and then silently toppled over the side of the boat. He lay floating, face down in the shallow waters.

An old woman, clutching her wooden staff, shouted angrily and limped forward hurling curses. Abdur Rahim and a few of the prince's attendants jumped into the boat and started clubbing the cowering boatmen with their shields and fists. Those at the stern, dived overboard and tried to swim away.

Caliph Khan swung his spear and sent it hurtling towards the rapidly stroking swimmers. A young boy, writhed in pain and thrashed over as the spear gored him across his back and emerged from his abdomen, the spear point carrying his intestinal entrails.

There was an immediate crescendo of wailing from the gathered womenfolk, with the unnerved children joining the uproar.

Enraged, Khusrau ordered, 'They need to be taught a lesson. Maybe, they have forgotten their allegiance to the Mughal throne. Set their huts afire!'

Jumping off their steeds, a few soldiers pushed the protesting women aside, and picking up the burning firewood from their open hearths, tossed it upon the thatched roofs. Within seconds, the roofs were ablaze, as the dry hay cackled and burnt freely.

Cows and buffaloes tethered inside their shed, shied in terror and stamped their hooves.

***

Killan, the *chowdhury's* son in law, was inspecting his fields, when the billowing smoke from the river bank drew his attention. Since he had ridden with the chowdhury's men last night, scouring the caravanseries and forest glades for the fugitive prince, the fire by the ferry aroused his suspicion.

Almost a kos away, the black plumes of smoke had not gone unnoticed. An armed posse of royal troops under Abdul Qasim Namkin were preparing to set camp for the night, when the breeze from the river carried the smell of burning hay and flesh. The troop commander hastily ordered his soldiers to mount and investigate.

In the sugarcane field, Dheeru, a young boy of sixteen, moved forward and stared at the violence being enacted. Ashen faced, he turned towards the others. 'I must do something. My sister is married to Shyamu Birha in that hamlet...'

'Wait. Let Killan Saha return with more men.'

Snatching the *lathi* from a fellow worker, Dheeru rushed forward.

Husain Beg smiled as he saw the half dozen semi naked farm hands rushing towards them with wooden staffs and scythes. Not waiting for his soldiers to accompany him, he charged headlong into them, delivering fatal blows from his heavy curved scimitar. Husain Beg leant down to cut Dheeru and smote him heavily across the skull. As Dheeru fell headlong, his body snared the hind legs of Husain Beg's horse, bringing it down in a shower of curses and terrified neighs.

Husain Beg scrambled up holding on to his steed's bridle, but the horse buckled and rolled onto its side. As Husain Beg looked at the bone protruding from the lower part of the horse's front leg, a searing pain shot up from his right calf. A sickle was half embedded in the flesh.

Drawing the sickle away, he limped towards the dying man who had thrown the sickle with his dying breath, and deliberately knelt on the man's chest, his leg armour crushing the man's ribs. Smiling into the man's stricken eyes, Husain Beg carved the man's jugular open with slow precision. Blood spewed in small fountains as the victim choked on his own blood and lay still.

'Riders! Afore!' shouted one of Khusrau's mounted guards as dust rose in the distance.

'Damn these infidels!' cursed Khusrau. 'Take the empty boat, NOW! We cannot wait any longer; this area is crawling with the emperor's troops and his chieftains. Abdur Rahim, do not waste time.'

A few soldiers jumped to cast off the mooring lines, as Abdur Rahim hastily had the horses pushed on board. Prince Khusrau, Caliph Khan, Abdur Rahim, Husain Beg Badakshi, and a score of handpicked soldiers climbed aboard, pushing the boat hastily into the current..

Abdul Qasim Namkin reined his horse just a spear flight away, and challenged the fugitives.

'In the name of His Majesty, Emperor Nuruddin Mohammed Salim Jahangir Padshah Ghazi, I demand your surrender.'

An arrow, sizzling from the longbow used by Caliph Khan struck Namkin's horse between the eyes. Without a sound, it sank on its knees. The imperial troops charged into the thin rebel line, as the boat carrying the prince drew farther away.

In the deepening twilight, Khusrau watched morosely as his adherents meekly surrendered to Namkin's troops. The prince's last glimpse was of his men kneeling in abject surrender, while his boat wavered in the untrained hands of his soldier-oarsmen.

***

Banks of the Chenab
Near Gujrewala.
29 April 1606
Sunrise.

The silence was eerie.

No one moved; not the prince on his sandbar stuck boat, nor the imperial troops lining the river banks.

Renowned Mughal warriors, Khwaja Khijr Khan and Hilal Khan had arrived late at night with a large contingent of Mughal cavalry and war elephants, and had chased the errant prince on his capricious boat. Abdul Qasim Namkin had marched all night along the shore, keeping the boat in sight, and was now arranging for boats to ferry his men across.

Prince Khusrau sat in the centre of the boat, enveloped on all sides with his men standing guard with drawn swords and cursed his luck. The large boat had struck a sandbar late into the night, and the prow had driven deep into the sand. His unproven soldiers had been unable to push it free. In fact, with each passing hour and the heavy load of horses and men on it, the boat seemed to sink deeper into the wet sand.

Khwaja Khijr Khan as the senior general signaled for an elephant to be brought over. He addressed the others, 'It seems there are about thirty people and eight horses on board, though I can't see the prince. Janab Namkin, please send a small section across to warn the *jagirdars* and their men gathered on the eastern bank to be ready for battle. '

Khijr Khwaja mounted a war elephant and, having waded a few paces into the river, shouted 'Hail, Your Highness, Prince Mirza Khusrau! We, the servants and soldiers of His Imperial Highness, seek your benevolent hand in ending this strife. We fear for your safety, Highness, and request you to please show your virtuous self, so that we may be assured that His Majesty's Light and Gift to the World, travels safe.'

Tired and despairing, the prince pushed his way to the stern, and said loudly, 'Make way. I wish to see my father, His Majesty, the Padshah Ghazi.'

As the boats, horses and elephants stopped a boat length away, Abdul Qasim Namkin and Khwaja Khijr Khan climbed down from their elephants, and swam across to another boat. With just six swordsmen on board, they approached the unfortunate prince and performed the kornish. Without a word being spoken, Khusrau stepped onto their boat. Immediately, the six soldiers moved forward and clapped him in heavy chains.

Incensed, prince Khusrau lunged at the nearest soldier headbutting him overboard. Khwaja Khijr put the point of his sword on the prince's jugular, 'Yield, prince. The emperor's orders are explicit—no kinship, no favours! I, personally, harbour no wish to harm you.'

Tears of humiliation, frustration, despair and rage flowed from his eyes, as he looked accusingly at the silently flowing river and cried, 'Thou hast wronged me, Chenab!'

* * *

Mirza Kamran's Biradari,
Near Lahore, West bank of Ravi,
01 May 1606.
04.30 a.m.

An intoxicated Jahangir snuggled his face into the silken brocade cover and wept in anguish. The emperor's chief eunuch, Qaid Akram, enfeebled over these many years, but, still as hardworking and diligent as ever, strained his mildly deaf ears to catch the unintelligible words of a grieving emperor.

Suffused with melancholy, Jahangir held onto the sleeves of Akram's *qaba* and made a plaintive sound, 'My old faithful... Do you remember those glorious summer months which I spent with my beloved Zehrun in these same rooms? What happy and precious moments were those, when I had my Anarkali with me. And also Firdaus, my long dead son!' There was an avalanche of body wracking sobs.

Flashback:

Mirza Kamran's Biradari,
Across the Ravi, Lahore.
Spring of 1598.

Lightly running her fingertips over Shehzade Salim's muscular chest, Nadira mused, 'I wonder how you will remember me, beloved? As Zehrunnisa, Nadira, or Anarkali?'

Holding her tenderly, prince Salim nuzzled her neck, 'Anarkali!' He paused, then whispered, 'I do not know why, Zehrun, but I have a feeling that posterity will remember you as Anarkali.'

'And you, my lord?'

'As Salim, the unfortunate lover of Anarkali.'

'And our son, Firdaus?'

Prince Salim fell silent. He stared hard at the flickering, dancing shadows on the gold rimmed walls. Their shifting shapes and impermanence offered no comfort to the silent prince.

'It seems Fate has decreed for him to be the eternal Mughal Mirage. Existing, but concealed.'

* * *

Present:

The senior eunuch rubbed his eyes with a corner of his turban, and moved to place a few more bolsters around the emperor. He needed all the rest that he could get.

In a few hours, the grieving emperor would have to punish his erring son, Khusrau.

* * *

The Gardens of Mirza Kamran's Baradari, 11.30 a.m.

A tight clutch of riders galloped away into the distance, bearing royal orders for the immediate arrest of the Sikh master, Guru Arjan Dev. The missive was to be carried without rest or respite, as the orders were to arrest him before next daybreak.

Emperor Jahangir, wearing a royal cloak of deep purple with a red band at his waist and matching turban, sat on a silver throne, with his Shahi Qur ranged behind him.

Jahangir turned his head as he heard the jangle of chains being dragged over stones.

In the age-old tradition of Genghis Khan, the prisoners were led in from the left. An unkempt and dishevelled Khusrau, stood chained in the centre with Abdul Rahim to his left and Husain Beg Badakshi to his right. Emperor Jahangir's face turned into a wrathful mask, as he surveyed the traitors trembling in front of him.

Prince Khusrau, with his hands and legs fettered, tried to throw himself at the emperor's feet. *'Padshah Ghazi, Noor-e-Khuda,* please forgive my trespasses, Sire, and allow me the protection of your...'

'Stand back, prince Khusrau,' thundered emperor Jahangir. 'You crave for my protection now? Have you no shame?'

Prince Khusrau babbled, 'Your Majesty... Father, I am your son, born with the blood of my revered mother Shah Begum of Amer and your valorous, world conquering blood in my veins! I seek forgiveness.' Tears flowed down Khusrau's cheeks.

'You have stained the blood of the Chugatais and the great Genghis Khan with your despicable acts of treason. Our ancestors conquered this land not by cutting our own arms and legs, but by using our concerted might against the infidels. You have betrayed that very essence, and you shall be punished.'

Weeping uncontrollably, Khusrau played his winning card 'If my revered mother would have been alive today...'

The emperor's face softened, and leaning forward, he cautioned, 'Silence, prince! You will not grovel and weep in my presence.'

Casting a contemptuous glance at the cowering figures of Abdur Rahim and Husain Beg, the emperor ordained, 'These treacherous curs shall be punished in a way that no one has been punished before. The shame will follow you through all the years that Allah has willed for this Earth. '

***

The next morning, on 02nd May 1606, Sheikh Abdur Rahim was sewn inside the carcass of an ass and Husain Beg Badakshi was stuffed inside the dead body of an ox, and were paraded through the streets of Lahore on sturdy donkeys. Husain Beg did not survive the ordeal, and Abdur Rahim was barely alive when he was taken out from the carcass just before midnight.

Earlier in the day, prince Khusrau was seated atop an old elephant on a simple *howdah* made of ragged linen, and was led from Mirza Kamran's garden towards the city. This stretch of two miles was lined on both sides by wooden stakes on which were impaled the remaining followers of Khusrau. Raza Bahadur Khan, an eunuch with a macabre psyche was seated behind the prince wielding a naked sword, and at each such stakes would prod the weeping prince to accept the last salutations of his treacherous band.

Numbed, paralysed, and anguished at this barbaric punishment, the prince slipped into a state of deep melancholy, from which he never fully recovered.

On the 07th of May, 1606, emperor Jahangir with his victorious generals and a chained son, entered the Shahi Qila of Lahore.

***

Maidan Diwan-e-Aam,
Shahi Qila, Lahore.
23 May 1606
09.30 a.m.

There was intense silence in the huge quadrangle as the Sikh Guru Arjan Dev was led onto a small thatch of grass, and made to sit cross legged. His five main disciples Bhai Bidhi Chand, Bhai Langah, Bhai Sangat, Bhai Rana and Bhai Jetha stood around him. All were simply dressed in white *chola*, pyjama, and a white turban wound tightly around the head.

Bhai Langah had been watching the growing crowd with distrust, and finally knelt by the Guru's side. 'Master,' spoke he, 'there is cruelty and treachery in the air. I fear for your life, Master, and implore you to leave this place, while we can.' The urgent notes had drawn the other disciples closer.

A peaceful smile was the Guru's answer.

A few minutes later, the blare of trumpets and the roll of naqqaras announced the arrival of the emperor. Jahangir, dressed in a simple white qaba of silk, worn with a golden sash around the waist, mounted the four steps to the canopied platform. His scabbard of green velvet encrusted with pearls and rubies matched the colours of his turban, where a pink heron feather jauntily stood upright in a small diamond aigrette.

The Mir Tozak's voice rose high, 'In the Court of His Majesty, Padshah Ghazi Salim Jahangir, we pray that you grant audience to the learned saint.' At the emperor's slight nod, he continued 'Today, the false *pir* stands accused of abetting a fugitive, and creating a parallel government in the *Suba* of Lahore.'

Leaning forward, Jahangir addressed the sage, 'Thou hast stained the robes of a saint, priest, by donning the garb of spiritualism, while all your efforts are directed towards procurement of wealth by dubious means. What sayest thou?'

'O, Emperor, I am a servant of the Eternal Self, and don't know spiritual garb! What crime have I committed to be brought thus to your Court?'

The emperor stared hard, and spoke coldly, 'You have spread sedition in the Realm, and stand accused of malfeasance by collecting taxes and levies from the populace, which belongs to the royal treasury. You have been vested with no powers or jagirs to collect any levies, yet your followers go around forcibly collecting taxes, which is the right of the State.'

'Is that all, Shahenshah?'

Jahangir glared, 'No,that is not all! You have spread sedition in the kingdom, and have conspired against your Sovereign Monarch. You have aided and abetted the traitor, prince Khusrau, by providing him shelter and five thousand rupees, to wage war against the majesty of my Empire. You put the infidel's caste mark on the prince's forehead and sullied the faith of a Mughal prince. Under the imperial law, it is punishable by death. Painful Death!

Guru Arjan Dev waited for the monarch to further vent his anger, but was just met with a stony glare. Smiling placidly, he replied 'First, let me record that I address you as Shahenshah only because it is a matter of Court protocol. For me, there is just one *Padshah,* who is Eternal, Glorious and Ineffable. You, me, and this world are mere passing thoughts.'

'Your accusations are false. We collect no taxes or levies. Our *masands,* acting as my representative, are charged with the propagation of our Sikh faith and the welfare of our followers and receive *Daswandh* from them. This, as your spies must have told you, is a voluntary contribution by a Sikh, similar to your *Zakat,* donated for the welfare of the community. There is no intrusion on the taxes compulsorily levied and collected by your officials, and if you have felt any diminishing of tax recoveries, then it is the avarice and corrupt practices of your state officials which is to be blamed.'

Several courtiers and minor officials bristled at the softly worded accusations of the white robed ascetic, and there were immediate shouts for retribution.

Sheikh Farid Bokhari, now titled Murtaza Khan, lisped, 'You have not answered His Majesty's question, Arjan Dev. Did you not put the *qashka* on prince Khusrau's forehead and help him with five thousand rupees, knowing fully well that he was a rebel against His Majesty, leading an armed uprising? Does that not make you an accomplice in treason?'

The hot-headed Bhai Jettha shook his fist at the Mir Bakshi, 'Make not these lofty statements, O Farid Bokhari! A cut of my sword has only lanced your lips and you babble like a pregnant monkey, lisping and stammering.' He shook his fist vigorously to enhance the effect. 'Any more lisping out of you and I will ensure that your dentures are sutured in your posterior!'

While the majority sniggered, Sheikh Farid Bokhari stood stunned at this unprecedented verbal assault in the monarch's presence. However, Khushkhabar Khan exploded, *'Lahoul vila kuubat!* Who dares to debase the majesty of the Sovereign's presence? Boot him out of here, quick!'

Jahangir put his golden cup of opium to his lips and sat patiently. He quite enjoyed these sudden fights of men and beasts, alike. Guru Arjan Dev raised a hand in blessing as Bhai Jettha was marched away by liveried soldiers, and turned to address the emperor again.

'O, Emperor, I did not provide shelter or give money to a rebel prince. I offered the warmth of my abode to a traveller steeped in fatigue and the travails of a long journey. I gave food to a hungry soul, who was not only hungry and thirsty, but had always felt famished for the love and protective arm of his father. I gave refuge to a young prince, whose grandfather had once graced my abode with his presence. It is in my faith, Shahenshah, to help the needy, the poor and the destitute; and the prince, that night, was a lost straggler with many hungry men and horses following in his wake. I did what any human would do—I offered them the warmth of my home and food from my kitchen.'

The Guru looked askance, as Farid Bokhari lisped, 'What about the money given? And the saffron mark?'

'I gave money to the prince from the Daswandh, of which I am the custodian. It is meant for distribution for the welfare of the community, and we make no discrimination on the basis of caste or religion. We are all His children, and for me the fugitive prince was just another fellow traveller in dire need of money, to feed and support the several hundred following him.'

Guru Arjan Dev paused and stared directly at Jahangir. 'You should know the feeling, Shahenshah. You were the first Mughal prince to rebel against his father, and prince Khusrau is only following in your footsteps, so why the ire?'

***

CHAPTER 11

FARYAD KOLAGH

(The Cry of the Raven)

Shahi Qila, Lahore.
23 May 1606
10.15 a.m.

Guru Arjan Dev's insinuations left the emperor apoplectic.

'Imposter, charlatan! How dare you accuse me of rebellion? My petition was for love, for Anarkali; not for the emperor's crown.' Shaking with terrible rage, the emperor shouted, 'Have him bound in chains and...'

'If it was not your greed for the royal crown, then why did you try to capture the royal fort at Agra in 1599, in your father's absence?'

Ignoring the ominous murmuring, the seer continued, 'You set up your own spurious empire in the Suba of Allahabad, with phoney ministers and the trappings of a phoney court! You marched with an army of seventy thousand against your father, but the fear of impending punishment halted your treacherous steps near Etawah in 1602. And, towards the end, you sent poisoned *pethas...*'.

Raging, the emperor screamed, 'Throw this criminal into the dungeons. Throw him, and let him rot!' Holding the arm of his gilded throne, he stood, and turned to the newly titled Murtaza Khan 'Sheikh Farid Bokhari! Confiscate all the properties of this charlatan, and unto thee, I give the dwelling abodes of this malicious criminal. All the lands of his hermitage and treasury now belong to the State.'

'Do not delude yourself, O Great Emperor, for nothing belongs to you but the colour of your deeds!'

Jahangir gripped the arms of his throne, and spat, 'Keep your loathsome words to yourself, and shun the garb of spiritual mastery! If you wish for clemency, then you must recant the unfaithful verses which are a part of the Granth Sahib, and I shall set you free.'

As his disciples surged forward in anger, the sage replied calmly, 'There is nothing unfaithful or blasphemous in the Granth Sahib, but it is the description and praise of the Supreme Being, who is the only True Monarch. Not a word can be altered or erased, because the Granth Sahib is a revelation of the Supreme One as seen by Guru Nanak Dev and all his successive Adepts. We mean no disrespect to any religion, for they all are paths to His Greater Glory.'

'Then you shall be punished!' Jahangir lurched to his feet. 'Sheikh Farid,' he shouted, 'kill him, but in the manner of the Timurids. *Siyasat-O-Yassa!* Not a drop of blood to be spilled!'

The imperial banner preceded the emperor, now tottering in rage and the desire for opium, across the vast lawns of the *Maidan-Diwan-e-Aam.*

Suddenly, with a shrill cry, a black raven swooped down and plucking the diamond aigrette with the pink heron feather from the emperor's turban, streaked rapidly away into the warm spring skies.

The raven continued to dip, soar and swivel, as the archers shot off a volley of arrows to no avail. Then with a sharp cry of ridicule, it hurtled away into the distance.

* * *

Bank of the Ravi,
Close to Shahi Qila, Lahore,
30 May 1606.
12.30 p.m.

The Guru stood buried in the burning sands up to his neck, his long hair and beard coated with matted blood, filth and sand.

Murtaza Khan, riding a huge bay stallion, motioned for his soldiers to bring forth and pour the cauldron of boiling oil on the sage's head, and inside the pit. As the burning oil seared the skin of Guru Arjan Dev, there rose a collective cry of horror from the assembled soldiers, but there was nary a sound from the Guru, only his lips moved silently.

Murtaza Khan commanded Qaisur Beg, 'Go and see what the infidel is muttering. Must be pleas for mercy.'

As a detail of soldiers moved towards the suffering master, a handful of Sikhs watching from atop a sand dune rushed forward to ensure the Guru's safety.

'Tera kiya meetha lage; Nam padarath Nanak mange!' whispered the savant softly.

Qaisur Beg rushed back to his master, 'Sire! The Guru repents not! He says that he enjoys the tribulations willed by his God, and only seeks to surrender in the name of Nanak. He is terribly burnt, Huzoor. I fear he will not last long...'

'The stubborn fool!' grated Murtaza Khan, then glanced towards the raised voices and clash of swords on the riverbank's periphery. 'What ails them?' he shouted loudly.

'Sire, they wish to meet their Guru.'

'It will be to our benefit to show a little mercy now. He has just hours to live,' advised Qaisur.

'So be it.' He gestured to his soldiers, 'bring them under escort.'

Guru Arjan Dev, with his scalp and facial skin badly singed could barely open his eyes, but he could discern the aura of his agitated, grieving disciples, and asked, 'Bhai Jetha! Bhai Piara! Are you there?'

Tears streaming down his cheeks, Bhai Langat leaned forward and said, '*Hazaaran Mubarakan, Saccha Padshah!* You truly are on your way to the Celestial Kingdom.'

The Adept's voice, melodious even in pain, spoke clearly, 'I fear none, and Death is but a friend in waiting. Do not grieve for me, O You Pious Band of Brothers, but set your hearts and efforts in promoting the sacred words of our Gurus.' He stopped talking, and his head drooped.

With a tremendous effort, he jerked his head up again, 'Now listen carefully. A few days back, I sent the fruit of a *bel* and five copper pice to my son, Hargovind, as a sign of his succession to the temporal seat, through Bhai Kheda Singh.' He winced in pain. 'Let Baba Budha do the anointment on an auspicious date, as he has done for all the Pious Gurus till date. Command the sixth Guru, Guru Hargovind, that I desire that he should sit on a throne and raise an army to defend our Faith, the poor and the deprived, to the best of his ability.' He paused for a few moments, then spoke,

'You, the Chosen Few, must not waver in your loyalty and should strengthen the young Guru, for he shall need you most, now that I shall be gone.'

Every Sikh was crying, though their bravery decreed that not a sob be heard, no lips quiverred, nor tears spill. Mustering the last of his reserves, he willed his voice to speak again, 'When you go home, do not tell Mata Ganga of all the cruelties inflicted on me. Please tell her to not abandon her body but to live, for Hargovind is but eleven years old, too young to be orphaned. I leave my body, but not her side. She must be a mother not only to our children, but to our Faith too, and a brave soldier in adversity. Tell her that I have just gone ahead, and regret the burden which I leave behind for her to bear. Now,' his voice fell, 'My time has come. Please request the general that I wish to bathe once in the holy river before I ...'

There was a flurry of activity as burly Sikhs started scraping the sand and widening the pit with their bare hands, their tears softening the sun-baked sand. Gingerly, they lifted the sage and made him sit on a hastily thrown shawl. Arjan Dev signalled for a turban to be wound around his head.

Helped by many, the Guru stood up and raised his scorched hands in benediction. The brave Sikhs cried silently as their Master staggered towards the swiftly flowing Ravi, his palms folded in prayer, his singed robes hissing as they encountered the cold waters of the river.

Suddenly, a black raven, escorted by a flight of falcons, peeled off from the blazing sky and swooped low over the sage. As it passed, it dropped a diamond aigrette with a pink heron feather into the folded palms of Guru Arjan Dev, who continued walking into the icy depths of the Ravi.

'Take me unto thy bosom, O Eternal Lord, and deliver me from this pain...'

The river Ravi was a witness to this last refrain from the grieving saint, as he was carried away by the swift current, never to be seen again.

The raven and falcons continued to raise raucous cries and circled overhead till there were no bubbles left.

In a swift move, they formed into a flying squadron and bearing in at man height, clawed the turban off Murtaza Khan and tore through the silk fabric of the Mughal flag, leaving a gaping hole behind.

As they soared away into the distant blue, their raucous cries of condemnation remained.

* * *

CHAPTER 12

DIG! TIG! FATEH!

(Degh! Tegh! Fateh!)

Prince Khurram's chambers,
Shahi Qila, Lahore.
22 June 1606.
Past 11 p.m.

The prince stirred in his sleep, as he felt the warmth of a body near his left flank. Controlling his breathing, he focused on getting his bearings right before making any move. With the speed and ferocity of lightning, Khurram drew the curved dagger from under his bolster and pressed it against the human form next to him.

A small gasp of fright escaped the young girl's lip, before the hand of prince Khurram clamped down roughly over her mouth and twisted her head. After a few moments, he eased the pressure slightly, as the semi naked feminine form and the cascade of long perfumed hair on his shoulders, registered in his sleep benumbed mind. He pulled the girl close to him, and was met by a pair of frightened doe-like eyes, framed by kohl.

'Who sent you here, girl?' The prince's voice was hard and demanding.

'I did, Sire,' replied Khoja Bhim, as he stepped inside the chamber. He kept his head bowed, 'Your Highness, there was a restlessness to your sleep, and I wondered if a little warmth could ease the strain and induce sleep. Please forgive me, Highness, if I have ever erred.'

The prince turned to look carefully at the scared, beautiful girl by his side. Her fair skin glowed in the dark, and the soft aroma of scented oils enveloped her lithe body. Her breasts, round and firm, rose and fell with each frightened breath. Khurram caressed the soft skin just below her navel and felt an excited tremor pass through her body.

'Khoja, you did well.' Khurram continued to softly stroke the skin near her pubic mound, 'Find me another one, with a little more age on her side.'

The eunuch withdrew silently. As the young girl moved away, Khurram pulled her back roughly, 'Where are you going, girl? Have you not learnt better than to leave without my permission?'

'A thousand pardons, Your Highness,' the voice was gentle and sweet, 'I thought Your Highness had no use for me. Maybe, I lack experience to please your majesty...'

'Be quiet, *kaneez.*' The prince's voice was gruff with passion as he rolled over on top and wedged her thighs apart with his knees.

His thrusts were long and hard as he recalled the ease with which Begum Ruqaiya had promised to speak to the emperor for an early engagement of the young prince with Arjumand Bano. Khurram smiled with satisfaction; a word from the Dowager Empress Ruqaiya would not go unheeded by the emperor.

He flipped the girl over and spread her buttocks.

* * *

Dera Da Arjan Dev,
Tarn Taran.
24 June 1606
7.00 a.m.

Hargovind, attired in simple loose trousers and a long frock in white, watched gloomily as Bhai Budha and a score of other Sikhs, escorted a lone rider into his presence. These past few weeks had been full of anguish and pain, as traveller after traveller had brought news of the inhumane treatment being meted out to Guru Arjan Dev at Lahore. Restrained by the Guru's departing words to his family and adherents, the Sikhs had abjured any direct retaliation, while praying for the Guru's early and safe return.

Bhai Budha's old wizened face was a mask of grief as he gestured for the new arrival to greet the Guru's young son, now stepping down from the raised platform on which he had been reciting the scriptures. To one corner of the walled compound, where a few simple huts stood, appeared the frail person of Maa Ganga Devi, the Guru's wife.

The Sikh traveller approached slowly, tears cascading down his cheeks to mingle with the dust and grime streaking his beard. Hargovind felt his legs shaking, fearing the worst, and cast a worried glance towards his mother standing by the hut. The Sikh made no move, just stood there, his weary body wracked with great heaving sobs.

The man looked upwards once at the sombre clouds darkening the sky, and reached deep inside his loose cloak. Crouching down on one knee, he proffered a bel fruit and five copper pice.

His voice quavered, 'Guru Hargovind, I bring these solemn symbols of Kingship from the Saccha Padshah, as his appointed heir. Take them and rule in his place. His soul now lives in thee.' A wail went up from the assembled disciples.

Hargovind reeled as the finality of the Guru's demise hit him. His first thought was for his mother, who was now sitting on the hard ground, head in her hands. As he started walking towards her with frozen steps, she held up her hand. Wiping her tears, she was on her feet and her voice was resolute, 'Hargovind, worry not for me. Your first, and only responsibility, is to our religion and adherents, whom thy father has left in your care. Bhai Kheda, what else did the Guru say?'

Bhai Kheda turned his gaze to the young boy, 'O Sage, these are his direct words addressed to you—"Hargovind, I have chosen thee to lead our people with piety, courage and fortitude."' Kheda's voice became stronger and louder, '"Let your hands be full of *Degh* for the poor, and *Tegh* for our enemies. Raise an army to the best of your ability, and sit on a throne, encrusted with the glitter of material wealth as also with the eternal gloss of piety and godliness. For both are a necessary part of our worldly life. Shield thy children with might and courage, and lead them with sagacity and love. This is Nanak's will. This is your Destiny."'

There was a sudden burst of sunshine as the clouds parted, and the firm words of the late Guru lingered much after Bhai Kheda had become silent. Budha Singhji, the venerable disciple from the time of the first Guru, bowed to the glowing Sun, and then to Hargovind, 'The Gods have parted the darkness brought upon by the late Guru's demise. Saccha Padshah lives again.'

On its own volition, the right hand of Sant Hargovind rose in benediction.

Bhai Jettha Masand, a six foot seven inches tall burly Sikh, raised his wooden staff and bellowed, *'Degh, Tegh, Fateh!'*

Sant Hargovind, just eleven years old, was brimming with determination and a new resolve. The grimness of the moment was transformed into a lustrous wave of hope, courage and fortitude, as two well-built followers knelt down and linked their arms together, forming a small perch. The young leader stepped onto it, and was held aloft.

***

Two hours later.

The angry clanging of the Dera's enormous bell had brought the villagers flocking to the ashram premises. More than five hundred adherents stood in a tight group, as Bhai Budha applied the vermilion mark on Guru Hargovind's forehead. Then, with great reverence, he picked up the rosary which the late Guru had entrusted to him before leaving for Lahore, and placed it in the extended palm of the young saint.

Guru Hargovind touched the rosary to his forehead and then wound it around his neck. Turning to the chief priest he said, 'Revered Bhai Budha ji, I shall live by the commandments of my Guru, as a soldier-saint. Invest me with a sword.'

Immediately, a disciple unwound his turban and tied it around the Guru's waist. A sword was hastily girded on the saint's right by the chief priest. Guru Hargovind smiled and pointed to the mistake, 'Revered priest, I am right-handed, hence, the sword should be on my left flank. But don't worry, bring me another sword.'

Guru Hargovind secured the second sword on his left, and spoke with measured authority.

'I speak the words and will of Nanak. I shall carry two swords, symbolising *Miri* and *Piri*. One shall enforce my temporal powers and the other shall enhance the spiritual path. We shall be a comity of soldiers with wealth, for one cannot do without the other. We shall strive to acquire great wealth as well as abide by the gospels laid down by our Nanaks. We shall fight for the weak, the deprived and the wronged. No friend or the indigent shall ever go hungry from our doorstep.' He stopped for a moment, and then raised his voice in a hoarse shout 'Degh for our friends, and Tegh for our enemies. Fateh for ourselves!'

The resounding cries of 'Degh, Tegh, Fateh!' could be heard in villages far and distant.

* * *

CHAPTER 13

TOLD TOUHOMAT

(The Birth of Delusions)

Mirza Kamran's Baradari,
West bank of Ravi, Lahore.
17 July 1606.
4.15 a.m.

The night breeze, laden with rain, had still not been tempered by the summer sun trying to break through the darkness on the horizon, as prince Khurram sauntered out of the sleeping pavilion. The encampment was slowly coming alive with the stables being the first to record the activities of the *syces* and the *bishtis.* The royal horses, restless for their morning run, were nodding their great heads and snorting softly.

His steps inadvertently turned towards the richly decorated set of rooms lining the western periphery, as the familiar scent of emperor Jahangir's *itr* came wafting along the early morning breeze. It was unusual for the emperor to be up so early, especially as last evening had seemed to be getting wilder with the arrival of a troupe from Hunza valley. Khurram was also surprised, when the emperor in consultation with Shereif Khan, had ordered for the *Diwan-i-khas* to be vacated by all, but for the members of the dancing troupe.

He entered the narrow corridor running around the suite of rooms generally used by the royal family for hunting the migratory birds in winters, and noted the neighing of horses nearby. As he walked towards the inner vestibule, he could hear the murmur of soft voices from within the main chamber. Cushioning his steps, he moved to the red sandstone wall with the marble filigree work.

His heart froze.

***

Khurram's eyes remained glued to the filigree, as the billowing silk curtains gave him fleeting glimpses of the tall, slender visitor being helped into the body armour of an Ahadi. He strained his eyes, but the plumed helmet and its face guard effectively obscured the face. For a fleeting moment, the exquisite face and large grey eyes turned towards the filigree, and Khurram recoiled in surprise.

He moved to the far end of the corridor, as the armour-clad visitor was led out by a group of soldiers, down the wide steps of the residence to where several other horsemen stood waiting around a few palanquins. An attendant stepped forward and fastened a red cloak on to the shoulder epaulettes, as the visitor swung his leg over a chestnut steed and gestured for the small group to follow him.

Khurram watched as the palanquin bearers hastily lifted the palanquins and started moving forward in their characteristic trot with quick short steps. Several riders closely arrayed themselves around the palanquins, and reined their horses on the downward slope of the ramp which led towards the river bank.

The prince's brow was furrowed as the posse of riders and palanquins, led by the red caped figure, were lost to sight amidst the forested slope and bends. Only the cadence of the palanquins' bells remained, long after the neighs and clatter of hooves had ceased.

There was a strange familiarity in the exquisite form of the visitor.

***

Bari Khwabgah,
Shahi Qila, Lahore.
04 August 1606.
10.30 p.m.

Qutubuddin Chishti was called to the private chamber of the emperor. Jahangir seemed to be in high spirits, and Qutubuddin, a childhood friend and milk brother of Jahangir, could not stop marvelling at the recent change and gaiety in the emperor's normally surly and cruel behaviour. Jahangir plucked a few grapes, and turning to the beautiful Persian attendant waiting on him, pushed the grapes inside her tight, silken bodice.

Chuckling with delight, he let his fingers wander over her breasts, rolling her hardening nipples under his thumb and kneading her fleshy orbs. Pulling her closer, he roughly tore her bodice away, and watched in glee as the grapes, almost squashed, spilled onto the rich carpet. With a roguish smile, he gestured for Qutubuddin Koka to get down on his knees and pick up the scattered grapes with his mouth.

A loud guffaw erupted from the emperor's mouth, as the spectacularly obese noble got down on his hands and knees, and an enormous fart erupted from his raised posterior. He waited, while Qutubuddin crawled around picking up grapes, absently pressing and kneading the taut breasts of the attendant.

After a few minutes, tired of the spectacle, Jahangir bade his friend sit. Curling his arm around the girl's naked waist, he slid his hand under the band of her silk trousers and cupped her buttocks. Qutubuddin Koka, inured to such intemperate actions of the emperor since his princely years, preferred to remain standing.

'I have a great task for you, Khubu,' the emperor referred to his friend's childhood name. 'A matter so delicate and important, that I can think of none other, but you, my milk brother!'

'*Zarre Naseeb, Shahenshah!* (My life is at your command, Sire!)' Khubu Chishti's voice rang clear, even as he tried to draw the emperor's attention to the presence of the royal attendant.

Emperor Salim Jahangir lifted her chin, and tracing his finger over her full lips, threatened mockingly, 'Worry not about this kaneez, Khubu. She would not like her limbs to be torn and fed to the alligators in the moat now, would you, girl?' His hands caressed her buttocks, even as his fingers grasped her throat and squeezed lightly. Voice hoarse with opium and lust, he rasped 'What is your name, girl?'

'Andaz, my lord.'

She shivered. The emperor's wanton acts of cruelty were well known. Disguising her fear, she snuggled her face into the silken folds of Jahangir's wine red qaba, draping her full thighs over his groin. Feeling the first sparks of lust, Jahangir roughly turned her over, and yanked her silk trousers down.

The girl lay silent, and heard the rustle of the emperor discarding his clothes. A few moments later, Andaz gasped with pain as she felt the engorged head of the emperor's member trying to force its way inside her. She raised her buttocks, even as Jahangir parted her cheeks and thrust hard. It took a few seconds for her to adjust to the painful intrusion. Wanting this ordeal to be over as quickly as possible, she decided to feign intense pleasure.

She arched her back, and with a quick flick of her wrists drew the emperor's hands under her aching breasts. Unsettled, Jahangir almost collapsed on her, as his willing fingers gripped her breasts and rolled his palms over her turgid nipples. Revelling in the sensuous contact of her lithe and smooth body, Jahangir increased his pace.

Qutubuddin Chishti could not avert his eyes from the copulating, writhing couple, and felt his own penis hardening. *Allah have mercy,* he thought, as he lowered his crossed hands to cover the evident bulge. The emperor would have him thrown in the dungeons, friendship be damned, if he ever found him coveting his harem. He lowered his eyes to the floor.

Amidst the lascivious thump of Jahangir's groin hitting the thrusting, pulsing buttocks of the beautiful attendant, the emperor turned towards his waiting courtier and said, 'Khubu, I am making you the Subedar of Bengal, the announcement for which shall be done in the *Diwan-e-Aam* tomorrow. You shall send Mirza Raja Man Singh back to the imperial court.' He nuzzled the girl's neck and ground his pelvis against her buttocks, which had turned a pale shade of pink with the constant, vigorous pounding on her bare flesh.

'You shall escort a very valuable asset of mine, which is closer to my heart than even the sacred memories of my illustrious father,

Arsh Ashiyani! You will guard it, protect it, and honour it with your life.' His panting grew stronger, as he increased the pace of his thrusts. Jahangir could feel his orgasm coming and his strokes became shorter and deeper. Feeling the gush of semen about to erupt, he could barely growl, 'Sher Afghan must be slain, and his widow, Mehrunnisa, brought to me. Now, this is what you must do enroute...'

* * *

Qudusiya Haveli,
Gali Kaghzian off Bazaar Hakimaan,
Walled City, Lahore.
06 August 1606.
Late evening.

Khwaja Wais Beg enjoyed his moments of pleasure with his sister-in-law, Andaz, ever since his wife Begum Qudusiya had suffered a paralytic stroke. It also helped, as being one of the favoured attendants to the emperor, she had access to a large array of court decisions and briefings done in the personal chambers and the Hall Of Personal Hearings, which had proven very useful in the past.

Andaz lay naked with her head resting on the broad muscular chest, her fingers languidly tracing the hard ridges of the shoulders. These short visits to her sister's home were a much-required palliative to her, with the pervading succour, warmth and love so nourishing after the harsh, insidious and formal settings of the royal harem. The constant plotting, gossip, and underlying jealousy within the imperial seraglio had led many of the inmates to premature nervous conditions, and in extreme cases, suspicious deaths.

She had been chosen as a personal attendant to the current emperor's harem at a very young age by Begum Salima Sultana, who always kept a sharp lookout for beautiful girls for her step son, knowing his predilection for wine, women, and opium.

Khwaja Wais also welcomed these sensuous sessions with his sister-in-law. A trained courtesan, she could provide such pleasure that for those few minutes every pain, every grain of sadness was forgotten in the tumult of their lovemaking. With her innate intelligence, and a *tawaif's* survival instinct, she sifted through the conversations and imperial commands, and faithfully conveyed all that she perceived to be of value to her incestuous lover.

Andaz grimaced, as she could still feel the tenderness in her buttocks where the emperor had entered her so vigorously the other night.

She sighed, and stretched her hand to smoothen the long locks of Wais Khan's hair, which lay plastered over his forehead. Wais Khan twined his fingers with hers, and drew it down to his groin. Andaz. smiled happily, as she could feel his erection growing in her palms. Raising herself on an elbow, she willed her lover to open his eyes. Indeed, the Khwaja was looking at her with half-lidded eyes!

'Wais, my love,' she cuddled closer. 'Do you know what Jahanpanah commanded the debauch Koka to do?'

'No. What?'

'Last Thursday evening, as Jahanpanah was engrossed in pounding my buttocks, he let slip a royal command to kill Ali Quli Khan Istalju.'

Wais Beg winced. He could not tolerate the thought of his beloved Andaz making love to another man, not even the emperor, and had admonished her several times not to discuss her harem activities with him. She, in turn, seemed to enjoy teasing him.

He looked worried. 'Do you mean the jagirdar of Burdwan, Sher Afghan, and his wife?'

'That is what I meant, lover!' was the coy answer.

He pushed her onto her back, and thought out loud, 'But, how can this be true? Sher Afghan has been rewarded by the emperor for his bravery, and his wife? Well, she is the daughter of Mirza Ghiyas Ud Din Beg Teherani, a court noble. He has roots in the royal court of Shah Abbas of Persia... What madness is this?' His eyes burned in the candlelight glow.

Andaz snuggled closer, pushing her full breasts onto his chest, 'And, there is more to it! You will not believe what the emperor has instructed Koka to do!'

She whispered in his ears, as he listened with growing incredulity.

Sleep eluded Khwaja Wais Beg as he waited for dawn to break.

***

A few days later...

Prince Khurram sat immobile on his horse, letting his gaze wander over the fields of ripe maize and barley. The unease over Khwaja Wais's startling disclosure had not settled even after four days, and the prince had spent many hours contemplating a course of action.

Khwaja Wais and his companion dismounted a good hundred paces away, and the Khwaja slowly unfolded his green turban from his face. Black folds partially covered the visage of the other rider, slender and fair, who walked with demure steps.

'Your Royal Highness, my sister-in-law, Andaz, bows at your feet.'

Khurram watched, stunned by the beauty of this *kenchen* as she unwound the black turban. Her fair, oval face with huge shining eyes, laced with curving dark eyebrows and full ruby lips, was pink in the heat of this August sun. The loose-fitting long shirt worn over tight linen trousers could not disguise the lithe, supple body beneath it. Khurram felt a familiar stirring in his groin.

'Khwaja Wais, you may leave us for a while. I shall seek the answers directly.' He extended his hand towards her.

The *Vakil* bowed and stepped back, watching helplessly as Andaz put her foot in the stirrups and clutching the prince's hand, was pulled onto the saddle. As she settled herself, sitting astride the saddle with the prince seated behind her, she could feel his engorged member nudging her buttocks.

Khurram wheeled the horse and cantered towards the dense thicket of trees, away from the rider's trail in the forest. Tightening the reins, he pulled her closer against himself, as he lightly wrapped an arm around her breasts and laid the other on her thigh. Andaz could feel the strong current of desire and strength flowing from the young prince, and responded by pushing back against his erection.

He nudged his steed towards a smallish tamarind tree with low boughs, and tossed his reins across, securing a loose knot. Nuzzling her nape and the thick waves of her perfumed hair, his fingers sought to tease her already rigid nipples. He whispered in her ear, 'Turn around, girl.' He lifted her by the waist, as she swung her legs around.

She gasped, as she sat astraddle with her face just inches away from the prince's, and her taut breasts lightly brushing his muscular chest. Smitten, Khurram gazed deep into her hazel eyes, and lifted her chin, 'How old are you, girl?'

'Nineteen, Your Highness.'

'Just the right age, *Nausheen!*'

There was a peculiar colour to her eyes which changed as often as her expressions. Now, burning with desire, they held the tumult of a midnight blue raging sea. Deftly, Khurram unlaced her linen trousers and grasping her hips, lowered her onto his inflamed penis. A moan escaped her, as the horse shifted to balance itself to the new cadence of the riders.

Suppressing his desire to mercilessly pound into her, Khurram held her down by the waist on his throbbing member, murmuring against her cheek, 'Andaz, tell me what happened that night between Jahanpanah and Sheikh Qutubuddin. Word for word.'

* * *

Shahi Qila, Lahore
Early September, 1606.

The events of the last two months had left Shehzade Khurram deeply worried. Parental love for the first born had again begun to surface as the monarch relented towards the rebellious prince Khusrau, and granted him full freedom within the fort walls. The arrival of the caped visitor a few weeks back had seemed to please the emperor, though his quest for wine and opium had not ebbed.

The Court was also pregnant with rumours that the Persian ruler, Shah Abbas, was mustering an enormous force to storm Qandahar, but Shereif Khan had vociferously opposed any troop movement, claiming that the Persians were being badly mauled in their war with the Turks, and would not venture into Al Hind.

Prince Khurram's eyes narrowed as he thought of the recent reluctance in his Vakil Khwaja Wais's demeanour ever since that tryst with his sister-in-law, Andaz, in the forest glades. Maybe it was time to show some imperial puissance?

The Northern Quadrangle,
Shahi Qila, Lahore,
Same evening.

There was a dangerous glint in the prince's eyes, as his words caused tremors in the motionless Vakil.

'Remember, Khwaja, that nothing is permanent in the royal court—not my grace, nor my favours. The only absolute permanence has to be your loyalty to me, as is my fealty to the Emperor and the Realm.' Khurram let his words hang in the gathering dusk.

Khwaja Wais fell to his knees as the harsh words of his patron continued, 'Your fate is inexorably tied to my destiny, Wais. Do you understand? Your safety, prosperity, even your life is at my pleasure Khwaja, hence, step with caution.'

'There are subtle shifts in the court, Khwaja, and certain dangerous alignments remain. Prince Khusrau will always be supported by his *mamu,* Mirza Raja Man Singh, and by his father-in-law, Mirza Aziz Koka. Also, he is the first born. On the other hand, *Shehzade* Pervez has just been engaged on 12 September to Jahan Banu Begum, the daughter of my late uncle, Mirza Murad, and the favours of the royal ladies and Akbarshahi nobles shall continue to protect and promote the ambitions of prince Pervez.'

'Which leaves me, an unprotected Timurid prince, born of a Rajput Marwar queen. The harem and the court may try to besmirch my claim to the throne by pointing fingers at the rabid feud between the Mughals and kings of Marwar. The death threat issued to my father upon his marriage to my mother by Kalyandas Rathore of Siwana has still not been forgotten, or forgiven, by the Mughal Court.' His expression bemused, he continued, 'I have to strengthen my position, Khwaja, for only then will your head be on your shoulders. My brothers will not let you live, if I do not survive.'

Khwaja, reeling from the unwarranted threats, silently wiped the collected tears, and ungirdled his sword. Eyes red and swimming with unshed tears, he placed his sword on the ground and spoke haltingly, 'I have never given you any reason to question my fidelity, Highness, and never have I strayed from your Auspicious Shadow. Allah knows that I have committed no breach of trust in word, thought or action, Sire.'

Khurram fixed the miserable Vakil with another cold stare. 'Khwaja, I know of your dalliance with your wife's sister for many months now. You have been very unwise, Khwaja, for you know the punishment reserved for adultery? And to fornicate with a woman from the emperor's own harem? Unthinkable! And, unpardonable. Whatever possessed you, Khwaja?'

Wais Beg seemed to crumple at Khurram's feet. He pushed his sword along the ground and with a great effort, steadied his voice 'Your Majesty, relieve me of my misery.' He nudged the sword forward.

Khurram ignored the sword, continuing his diatribe, 'You are aware of the court politics—Prince Khusrau has rebelled against His Majesty, the Padshah Ghazi, and has earned the wrath of our

Timurid ancestors. Prince Pervez continues to slither from one command to another without achieving anything. Do you see either of them succeeding our illustrious monarch, may he live long?'

Khwaja raised himself. 'I behold the future emperor of Hindustan, blessed are my eyes!'

Khurram beckoned him to stand. 'Girdle your sword, Khwaja, your services will be recognized. I shall speak with the Dowager Queen, Begum Ruquaih Sultana, to arrange Andaz's release from the emperor's duty. And, should you need to dispose of your ailing wife to cement your new marriage, you shall have my support.'

Khwaja scrambled to his feet, and bowed low. His voice hoarse with relief, he could only manage 'A thousand graces be upon you, Prince. May your reign be long, and splendorous!'

'Just remember, Khwaja. I own you.'

* * *

Lahore.

On the 02 of October 1606, the narrow, paved streets of the Walled City were littered with the refuse and debris of a passing army. The citizens witnessed the departure of Sheikh Qutubuddin Chishti to the far-off Suba of Bengal.

Most of the watching populace were astonished at the unprecedented sight of a large contingent of the emperor's own bodyguards accompanying the caravan.

Just beyond Lahore, the caravan broke into two parts. The designated Subedar, with a small band of riders on swift horses and the full body of the imperial bodyguards, rode out at breakneck speed. The remaining caravan plodded along at their usual pace of eight to ten *kos* in a day.

Sheikh Qutubuddin Chishti, with his small retinue, reached the Mughal capital of Bengal—Rajmahal, and assumed the Governorship on 04 November 1606. The remaining posse of riders and royal troops, preferred to billet in the densely forested tracts of the *Damin-i-koh* mountain ranges, unseen and unheard.

* * *

CHAPTER 14

ARVAH RAQSAN

(The Dancing Wraiths)

Sheikhpura,
Hunting Lodge,
10 October 1606
10.45 a.m.

Emperor Jahangir looked fatigued as he lay against the bolsters, his imperial turban by his side. The morning hunt had not been interesting, as the lone tiger spotted was able to escape due to the mahout's recklessness, and cheetals and spotted deer held no interest for him today. The insinuations being made by Khurram deepened his worries.

'Majesty, the palace is full of rumours that a female *djinn* has been frequenting the imperial quarters. The slaves and eunuchs are swearing that they have seen caped, silent figures gliding swiftly through the palace corridors.'

'This is all nonsense, Khurram. A similar story was floated for the *Shahi Qila* at Agra many years ago—that the spirits of my elder siblings, Fatima Bano Begum, Hassan and Hussain, Peace Be Upon

Them, frequented the corridors and the chambers around the royal courtyard. This was even before my birth...'

'And it led to Shah Baba to abandon the Agra fort and establish the new city of Fatehpur Sikri,' interjected Khurram uncharacteristically.

Jahangir looked at him with quizzical annoyance. Interjections in the presence of the emperor were unusual, especially from prince Khurram, a rigid follower of court protocol.

'Your Majesty,' blurted Khurram, 'I have seen them with my own eyes. A few weeks back when we were encamped at Mirza Kamran's Baradari, I did see a few veiled figures near the river bank.'

Jahangir's eyes narrowed, 'What did you see?'

'Sire, I saw a veiled woman, dressed in red, gliding along the marbled forecourt of the *baradari* and down the steps to the riverbank.' He paused, and then passing his hands over his eyes, muttered 'She left behind a fragrance, something very familiar, but I cannot exactly explain it to you, Majesty.'

'And then?'

Prince Khurram lowered his eyes, and with a small shiver, said 'She was escorted by a body of ghostly horsemen, and they silently rode away and disappeared into the mist.'

Emperor Jahangir waved a derisive hand 'There are no phantoms or dancing wraiths here, Khurram. She must have been one of the royal begums.'

Prince Khurram raised his eyes, and with just the hint of a conspiratorial smile, concluded, 'I am sure she was, Majesty. From the past.'

Their eyes met and locked.

Jahangir weighed his next words very carefully. 'What is it that you desire from me, Khurram?'

'You are omniscient, Majesty—just my matrimonial alliance with Arjumand Bano, Sire!'

'So be it!' intoned Jahangir tersely.

'For the moment, it will suffice,' replied Khurram tartly.

* * *

The next day,
11 October 1606,
Walled City, Lahore.

There was happiness in the air, and the nip of a cold winter morning was allayed by the sounds of festive music and the meandering warmth from the burning hearths of sweetmeat shops and small food shops, tucked between the bigger shops of jewellery, utensils and winter clothes.

Early this morning, the nobles had assembled in the *Diwan-e-Aam* and were surprised to find that overnight the massive quadrangle to the south of the royal dais had been decorated. The enormous tent of *Maidan-e-Diwan-e-Aam* was festooned with rolls of silk in gossamer pink and gold, stretching under the roof and on the pillars supporting it. Strands of silver and gold ribbons hung like golden raindrops over the colourful turbans and dresses of the court nobles.

The sonorous voice of the royal herald rang out, as the green flag with a golden crouching lion preceded the emperor, '*Ba-adab, Ba-mulaizah, Hoshiar! Padshah-e-Ghazi, Amir-i-Adl, Mirza*

Nuruddin Baig Mohammed Khan Salim Jahangir tashreef farma!'

Asaf Khan Qazwini, officiating as the *Mir Tozak*, unrolled a red scroll with gold tassels, and turning to the emperor, performed an elaborate kornish. At the emperor's slight nod, he addressed the assembly.

'Know all men, that His Imperial Majesty Padshah Ghazi Nuruddin Baig Mohammed Salim Jahangir has honoured the house of Khwaja Ghiyasuddin Beg Teherani, an honoured courtier of the Realm, by accepting the hand of his granddaughter, Arjumand Bano, for prince Khurram Taimur. That the Grace of Allah is invoked upon this happy alliance. *Padshah Salamat! Hukumat Salamat!'*

The tented hall erupted with congratulatory cries and salutations. Some of the senior lords were discomfited by the use of the suffix 'Taimur'; it had not been used in recent memory, and was indicative of momentous decisions in the offing.

Khwaja Ghiyasuddin Beg Teherani and his son, Mirza Abul Hasan Teherani looked at each other in bewildered silence, as congratulations burst forth from all sides.

***

Chambers of Begum Salima Sultana,
Shahi Qila, Lahore.
Same day, 11.45 a.m.

Emperor Jahangir politely declined the silver tumbler of warm, sweetened almond milk being proffered and stared sullenly at his gold braided moccasins. The past twenty-four hours had been tumultuous, and had mentally and physically worn him down. His hasty departure from Sheikhpura, and the continuous ride of ten kos to the Shahi Qila had definitely destroyed his opium induced good humour. The emperor was cross, and worried.

Begum Salima Sultana leaned back against the bolster, and chose her words carefully. 'Majesty, your sudden decision to announce prince Khurram's betrothal to Arjumand has taken us all by surprise. I am sure there must have been overriding considerations behind this decision.' She waited for Jahangir to respond, but he merely shifted his gaze to the rich borders of the Persian rug. Taking a pull at her silver hookah, she delicately let the smoke rings escape in small perfumed wisps from her bejeweled nose.

The emperor crossed his arms, 'It was a conscious decision, Begum Sahiba. It is also what the Dowager Empress, Begum Ruqaiah wanted. She had communicated as such a few months back, at Khurram's insistence.'

Begum Salima looked at him keenly, and pointedly asked, 'I know you better than anyone, Sheikhu,' she smiled as emperor Jahangir looked up at the mention of his childhood name, 'there is definitely more to this than Her Highness' wish.'

'I have been watching Khurram closely, Begum Sahiba, over these past few months. After all, with prince Khusrau in disgrace and Pervez on the Mewar campaign, the Court's attention is on Khurram. He is fourteen now, and needs female company.' He stopped and looked squarely at the Begum, 'His fantasies are running wild. He chases ghostly apparitions in red capes who glide over marbled floors, and raises the specter of catastrophe befalling the empire, if this ghost, this djinn is not locked away.'

The widowed queen smiled faintly, 'Even I have heard rumours in the *zenanakhana* about some ghostly figures around the royal harem. You have enough romantic skeletons buried in your garden, Sheikhu!'

Emperor Jahangir looked speculatively at her; Begum Salima Sultana had definitely been his closest confidante and co-conspirator in the past, and could certainly be trusted with impending events—he did need his own Hand within the harem. Jahangir leant forward, and resting his elbows on the silk bolster, began to speak in cautious whispers.

Begum Salima shivered as the full import of the emperor's words hit her. Her hands shook as she raised them in supplication.

'Ya Allah,' she muttered, 'a subterfuge like this has never been implemented before. We put our trust in Thee, and pray that this action shall not destroy the empire or this Timurid dynasty. Ameen!'

* * *

Old Street near Morchi Darwaza
Mohalla Banduk Saz, Walled City, Lahore.
17 December 1606
06.20 p.m.

The evening had turned dark and cold just as the sun had set. Witheringly algid and dry winds blew from the Hindu Kush range on the north, and the Suleiman range to the south east, forcing the populace to find warmth and succour inside their homes. In such an evening, emperor Salim Jahangir rode out on his favourite elephant, *Hawai*.

Preceding the emperor's elephant were a squadron of mounted horsemen, riding with their lances held across their chests. *Gurj-burdars* with their golden maces ran alongside the royal elephant, pushing and shoving their way through the gawking pedestrians. The emperor sat in his golden howdah, surrounded by vessels containing roasted meat, dry fruits and silver decanters of wine, happily devouring the roast and throwing half eaten pieces to the small crowd of destitutes and children running behind.

Trailing the monarch were a string of elephants carrying musicians and cooks. While the musicians played a symphony of evening ragas, the cooks were busy tending to their copper wares holding fragrant rice with meatballs, aromatic curries and a huge golden salver with pickles and spicy onion rings.

As the road curved towards Mubarak Haveli, there sat a group of *'Be-Qaid'* fakirs, rolling their smoking pots of opium and cannabis. These roving mendicants called themselves as 'liberated' and did not care much for material things or worldly ties. They were known to be fearless and bold, and could cause a huge uproar if crossed. Enormous turbans, with fancy feathers and strings of beads, were their only decoration.

They watched warily as the royal procession slowly wound its way towards them.

While the horsemen were careful in skirting the circle of *Be-Qaid* fakirs, the mace bearers waded into the motley group of squatting *fakirs,* raining blows with their maces. 'Clear the way, O, you sodden lumps! Clear the way, for His Imperial Majesty' rang the harsh words.

In a trice, some of the sober fakirs were grappling, pushing and shoving the mace bearers. Their long wooden staves were used with sufficient might and finesse to lay a few of the royal runners writhing in pain, clutching their legs, knees and abdomen. Some of the more spirited ones had heated one end of their wooden staffs in the fire pit, and then wildly chased the gurjbardars, threatening to brand their posteriors.

The emperor's elephant, *Hawai*, was trumpeting loudly and shaking his great head, when out stepped an ascetic and loudly challenged the monarch. 'Hail, Emperor of Mortals, wherein dost thou ride with such aplomb and show? Thou hast perched yourself on an elephant high, and blind are thee to the suffering around you? Step down, O King, and listen to what I have to say.'

The mounted soldiers had already pushed their way between the furious mendicants and the royal elephant, when Jahangir commanded his *mahout* to make the elephant kneel. A great shout went up from the assembled fakirs.

Emperor Jahangir dismounted slowly, gripping the rails of the hastily put silver steps. The cavalry dismounted too, but Jahangir waved them away.

The mendicants became quiet, as they warily watched the emperor walking towards their group. Jahangir, flush with opium induced happiness, called merrily to this assorted group of libertines, 'Hey, Pious Men, what ails thee that you create such a furore in the presence of your emperor?'

A *Be-Qaid* with his turban askew, and clutching his sides where a macebearer had landed a heavy blow, countered with passion, 'You may be emperor to these sorry souls around you,' he gestured to the silent group of soldiers and royal attendants, 'but, you are certainly not emperor to us. We are *Be-Qaids,* unfettered and free, answerable to none but Allah above. He who provides for us and for you, O King! You only sit atop a mighty elephant, and gorge on food and wine, while your poor subjects and little children run after thee, desperate for morsels? Is this your Kingship?'

Jahangir had tears in his eyes, and his cheeks quivered in the first paroxysm of grief, when another fakir shouted, 'You are nothing but a bag of bones and flesh, destined to decay in the very earth, which you trample with this mighty beast.'

These words were catastrophic for the emperor in his opium afflicted state. He sank to his knees, and cried in great howls of violent grief.

The *Be-Qaids,* unnerved by the emperor's wailing, and susceptible to melodramatic relief in their cannabis-ridden state, also dissolved in tears amidst great shrieks and body wracking sobs.

The emperor and the destitutes were momentarily united in their Cannabis induced grief!

***

Many hours later, a listless and inebriated Jahangir was carried back on his elephant, while the fakirs slept soundly, well fed from the royal cauldrons of meat and rice.

***

The Haveli of Itmad-Ud-Daulah,
Rarra Maidan, Eastern Circuit,
Lahore.
29 December 1606
3 p.m.

The emperor looked at the glum faces of Sheikh Ghiyasuddin Itmad-Ud-Daulah and his son, Abu'l Hasan, as they stood with bowed heads amidst the mountain of gold, copper and silver vessels.

Just behind the ornamental screen of golden silk and brocade could be seen the hushed figures of the Sheikh's harem—his wives, daughters, and daughters in law. The emperor's refusal to taste even a morsel of food in their house was a primary sign of imperial disfavour, and could presage the ruination of their dynasty. The emperor's words of comfort and royal favour failed to assuage the family members.

Begum Asmat, the Sheikh's chief wife, spoke in a cultured voice from behind the screen, '*Alampanah,* you have graced our house with your imperial splendour, for which we shall be eternally grateful. Where have we erred, my lord, that you decline to even touch the food that we have cooked with our own hands? My sons and I have tasted each dish in your presence to banish any doubts of poisoning, Allah forbid.' Her voice broke, 'Ever since we received your farmaan over forty-eight hours ago, we have been toiling in the kitchen...'

Jahangir was moved by the simple eloquence of this cultured lady, and he addressed her husband 'Ghiyas Beg, please do assure your Begum that I am restrained by royal protocol, and not by any other factor. Please make her understand that my visit today was of my own choosing, setting aside royal protocol, only to apprise you that many imperial favours await you and your sons. Extraordinary favours.'

The emperor paused, as he looked at the faint return of joy in their faces. 'I wanted to personally inform you, Sheikh. You shall have riches and power beyond your dreams. You have only to devote yourself to the welfare of the empire, even if it may mean personal sacrifices.' Jahangir's eyes bored into their eyes.

Ghiyas Beg bowed low, quickly touching his palm to the ground and then bringing it up to his forehead. 'Your Majesty,' he said, 'My life and my hours are sworn to your service. You will never find me, or my sons deficient in trust or service.'

Feigning reluctance, Jahangir gestured towards the vessels of gold filled with aromatic dishes and observed, 'Ghiyasuddin, please inform your Begum that I cannot refuse her hospitality, and shall definitely partake a meal.'

Heartfelt laudations of *'Hazaarah, Hazaarah Shukar, Rehem-Dil Alampanah'* filled the large vaulted hall.

***

The following day, 30 December 1606, a small detail of court officials headed by the Mir Tozak and Sipahsalar, carried a Shahi Farmaan to the house of Ghiyas Beg Itmad-Ud-Daulah.

Arjumand Bano would be engaged to prince Khurram on Wednesday, 28 March 1607.

***

CHAPTER 15

'BA AHAN DAR RAGNPEHEIMAN'

('With Iron in our Veins.')

Lookout's Shelter,
Arghandab River Valley,
West of Kandahar,
08 January 1607
06.40 p.m.

The two shepherds were huddled together under their sheepskin rugs, afraid to light a fire as their location would be compromised. A few hours ago, they had watched with interest as a small posse of horse riders had appeared amongst the distant stony cliffs along the banks of the Arghandab river.

After about half an hour, a larger body of men had turned up, with a great many horses and soldiers travelling on foot. Shahqaum, the eagle-eyed shepherd, murmured 'Scratch my arse.. these are surely not innocent traders. Aalam, come quick!'

Aalam Beg, the senior of the two, inched closer to the rough wall and peered in the direction that Shahqaum was looking at so intently. In a few moments, his vision had adjusted to the distant site, and he could make out the great pile of swords, javelins and shields which were being unloaded from the pack horses and the score of mules, now tethered.

Aalam Beg, muttered aloud, 'They are too well armed to be traders or travellers, yet, they carry no flags or war drums to single them out as soldiers. Who are they? And, what brings them here?'

They sat together, huddled, silent companions in the wintry wastes of these stony mountains, when Shahqaum reluctantly took out his arm from the warmth of the rug and pointed once more in the distance. Aalam strained to see, and then a raucous oath erupted from him.

Way back in the shadow of the river valley, and shielded by the darkness and rising mist, there stretched a river of small, soft glowing lights. Even to an untrained eye, the sight of a sizable war camp was evident.

***

Early next morning, Aalam Beg was on his way to alert the garrison at Kandahar, a day's march away.

***

Northern ramparts,
Qila Kandahar,
24 January 1607
Dusk.

There was the thunderous roar of cannons as the Persian artillery, ranged in a crude semicircle, fired their first barrage in unison.

Great walls of dust arose as the iron balls thudded short of the fort into the stony plain below.

The Mughal Fort Commander, Shah Beg Arghun, spat out a thick wad of cannabis, glaring at the Persians as they slowly went around their business of arming and firing their cannons. 'It seems these lazy louts are in no hurry.' Shah Beg looked disgustedly at his senior *Topchi*, and continued, 'Ismail, let us put some vigour back in their tired limbs. Fire a salvo right over their heads into the forward tents.'

Ismail Jubair, the gigantic Pashtun with an incredible inventory of abuses, shouted to his cannoneers, 'Raise the embrasures, and lift the barrels. This volley must singe their pubic hair.'

The next volley was right in the middle of the Persian ranks.

'Sons of whores, seed of a donkey, move your cannons forward, and FIRE! Do not rush back... move forward, move forward.' The Persian commander's voice drowned in the pandemonium of crashing cannon shots, bellow of animals and the frightened shouts of the soldiers, as cannons and wooden boxes of ammunition were unceremoniously pushed backwards. The Persian Topchi swung his horse into the melee and started clubbing the troops with the hilt and broadside of his sword, all the while exhorting and threatening his men to turn around.

The Topchi leaned forward to kick and smite yet another band of fleeing soldiers, when a couple of his own troopers leapt on him from behind, unsettling him from the saddle and throwing him to the ground. As he hit the ground, he tried to roll to his right and reach for the sword lying a few paces away, when one of the men pinned his head to the ground with his knee, and sliced his jugular with his dagger.

Shah Beg Khan, standing on the foremost parapet, leant on the rough-hewn walls and called out to Ismail who was busy directing his cannoneers, 'Hey, Ismail Pathan, you see the soldiery of this sorry mass of stragglers? This is what happens when you put fruits, beans, meat and wood in the same cauldron to cook... an unpalatable mess! These Seistanis could never get along with Khorsanis, and the Herats are enemies of all. But here they are, a pitiable mass of cowardly lice. Ismail, let us give them something to remember for generations together... let us fight with iron in our veins!'

The huge Pashtun's smile was more terrifying than the cannonade.

***

Siege
Qila Kandahar,
Same night, about 9 pm.

Hosayn Khan Shamlu, the governor of Herat, sat smoking cannabis from his *galyan*, the Persian form of *hookah.*

Hosayn Khan's anxiety and misery had increased with every passing day of the siege. What he had considered to be a short military assault on a weak and truncated Mughal garrison, had emerged as a debilitating blockade of a resolute foe.

Suddenly, there was a great shout from outside, and the sentry commander rushed in. '*Sipah-salar*, you must see this to believe it! The Devil, Shah Beg Khan, is dancing on the parapet!'

Hosayn Khan stumbled out. Transfixed, he watched as the Mughal *Qiledar* Shah Beg Khan Arghun, surrounded by a bunch of inebriated, clapping soldiers thrust and ground his pelvis in a grotesque imitation of the Turqi belly dance. The top of the circular bastion was lit up by a dozen long handled mashals, and a small clutch of drum beaters tried to match the weird cadence of Shah Beg's pelvic gyrations. Noticing that he had the attention of the besiegers, Shah Beg turned towards their encampment and started taking off his leather smock.

The Safavid general called out, 'Shoot lighted arrows at that madman, and ...' he turned towards his artillery men standing despondently, 'Prepare and fire the heavy cannons. Now!'

With their commander slain a few hours earlier, the *Top-andaz* were a despairing lot. Reluctantly, they started hitching their cannons to mules and oxen to move them forward. The archers had by now sent a volley of lighted arrows towards the citadel, and they cut a fiery tract across the sky.

By now, Shah Beg Khan was divested of his clothing and stood naked with his engorged penis in his hand, moving his hand up and down the shaft, insulting the Persians in a most primitive way. Many of his soldiers were also holding their penises and taunting the besiegers.

Ismail Beg stood near *Jung Bahadur*, the heavy copper-iron cannon on the left bastion, and pointed towards the right flank of the Persian war camp. 'Do you see that huge tented quadrangle near the water tank? That is their store for cannon shots and gunpowder. One careful, steady shot, and they shall be blown to Kingdom come.

In a matter of seconds, at least two cannonballs exploded right in the midst of the huge tented enclosure. There was a tremendous roar, and the earth seemed to shake as munitions went up in a huge ball of flames. Men and animals were thrown around like little dismembered dolls, and gusts of hot wind and thunderous explosions continued for the next several minutes.

Hosayn Khan sat down on his haunches amidst the screaming, terrified horde of soldiers.

'Shah Beg Khan is blessed by the Devil. He is a djinn... I cannot fight a djinn!' His heaving sobs and tears ridden dirt-streaked beard was a call to return.

***

Early next morning, the war camp of Hosayn Khan Shamlu, governor of Herat and the field commander of these diverse forces, was being unpegged. The war banners were being furled, while the pack animals were being brought forward and cavalry withdrawn.

Only a few squadrons of cavalry and detachments of foot soldiers were left in the vanguard to repel any attack from the Mughal garrison, while the main body became busy in moving camp.

***

Toshakhana- The Imperial Treasury,
Shahi Qila, Lahore.
12 March 1607.
3 p.m.

There was rapid knocking on the closed door, and Ram Das Kachhawa, after a brief exchange, approached the emperor, 'Your Majesty, there is a messenger from Kandahar. The imperial forces under Mirza Jani Beg Tarkhan reached Kandahar by the middle of

February, but the Persian forces had retreated earlier, deterred by the fierce engagement of the Mughal garrison there.'

A faint smile played upon the emperor's lips, 'With *Chaar Lazeez Khor* Shah Beg Khan as the Citadel Commander, I can well imagine the plight of Shah Abbas's generals and troops!'

The faint smile turned into a laugh, and then into a loud guffaw, as Jahangir recalled the temerity of Shah Beg Khan Arghun on his Ascension Day, comparing all the assembled nobles and Court Grandees to his own pubic hair. Despairing at such a blatant violation of court protocol, Jahangir had been forced to exile his bravest commander to the far-off citadel of Kandahar.

* * *

Khwabgah,
Jahangiri Quarters, Shahi Qila,
Lahore.
14 March 1607
Late evening.

Emperor Jahangir straightened the curled edges of the parchment, and pulled the silver candle stand closer. He had hurried back from the Hall of Private Audience as soon as Qutubuddin Koka's emissary had arrived from Bengal with the concealed parchment in a sealed, chained and padlocked leather pouch slung across his chest. Unlike other royal messengers, he had been escorted by a score of cavalries. To make the journey less conspicuous through the notoriously murderous badlands of Bhojpur and Rohtas in Bihar, the local chieftains had been asked to provide adequate security.

His eyes darted over the words written by his childhood friend in his broad scrawl, which so resembled his mammoth girth.

'In the service of His Imperial Majesty,
The Most Benevolent and Just,
Shah Nuruddin Salim Jahangir Padshah Ghazi

Hail, The Emperor, The Mightiest and Just,

The grace of your reign extends far and wide, and the Subas of Bengal and Bihar prosper under your benevolent hand. You will be glad to know, Sire, that the harvest has been good and the royal cess collections will not be disappointing. All other matters of State follow in the regular fortnightly Dak.

Your Majesty, the monsoon consultations with the Jagirdar of Burdwan has been confirmed for 30 March Friday. I am fortunate indeed to render this service on the auspicious day of Juma, and pray that it brings immense happiness and joy in your life, my foster brother, the Sultan-e- Hind!

Be assured, Your Imperial Majesty, that the small work entrusted to me of replacing one gem with the other shall also be attended to expeditiously, once the monsoon arrangements are in place.

This may be my last missive to you in a long while, Majesty—I shall now write to you only after all pending aspects have been settled to your satisfaction.

The mango trees here are full with the reddish white flowers, and may ripen early. I shall personally select and send the best of 'himsagar' and 'malda' mangoes as a shipload, but shall sincerely miss our summer sojourns immersed in mangoes!'

Jahangir's eyes misted over as he recalled the 'mango afternoons' as a prince, when he and Khubu spent hours together gorging on mangoes sent from all over the realm; what carefree days were those! The emperor smiled, as Mirza Qutubuddin's childhood's name, 'Khubu', came rushing back at him. He continued to read.

'It is hoped, Your Majesty, that you shall shower me with the same love and affection that we shared as children, and that neither the years nor the weight of Kingship will dim your love for me... With such fond hopes,

I remain,

Your Imperial Servant
& Faithful Hand,
Khubu Chishti
Subedar of Bengal & Bihar
21 February 1607.

Jahangir sighed deeply, pleased, yet a little nervous—the 'monsoon arrangements' was a code developed between the emperor and Qutubuddin to signify the murder of Sher Afghan, the Jagirdar of Burdwan and the husband of Mehrunnisa, the most beautiful and coveted woman of her Time.

Navroz was but a week away, and Khurram's engagement ceremony was just a week after that; so much had to be done, and hardly any time!

***

Having raised Khurram's *mansab* to 8000 Zat/ 5000 Sowars, he solemnised Khurram's engagement to Arjumand on 28th March, 1607.

On Friday, 30 March 1607, he left Lahore for Kabul. The royal court moved with him.

***

CHAPTER 16

RODKHANEH SHIR BARAYE CPEHMISHEH RAFTEH EST

(The River of Milk is Gone Forever)

The camp of Qutubuddin Koka,
Purba Bardhman, Burdwan.
30 March 1607.
8 a.m.

Subedar Qutubuddin Khan Koka nudged his horse under the shade of a tamarind tree, and delicately scraped out a little wad of moist cannabis from a ruby encrusted silver box.

Standing behind a clump of tall, razor-sharp wild grass, Sher Afghan surveyed the Subedar's assemblage from afar. Qutubuddin's massive form could be seen surrounded by at least a score of attendants and soldiers, all bearing arms. He waited a few more minutes, and then guided his steed out of the thicket into a lazy trot.

Qutubuddin quickly wheeled his horse and watched Sher Afghan approach with two grooms. He cautioned Haider Malik, his trusted Kashmiri *Waqia-navees,* 'Haider, Sher Afghan is suspicious and alert. Let him come close enough. Then surround him, and slay him.'

Haider Malik nodded.

As Sher Afghan rode nearer, his anger flared. Lumbering towards him was a war elephant, guided by two mahouts and with a spiked chain tucked in its trunk—the classic manoeuvre of an attack elephant. He nudged his horse into a canter and drew his sword.

Qutubuddin watched as the elephant picked up pace, lowering its great head and cutting diagonally across mustard fields to intercept Sher Afghan. The Jagirdar swerved left, away from the charging beast, and cut a wide swathe towards the governor, who was now closely guarded by his troops and attendants.

When just a few horse lengths remained between them, Sher Afghan shouted, 'What evil do you have in your heart, *O Kokultash?*'

Qutubuddin rode forward with a raised hand to assure the furious Afghan, when suddenly the chasing elephant bellowed in rage. The cinder black stallion of Sher Khan bolted, and tore forward. Instinctively, Sher Afghan leaned to his right and cut an arc with his sword.

Qutubuddin, caught unawares, could merely manage to sway left in his saddle. The broadsword sliced his abdomen, and his intestines spilled out. Shocked and speechless, he stared at the blood gushing out from his stomach, and gingerly put his hands on his stomach, trying to stuff back his hanging intestines.

Amba Khan, a Kashmiri steward of Qutubuddin, immediately swung at Sher Khan's head and managed a glancing blow. Enraged, Sher Afghan turned around and half standing in the stirrups, delivered a double handed vertical blow, slicing Amba Khan's head in half. Pressing his knees into the horse's flank, Sher Khan tried to gallop away, but his escape was barred by the snorting, shaking form of the war elephant. Whipping his trunk from side to side, *Bandhu,* the war elephant, advanced on the neighing, pawing horse and its rider.

Raising its trunk high, it brought it down with terrible force on the horse, which buckled under the assault. The spiked chain narrowly missed Sher Afghan but cut deeply into the face and tender nostrils of the fallen stallion, cleaving his nostrils and lips into two bloody parts, dangling on either side of its face.

Frenzied with pain, the stallion thrashed on the dry ground. Meanwhile, Haider Malik and Yakub Khan having recovered sufficiently from the sudden attack on Koka, rushed towards Sher Afghan. Yakub, coming from behind Sher Khan's left shoulder, gave a crushing blow with his sword at the Jagirdar's nape. Haider Malik also swung at Sher Afghan's torso, but it was Yakub Khan's second blow which neatly severed Sher Khan's head.

Qutubuddin lurched in his saddle, holding his guts with his hands. His benumbed eyes could hardly register the mangling of Sher Afghan's body by his enraged troopers.

Eyes smarting with fury and pain, Yakub Khan waved his sword in the air, 'Death to the traitor's family! Death to our enemies!' In a split second, he had spurred his horse towards the fortress of Sher Afghan.

Haider Malik chased after him.

* * *

Sher Afghan Garh,
Taluk Andal,
8.45 a.m.
Same day.

The old servant, rushing down the stairs in abject fright, screamed, '*Ammi Begum*, our master is gone!' A sob escaped his quivering lips. 'There are riders riding furiously this way... they would not have dared if Sher Khan was alive.'

Just then, Mehrunnisa, the beautiful wife of Sher Afghan ran out, and shook Rafiq, 'What happened?' Rafiq dissolved in tears.

Her bewildered eyes turned towards her mother-in-law, '*Ammi jaan*, what is the matter? Why dost thou shaketh so? Please...' Her face crumpled as she saw the old lady shaking in grief, her cheeks lined with cascading tears.

'Ya Allah!' screamed Mehrunnisa, as the import of the circumstance hit her. She sat down on her haunches, holding her head in her hands.

Several of the attendants, and a few soldiers were gathering in the verandah, fear writ large on their faces.

The old lady limped forward, and unable to bend down, prodded Mehrunnisa with her silver cane, 'Biwi, this is no time to grieve, nor lose your senses. You must escape before they get here.' She called to the old faithful, 'Rafiq, take a few guards with you and escort Begum Sahiba and Ladlii to the nearest garrison at Asansol. Seek refuge in the name of Mirza Ghiyas Beg of the Imperial Court at Lahore.' She beckoned the female attendants.

Mehrunnisa gasped as the slave girls pulled her to her feet. She found her voice, 'Leave me,' she said in a haze, 'Help Ammi jaan with her things.'

Her mother-in-law took her firmly by the hand, and commanded 'There is no time to pack, just go! My time has come; I have suckled Sher Khan and will never leave him behind.' She tried to push Mehrunnisa towards the back door of the haveli. 'Beti, you must escape for you carry Sher Khan's legacy in your arms—defend Ladlii as you would defend your honour; let no harm come to her. She is all that we have left of Ali Quli Khan Istalju.'

Just then, Sher Afghan's younger brother, Qamar Sultan entered from the back door, panting with fear and exertion. Before he could say anything, the resolute old dowager called out to her surviving son, 'Sultan, dwell not here for it is unsafe. Take Mehrunnisa and Ladlii to Asansol fort. I shall come with Sher Afghan.'

'But, Ammi, I have just heard that...'

The grieving mother thundered, 'Sultan, this is not the time to argue, or dither. Find a safe refuge... I shall follow soon.'

Qamar hesitated for just a second, and then rushed out, calling for swift horses to be brought around to the back near the big lake.

'Khuda Hafiz, Sultan,' murmured the old matron. She looked upwards at the clear blue spring sky, and intoned *'Allah, rehem kar!'*

* * *

As Haider Malik crossed the low stone wall, marking the outer boundary of Sher Khan's haveli, he espied a few fleeing figures through the forest on the lake's far side. He reined in his horse, and looked at the distant figures, shielding his eyes from the sun.

He raced his horse around the huge pond's muddy shores, and cut across the mango grove, which had seemed like a forest from afar. Riding low over his steed's neck to avoid the low hanging branches, he quickly wheeled his horse around, when he heard the low keening moan of a woman in grief.

Rafiq, the old servant, stepped forward clumsily holding a long sword. Just behind him were Qamar Sultan and the veiled form of a woman with a small child clasped to her breast. Haider dismounted, and walked forward with his empty hands held in front, offering peace. From the periphery rose several soldiers and surrounded him.

Haider spoke gently, 'Please, I mean no harm. I am the *Waqia-navees* of the Subedar. My name is Haider Malik and I have come searching for you, Begum Sahiba, at the express orders of my lord.'

Qamar Sultan stepped up, and asked tersely, 'What has happened, Malik?'

Haider Malik lowered his eyes, 'I do not know you, Sire...'

'I am Qamar Sultan, the younger brother of Sher Afghan.'

'Sire, there was an altercation between Subedar and Janab Sher Afghan, due to a misunderstanding raised by the local *karori* regarding tax collections. During the heated argument, Sher Khan's hand went towards his sword, and unwittingly a few of our soldiers attacked him. But the governor stopped them before any grievous harm could be done.'

'But, where is my lord?' asked a tremulous Mehrunnisa.

'Your Grace, both the Subedar and Sher Afghan were slightly injured in the fracas. They have both retired to the official quarters at Burdwan, and I have been expressly sent to escort you in safety.'

Tears of joy welled up in her eyes, and she raised her hands in supplication to the heavens above. However, Qamar was not convinced.

'We have heard a different story that Qutubuddin connived to have my brother murdered?'

'Sire, these are canards being spread by the treacherous karori. He was unable to embezzle imperial funds because of the jagirdar's honesty. Hence, he arranged for several complainants to file their petitions before the Subedar. Sire, this is why it is imperative that I escort you all to safety before they hatch another plan to harm Sher Khan and his family.'

Fearing for her daughter's safety, Mehrunnisa ordered, 'Qamran, we ride to Burdwan. I must see my lord and take care of his wounds. Even Ladlii would be safer there. If you wish, you can go back to the haveli and be with Ammi. I shall go with Haider Malik.'

Qamar caught a horse's bridle and helped Mehrunnisa aloft. He took the silent and terrified Ladlii into his own arms, and mounted a horse.

As the small party wound its way to the *daftarkhana*, it was met by a strong escort of imperial guards. The personal attendants and guards of Sher Afghan accompanying Mehrunnisa were herded towards the fortified square buildings of the Subedar's office, while Mehrunnisa, Ladlii and Qamar were brought to the house of Ashq Jolaha, a close confidant of Haider Malik.

Upon reaching, Mehrunnisa and her daughter were taken inside the zenanakhana while Qamar Sultan was bound in chains and fetters, and dragged to an outhouse. Bewildered and frightened, he was thrown inside a dark and smelly room. Rodents, as big as mongoose, skittered out to welcome their new guest.

Mehrunnisa swooned in despair, as she heard Haider Malik threaten, 'Times will never be the same again for you. Sher Afghan is dead, and you will do well for yourself and your daughter, if you keep your wits about you and make no foolish attempts at escape or revenge. Day after, you shall be moved to my house to spend your forty days of mourning. Any imprudent action of yours, and you will see your daughter's hair sutured into her scalp.'

***

Subedar's camp,
Just outside Burdwan,
8.20 p.m.
Same night.

Qutubuddin Chishti died about twelve hours after the skirmish, when the camp was just about to have their evening meal.

The cooking fires were quickly doused and an eerie silence descended upon the huddled tents.

Haider Malik, the Waqia-navees, sat with great trepidation to write the mandatory note to the royal court. He felt sorry for the messenger who would carry this missive and would become the subject of the emperor's wrath.

With a sigh, he dipped his quill, and began to write...

'In service of the Sultan-i-Hind, Sultanat Mughaliya,
The River of Milk has Gone Forever...'

***

Small hut of Pir Shahbaz Hamadan
Shahpur Mircha, near Baghi, Bihar.
12 June 1607.
04.50 a.m.

The screened wagon cart slewed heavily over the mud tracks now turned to slush with the first showers, presaging a good monsoon this year. Mehrunnisa, after having spent forty days of mourning in the house of Haider Malik had left Burdwan for Agra on the 15 May 1607. An imperial farmaan had been received, ordering the widow to return to the protection of the royal court at Agra, and Islam Khan, a close relative of the slain Subedar Qutubuddin Chishti, was entrusted to escort her with a heavy contingent of cavalry and foot soldiers.

These past few weeks had lain Mehrunnisa low with apprehension and fear; fear of what fate had for her in store at the royal court—whether she would be accepted or surreptitiously pushed from a pavilion? The Mughal harem was infamous for its swift executions and convenient disappearances! Would Ghiyas Beg and Begum Asmat accept her as a widowed daughter returning home? Ladlii's reticence and constant melancholia had become a cause of worry to Mehrunnisa, as she had slipped into absolute silence and surliness after Sher Afghan's murder, and nothing seemed to cheer her.

While camping at the small hamlet of Baghi last night, she was told of a highly venerated Moslem fakir who resided in the adjoining village of Shahpur Mircha, barely a kos and a half from the camp. He had the gift of divining the future, so the villagers spoke. Islam Khan readily agreed to her request, and the camp broke very early the next morning.

Mehrunnisa peeked from behind the jute screen as the cart drew to a halt. The aged seer rose from his prayer mat, and carefully rolled it. He looked once at the mounted soldiers and then quietly shuffled inside his small hut.

Mehrunnisa raised her eyes, and was shocked at the astounding shimmer in the fakir's eyes. Stunned, she could not escape the magnetism of those eyes and continued to stare.

Pir Shahbaz Hamadan, a direct descendant of Mir Sayyed Ali Hamadani, the revered saint who lived almost two hundred years ago, looked at her nervously wringing fingers and spoke softly, assuring her.

'You have embarked on a journey of great munificence, my child. I know there are great worries and burdens on your mind, but why do you fret? You are protected by Pirs and fakirs.... The stars and the moon watch over you, child.' He looked at her, and then turned his gaze towards the rosary beads hung on the wall, continuing with a soft cadence. 'Your Destiny awaits you—Widowhood is not for you. Go in peace, and forget not those who helped you in your darkest hours. The Time has now come for you to become the Empress, my child.'

There was silence as the ascetic stopped speaking. His eyes were closed, and he leant against the coarse wall. Mehrunnisa stood, and with a solemn salutation left the hermit's abode.

* * *

That night, as the cavalcade was being ferried across the Ganges towards Patna, a hefty Afghan fettered and bound with chains, and with a heavy boulder strapped to his chest, was quietly pushed back over the stern.

He sank without a trace, the black waters hastening to hide the rising bubbles.

It was Qumar Sultan, the slain Sher Afghan's brother.

* * *

CHAPTER 17

FARYADEHAYI AZ ZHERFAYE TARIKI

(Shrieks from the Abyss of Darkness)

Caravanserai,
Bankipur, Patna
13 June 1607.
A few minutes to midnight.

Mehrunnisa felt stifled in the large, ornate room of the caravanserai. The sultry June night promised the freshness of rain, but the night sky remained clear, with an occasional owl scooting across the half-waned moon. The rippling of the Ganges could be felt, the dark waters gently lapping against the caravanserai's rear walls.

The horror of Qumar's sudden disappearance and certain death had hung heavy on the camp since morning. Islam Kham had ordered a three-day halt at Patna for supplies and provisions, and it was also rumoured that a small squadron of cavalry from Surajpura would be joining shortly as additional escort through the troubled lands of Bhojpur.

Ladlii, her two-year-old daughter, whimpered as she picked up her small delicate form and walked out into the cool breeze of the veranda. She leant against a carved pillar and the smell of fresh hay, animal sweat and smouldering cooking fires so peculiar to every traveller's inn wafted softly in the air.

Mehrunnisa's eyes were drawn towards a sudden movement, just behind the large flaming torch. She strained her eyes, but the glow from the torch shadowed everything in its lee. A black silhouette again flitted from behind a pillar, sword blade flashing. Mehrunnisa, restless and apprehensive, screamed.

Terrified, she watched as several shadows sprang up and raced across the courtyard. Clutching Ladlii to her breast, she turned and fled towards her room.

'Help!' she cried. 'Islam Khan, help... somebody, please help!'

Shouldering the door open, she thrust Ladlii into the arms of the child's bewildered maid, and flung herself upon the door, bolting it with a swiftness born out of fear. She gestured to the maid, '*Dhai,* pick up that wooden block and wedge it here.'

As the wooden bar was wedged between the iron clasps on the doorframes, there was a mighty crash and the door shuddered on its hinges. Crying with fear, Mehrunnisa threw her weight against the door, when suddenly the middle plank was splintered by a sword thrust, just inches from her midriff. She shrank back in fear.

Loud shouts and the sound of running boots could be heard outside. In seconds, the veranda was teeming with soldiers and the clash of swords. Mehrunnisa huddled in a corner behind a large wooden trunk with Ladlii in her arms, as abusive oaths and anguished shrieks of the soldiers continued unabated.

After a few minutes, the clamour of arms died down, and there was an urgent knock on the splintered door.

'Your Grace, open the door. It is safe now.'

Islam Khan and a few soldiers rushed in; blood and flesh plastered on their swords. The escort commander spoke rapidly, 'My Lady, you must come quickly and hear this...'

Transfixed, Mehrunnisa ran outside. On the floor, bleeding and badly hurt, was held a man wearing a coarse grey cloak. His beard was matted with blood dribbling from his lacerated face and his right arm lay crooked, as if someone had wrenched it out of its socket. A large, heavy soldier had his knee in the man's back and held his neck in a deadlock.

Islam Khan snarled at him, 'Say again your name and your purpose, wretch!'

The man growled back, 'My name is Mirza Mohammed Uzbeg. I am from the Patna garrison...'

'And your slain comrades?'

'Patna garrison.'

'Show a little more respect, Uzbeg! Who sent you, and what was your purpose?'

'We came here at the behest of Mohammed Shareif, son of Ghiyas Beg *Itmaduddaulah*. To kill this villainous woman.' The man spat blood as he tried to turn his head and glare at Mehrunnisa.

'You mean, Shareif sent you here to have his own sister killed? With Itmaduddaulah's knowledge?' Islam Khan asked with pretended incredulity, as Mehrunnisa looked at the unfolding drama with terrified eyes.

'What sister? She is the Devil Incarnate...' the fallen assailant spat, rolling his hate filled eyes towards the almost delirious Begum.

'Enough!' commanded Islam Khan. 'Let him go.'

The giant removed his knee. The man leant forward on his knees gasping for breath.

Islam Khan's sword hurtled through the air and sent the prisoner's head rolling. A gush of sickening warm blood gurgled from the stem of his neck, as his body toppled in its own puddle of blood and shreds of muscle and flesh.

Mehrunnisa swooned and fell on the stony veranda. Ladlii remained safe in the shrieks of the petrified maid.

***

On 01 July 1607, Islam Khan advanced towards Agra with Sher Afghan's family in protective custody.

***

The Royal Chambers,
Lower Fort, Bala Hissar,
15 July 1607
11 p.m.

Emperor Jahangir sat quietly in the darkened room. Most of the candles had been extinguished, and only a pair burnt in a small alcove by the door. Prince Khurram stood silently, hands clasped in front, waiting for the emperor to speak.

'Khurram.'

The prince raised his eyes. 'Yes, Your Majesty?'

'You must have heard of the attack by Itmaduddaulah's men on the royal troops at Patna?'

'Yes, Your Majesty.' After a brief pause, Khurram ventured to ask, 'Sire, the attack makes no sense. Islam Khan was not escorting the royal treasure, nor was any royal traveling. Why would Itmaduddaulah invite the emperor's wrath by doing something so silly, and without motive?'

Jahangir's voice rasped, 'Sher Afghan's widow, Mehrunnisa, and her infant daughter are travelling with the troops. I have commanded their presence at the Agra Fort, to be under my royal protection.'

'This is a ploy by some disgruntled family members to besmirch my name,' continued Jahangir. 'They are spreading rumours that I had Sher Afghan killed, and want to further smear it with his widow's blood!' He stood up in agitation.

Jahangir's hand went to the dagger tucked in his patta, and his voice rose, 'Do you see, Khurram? The family of your beloved Arjumand is plotting against my Majesty? Her grandfather, Itmaduddaulah, her uncle Shareif, even her own father Abu'l Hasan have been conspiring against me! The whole family is a clutch of shameless devils, usurpers, and ungrateful wretches.' He paused, then screamed 'I shall have them flayed, and executed. And you, Khurram, shall have nothing to do with a daughter of that family. Your betrothal is now void by royal command.'

'Mercy, Sire, mercy!' whispered Khurram, stupefied.

'Mercy is of the weak, Khurram. The traitors are in our midst, here, which is why I had the messengers flung over the wall. No leaks, no gossip. The story stays with us, or it will rip our kingdom apart.'

Fearful of his own life unravelling, Khurram knelt down and laid his head on his father's lap. 'Your Majesty, forgive my words. Punish the guilty, if you must, but spare the innocent Arjumand Bano. Sire, I love her with all my passion and my heart, Padshah Ghazi, and who better than you to understand true love? Was not the mighty Mughal empire swayed when your beloved Anarkali was so cruelly snatched away from you? Enbricked in a cold, heartless wall? Did you not brave the wrath of Shah Baba, the mightiest monarch of all times, and embark upon a rebellion which almost decimated the empire in two? Let not history repeat itself, Sire, for you are most just and forgiving. Mercy, Padshah Ghazi, mercy!'

Jahangir lifted the tear-streaked face of Khurram.

'History will not be repeated, Khurram. But, as we camp by the Surkhab, here is what you must do...'

History was to be shamed.

***

Royal Camp by the river Surkhab,
One kos North West of Jalalabad,
12 September 1607
An hour to midnight.

For a change, emperor Jahangir was not inebriated.

Though Jodha Bai, his favourite queen of the moment was seated next to him, decorously feeding morsels of roasted mutton with spiced reels of onions and juicy black grapes, Jahangir's eyes continuously flicked towards the main tent flap. It was as if he was expecting someone to arrive.

Jagat Gosain was the Empress Consort of Salim Jahangir, but was more popularly known by her sobriquet 'Jodha Bai'. Only in the official records was she referred to as Taj Bibi or the Crown Begum, the title granted to her upon the birth of her son, Khurram, by her father-in-law and emperor, Akbar, in 1592. Because of her beauty, charm, and quick wit she was quite the favourite with her husband, emperor Jahangir, who would provoke her with salacious stories of the court grandees. In return, Jagat Gosain, would regale him with the rustic dramatization of harem gossip.

There was a sudden commotion outside, and a flustered Jawahir Khan rushed in. 'Your Majesty, it is His Highness Prince Khurram. He requests an audience with you, Jahanpanah.'

'Then send him in, Khwaja!'

'He carries a sword, Majesty, and refuses to part with it.'

Empress Jagat Gosain laughed and said, 'Remove that expression of intense pain from your face, Khwajasera! He is our son, send him in.'

In a trice, prince Khurram was inside the tent, open sword in hand. Bowing low with salutations, he spluttered, 'Your Majesty, forgive this intrusion! Matter is urgent, sire, and I need to speak in privacy.'

Jahangir nodded to the attending servants and slaves, 'Takhliya!'

'Majesty, I have just been informed by my Diwan, Khwaja Wais, that there is a plan afoot to murder you tomorrow, sire... kill you, father...'

Fear was writ large on Begum's face as she clutched the emperor's arm. Jahangir was leaning forward now, his eyes aglitter. 'Slow down, son. Say what you have to say, slowly and from the beginning.'

'Your Majesty, my Diwan, Khwaja Wais heard from a dancing girl, Andaz Bano, that there are some here, who are planning to murder you while duck hunting tomorrow, on the Surkhab river.'

'And how does this girl know? Isn't she the one who was released from my imperial duties a few months back?'

'Yes, My Lord ... the same one. She is often visited by Fath 'Ullah, the son of Hakim Abu'l Fateh. Yesterday, while drunk, Fath 'Ullah boasted to this kenchen that there are several nobles who want the disgraced prince Khusrau to become emperor. With the active support of prince Khusrau and his father-in-law, Mirza Aziz Koka, the traitors have hatched this plot, sire.'

'Who else is involved?' The emperor's voice was grim.

Khurram lowered his sword, and said ruefully, 'Your Majesty, it emanates from the prison cell of prince Khusrau, abetted by Mirza Aziz Koka. It is also now known that Mohammed Shareif, the elder son of Itmaduddaulah, and Nuruddin, nephew of Itmaduddaulah are actively involved in this treacherous plan. It is said that your favourite eunuch Itibar Khan and the Turk, Bedagh Khan would be the chief assassins. *Abba Huzoor,* allow me to...'

Jahangir interrupted him, 'What ails Itmaduddaulah and his sons? How will they benefit?'

'Majesty, they are spreading rumours that Sher Afghan's slaying was ordered by you. That you covet their daughter, Mehrunnisa, Sher Afghan's widow. It is also possible that Mirza Aziz Koka with his slippery silver tongue, has promised them jewels and power.'

'What are you saying, Khurram?' demanded Jodha Bai in alarm. 'You are engaged to Arjumand, his granddaughter!'

'Forgive me, Empress, but the safety of Jahanpanah is paramount to me. All other relationships are secondary.'

Jahangir got up and hugged Khurram, 'You are my true son and heir. My revered father had correctly predicted that you will bring eternal fame to our dynasty. You did well, Khurram, you did well. Now, let's destroy these traitors.'

He turned and shouted, 'Khwajasera! Call the Yatish Begi, and double the guards. My own Ahadis and a contingent of Jodhpur swords will guard the royal camp. Prince Khurram will remain with me. Go!'

The tents of Itmaduddaulah's family and a few other identified conspirators were ransacked and then set on fire. The families, including women and children, were huddled together in a circle, and spent the night under a September downpour.

Prince Khusrau was roused from his tent, manacled and dragged to the tent of Mahabat Khan. They both spent the night glaring balefully at each other.

Jahangir clasped Khurram to his chest, and whispered in his ear, 'You are a better actor, Khurram, than I thought!'

***

The Royal Court,
Camp by the Surkhab river,
14 September 1607
11 a.m.

The entire court was assembled in the huge ground in front of the emperor's crimson tent. The last thirty-six hours had seen the most fearsome reprisals and arrests of several young men with ties to imperial nobility and high offices.

The disclosure of an assassination conspiracy on the emperor's life had been met with shock and unbridled fear. Since the conspiracy had been unearthed by prince Khurram, its source, spread and effect were unknown to apprehensive nobility.

The emperor's eyes swivelled left, where the prisoners stood in fetters. He had wanted to punish many as an exemplary deterrent to other subversives, but Salabat Khan counselled restraint. The monarchy was yet fragile, and an extensive punitive campaign would tear the fabric of loyalty and rock the empire. Fath' Ullah Khan, Bedagh Khan Turkman, Khwaja Itibar Khan and a dozen more stood in abject misery. Salim Jahangir shifted his gaze towards Mirza Ghiyas Beg, standing old and forlorn with his three sons and a nephew, trussed in ropes, but not in iron fetters.

Jahangir looked to his right—the forty executioners with their leather smocks, noose, sword, and spears as dictated by Mughal court protocol, waited for the emperor's signal—a quick flick of the right wrist.

Satisfied, he nodded to the Mir Tozak.

'In the presence of His Majesty, Nuruddin Mohammed Beg Padshah Ghazi, Slayer of Evil and God's Own Shadow on Earth, are the conspirators of a dastardly crime against our Sovereign and The State.'

The baritone rose higher, 'All of them have been covertly abetting and planning to indulge in regicide against their own emperor, and put on throne, the disgraced prince Khusrau.' He picked up a sheaf of paper and held it aloft, 'These letters written with the ink of high treason have been recovered from the person of khwaja Itibar Khan, all addressed to these traitors and the treacherous prince...'

'That's a lie, my lord...' screamed Itibar Khan, trying to push forward.

There was a quick flick of the emperor's wrist, and an executioner charged forward, spear extended. He collided head on with Itibar Khan, impaling him on his spear and clearly lifting him off the ground. His momentum carried the skewered convict backwards, scattering the soldiers and onlookers. As Itibar Khan gurgled blood, the executioner put his iron shod boots on his neck and twisted the spear. The fetid smell of faeces and intestinal debris burst forth.

The emperor rose from his silver throne, and addressed the felons. 'Bedagh Khan Turkman, you shall join your treacherous comrade in hell.' Immediately, another of the executioners rushed forward and beheaded the petrified Turk.

Jahangir turned towards Mirza Ghiyas Beg, 'Itmaduddaulah, in view of your services to my revered father, and the high esteem in which I hold you, your life shall be spared. However, you shall remain in the custody of Dayanat Khan, and you are forbidden from the Court. Your sons Mirza Abu'l Hasan and Mirza Shapur shall be spared too, as the taint which smears your other family members, has not touched them. Release them.'

Jahangir looked pointedly at prince Khurram, who bowed low in obsequiousness.

'However, your eldest son Mohammed Shareif and nephew, Nuruddin, are the ring leaders of this band of traitors. They deserve to die.' Again, the wrist flicked.

Itmaduddaulah's tall frame, lean with almost sixty winters behind him, crumpled to the ground, sobbing. A few feet away, the heads of his eldest son and nephew twitched in the dust.

Nuruddin Jahangir's scornful eyes now turned towards the trembling Fath' Ullah, sitting on his haunches, unable to stand. 'And you, Fath 'Ullah, in consideration of your father, Hakim Abu'l Fateh's services to Arsh Ashiyani, your life is being spared. But, every morning, you shall be seated on an ass, facing the tail and paraded through every town and village. You were seeking fame; now infamy seeks you!'

'The others I release, as a gesture of goodwill to those who depend on you for their living. Let no man, woman or child ever say that I was unjust and cruel.'

The crowd stood silent.

Jahangir looked at the sullen, grieving mass and spoke again, 'You are silent and resentful because I have not punished my own son, prince Khusrau, the vessel of high treason? Fret not, because a fate worse than Death awaits him!'

***

That night, in the quietude of a grieving camp, the emperor's childhood friend and valiant commander, Mahabat Khan entered the tent of Prince Khusrau, and with the help of four accomplices, strapped the grappling prince to a long wooden bench.

Heating two slim iron skewers in the flames of the burning mashaal, Mahabat Khan pierced first the right and then the left eye of this Mughal prince.

The shrieks rose high, but fell sadly into the abyss of darkness.

Mahabat Khan, his Rajput soul gladdened by inflicting this grievous harm on a Mughal prince, walked out with a malevolent guffaw.

Prince Khusrau's wife, Beti Jaan, tried to commit suicide by setting herself on fire. No harm came to her. Her attendants doused the fire.

As dawn was breaking, two sentries stretched their aching limbs by the banks of the river Surkhab, one of them, splashing water on his face, commented drily, 'The Surkhab has today lived up to its name. It is red with innocent blood!'

***

In one fallacious and putrid drama, Jahangir had effectively destroyed prince Khusrau's ambition of adorning the throne, and prince Khurram's innocent persona.

***

CHAPTER 18

DAFN YEH ROYAYE ZIBA:

(The Burial of a Beautiful Dream)

The *Haveli* of Itmaduddaulah,
Yamuna riverfront, Agra.
21 October 1607.
2.30 p.m.

Mirza Ghiyas Beg, entitled Itmaduddaulah, sat morosely by the small pond, his gaze unwavering on the pink and white water lilies, which Mehrunnisa had so adored. Almost thirteen years ago she had left this house as a beautiful, blushing bride of the brave warrior Sher Afghan; Oh, how the tides had turned! He could still see the little girl child, as pink as a Persian rose, pushing the water lilies with her pretty feet, and the haughty lilies coming back again and again to brush against her playful toes. Tears were not long in coming.

The tenor inside was no better. His wife, Begum Asmat, was inconsolable, as she swung between two extremes of love and helplessness. For the last five months she had floundered in waves of self-pity and then monumental anger, at Destiny's perceived injustice.

Itmaduddaulah shook his head to clear the anguished cries of a wronged mother. Asmat's helpless lamentations of 'What use is that girl to us now? We had given our daughter, and now we are getting the living carcass of a woman despised!' had always grieved him. Her wails would escalate into 'I lost my daughter the day we married her to Sher Afghan. This was destined to happen... Cursed is my womb!'

Ghiyas Beg steeled his heart and walked into his house. It was better that the news be broken by him, rather than have it conveyed through the rancid gossip of retainers. His eyes swept the large sitting area of the harem, where Asmat sat with other female members of the large extended family.

Ghiyas bent down and touched her face. As Asmat raised her red, swollen eyes, Ghiyas could not but shudder at the depths of misery and anger in those eyes. Letting her warm tears collect in the hollow of his cuddling palm, he gently spoke 'Asmat, by royal command, the palanquin has been sent to the royal palace. She will serve under *A'la Begum* Salima Sultana.'

'That witch!'

After a few seconds, Asmat Begum's voice quavered between hope and despair, 'And, what about Ladlii?'

'I am afraid she will have to stay at the palace, too.'

Asmat Begum took off her silver embroidered slippers and flung it with all her might at the portrait of Dowager Empress Salima Sultana hung on the opposite wall.

The begum's frozen smile seemed to become wider...

***

Toshakhana,
Shahi Qila, Lahore.
12 January 1608.
11 a.m.

Emperor Salim Jahangir stood back and watched as the heavy iron doors were pulled shut, and three heavy iron bars were slid into place and secured by padlocks as big as coconuts. Eight imperial guards with swords, spears, and battle-axes flanked the iron doors, as a dozen more stood by the colonnaded pillars.

The Mir Bakshi in a ceremonial ritual offered the set of three keys to the monarch, who just as solemnly touched them and returned them to the safe custody of the Mir Bakshi. The three *Ulemas* witness to such events when invited, softly intoned the Quranic blessings.

Jahangir walked towards Akbari Mahal for an early cup of wine, when the Lahore deputies, Said Khan Chagatai and Quli Khan stepped out of the shadows and performed the kornish.

'Yes! What is it that cannot wait for the assembly tomorrow?'

'A thousand pardons, Alampanah, for this intrusion. We shall appear in the assembly tomorrow.'

Jahangir's tone was peremptory. 'Speak, now that you are already here, and have my attention.'

Said Khan Chagati bowed low. 'Your Majesty, the Sikhs seem to have learnt no lesson from the chastisements of the past. The new Guru, Hargovind, is a step ahead of his slain father. He girds two swords, one for worldly power and the other for spiritual power, and sends out his followers to collect taxes from the realm.'

The emperor snorted in derision, 'Have his followers rounded up and beaten. In every village that they have collected tax from.'

Quli Khan of massive proportions, piped in, 'And, that is not all, Majesty! His war cry is 'Degh, Tegh, Fateh!'

'What does that mean?'

'Jahanpanah, it means "Food for our friends, sword for our enemies, and victory for us!"

'Have him arrested for sedition and high treason. Then throw him in the dungeons of Gwalior Fort to rot.' He walked quickly towards the third of his twelfth wine-opium cup of the day.

***

Khwabgah,
Shahi Qila, Lahore.
17 January 1608
Close to midnight.

The emperor imbibed no warmth from the perfumed body of the concubine wrapped around him. He would have much preferred the warmth and sensuous touch of wine upon his lips, than the arduous pretensions of sexual ecstasy with a demanding partner. Jahangir's eyes moved towards the silver goblet, and he reached across the sleeping form; at least, the wine and opium were so easy to live with—they demanded no gratification, but gave relief from misery and unbridled happiness. True friends!

Yaseena, the Azerbaizanian concubine, stirred in her sleep as she felt Jahangir's arm across her. Snuggling down in the warm comfort of the Persian quilt, she moved her buttocks against the emperor's thighs. Jahangir, enthused by the wine made warm from the candle burning beside the goblet, turned on his side and pushed against her hips. Yaseena, feeling his ardour growing against her rump, guided his hands to her breast.

An hour later, a dishevelled emperor sat in the ante room, used mainly for secret meetings, with a rolled parchment spread before him. He called out for his chief eunuch, 'Khojasera, send Yaseena back to her chambers, and please ask prince Khurram to come and see me, immediately.'

'At once, Your Majesty.'

A few minutes later, a worried prince Khurram walked briskly in. 'Your Majesty, you sent for me? I trust all is well?'

'Do sit down, Khurram. There is much that dwells on my mind.' The emperor spoke after a pause, 'You know, the family of Itmaduddaulah has still not reconciled with the altered state of affairs. They still continue to hold me responsible for what happened at Burdwan.'

'Majesty, those punishments...'

'It has quelled their dissent for the moment, but rumours abound. Our khufiya navees, in touch with their servants, have revealed that there is tremendous turmoil in the harem. The women are demanding a public hearing in the *Diwan-e-Aam,* and the Begum, Asmat, has threatened to ring the *Zanzeer-e-Adl,* next Thursday.'

Khurram remained silent. Jahangir pointed to the royal parchment spread next to the candelabra. 'Begum Sahiba, has sent this epistle. You may read it.'

Khurram straightened the crinkled parchment.

Qila Agra,
29 October 1607.

A thousand blessings of Allah,
On The Most Fortunate Emperor
And Adored Son, Jewel of The Timurids,
Nuruddin Mohammed Salim Jahangir!

Dear Son,

With the Grace of Allah, Mehrunnisa Begum and her daughter, Ladlii, reached the Shahi Qila safely a week back. There was the usual torpidity after a long journey, especially in the infant daughter, although Mehrunnisa seemed none too worse after the long journey.

Islam Khan is to be commended for having deftly handled a ticklish situation, an event so blighted that it could have tarnished our reputation forever. You may like to reward him as you reach the Royal Court at Agra.

As per your instructions, Mehrunnisa was brought directly to my royal quarters completely veiled and in strict secrecy, using the secret alleyways of Ankh Mi'chauli and the underground passages of Jahangiri Mahal. Do not worry, your wife Jodh Bai was busy worshipping her several gods as the palanquin passed through the forecourt, whereupon it was escorted by my personal bodyguards. I have had her placed in a set of rooms at the end of the corridor, close to my apartment.

A word of caution, though! The harem is rife with curiosity and sinister rumours of Mehrunnisa being a conspirator in her husband's murder. Though unsaid for fear of reprisal, your glorious name may also be dragged into this murky drama. In our harem discussions, I have let it be known that Itmaduddaulah's family has turned their backs on her, fearing accusations and infamy clinging to her. I have also made it clear that she is under my protection and will spend the next one year in mourning, and in seclusion. This will take care of the initial troubles envisaged.

Please do not tarry long at Lahore; your august presence is required at Darul Hukumat, too!

I close this missive now, with Allah's choicest blessings on you, and much love and blessings to prince Khusrau and Khurram!

Begum Salima Sultana,
Shahi Mahal Khas
Qila Agra.

Khurram folded the letter and slid it under the heavy candelabra. His eyes met Jahangir's.

'Majesty, you were mentioning Begum Asmat...'

'Yes?'

'Maybe, a little communion with them in the depths of Bengali Mahal will settle their resistance. Once and for all.'

'Whom should I task this with?' Jahangir's eyes were questioning.

'I would be happy to do this, Shahenshah Huzoor!'

'Yes, Khurram. You must be present as my Royal Command. However, let Mahabat Khan handle the filthy part. He singularly hates Itmaduddaulah, and will get the desired result. He is heartless too!'

Khurram's thoughts raced towards his elder brother, Khusrau. Mahabat Khan had definitely done a good job in ruining his eyesight forever. Not a man to be crossed, noted Khurram.

***

The Dungeons,
Bengali Mahal, Agra Fort.
27 March 1608.
8 p.m.

Prince Khurram felt sorry for the dozen or so family members of Mirza Ghiyas Beg Itmaduddaulah who stood around in a semicircle. The vast chamber of the dungeon was dank and smelt of sweat and faeces. The single flaming torch near the steps only highlighted the staircase and freedom beyond, while the cavernous room remained dark and scary.

Itmaduddaulah had arrived at the Shahi Qila in response to the royal summons for dinner. They preferred to believe that the ignominy of the assassination attempt had been put behind, and a new chapter would unfold with the impending marriage of Arjumand with prince Khurram.

As their retinue had entered from the Dilli Gate, and ascended the Elephant Ramp, they were met by armed troopers of Mahabat Khan and prince Khurram. Abu'l Hasan and his daughter Arjumand were made to stand aside, and the rest were herded towards Bengali Mahal, which touched corners with Macchhi Bhawan and Jahangiri Mahal on either side. Taking a shallow incline to the right, they walked to the iron barred staircase which descended into the dungeons below. Bewildered and discomfited,

Ghiyas Beg and his younger son, Ibrahim Khan, reached for their daggers, when several troopers surrounded them and wrenched the weapons away. Itiqad Khan, the third son, meekly allowed his sword to be taken.

Angrily, Ghiyas Beg accosted Mahabat Khan, 'What is the meaning of this perfidy, Khan? You have lured us to our deaths? Will your treachery and debauchery never end? Who has...'

Mahabat Khan moved swiftly and gave a hard shove. Itmaduddaulah staggered back but was steadied by his sons. In a flash, Asmat begum lifted her veil and darted towards Mahabat Khan, a small jeweled dagger clutched in her hands. She let out a sharp cry of pain as Mahabat reached forward and twisted her wrist; the dagger fell.

Mahabat Khan dragged Itmaduddaulah aside, and put a dagger just below his ear, almost drawing blood, 'Tell your womenfolk to behave like ladies. You would not like me to undress them and check for weapons, would you?' His eyes were as hard as stone.

He let go of Ghiyas Beg's collar, as the ageing noble turned towards his wife, and spoke, his voice choking, 'Be resigned, Asmat. Our time has come. They have taken our daughter, and now they shall take us.'

Dewanji Begum, wife of Abu'l Hasan, started crying loudly, as she held onto the hands of her seven-year-old son, Abu Talib.

They entered the vault and found prince Khurram sitting on a silver chair. He cleared his throat, 'I am here as the Royal Command of my father. The words that you will hear are the emperor's own, and your compliance to them will guarantee your safety and prosperity.' He stopped to gauge their reaction. Satisfied that he had their complete attention, he motioned for Mahabat Khan to speak.

Mahabat wasted no words. 'I speak by royal command. It has been brought to the emperor's notice that members of your family continue to spread rumours about His Majesty's involvement in Sher Afghan's death. You know the circumstances very well. When called for a dialogue on the tardy governance of his jagir, Sher Afghan raised the sword of rebellion and struck the Governor Qutubuddin Koka in the abdomen, fatally wounding him. The Subedar's attendants then rightfully cut him down to pieces. Have you heard anything else?' His eyes bore into the huddled group.

There was complete silence.

'His Majesty will not condone any further seditious lies emanating from your family, colleagues or servants. If there is ever a squeak to the contrary, or even the wisp of an insinuation regarding His Majesty's interest in Sher Afghan's death, then I swear that I will personally dismember each one of you.' He strode up to a sobbing Dewanji Begum, and murmured, 'And, I shall take the women for my pleasure.'

'The emperor has already taken our daughter, and snuffed the life out of her,' wailed a distraught Asmat Begum, 'What more do I have...'

Mahabat Khan snatched Abu'l Talib from his mother's grasp, and took a step back. Fixing his eyes on the petrified group, he cautioned 'You see me today? I wear nothing but a new, unstitched garment, and almond oil purified over the sacred fire. I am ready to make a sacrifice to keep my vow to my Deity.' He jerked the seven-year-old Abu'l Talib against his left thigh and placed the dagger on his throat. The young child's eyes had rolled up in terror and his chest was heaving with fear. His swooning mother, Dewanji Begum was being held upright by her mother- in-law and Ibrahim.

He caressed the dagger across the child's throat, and remarked 'An innocent child's blood is most relished by my deity. So, are you willing to forget the unfortunate incident, and invite prosperity, or do I assuage my deity's thirst?' He moved the dagger a little, and a thin line of blood appeared.

Itmaduddaulah fell on his knees, hands clasped in subjugation. Tears streamed down his face, as he uttered between sobs 'Please let the child go. We shall abide by the emperor's wishes, and never again will this sinful subject be addressed again by me and my family. I swear on the Holy Qoran!'

Mahabat let the child go. He turned towards Khurram, 'Your Highness. Our work here is done.'

Khurram nodded. 'Have them sent to Macchhi Bhawan, where the emperor awaits them for dinner.'

***

Royal Suite,
Macchi Bhawan, Agra Fort.
Around the same time.

Emperor Jahangir continued his monologue in the same jovial note, 'So you see, Abu'l Hasan, there is nothing to gain by dwelling on Sher Afghan's death, but much to gain by forgetting it. Arjumand is already betrothed to prince Khurram, and who knows, she may well become the Queen of Hindustan, *MashaAllah!'* He slapped his thigh in merriment, 'And then, you, Mirza Abu'l may well become the *Vizier-e-kul!'*

He turned his attention to Arjumand, standing shyly by her father's side. 'Come here, my child,' he beckoned. She took a step forward and stood, head lowered. Jahangir leant forward, and taking a huge necklace of diamonds and rubies from around his neck, put it in her palms. 'May your life be as lustrous as these diamonds,' he blessed.

A smiling father and daughter performed the kornish. The deal was sealed.

* * *

CHAPTER 19

BEGOZAR TUFAN BEGZARD

(Let the Storm Pass)

Dungeons,
Gwalior Fort,
21 June 1608
8.45 p.m.

The guards went around unshackling the prisoners, and dousing the wall torches. At night, the inmates were not fettered to the wall brackets or manacled, but a long chain was looped around their ankles and passed over a group of five-six prisoners, enabling them comparative ease at night.

There were two exceptions—the thirteen-year-old Guru Hargovind and the octogenarian Baiju Bawra, the senile bard. They were neither fettered nor confined to any particular vault of the dungeons, but sat and slept wherever they felt welcome. Their reasons were different, too. While Guru Hargovind was much sought after for his words of wisdom and succour, Baiju roamed free, because no single group of prisoners was willing to live with his scary caterwauling at night. When questioned, implored and ultimately threatened by his fellow prisoners for his beatific singing during daylight, and beastly screeching at night, Baiju the Mad Bard would innocently say 'To scare the rodents, the ghosts and the imperial guards!'

As the remaining long torches quivered with their diminishing flames, the first long melodious notes of Raag Jaijavanti sprang from the unlit recesses of the darkened vaults. Guru Hargovind sat on a large block of rough stone, his white robes and turban a beacon of goodness in the vile depths of this fort, singing effortlessly. As the Guru's tenor wound its way over the highs and rapid, staccato low notes, there emerged the unmistakable sound of the four stringed *tanpura* merging seamlessly into the vocal verse. Guru Hargovind smiled in the darkness; Baiju was up to his usual tricks—for only he could so faultlessly conjure up the melodic notes of a tanpura with his vocal chords!

***

Imperial Suite of Begum Salima Sultana,
Jahangiri Mahal, riverside, Agra Fort,
02 July 1608
Just past midnight.

The late monsoons had arrived with a fanfare—the steady thud of heavy rain drops beat a fast tattoo on the stone courtyard and arch overhangs, thrashing the stored heat of several months into submission.

The emperor was exulting in the companionship of Mehrunnisa. His visits to the private suites of the royal seraglio had become more frequent now, and many nights were spent there in the arms of the beguiling widow, ever since his return from Lahore.

The mask of being a Lady in Waiting to the Dowager Empress had its own advantages for Mehrunnisa, as several trysts with the emperor had remained veiled from the other royal concubines and inmates. But, not for long.

This evening, Salim Jahangir had retired late from the *Diwan-e-Khas* and had gone directly to the chambers of Begum Salima, where he had spent the good part of an hour partaking wine with roasted meat, and discussing the ill health of the senior queen, Ruqaiah Begum. As the sentries sounded the gong for the midnight hour, he had excused himself and hurried along the private passage to Mehrunnisa's suite of rooms at the end of the corridor.

Jahangir found her sitting demurely, delectably clad in the thinnest of sheer muslin, her beautiful figure alluring in the flickering glow of a hundred candles. A large decanter of silver and jade was kept beside her, along with a vessel of gold, covered with silver tassels. The sickly-sweet smell of opium hung heavy.

Jahangir strode forward, and roughly clasped her to his chest, his hands roaming over the contours of her shapely buttocks. Mehrunnisa pushed slightly away, and with a mischievous smile, asked 'Jahanpanah, a cup of wine and opium for you?'

Jahangir guided her fingers to his hardness under the qaba. 'The moth needs no urging,' he said, 'when the flame burns so strong! Mehrun, I am intoxicated by these grey eyes of yours. Let me drown in them tonight.'

Not a word was said, as scantily clad nubile young attendants hurried forward to undress them. The Mahaldar who had been waiting in the shadows with the emperor's chief eunuch, Firoz Khan, silently gestured for the candles to be extinguished and the attendants to leave the room, except Bahar and Nawa, the two beautiful dancing girls whom Jahangir had brought forth from Illahabas in 1604. They were adept in the art of love making and could excite the emperor out of his opium induced sexual lethargy.

They gently massaged the emperor's thighs and back as he slid beside Mehrunnisa, and draped his legs over her. She closed her eyes and sighed blissfully, as Jahangir kissed the tip of her nose and then trailed his mouth to find the alluring softness of her slightly parted lips. Forcing his tongue inside, he moved over her, the tips of her engorged nipples hard against his chest. She tried to caress his back, but Jahangir clasped her wrists and stretched her arms behind her head. Suffused with lust, she arched her back and thrust against Salim's rigid penis. Bahar, her fingers hovering on the emperor's thigh, quickly guided his member inside.

The emperor was stretched between the shapely thighs of Mehrunnisa, and was pleasuring her with deep hard strokes. She, thrilled by the ecstasy of the moment, had completely given herself up to the sensuous arousal and raised her hips to meet him, thrust for thrust. Sweating, panting and delightfully delirious, Jahangir gave one final hard shove and exploded inside her, his voice high in orgasmic relief, 'Ohh, Zehrun-nnisa, my beloved Anarkali, I want to come deep inside you. Ahhh...'

There was complete silence in the room, as if all breathing had stopped.

A rattled Mehrunnisa pushed Jahangir away and gathering her tresses, said crossly, 'Jahanpanah! This nonsense of Anarkali has to stop. She is dead and gone. As is my husband, Sher Afghan... If you can't bury her from your thoughts, then let me mourn my days in peace.'

Jahangir was truly apologetic, 'Forgive me, Mehrun. I know not what possessed me, believe me,' he stopped, and spoke softly again, 'Anarkali died nine years ago, a wronged woman, maybe that is why she haunts me? But it will never happen again, I promise.' He reached for her hand.

'It will be calamitous for us, Your Majesty. The curse of a wronged woman can make the heavens fall, remember that.'

Jahangir's mind darted back to the curse of the Persian widow of the deceased Vizier Sheikh Abu'l Fazl Allami. He shivered.

Bahar and Nawa had melted into the shadows. Would the 'Curse of The Mughals' erupt again?

***

A few days later.
Deserted Corridor,
Near the old 'Baoli', Agra Fort
Close to midnight.

The four slaves rested against the carved pillars of the stepwell, slowly thumbing the tobacco into their palms. Despite their menial position, their shoulders and legs were well muscled, almost like wrestlers. Maybe, it was because of their labour with the oxen and the water wheel that they had developed thus. Right now, they rested their tired limbs and found succour in the small wads of tobacco wedged inside their mouths. The pair of oxen also slowly masticated on the long stalks of hay kept in front. Once in a while, they would cast baleful glances at the heavy water wheel and the somnolent slaves, stoically awaiting their turn to churn the huge water wheel again.

Soorma, a young slave from Bengal, spoke aloud, 'Have you heard of the emperor's new mistress? The one who has come from Burdwan?'

'No.'

'Well, if harem rumours are to be believed, then she is none other than the unfortunate Anarkali,' opined the young slave, pompously.

Muthoo, the senior slave, opened his eyes and queried, 'What is the source of your inspirational stories, Soorma?'

'Oh, I met one of the slave girls in the market yesterday. Bought her a pair of pink bangles and then took her behind the tavern. Ah, the blissful humping...'

Muthoo turned viciously onto Soorma and banged his head against the pillar, hissing 'You keep your 'humping' to yourself, and your tongue within your loincloth. You will get all of us into trouble.' His white eyeballs strained in his black face, 'You remember prince Khusrau? Being blinded?' He hit Soorma on the head for good measure, 'You remember Kalyan Mal, son of Raja Bikramjit—how his tongue was cut and fed to the royal dogs?' Furious, he gave another clout on the young slave's head.

Soorma covered his face fearing another slap. He blabbered, 'I am sorry, very sorry, Muthoo Raja.'

Another slave, big, black and brawny got up and went behind the pillar. He caught Soorma's head in an iron grip and twisted savagely. The neck snapped.

Muthoo sighed and went down to call the Yatish Begi. In a few hours, it would be time to churn the water wheel again—a fresh pair of hands were needed.

***

With imperial consent, the Yatish Begi lost no time in executing the four slaves whose innocuous words had caused so much consternation to a drunk emperor.

An hour later, four bodies were loaded in a cart and sent through the busy streets of Agra. A braying donkey pulled the cart, announcing the betrayal of imperial trust.

That night, as emperor Jahangir sat alone with his decanter of opium mixed wine, tears rolled freely. The eunuchs and personal attendants had not seen the emperor in such grief before, not even when Padshah Akbar passed away.

For many minutes, a silent Jahangir stared into the burgundy depths of his wine cup. Finally, he called for the Waqia-navees to be sent in.

The court chronicler sat on his knees, his parchment spread in front.

The emperor's voice was full of grief and forlorn love. 'Waqia-navees, record this for posterity, so that my beloved Anarkali be remembered thus:

Ta qayamat shukr goyam, kard gar khwish ra,
Ah! Gar man baz beenam rui yar khwish ra!'

An audible sob escaped the monarch's lips.

The chronicler wrote swiftly—'Ah! If I could behold the face of my beloved once more,

I would give thanks unto my God till the Day of Resurrection!'

* * *

The Royal Seraglio,
Agra Fort,
01 August 1608
06.15 a.m.

Begum Salima Sultan had entered emperor Jahangir's suite of rooms, just as he was about to proceed for *Jharokha darshan*. The worried creases on her porcelain-like forehead augured trouble.

She sat on a low silver diwan and waved the attendants away. Jahangir watched silently.

'Farzand, there is trouble brewing in the harem. Mehrunnisa's arrival seems to have stirred a viper's burrow.' Jahangir just raised his eyebrows.

'Your queen, Jagat Gosain, has the tongue of a viper!' continued the Begum with indignation.

'And also, the fangs of a *krait!*' commented the monarch drily, remembering the time in 1594 when she had taken a dagger to the now deceased Padshah Ghazi's throat for trying to molest her in the corridors of Shahi Qila, Lahore. Akbar had made light of the incident and called her a 'feisty Rathore!'

'Yes. No wonder she is so dark with all that venom inside her' added Salima begum crossly. She studied the large emerald ring on her finger before continuing more formally, 'Your Majesty, ever since Mehrunnisa has stepped inside this auspicious abode, the Rajput queens and concubines have become very vocal and aggressive,' she looked directly at her step son. 'Maybe it is the quantum of time that you spend with Mehrun, and neglect the others, which is causing this minor uprising in the harem.'

In her agitation, she drew two quick, large puffs and spoke between coughs, 'I think it was Malika Shikar Begum who first instigated these quarrelsome women.' Her fine Persian traits were clearly offended by the brassy ladies of Rajputana. Her voice rose 'Her taunt of Rajput women being unable to satisfy their men was quickly carried by slave girls and attendants, only to bring forth a retaliatory barrage of obscenities in different dialects, and the most gross invective—that all Iranians and women from behind the Hindukush have to fornicate with wolves and mountain goats, because their men are busy slitting each other's throat!' Her knuckles were white with suppressed rage.

'Begum Jagat Gosain lost no time in cutting it deep. She was heard exclaiming by quite a few, that if someone is interested in only having stale leftovers, then what can the women do?' She waited for Jahangir's response.

The slur was not lost on the emperor. Mehrunnisa was after all a dead man's widow, having borne a child. He could feel the bile rise up in his throat, and he grimaced.

Salima Sultana was quick to fathom the emperor's oncoming uncontrollable rage; it had been the cause of many a debacle in Jahangir's life. She leaned forward and took his hand.

'Your Majesty, this is not the time to punish, but to wait and let the storm pass. Any punitive action now will only bring more attention upon Mehrunnisa and you, which we cannot afford. If you wish, I have a plan.'

Jahangir squeezed her hands. Even the all-powerful Arsh Ashiyani had sought her advice from time to time.

She lowered her voice. 'Your Majesty, you must dethrone Ruqaiah begum as Padshah Begum. She is none too happy with Mehrunnisa's arrival and feels that you have betrayed your father's will once again. This is the right time... otherwise, she will become fairly well ensconced once again. Right now, with Arsh Ashiyani's death, the fight has gone out of her, and she is half expecting to be sent into retirement.'

The emperor waited for what he knew would be coming. Begum Salima would propose her own name.

'You should make your new queen, Saliha Bano Begum, as your Begum Padshah. She is barely fifteen years old and has been married recently to you—she is comparatively innocent of harem intrigues! She comes from a family of royal *Khanzadas,* hence, her elevation shall be welcomed by the Mughal nobility too. The Rajputs dare not raise their voice. Also, while Saliha will bask in her unprecedented good fortune, it will keep the attention away from Mehrunnisa.'

Jahangir raised her bejewelled fingers to his lips, and kissed them reverently.

Masterstroke!

* * *

A week later, in a solemn ceremony, the Dowager Empress Begum Ruqaiah Sultana, gracefully handed over the heavy *Muhr Uzek* to the new Padshah Begum Saliha Bano, and quietly stepped back. Emperor Jahangir could not raise his eyes out of shame, and thus missed her final salutations.

Prince Khurram held his foster mother's hand as he slowly walked with his adored Shah Baba's favourite queen to her royal suite.

* * *

That night prince Khurram indulged in rough, cruel sex. He had the beautiful Kashmiri slave girl with the luscious thighs and full breasts pressed against the metal studs on the door. She had her thighs wrapped around his waist and clung to his shoulders. Each time that he thrust savagely into her a small whimper of pain would escape her lips. Her back was red with welts, and her spinal cord hurt.

Khurram removed one of his hands from beneath her heaving buttocks, and mauled her breasts. Breathing heavily with lust and exertion, he continued to murmur, 'Mehrunnisa, I will impale you one day for all your deceit and treachery! I will, I will!'

***

Shikargaah,
Eight kos west of Agra
18 August 1608
10.30 p.m.

An inebriated emperor fought hard to remain focused on the issue at hand. The hunt had not been satisfactory today, just a few antelopes and wild boars. The big game had eluded the royal party and the solitary leopard that was sighted had rushed past at blinding speed.

Prince Khurram's thoughts were elsewhere, and were mightily troubled. If the emperor decided to push forth with his proposal, then his own life, personal as well as official, would be decidedly compromised.

Jahangir, bleary eyed and belching, tried to reason with a recalcitrant prince. 'Khurram, you know that Khwaja Wais and that dancing girl, Andaz, to whom you have taken such a fancy, are the only loose ends. And, we cannot afford to have loose ends, Khurram.'

A despairing Khurram could only protest meekly, 'But, Your Majesty, Khwaja Wais is my Vakil, and I had promised him protection in this matter.'

Jahangir's voice turned hard, 'Who are you to offer protection, Khurram, when you cannot even protect yourself?' He raised his voice, 'Ahadi!'

Immediately, several of the emperor's personal bodyguards in crimson and purple rushed in. Khurram glanced at their weapons and armour, and knew that they had been briefed for such an eventuality. He lowered his eyes.

'Do not worry, Khurram.' The emperor tried to soften his voice, 'You can choose any mansabdar to be your minister. I would suggest Mulla Shukrullah to take Khwaja's place; he is well versed in the spiritual and temporal aspects, and will bind the hard core Mussalmans together. The kenchen is just another bone to be chewed upon, and not made into a necklace. Do you understand?'

Khurram nodded.

'Now, go and rest. Tomorrow should be a good hunt. For both, you and me.' The emperor's words were deliberately slurred, but not their intent.

* * *

Early next morning, with the darkness still to melt, the hunt began on an ominous note. Khwaja Wais riding ahead with *Qarawal Begi* was struck in the throat with an arrow. The large tip had clearly riven his jugular, and the Khwaja toppled off his steed, unable to speak, gurgling blood in his death throes.

The other horsemen quickly drew their weapons and a shout went up, only to be drowned by the blare of trumpets announcing the sighting of a tiger or a lion.

The big game hunt had indeed begun.

* * *

A fortnight later, far away in the North West, a beautiful concubine was murdered in her sleep at Shahi Qila, Lahore, and her body buried in a shallow grave filled with filth and human excreta. For good measure, a sack full of beetles and crickets were thrown in the grave to hasten decomposition.

* * *

By the middle of September, emperor Jahangir had decided to have a mausoleum built for his fragmentary love; now, at least, Anarkali would have a permanent abode.

Prince Khurram was given the task of having it built, and the emperor's final words had been, 'You shall have the mausoleum done from your own accounts; the imperial ledgers will not show any expense. Let not the mausoleum be too grand that it becomes an eyesore for the other jealous and inimical factions, and be aware, Khurram, that it takes the longest time to finish, for my love for her is yet not dead.'

The work on the mausoleum began in the same year—1608 AD *(1016 Hijri.)*

It took eight years to finish this simple octagonal mausoleum in the year 1615 AD *(1024 Hijri)*. Inexplicable in the case of Mughals, the most prolific builders!

* * *

CHAPTER 20

ESTEKHANNPEHEI SARSOKHT RA DAFAN KONID!

(Bury the Stubborn Bones!)

'Bismillah', The Royal Barge,
River Jumna,
18 April 1609
8.15 p.m.

Jahangir stared at the solemn, worried faces of his queen and son, and revelled in his harsh words 'I am putting Itmaduddaulah's family in disgrace, till such time as they realise the folly of their ways. I also decree that Arjumand will not be your first wife—her family does not deserve that honour. You shall have another bride.'

Stunned, prince Khurram rose in anger, 'Forgive me, *Abba Huzoor*, but we had decided on this even before Sher Afghan was killed! Your Majesty,' he added with more vigour, 'We agreed on Mehrunnisa's arrival and status within the royal harem, Alampanah, and I have fortified every action and thought of yours with my unwavering loyalty. Now, why *this?*'

'It is for your own good, Khurram. You cannot inherit an empire where sedition and serpents thrive. They need to be quashed.'

'Just as your licentious liaisons and progeny from that dancer Anarkali were quashed by emperor Akbar?' asked Jodha Bai venomously.

Jahangir's face turned hideous in wrath, as he lunged at his begum. 'Shut up, Jodh bai, you vile woman! Get out of my sight!'

He roared at Mahabat Khan standing a dozen paces away, 'Turn back the barge.' He gestured angrily towards the following crafts, 'The begum needs to get back to the harem. Have her escorted back in one of the royal boats.'

A few minutes later, Khurram was left alone with the emperor.

'I shall seek a loyal bride for you, from one of the royal families, Khurram. My actions are not without reason.'

'My complete acceptance of your orders and betrayal of others, including prince Khusrau, Abba Huzoor, are also for a reason.' Khurram left the meaning unsaid.

'You want the throne?'

'Not the throne, Alampanah, but your assurance that when the time comes, you will anoint me your successor.'

'You are testing my affection, Khurram. You do not threaten me—you should not threaten me,' Jahangir gestured towards the dark swirling waters of the Jumna, 'Many have drowned, weighed down by the sins of their ambitions.'

'Then let it be so,' countered Khurram, hotly. 'Please order Mahabat Khan to cleave me in half, and then fling me over the hull. But remember this, my revered father, your lovely Mehrunnisa and Begum Salima Sultana will die before you reach the harem. My mother was anticipating some devious action by you, and had alerted her attendants from Jodhpur, to do the needful if either one of us was not to return. These Jodhpuri Rathores are ferocious and unforgiving, father, as you must remember?'

Jahangir looked at the sudden icy glint in Khurram's eyes, and his thoughts went back to the summer of 1586, when several Rathore chiefs had vehemently opposed the marriage of a Jodhpur princess to a Muslim, and had taken to arms!

Jahangir considered the odds. Khurram *was* the worthiest of his sons, and he had blindly supported and carried off all that was demanded of him, treacherous or otherwise. What was the harm in keeping your right arm warm? The moment was politic to concede.

Jahangir walked forward, and in one of his famous turnarounds, clasped Khurram close to his chest, 'You are learning well, Khurram. The throne definitely shall be yours one day. You have the emperor's word!'

Khurram bent low and performed the kornish, 'You truly are the Sovereign Lord of Justice, jahanpanah!'

And the King of Chameleons! he thought wryly to himself.

***

With the safe return of Begum Jagat Gosain and prince Khurram to the royal seraglio, there was a perceptible drop in the tense atmosphere of the harem. The curved daggers being openly worn by the Jodhpur attendants and slaves was now no more on display.

The *Mahaldar* sent an urgent note to the emperor. Late that night, into early morning, the daggers and other assorted weapons from the Rajput wing of the royal harem were confiscated by the Tatar guards.

All martial contingents on palace duty from Marwar were routed to other far off chowkis.

Raja Sur Singh of Jodhpur, Marwar, was summoned to the Imperial Court and admonished.

***

The Royal Offices,
West of Diwan-e-Aam,
Agra Fort.
27 May 1609.

Prince Khurram checked the parchment with his keen eye for architectural detail, and stabbed a finger at the jutting minarets.

'Kasim Khan, there is no need for these high minarets. This is not a celebratory building. We shall go by the emperor's wishes, and keep it simple and austere.'

'Understood, Your Highness.'

'Remember this, Kasim Khan—The emperor desires this couplet to be inscribed on the sarcophagus.' Khurram handed over a rolled leaf with a gold border, the finely etched script visible through the thin leaf.

'It shall be done, Your Highness. There is one more thing.'

'What?'

'When we lay the gravestone, which body will be buried?'

Khurram looked at him long and hard. The Chief Architect seemed genuinely puzzled.

'You will bury Anarkali's body! Who else?'

Kasim Khan shook his head, 'Your Highness, it has been almost ten years now. There would be nothing left, but some stubborn bones. The limestone in the walls would have devoured the bones, too.'

'Then bury the stubborn bones!' Prince Khurram's voice was cold and menacing.

***

The Royal Forecourt,
Macchhi Bhawan, Agra Fort.
07 September 1609.
12.30 p.m.
Just after *Zuhr namaz.*

The open forecourt was covered with several large tents in purple, red and gold. The golden strings and ribbons were strung around the palace grounds right from the Akbari Gate at the entrance to the Khijr Gate in the rear. All the royal buildings were festooned with bright streamers in pink and gold, and camel mounted musicians played the auspicious tune.

It was time now for the emperor and the royal ladies to grace the engagement ceremony of prince Khurram with Hamida Bano Begum, daughter of Mirza Muzaffar Husain Safavi of Kandahar, the great grandson of Shah Tahmasp of Persia.

Shortly thereafter, there was a blare of trumpets and the roll of drums announcing the emperor's arrival. From the wide staircase near the Daftarkhana emerged Padshah Ghazi Sahib-i-Islam Nuruddin Mohammed Salim Jahangir, followed by the young prince Khurram and the emperor's Shahi Qur.

Jahangir looked around. His chief generals and court grandees were in attendance, as well as the members of the extended royal family. To Jahangir's delight, the mammoth tent seemed to be a carnival of colours with the bright red, pink and yellow of the Rajput turbans being challenged by the green, black and gold turbans of the Persians, Afghans and Turks.

The Chief Herald's stentorian voice rang out, 'Under the auspicious gaze of our Sovereign, *Mir-i-Asbab,* Defender Of The Faith, Mountain Of Virtues, and The King Of Kings, *Nuruddin Mohammed Salim Jahangir Padshah Ghazi,* does the engagement ceremony of our beloved *Chirag-i-Kul, Roshan-e-Zamana His Royal Highness Prince Khurram* be solemnised with The Most Virtuous and Dignified Hamida Bano, Daughter of Mirza Muzaffar Hussain Safavi of Kandahar, from The House Of Safavids! *Thus, Allah Be the Witness!'*

From the entrance streamed a double file of Persians from Kandahar, resplendent in their violet conical hats with a toggle dangling from one end, bearing trays of gold and silver heaped with glittering jewels, bejewelled weapons and fine brocaded cloth.

The first tray carrying a beautiful ruby and sapphire encrusted sword was brought before the emperor. The Kandahari attendant spoke loudly and clearly, 'As a sign of eternal peace and friendship between the two great Kingdoms of Hindustan and Faras, I bring this jewelled sword from the personal armour of Mirza Muzaffar Husain Safavi, lineal descendant of The Most Magnificent Shah Tahmasp of Persia.'

Emperor Jahangir touched it and signalled for the sword to be girded around prince Khurram's waist. The wedding alliance had been ceremonially accepted.

For the next one hour, the bridal offerings continued to be presented to a bemused emperor. He wanted to get away, for his cup of opium and wine could not be left unattended. After all, they offered more mirth and succour than these gleaming heaps of priceless jewels!

***

The next day, Jahanagir did not forget to instruct his *Waqia-Navees*, 'The daughter of Mirza Muzaffar Husain Safavi shares the same name as my revered grandmother, Hamida Bano Begum *Mariam Makani*. Therefore, be aware that never in the court records will the first Begum of prince Khurram be ever referred to by her maiden name. History should only know her as Kandahari Begum.'

***

Diwan-e-Aam,
Agra Fort,
10th May 1610.
09.30 a.m.

There was consternation in the Hall of Public Audience.

The report from Patna's *Khufiya Navees* indicated that a young village ruffian by the name of Qutub, with defective eyes, had been impersonating the blind prince Khusrau and had raised a large force of village louts and bandits. Seeking the people's support, his band of brigands and thugs stormed the fort at Patna, which in the absence of Subedar Afzal Khan, had been surrendered by the garrison without a fight.

Most embarrassingly, the Bakshi, Sheikh Banarasi and the Vaqil, Ghyas Beg, had fled on river boats from the rear entrance.

Subedar Afzal Khan returned from his personal jagir of Gorakhpur and defeated the rebels. Qutub, the impersonator, was cut into small pieces and fed to the dogs.

The Khufiya Navees also wrote that the imperial soldiers were amazed at the striking resemblance that one of Subedar's squires had with prince Khurram. The only thing missing from the lookalike's face were the pock marks so evident on prince Khurram's face.

The emperor's interest was piqued. Lookalike for both prince Khusrau and prince Khurram?

'Send a Shahi Farmaan to Subedar Afzal Khan, commanding his earliest presence at the Royal Court. The cowardly Sheikh Banarasi and Ghyas Beg are both to be stuffed in the carcasses of donkeys and thrown into the river Pun Pun,' thundered Jahangir.

'As for this Khufiya Navees, have him thrown into the Ganges for referring to the pock marks on prince Khurram's face!'

***

On May 29th, 1610, Abdur Rehman Afzal Khan died near Chunar, enroute to the Royal Court at Agra. The hard riding from Gorakhpur to Patna, and then again from Patna to Agra, had worsened a tender lump in his testicles, which became infected and soon spread as pus filled eruptions all over his body. It resulted in his painful death.

His few attendants, fearing the emperor's wrath, either submitted to the nearest Mughal fort, or merged into the populace of distant Subas.

***

Forecourt of Diwan-e-Aam,
Agra Fort,
05 September 1610
8 a.m.

The forecourt in front of the *Diwan-e-Aam* was vibrant with the mellifluous notes of the lute, cello, clavichords and harps, while small kettle drums kept up their skittering rhythm with the lyrical flow of the unfamiliar tunes. These western musical instruments were unknown to the Mughal court, and were a cause of great merriment, especially amongst the harem ladies. The Jesuit priests, encouraged by all the attention, were playing with great gusto and swaying to the cadence.

Emperor Jahangir sat on his throne, with Khurram standing by his side. Most of the royal ladies were thronging the anterooms to get a glimpse of this peculiar parade, which was about to start.

At the head of the parade was a young Jesuit monk carrying an enormous cross made of silver, and silver bells hung from his vest, making a merry chime as he walked. Behind him came another priest carrying a silver jar of Holy Water, which he ever so often sprinkled on the assembly with a small feather quill. A group of nine young priests, robed in red silk, played the instruments.

About three dozen Christians, recently converted, walked behind, clapping and dancing to the tune. Father Pinhiero, the Head Priest, walked slowly just in front of the elephants, on which rode princes Tahmuras, Hoshang, and Baisanghar. The senior priest carried a small cross of gold which he kept close to his chest, and chanted verses in chaste Latin to ward off evil.

The princes, miserable, threatened and bemused, sat atop the elephants, dejectedly throwing coins of silver to the surrounding crowd. They knew their rights, titles and privileges as Timurid princes had been compromised forever, and that they could never again lay claim to the Mughal throne.

As Jahangir watched the rakish procession recede behind the abutting walls of the ramp, he turned towards Khurram and proudly announced, 'Thence ride the first of your rivals into oblivion! These three princes, sons of my deceased brother prince Daniyal, are now encased in the ignominy of apostasy, and can *never* lay claim to the Timurid throne. With Khusrau blinded, only your brother Pervez and Khusrau's son, Dawar Baksh, need to be neutralised.' He looked conspiratorially at his son, and patted his shoulder. 'All in good time!' he assured.

Prince Khurram's smile carried vicious malevolence, but with a low bow of servility he exclaimed, 'Revered Father, may you live long, and may I have the good fortune to serve your every command! Alampanah! I promise thee; my blood shall flow for you, but never a word about the fallen widow.'

* * *

That evening, the three Timurid princes walked through the aisle of the Agra Church amidst sprinkling of frankincense and baptismal water, serenaded by hymns in Latin and the euphoric congregation.

Wearing robes of crimson silk with gold crosses hung around their necks, their Timurid ancestry was dissolved forever. Prince Hoshang became Don Henrique, prince Tahmuras became Don Felipe and prince Baisanghar was baptised as Don Carlos.

And, that night in the sunken crypt at Kabul, the old frayed bones of Babur creaked in dismay.

***

CHAPTER 21

DAMAN AZADI

(The Hem of Freedom)

Diwan-e-Khas,
Agra Fort,
10 September 1610.
3 p.m.

Emperor Jahangir peered morosely into his ruby encrusted silver glass, the sparkling wine holding no immediate allure for him.

The reports reaching from Gwalior did not bode well. The imprisoned Sikh Guru had become very popular, and devotees from distant lands were coming and touching the fort walls in veneration. Many groups had encamped just outside the fort and were holding continuous vigils and singing hymns.

The fort garrison had also sent several reports of Guru Hargovind's sagacity and miraculous powers. The fort commander had mentioned that no harsh measures could be taken against the Sikh Guru as none of the troops were ready to lay a finger on him. The *Qiledar* also suggested clemency for the sage.

Abdullah Khan, divining the cause of the emperor's morosity, suggested diffidently, 'Your Majesty, it would be advisable to release Guru Hargovind as a goodwill gesture during the forthcoming marriage of prince Khurram next month. It will be seen as a gracious act by the Hindus and Sikhs, and the immediate period will be of peace and harmony.'

Salim Jahangir nodded his assent to the limpid wine in his glass.

***

The dungeons below Man Mandir Palace,
Gwalior Fort.
8 October 1610
10 a.m.

'I came here at the emperor's behest. But I will leave of my own sweet will.' Guru Hargovind sat calmly on the polished stone slab, but his words were like steel.

The fort commander tried to placate the sage, 'Sire, it is the emperor's command that I release you forthwith.'

'Please tell your emperor that I have done nothing to earn this reprieve.' He twirled the ends of his simple turban, and gestured towards the throng of condemned men sitting around him. 'Tell him that I am as guilty or as innocent as these poor people, and if he wishes to set me free, then he must also let the other prisoners go free. I will not walk into Freedom alone.'

Despairing, the fort commander tried one last time, 'Sire, is there no way I can persuade you...'

'No, Lashkar Khan.'

***

Gwalior Fort,
A few days later.

Lashkar Khan with a few guards entered the small dungeon which served as the Guru's abode, bearing trays of sweets and rich silken robes.

The fort commander bowed slightly. 'Your Grace, the emperor has agreed to your request.' He gestured for a golden scroll to be brought forward.

Touching the scroll to his forehead thrice, he unrolled it with the utmost respect. His voice was loud and clear as he read the Shahi Farmaan.

'To Whom It may Concern:

Blessed by the Majesty of His Imperial Highness, Padshah Ghazi Nuruddin Mohammed Shah Jahangir, Mir-e-Adl and Benefactor Of The Poor, this Royal Decree herewith commands that Sant Hargobind incarcerated in Gwalior Fort shall be set free on 11 Sha'ban 1019 Hijri, on the auspicious occasion of the marriage of Shehzade Khurram.

It is further decreed that as many fortunate prisoners as can hold the hem of the saint's robe, shall be allowed to walk free.

Issued By Royal Command.
Shahi Qila Agra.
27 Rajab 1019 AH

* * *

Main door
Man Mandir Palace,
Gwalior Fort.
29 October 1610 (11 Sha'ban 1019 AH)
6:30 am

The entire garrison had assembled in the forecourt of the palace, as crowds continued to swell on the narrow, winding road leading up to the main gates of the fort. The news of the saint's impending release from jail had spread like wildfire, and there was a mammoth gathering of Sikhs sporting ochre turbans across Gwalior.

The brass decorated massive wooden doors creaked open and the young, lean Guru walked slowly forward, resplendent in a pure white robe with a gold and orange sash tied around his waist. Girdled on either side, were his bejewelled Temporal Miri and Spiritual Piri swords.

A great roar went up from beyond the fort walls, as the assembled garrison struck their shields in spontaneous welcome.

With a slight smile adorning his lips, Guru Hargobind strode forward. Holding the hem of his specially created gargantuan robe, walked fifty-two Indian princes to freedom!

* * *

The same day
Agra Fort

Since before dawn, there was an electric rush of gaiety and happiness in the air. Even the high forbidding walls of the fort were looking joyous today, bedecked as they were in ribbons of gold, red and green and the Royal Standard with the couchant lion proudly flew from every arch of the massive fortified walls. In fact, the celebratory preparations had been going on for the last fortnight or more, as the royal court prepared to celebrate the first marriage of the emperor's favourite son and heir apparent, prince Khurram.

The strains of auspicious wedding *ragas* had heralded the morning sun, and today, the *shehnai* players held precedence over others; there was nothing more welcome in a wedding household than the sharp, sweet notes of the shehnai. The feasting had started a week earlier, with specialist cooks from the far-off lands of Persia and the northwest territories joining their compatriots from the vast dominions of the Mughal empire. Mammoth cauldrons of rice and mutton curry were placed across the city to feed the indigent and the citizens, while the royal kitchen had spread to engulf vast areas of the fort. The fragrance of cooked venison, beef, mutton, partridges, and quails, exotic vegetables, fruits and spices, mixed with the softness of saffron and the cutting aroma of roasted mace hung over the city in an enveloping embrace.

Within the palace there was the lilt of melody and the rhythm of dancing feet. Small groups of courtesans and performing girls burst into spontaneous dance as the spirit of joy and festivity flitted from one decorated pillar to the other. The more adventurous of these, tried to draw the royal ladies into the swirling circles of twirling feet and tinkling ankle-bells.

Just as the faithful finished their *Asar Namaz,* emperor Jahangir stepped out into the royal forecourt festooned with gold and silver streamers. The royal ladies, resplendent in their glittering attire stood in a semicircle with their attendants holding silver flasks of fragrance and trays heaped with silver and gold coins.

Prince Khurram, in a tunic of gold brocade with a burgundy cloak of finest silk trimmed with small rubies and diamonds was led forward by the Dowager Empress Begum Ruqaiah Sultana. Prince Khuram's mother, Rani Jagat Gosain or Jodha bai as she was popularly known, draped in her traditional Jodhpuri saree in red and yellow silk followed.

The monarch stepped forward and held Khurram's face in his hands, smiling, as he took off a sparkling necklace of rubies and diamonds from his neck and placed it around Khurram's. Tears swelled up in Begum Ruqaiah's eyes as she saw her step son and foster son standing together, living embodiments of her beloved husband Arsh Ashiyani Akbar.

The Mir Bakshi stepped forward holding a tray. Emperor Jahangir lifted the *sehra* made of white jasmine interspersed with small diamonds, rubies, and sapphires and placed it upon the prince's turban. Rani Jodha Bai, flanked by ten attendants to make an auspicious eleven, performed the traditional *aarti* of her husband and son, even as rose petals and sprays of itr showered upon them.

To frenzied cries of '*Padshah Salamat, Hukumat Salamat*' the royal bridal party moved out of the royal palace to the mansion of Mirza Muzzafar Husain Safavi.

The bride was to be forever known as Kandahari Begum.

As the procession moved past the narrow steps of Jahangiri Mahal, an eunuch observed drily, 'There shall be no virtue attached to this marriage. The sapphires in the sehra will ensure this!'

***

CHAPTER 22

NAGHOUSIACPEHEI KHAMWSHI RASVAYI

(The Silent Bells of Disgrace)

Haveli of Khan-e-Khana Abdur Rahim,
Kannauj,
04 October 1610
4 p.m.

Khan-e-Khana Abdur Rahim stared gloomily at the lush mustard fields all around him; they brought him no joy. The harsh treatment at the royal court in Agra, and Jahangir's contemptuous words had robbed much of his joy lately. That he was a victim of Circumstance and the combined ineptness of the Mughal commanders in Deccan, softened not the emperor's words, who personally held him responsible for the debacle and had him recalled from Burhanpur to Agra. Then, in disgrace, he was sent to bide his time in his jagir at Kannauj, near Kanpur.

His steed, Mastaan, snorted and shifted his feet nervously, turning his head towards the muddy tract leading to thc fortified mansion. Khane-e-Khana followed his gaze, and saw a small posse of horsemen riding his way, the Mughal Standard flying in the fore. Careful not to damage the mustard crop, the group of horsemen rode single file now, following the raised wedges of field demarcations.

Abdur Rahim tightened his grip on the reins, quieting his nervous horse. A few moments later, the chief rider dismounted and performed the taslim.

'Sire, we are from the retinue of Sardar Afzal Khan, Subedar of Patna.'

A delighted smile spread across Khan-e-Khana's face as he heard the name of his long-lost friend's son. Afzal Khan's father, Sheikh Abu'l Fazl Ibn Mubarak was one of his closest friends, and Abdur Rehman his ablest son. Subsequent to his coronation, emperor Jahangir atoning for his unforgivable sin of having Sheikh Abu'l Fazl murdered, entitled Abdur Rehman as Afzal Khan and made him the Subedar of Patna. Khan-e-Khana's eyes softened as he remembered the wonderful, spirited days in emperor Akbar's company, and the wise, valiant men who surrounded him.

The general nodded, and asked with good humour, 'Where resides my friend, Afzal Khan?'

'The Subedar Huzoor was encamped at Bhojpur when we left.' The man fell silent.

'And?'

The man raised his eyes, and with evident misery answered, 'Sire, Subedar Huzoor is not keeping too well. There are sores all over his body, and he is in considerable pain.'

'Have not the royal physicians been called for?'

'Sire, the emperor himself sent a hakim from the dark-skinned land of Abyssinia, but even he could not cure him. He said that one of the wounds sustained near river Pun Pun in the clash with the false imposter had turned fetid and poisonous, thus spreading its venom through his entire body.'

Abdur Rahim nodded. 'What brings you here, sowar?'

'My Lord, Subedar Huzoor has sent a personal letter for you, with a recommendation that I hand it to you in private.' He held Khan-e-Khana's gaze.

Rahim turned his horse around, and asked over his shoulder, 'How many of you are here?'

'We are six hundred and forty troopers, Sire. I rode ahead with just my bugler and the royal standard. The main force awaits outside your haveli's gates.'

Abdur Rahim did not let his puzzlement show. Such a large contingent for a mere missive?

***

Though the silver encased lamps burnt with a steady glow, there was tremendous disquiet in Khan-e-Khana's breast. Beads of perspiration stood on his brow despite the October chill, and a slight tremor ruffled the several parchments which lay clutched in his hands.

Abdur Rahim lurched to his feet and sought another chair, drawing the thick silver candle stand closer. He rubbed his eyes, willing the written words to rearrange themselves into something less unsettling. But the words remained.

***

The suites of Salima Sultana
Agra Fort,
07 February 1611
11.35 p.m.

An inebriated Jahangir was escorted into one of the rooms kept especially decorated for his frequent trysts with Mehrunnisa, in Begum Salima Sultana's royal apartment. In a way, her suite of rooms were larger than the Dowager Empress' and were richer with gilded chairs and heavy brocaded tapestries.

Mehrunnisa, sitting demurely on a corner of the wide silver braced bed, rose and performed the kornish. Taking the emperor's arms, she gestured for the eunuchs to step back and her own maidens to help her.

Emperor Jahangir nuzzled her long, slender neck and murmured softly into her ears, 'How will you carry me, little pigeon, with the weight of the empire on my shoulders?' His left palm cupped her breast.

'As the dove carries the falcon, Your Majesty! By allurement, and then by sacrificing one's life to nourish the other!'

'Oh, Mehrunnisa! Your words are like magic... they soothe and they ignite at the same time!' The emperor toppled onto the bed, pulling Mehrunnisa across.

The maidens swiftly took off his pointed leather shoes and the outer robe of thick brocade. Mehrunnisa gently slipped the bejewelled turban off, and with great reverence set it on a golden salver. Her hands slipped inside the silken tunic and gently played along the hard ridges just below his nipple.

Jahangir tightened his hold and let his hands roam over her back and softly rounded buttocks, drawing her closer. Mehrunnisa lowered her face, searching for his lips, which carried the faint, sweet smell of Samarqand wine. The emperor's response was electric, his lips chewing hungrily on her lips even as her perfumed tresses framed his face. He brought his hand under her breasts and searched for her hardening nipples.

Mehrun knew that the monarch's vigour would be short lived; the numbness of the wine and opium would soon take over his sexual energy, and thus, her fingers travelled quickly downwards to fondle and caress his hardening member. Disentangling herself, she moved down to take him in her mouth, but he sat bolt upright.

'No, my beloved! Let me pleasure you today. It has been ages since I tasted you, and today calls for a special celebration.'

Mehrunnisa sighed with pleasure as Jahangir put his face between her wide spread thighs and nibbled gently.

She arched her pelvis against his face and held it between her straining thighs. Amidst the laboured breathing, she asked 'What is the celebration today, Alampanah?'

Jahangir turned his head to lick the insides of her thighs, exclaiming 'Our plight is over, Mehrunnisa! Ghiyas Beg and others have submitted, my beautiful sensuous lady, and have conveyed their acceptance of you in their lives again. Our love shall not have to be cloaked in sheets of shame, Mehrun. You shall be the Queen of this empire and the *Malika* of my heart, sweetheart!'

Mehrunnisa could not believe the spoken words. Oh, what a relief it was after these four years of sullying infamy, barbed taunts, and these surreptitious trysts like an alley whore. She moved her hands to cradle Jahangir's head and pressed it against her swollen clitoris, moaning with pleasure as his hands went beneath her raised buttocks and his tongue lashed deep within her.

Half an hour later as they lay in each other's arms, spent and satisfied, Jahangir spoke softly as he caressed the curve of her breasts. 'I shall confer with the *Ulemas* tomorrow, and will command them to fix an auspicious date as early as possible. But, be aware, Zehrun, that I shall keep our marriage a low-key affair.'

'I am Mehrunnisa, Your Majesty. Your Zehrunnisa died more than a decade earlier, remember? Bricked alive in the Lahore gardens?'

After a short, pensive pause, she spoke again 'I harbour no fantasies of a grand, imperial wedding, Your Majesty. After all, what can a despised widow aspire for? It is enough, Shahenshah, that you find me worthy of your gaze... I need nothing more.'

Quietly, she turned her face and laid her cheek on his muscled shoulder, languidly draping her arms across his broad chest.

Almost an hour later, much past the midnight hour, she heard his words through the mists of slumber, 'We have to tread very carefully, Anarkali! The world is against us.'

She shook her head in slumberous despair. When would the emperor get over his Anarkali obsession?

***

Royal Seraglio,
Suite of the Dowager Empress,
Agra Fort
25 May 1611

Arjumand Bano's breath was shallow and fast, her gaze decorously lowered as prince Khurram stood just inches away from her heaving breasts. The prince, enjoying her discomfiture, brushed his lips against her forehead.

With a sharp gasp, Arjumand shrank against the marbled pillar, her hands involuntarily rising to rest on Khurram's chest.

'Please, not here, my lord. Not now.'

'Why? This is as good a time as any!'

She lowered her head, 'Please, Your Highness. There are so many people here, what will they say?'

Khurram swung his gaze around at the royals assembled around a jubilant emperor and a blushing, beautiful Mehrunnisa attired in bridal finery. The whole palace was bedecked with streamers of gold and silver, tassels and braids spun out of golden brocade and silks, and the rich carpets encrusted with precious stones. The royal ladies, concubines and the harem inmates were all in their finest costumes and jewellery to celebrate the emperor's twenty fifth marriage.

Khurram stepped closer, the hilt of his dagger almost pushing into Arjumand's stomach, and spoke languorously, 'Who will bother about us today, Arjumand? They are too busy fawning over the new bride and His Majesty.' He lifted her chin and sought her lips with his own.

She trembled at his touch, but could not deny the pleasure that his searching tongue brought deep within her. Her fingers tightened against his chest as she hesitantly intercepted his roving tongue with her own and tightened her embrace. Prince Khurram, aflame with desire, pushed his groin against her and let his hand drop to her breast, pinching her swollen nipples.

With a sharp gasp, Arjumand broke the kiss. 'This is not right, Your Highness! Forgive me, but this is not right.' Tears welled over her beautiful eyes.

'Oh, Arjumand! How I have waited these last four years for a glimpse of you...'

A short sob escaped her, and wiping her tears with the end of her pink scarf, she took a moment to compose herself. 'I suffered as much as you did, Sire, maybe more. I was laid bereft of hope, happiness, and the will to live. It was only *Baba Huzoor's* comforting words and hand which saw me through these troubled years.'

'And the comfort of my arms around you!'

She remained silent, then replied softly 'Honestly, Your Highness, it was not your arms which provided support.' She looked up to see his reaction, and found only puzzlement in his eyes.

'I had lost faith in Allah and all things virtuous when you married Hamida Bano Begum.'

'Kandahari Begum!' said Khurram tersely.

At her puzzled frown, his tone remained brusque as he explained, 'In our history, she will only be known as Kandahari Begum. She has no other name, and no other role. The only Hamida Bano Begum in our history will be Shah Baba's revered mother, no one else.'

'She carries your child, Your Highness!'

'Yes! I performed my conjugal duty as a husband.'

'May she be blessed with a son!'

'Ameen,' replied Khurram automatically, amazed at her generosity. In the Mughal harem, the birth of a son was a propitious event guaranteeing imperial benevolence and was rarely wished upon anyone, especially a rival wife.

He changed the subject, 'Tell me, my Fairy Princess, what kept you occupied these four years?'

'The love and care received from my Baba Huzoor, even though he was himself being chastised as a common criminal.' Her gentle eyes dimmed with silent accusations, and tears welled up.

Then, she looked up, and said defiantly, 'I also learnt the Holy Quran by heart.'

'Oh! You are a *Hafiz* then?' teased the prince.

'My piety lies in my heart, my Lord. Not on my tongue.'

Stumped, Khurram looked deep into her blue eyes, brimming with hurt, pain, piety, and unconditional love.

Overwhelmed with love for this lovely girl-woman, he took her soft hands decorated with a simple design in henna, and promised 'Arjumand, we shall be married within a year, come Hell or High Water. Let Allah be my witness.'

'May Allah will it so!'

Khurram and Arjumand, oblivious to the wedding bells of disgrace chiming silently around the bewitched emperor and his wife by plunder, locked eyes as they spun webs and dreams of a magical future.

***

CHAPTER 23

'MA ZADEH SHODEGIM TA BA NIROYE BAZVANEMAN FARMAN BARANIM'

('We Are Born to Command by the Force of Our Arms')

The Bridal Suite,
Imperial Palace, Agra Fort
10 May 1612
11.30 p.m.

'Subhan Allah!'

Khurram was suffused with delight as he beheld the face of Begum Arjumand Bano, lifting the red and gold veil of a new bride. In the age-old tradition, he put a gold *mohur* in her palm, and with a curt *'Takhliya'* sent the attendants away.

The large vaulted room glittered with the decorations done entirely in gold. A canopy of gold *zardozi* threads covered the silver bed, the four posts of which had been wound with thin sheets of sequined golden silk. Screening the wide windows were wet sheets of golden gossamer to cool the river breeze blowing in.

Shining brightly on the midnight blue high vaulted roof were stars created by using real gold inlays and semiprecious stones. Reflecting the glow of myriad silver and golden lamps burning beneath, they shimmered as the celestial sky above.

Lost in the radiance of her beauty, Khurram continued to gaze long into her eyes—eyes that were mirrors of love and piety.

'Oh, Arjumand! My sweet beloved! What beauty lies in your eyes and face. These dainty hands and ruby lips....'

A sweet, tinkling laugh, and Arjumand clasped Khurram's hand. 'My Lord Liege, if you feel that I am beautiful, it is only because I reflect your love.'

Khurram, enraptured and overcome with passion, wrapped his arms around her slim waist and gently lowered her onto the petal bedecked bed. Arjumand, blushing and breathing hard, caressed Khurram's face as he lay across her, careful not to crush her. She could feel his muscular thighs wedged against her and his hands softly brushing the contours of her shoulder and breast.

There was an odd scent to prince Khurram's hand, and it was not long before she spoke up, 'I love the scent of apples on your hands, My Lord. I have never come across this Itr before.'

'It is not an Itr, Arjumand.'

'But the scent is so strong!'

Khurram delicately touched her lips, 'I was blessed by a virgin whom I took, and she in turn had been blessed by a faqir whose thirst she had quenched. The scent of apples will stay with me till I live. It will start fading away as my end draws near.'

Arjumand shuddered and turned her face away. 'Ya Allah! Banish such morbid thoughts on our wedding night.'

'Yes' breathed Khurram, as he pressed his lips against her turgid nipple, 'banish such thoughts!'

* * *

The senior begums and maids were glad to find bloodstains on the bridal bedsheet, the next morning. The deflowering of a virgin queen always brought good luck to the Mughals.

* * *

Second Kos Minar,
Ajmere-Chittorgarh route,
11.45 a.m.
26 December 1613.

Khurram's war elephant *Bal Sundar* trumpeted in delight as it neared Begum Ruqaiah's caparisoned elephant. It was the first time it had laid eyes on Begum Ruqaiah after emperor Akbar's death, and his elephantine memory had not forgotten the many marches and hunts when Begum Ruqaiah had shared the ride on his back with emperor Akbar.

Slowly, the elephants sidled together and a golden hook was attached to keep the pachyderms abreast.

Prince Khurram, dressed in the armour and spiked helmet of battle, leaned forward and performed four taslims to the Dowager Empress.

Corpulent in frame, but with all the beauty of her Turkish ancestors, Begum Ruqaiah's happiness was writ large on her smiling face. When Akbar had placed a six-day old Khurram in her arms, she had loved and raised him as the child she never had. Acutely aware of astrologer Gobind's prediction about prince Khurram's destiny as the most resplendent of the Mughal emperors, she had used all her might as the Empress Consort to keep prince Khurram safe from harem intrigues and harm.

She returned the prince's salutation with a shower of miniature flowers made of gold, and raised a salver with a golden lamp, holding a large, thick wick. 'Shehzade Khurram, as you embark on your first independent war campaign against Mewar, you carry not just the hopes and aspirations of your deceased *Shah Baba Arsh Ashiyani Jalaluddin Mohammed Akbar,* but of the Empire itself!'

Prince Khurram could feel the tears gathering. Quickly, he extended his sword and rested it over the flame, an age-old testimony of allegiance.

'Go forth, Shehzade Khurram, and seize your Destiny. Walk in the armour of Arsh Ashiyani and replicate his creed: Be Glorious in Battle, but, Generous to the Vanquished; Give Diplomacy a Chance, and Sword, only if required; Never underestimate the enemy and overestimate yourself. Now, go with Allah, Khurram—I shall keep this lamp burning till I hear of your victory. *Allah Hafiz!*'

Tears of joy flowed down the Dowager Empress' cheeks as she saw the vast contingents of cavalry, infantry, elephant and artillery corps following the young prince's banner. Watching the receding figure of prince Khurram, she was so reminded of the young, valorous fourteen-year-old Akbar whom she had married so long ago.

A richly caparisoned elephant with a gilded, screened howdah stopped momentarily in front of Begum Ruqaiah's elephant, and a delicate, fair hand appeared in taslim. Begum Ruqaiah showered gold petals again as Arjumand Bano Begum, heavily pregnant with her first child, followed her husband into battle.

***

Small hillock,
Gogunda, 10 kos NW of Udaipur.
20 February 1614.
9.10 p.m.

Prince Khurram wheeled his horse around. The enemy camp in the far distance was not a cause of worry; hardly two scores of cooking fires had been counted which indicated a strength between seven hundred to a thousand strong troops. He had more than seven thousand troops in his camp, excluding his personal bodyguard of six hundred Ahadis.

His horse slithered and snorted as it tried to navigate the rock-strewn escarpment in darkness. Khurram, impatient to call a war council, reined in as he saw a man being dragged towards him.

'What is it?' snapped Khurram.

'Your Highness, this man is a Mewari spy, masquerading as a cook in the soldier's kitchen.'

Khurram looked at him closely. 'Is it true, traitor?'

The man with a heavily bruised face, lisped 'I am not a traitor, Huzoor! I am willing to give information. For a price.'

Khurram let out a loud guffaw as others around him snickered, 'Traitor, do you realise I can have your head, thus, where is the question of your price?'

The man nodded evidently in pain, 'Information bought is always true. If you beat me for it, I will say whatever you want to hear, which may not be true.' He spat out a small gob of congealed blood.

'True, traitor. What is your price?'

'Five gold mohurs.'

Khurram spurred his horse into a trot. 'Bring him to me. He shall get what he deserves.'

Half an hour later, the manacled spy was pushed inside prince Khurram's war tent, where a refreshed Khurram sat with Fidai Khan the Mir Bakshi, and a few other generals.

Mir Taqi, his huge form a physical fright in itself, almost bellowed 'What brings you here, spy? Gold or Death?'

The manacled prisoner addressed the prince. 'My name is Hukum Singh, and I am from the village of Chavand.' The imperial officers exchanged glances; they had a war camp there. 'If it may please the prince so, I would like to narrate a story.'

'We are not here to listen to your stories,' growled Mir Taqi.

Unperturbed, the man continued, 'The royal prince has more brains than you do, O Mountain of Wobbly Flesh, for he understands that there dwell many lessons in a story well told.'

Intrigued, Khurram gestured for a livid Mir Taqi to refrain from clobbering the prisoner into a pulp. Settling his sword by his side, he nodded his assent.

'Thank you, Your Highness. The story begins from the time Prince Pervez came to vanquish Mewar, just after the emperor's coronation.'

'It was towards late June, when rains had just started, and the parched earth of Mewar received a little respite. Then soon after, rolled in prince Pervez with a force of 20,000 horses and 25,000 swords, aided by such fearsome generals as Asaf Khan Jaffer Beg and Mamuri. Time rolled by and the Mughals had not achieved much, preferring to lay huge war camps rather than fight. Similarly, Rana Amar Singh, softened by years of peace after Maharana's death in 1597, was loathe to fight.'

'So, Rajput bravery is just lyrical prose, spun by your bards?' snickered Saif Khan Barha.

Ignoring the barb, Hukum Singh continued, 'As I said, Rana was loath to go to war...'

Rana Amar Singh's Palace,
Udaipur.
27 June 1606.
Mid-morning.

The Chief Attendant entered the ornate throne room, and bowing low, announced, 'Amma, there are several chiefs wanting to see you.'

Rana Amar Singh waved the beautiful concubine away, and wiped the drops of wine from his flowing moustache, 'What is it that they desire, Kishen Singh?'

The attendant kept his eyes lowered, 'I have no knowledge, Amma, but they seem agitated.'

'Another delegation demanding war,' scoffed the Rana wearily.

Many nobles of Mewar from the first and second ranks of Sardars filed into the room, and stood silently.

From their sombre looks, the Rana could presage their intentions, and to defuse the cold discomfort of their presence, spoke merrily 'Oh, I see the Jhalas, Chundawats and Ranawats have all come together this day!' He gestured towards the sixteen ornate chairs placed on either side of the aisle leading to the throne, 'Pray, take your seats, and state your purpose.'

The Raj of Bari Sadri, senior most amongst the first rank of Sardars, stepped forth 'Khamaghani, Amma! The time now is not to sit and deliberate, but to wield our swords and wreck the Mughal army, even as they prepare to attack us.'

'Oh, come now, Jhala! Have we not had enough of this war and destruction over the last fifty years? Have we not lost fathers, brothers and sons? Have not our fields withered and women widowed in this demonic enterprise?' The Rana looked around and continued, 'The Maharana fought for almost twenty-five years and was forced to live amongst rocks and ate rotis made of grass... to what end?

Sensing the belligerence in the assembled chiefs, he softened his tone, 'Now, Chiefs of Mewar, look at your mansions—they are aglitter again with laughter and children. Your granaries are full...'

The Thakur of Ghanerao interrupted, 'Rana, our granaries are full but so are our hearts full of sorrow! This life of leisure is not what we promised the Maharana on his deathbed.'

Raj Rana of Delawar, a Jhala of massive proportions, stepped forth and raised his sword of almost six feet, 'Amma, what good are our mansions and granaries when our souls are bereft of pride?' His sword seemed to almost touch the chandelier in the high-ceilinged room.

Rana's voice hardened, 'You have forgotten the trials and tribulations of war with the peace which I have bestowed on this war-ravaged land! Go back to your jagirs and waiting women, this land will not be widowed again.'

Rawat Jeth Singh Chundawat of Salumbra could restrain himself no further. He pushed forward, his face red with indignation, 'Rana, you have forgotten the oath which we, Chiefs of Mewar, made to your father on his dying breath! We promised that no mansions will be built till we have restored Mewar to its former glory. We prefer to struggle for freedom rather than embrace the comfort of servitude, Amma!'

Rana Amar Singh turned his face away, and said dismissively, 'Go back to Salumbra, Chief. Invite not war and calamity upon our people.'

Apoplectic with anger, the Chundawat of Salumbra picked up a brass carpet knob and hurled it with great force at a beautiful framed mirror, shattering it into small slivers. Bounding up the seven steps to the throne, he clutched Rana Amar Singh by his arms.

Bewildered and furious, the Rana shouted, 'How dare you touch me, Chundawat? Have you forgotten your place?'

Without answering, Jeth Singh Chundawat continued to drag the Rana down the steps.

Shouting to be heard in the furore, the Rawat of Salumbra exclaimed, 'To horse, Chiefs, to horse, and preserve this son of Maharana Pratap from infamy!'

To cries of 'Jai Mewar' Rana Amar Singh was dragged and pushed to the forecourt, where he was made to sit on a horse. The other valiant chiefs of Mewar riding in close echelon descended the ridge, and came near the temple of Eklingji. Here, a tearful Rana turned towards his nobles.

Ashamed and inspired, his dark face glinted with passion as he twirled his moustache. His words rang clear.

'Forgive me, O valorous Chiefs of Mewar. I forgot my duty. I forgot Mewar. It shall never happen again.' Tears streamed down his dark cheeks.

'I am the eldest of the Maharana's sons, and am the Rana of Mewar. I promise you, O Valiant Chiefs, that I shall not rest till I have extinguished the Mughals. You will never find me wavering, or my arms weak! We shall wage war, as the world has never seen.

To horse! To arms, Chiefs, and never shall you have reason to regret your late sovereign!'

The forests and mountains reverberated with cries of 'Jai Mewar' as battle hardened Rajput chiefs thundered across the countryside, inviting Victory or Death.'

The spy looked up at prince Khurram.

'Why do you tell us this story, Traitor?' enquired Khurram.

'Because, over the ridge sits the Chundawat of Gogunda, waiting to slice you into pieces.'

Livid at the implied threat and insult, a furious prince Khurram stepped forward and severed the man's head from his body.

Mir Taqi kicked the fallen head out of the decorated tent.

***

Gogunda War Camp
21 February 1614
8 a.m.

Bhairon Singh Mangli, the Chief War Herald, stood upon two planks of thick wood. Not that he needed it; He was nearly seven feet tall and three feet wide at the shoulders, with a voice that could boom through the din of battle. It was his job to relay imperial commands and shout spirited war cries in the thick of battle. Today, he had been summoned to relay the words of young prince Khurram to the seven thousand troops gathered now.

Bhairon Singh looked on as prince Khurram took the proffered plumed helmet from his attendant, and settled it upon his head. He looked magnificent, Bhairon thought, with the red and white plume flowing majestically behind his glinting helmet of iron and silver.

Khurram spiked his horse forward, and casting a long, searching glance over the gathered troops, began to speak in the commanding voice of a conqueror.

'My fellow Commanders and Soldiers,

I speak to you on behalf of Emperor Nuruddin Mohammed Padshah Ghazi, may his life be long and illustrious!'

Bhairon Singh bellowed the words further down, 'My fellow Commanders and Soldiers...'

'Padshah Salamat!' thundered a thousand voices.

'We have been chosen to lead this campaign to bring Mewar to its knees—and we have been chosen for a reason.

We are to engage with a foe who is most wily, and who has no regard for Life. The funeral pyre for him is a holy adobe, which he wishes to adorn. He gives no quarter, and asks for none...In the Battle of Khanwa in 1526 against my illustrious forefather, Padshah Zahiruddin Babur, these mad Rajputs had stuffed their bodies into the mouths of our cannons to quell our fire. But still we won! Twenty thousand of us against their eighty thousand!

Why?

Because we fought as one, and not as the seventy-six different Rajput chiefs who had come together under Rana Sanga's banner, each with his own agenda and personal vendetta.

We had one aim—Conquer Hindustan!

Today, my fellow soldiers, our goal is the same—Conquer Mewar!

To this goal we are sworn, and this goal we shall achieve. End is the only consideration; means can be any.

We shall fight fire with fire, poison with poison. If they are willing to embrace Death, then we shall provide it to them. If they wish to fight and struggle in the jungles without food and shelter, we shall provide that too! We shall burn their fields, poison their wells, capture their women and raze their dwellings till even the clouds above call for mercy.

Remember, we are born to rule by the force of our arms, and nothing is going to stop us.

There shall be no conciliation, and no respite, till we have achieved total victory.'

There was absolute silence as the troops stood transfixed by the oratory and majesty of the young prince. His eyes glinting, Khurram raised his sword and shouted, 'Fateh!'

Boomed Bhairon, 'Fateh!'

The hills of Gogunda reverberated with the clash of swords and shouts of 'Fateh! Fateh!'

***

Prince Khurram's War Tent
Gogunda.
Same night.

'I still believe, Your Highness, that Mewar cannot be won by arms. We must find other means to induce them to accept our overlordship.'

'Khane Azam, we hold you in utmost respect, but your advice at the moment is unwise. Mewar understands only one language—war!'

'If that be the case, Your Highness, then why have we not been able to subjugate them these last forty years? We have been fighting since long, and I have seen no crushing defeat of Mewar!' The patronising, sarcastic words of the irascible Khane Azam seared Khurram.

'We did not crush Mewar, Khane Azam, because dithering old fools like you kept slipping up on opportunities. You were fed and kept fashionable at the expense of the emperor's war chest, and you never had to go without food or sleep. You never had to endure the anguish of not knowing whether your womenfolk were safe or lay raped. You sat atop elephants and directed battle while eating walnuts and raisins! All that will stop now. You shall lead from the front now, and you shall scorch Mewar!' The other nobles in the room were aghast at the prince's fury.

'Have I made myself clear?' enquired a frothing prince.

'Absolutely, Your Majesty!' countered Mirza Aziz Koka calmly, as he retreated from the tent, bowing slightly.

Despairing at Khane Azam's insouciance, Khurram threw his gauntlet into the burning fireplace.

'This little twig of a prince will teach me how to fight now, eh?' queried a petulant Khane Azam to himself, as he made his way back to his tent.

* * *

War Camp-Gogunda,
Detention Tents,
10 March 1614.

Prince Khuram's first question as he rode into the Imperial war camp was to enquire about Khane Azam.

'Where is he being held?'

'As per your orders, Highness, he has been moved to the Detention Tents at the rear.'

Wheeling his horse around, Khurram cantered towards the prison tents, where all deserters, drunks and villainous scum were held captive. The prince dismounted before a lone tent set slightly apart, and guarded by Ahadis.

Mirza Aziz Koka rose quickly from his silver stool as prince Khurram entered the sparsely furnished tent, and performed the kornish.

'Khane Azam, I was left with no choice but to remove you from command.' The prince's voice was weary.

'Shehzade, it would have been better if you had called me personally and punished me. Maybe, given me a chance to place my views before you.' Mirza's voice was tremulous.

'Khane Azam, I gave you all the license you needed to get our war plan into swift action, but you dithered. Not only did you not make sufficient efforts, but you deliberately questioned every move, criticised every action and mocked the chiefs who were striving so hard to carry forth our orders. With your demonstrated indifference and callous words, you demolished the fighting spirit of our troops.'

'That is not true, Your Highness. I merely...'

'Mirza, you refused to give a thousand cavalry to Saif Khan Barha as he set out to cut the Mewari scouts from rushing back into the hills. Because of your lack of military wisdom, or spite, Allah knows better, we were unable to massacre them en-masse. Had you done your duty, none of them would have escaped, and carried information about us. Your intransigence had grown to such a level where it became almost treasonable.' Khurram let his words hang.

It had the desired effect. Treason only invited the death penalty as Mirza knew well, and his voice became softer, and words mellow. 'If I have erred in your eyes, I beg a thousand pardons, my prince. I yield to your command.' He hung his head.

Prince Khurram wanted to end this quickly; it had been a long tiring day. As he turned to leave, his eyes fell on a young eunuch standing near the rear flaps, with bruises on his face.

'You, boy! Who are you?'

The prison guard commander answered, 'Your Highness, he is an attendant eunuch of Khane Azam. He fought like a tiger when we went to arrest Khane Azam, and injured several of our guards. He quietened only when we told him that we were carrying out your orders.'

Khurram looked speculatively at the young, bruised eunuch. Tall, muscular, and dark, his eyes shone bright.

'What is your name, boy?'

'Wafa, Your Highness.'

'Faithful! Well, why did you resist the royal guards?'

'Your Highness, I was protecting my master. But, when I heard the orders came from you, I quit battering your guards. My foremost loyalty is with the emperor, and his Wali Ahad.' His simple words brought a smile to Prince Khurram's lips.

'Ameen!' intoned the guards as Khane Azam tried to ingratiate himself with the prince, 'Your Highness, the eunuchs are blessed by The Divine—their words are prophetic! He has called you the Wali Ahad, and may his words ring true.'

Khurram melted. He commanded the senior guard 'Let Khane Azam have all the comforts to which he is entitled, including his food from the royal kitchens. See that he wants for nothing.'

Mirza genuflected as the prince strode out. A moment later, the prince's voice could be heard commanding his aide, 'Have Wafa sent to my service.'

***

CHAPTER 24

'MIVAR, BARAYE TO, MAN KHON MIRIZAM!'

('Mewar, for Thee, I Bleed!')

Forest Tracts near Chavand,
5 Kos North of Udaipur
17 March 1614
5.40 a.m.

Prince Khurram leant against the huge gnarled roots of the ancient mango tree, and watched as the boy-eunuch Wafa rubbed the reddish oil on his calves and soles of the feet. The prince with his reconnaissance troops had scoured the clefts and crags of the surrounding Aravalli hills all night, searching for the dozen or so hideouts established by Maharana Pratap after his defeat at Haldighati.

They had found three of the supposed sixteen hideouts, and signs of hasty retreat were evident in the remnants of iron trunks, weapons and utensils left behind. The continuous scaling over rough terrain had strained his muscles and Khurram now enjoyed the administration of the reddish, warm oil which seemed to draw the pain away. To stay awake, he asked the young eunuch, 'Wafa, how did you come into the service of Khane Azam?'

'My mother was a bangle seller, Your Highness, and we used to visit the mansions of the rich nobles.'

'So, you were not born a eunuch, were you?'

'No, Your Highness!'

Prince Khurram sat up straighter. 'What happened, boy?'

Wafa kept silent. This time the prince's voice was sharp, 'I asked you a question, boy.'

'A thousand pardons, Your Majesty!' There was fear in his voice now. 'I am afraid you will have me whipped and thrown to the tigers and crocodiles in the moat.'

'You shall be whipped only if you lie. And forget the crocodiles! You are a long way from Agra Fort.'

Wafa kneeled in front of Khurram, 'Your Majesty, I was barely six years old and we had gone to the mansion of the learned Khane Azam. It was around the time when Emperor Akbar was seriously ill and was about to die. I was with my mother in the *zenanakhana* for many hours as the ladies kept trying new bangles, and after a while, thoroughly bored, I wandered off to explore—the house was so richly decorated and there were big vessels piled high with fruits and cashews and raisins kept everywhere. No one stopped me, and I merrily explored the palatial house.' He grew silent.

Khurram extended his legs to be oiled.

'I entered a room, Your Highness, which was larger and more ornately decorated than the others. Mirza Huzoor Khane Azam and a large man with thick moustaches were sitting on a diwan and talking. Frightened, I hid behind the heavy tapestry, but I could hear everything.' He looked at the prince in trepidation.

Khurram just flexed his knee and stared hard at Wafa. He muttered softly 'Your Highness, they were discussing the emperor's impending death and were talking of installing prince Khusrau as the new emperor. Scared, I pulled hard on the thick curtain and it crashed on my head! The next thing I knew, I was being thrashed and then I heard Khane Azam order his bodyguards to castrate me and send me away to Bengal with Raja Mansingh.' His voice was quivering as he looked up.

Prince Khurram's voice was hard, 'What else did they discuss?'

Prince Khurram listened intently as Wafa recounted the evil designs of that afternoon. His voice had turned to steel. 'Why did you not inform me earlier, Wafa?'

Quailing, the boy replied 'Your Highness, the senior eunuchs and servants had warned me never to speak in your presence without being asked to, else you would have me trampled upon by an elephant!'

His bloodshot eyes glinting, Khurram commanded 'Ask someone to send the Waqia Navees at once. And you, Wafa!'

'Sire?'

'Your name means Faithful. Will you be faithful to me?'

'To my last breath, Your Highness.'

***

That evening Prince Khurram sent a missive to emperor Jahangir requesting the urgent recall of Mirza Aziz Koka Khane Azam to the royal court and immediate incarceration.

Mahabat Khan brought Khane Azam to the royal court at Ajmere on 05 April 1614, from where he was then sent to be imprisoned at Gwalior Fort on 09 April 1614.

Raja Mansingh had already died the year before.

Emperor Jahangir could not believe the depths to which these two gallant Akbarshahi nobles had stooped to thwart his ascension. Stung, he cried several cups of tears into several cups of wine and opium!

***

The hamlet of Chavand,
18 Kos South of Udaipur,
04 September 1614,
08.35 a.m.

From the slope of the mud and brick fort of Maharana Pratap leapt hundreds of Rajput warriors, with full throated war cries of *'Eklingji ki Jai!'* upon the Mughal cavalry and foot soldiers. Swords clashed and lances ripped through the air as frenzied Jhalas and Ranawats tore into the imperial echelons.

High above, from the battlements and crenelations of the fort, ferocious Bhil archers shot fusillades of arrows into the midst of the Mughal riders. A special group of archers with thicker, poisoned arrows were shooting at horses to maim and waste them, their riders falling headlong into the maelstrom of bucking, butchering warriors. Young boys, hardly into their teens, crouched low with broad bladed swords and swiped mightily at the fore and hindlegs of the rushing Mughal cavalry—the horses buckled and fell. The young boys then leapt upon the fallen riders and ran their sword through. At times, it took two or even three youngsters to kill a fully armed soldier.

As the foot soldiers charging behind the Mughal cavalry entered the fray, the battle became more vicious and gruesome. Battle hardened Mughal troops, in heavy armour, grouped themselves in tight formations and then charged into the widely dispersed Rajputs, separating them and then cutting them down.

The Jhala of Bari Sadri along with the Rathore of Ghanerao, who had been waiting behind the small hillock to the East of Maharana's old fort, now charged forth with their cavalry shouting blood curdling cries of 'Jai Mewar!'. Instantaneously, Sarfaraz Khan and Fidai Khan—the Mir Bakshi, disengaged from the main body of troops and rushed towards the Rajput riders.

Thunderous roars of 'Allahu Akbar' were met with sky ravaging cries of 'Jai Mewar' as steel met steel and armour-clad horses thudded into one another.

Suddenly, an arrow flight to the west, where the cenotaph of the late Maharana Pratap had been hastily raised two decades ago, a lone Bard climbed onto the cenotaph's dome and raised the crimson flag of Mewar with the symbolic Sun and Dagger in gold. His baritone, rich with fortitude and passion, carried in strong strains to the battling Rajputs:

'Mewar, Tharo wo puut kathe,
Wo Maharana Pratap kathe?'

For a moment, the Rajput swords held still, and then the Rao of Bedla riding a black stallion pointed his sword towards the Rana's cenotaph and the lone Crimson Flag of Mewar fluttering in the hands of the solitary bard, and shouted:

'Dekh, Dekh, Kaun Aayo?'

A thousand valorous voices rose as one—*'Maha-rana Pratap Aayo!'*

And then the clouds burst with the thunderous war cries of the Rajputs and their avenging swords. It was as if a tornado had risen from the dusty plains of Chavand bearing the Crimson of Mewar, and was enveloping the Mughals in its deathly embrace. The Rajputs, spurred beyond boundaries of bravery, heaved, surged and pushed the Imperial forces back.

The Bhil archers, now unable to shoot arrows into the mixed cauldron of Mewari and Mughal troops, swooped down from the battlements with their gaily decorated swords and fearsome cries of *'Jai Bhairoba'* and *'Jai VaghDev!'* and cut into the flanks of the retreating Mughals. Hemmed in from three sides, the Mughals fled towards the cenotaph and then veered North, where the hamlet of Chavand lay.

A Mughal archer rushing past, shot a barrage of arrows at the bard who was clinging to the cenotaph's dome, clutching the Mewar flag. An arrow pierced the bard's throat and came out from the other side. Ramlochan, the bard of Chavand gained immortality as with his dying breath, he wrapped his arms across the dome's spire cuddling the fluttering flag of Mewar.

The arrow transfixed across his throat was like a blood vane, pointing towards the fleeing Mughal army.

An injured Saif Khan Barha veered towards the hamlet of Chavand and ordered his troops, 'Burn all the houses; raze everything to the ground. Spare no man, woman or child!'

With the Rajputs in hot pursuit, they tarried not in the hamlet but rushed through it, throwing lighted torches onto the thatched huts and haystacks, lancing any man, woman or child who was foolish enough to cross their path.

***

Prince Khurram, when apprised of the battle's outcome, realised that this foe could not be subdued by sword alone, nor with diplomacy. It needed a more venomous approach.

The next day, all field commanders were issued with orders to poison every well, tank and pond and to 'scorch the earth of Mewar into rubble and ashes.'

For the next four months, Mewar remained poisoned and scorched, but unconquered still!

***

Eklingji Temple,
5 Kos North of Udaipur
26 January 1615
9 a.m.

Rana Amar Singh leant forward and touched the circular cradle of the deity with his helmeted head.

It was time to surrender.

'Eklingji Maharaj, forgive me for the dishonour which I have brought to this great land of Bappa Rawal and Maharana Pratap, but bless my people to be happy and prosperous again.'

The tremble was not just in the Rana's parting words. Honour and Chivalry too trembled in their dying throes.

As the grieving Rana and his despairing warriors rode out, Rana Amar Singh signalled for the Mewar flag to be lowered and furled. Stricken, the flag bearer looked at the tear besmirched face of his sovereign and held the flag at port arms.

A Hada chieftain, his pride and honour destroyed, could bear the indignity no more. He unsheathed his sword, and resting the hilt against his saddle's pommel, drove himself forward.

As the sword entered his chest and came out from between the shoulders, he lurched and swayed, and with a final rush of breath galloped to the standard bearer and nudged the flag upright.

As the crimson flag of Mewar fluttered proudly once more, the brave Hada fell, gasping his last words in bloody froth 'Mewar, for thee, I bleed!'

* * *

Two days later, Rana Amar Singh sent his uncle Shubh Karan and his Principal Officer, Hari Das Jhala with a peace proposal to the camp of prince Khurram.

Prince Khurram received the envoys with great decorum and having read through the proposed terms, assured a favourable response.

The next day, prince Khurram forwarded the Rana's letter with recommendations in the strongest possible terms, to the royal court at Ajmere.

Padshah Ghazi Nuruddin Mohammed Salim Jahangir readily accepted the recommendations, and with a thousand invocations of gratitude to the All-Merciful Allah, affixed his own right palm to the treaty as a measure of everlasting trust.

The kingdom of Mewar was exempted from marrying their women to the royal court or sending them to the royal seraglio; The Rana of Mewar would never have to attend the Mughal court in person, his representative would suffice; their territories would be given back to them and they would rule it independently, maintaining a contingent of just 1500 horses in the imperial cavalry; and, they would not have to pay an annual tribute.

Chittaurgarh could never be rebuilt, but peace would prevail.

***

CHAPTER 25

GUL AWWALIN GULISTAAN SHAHI

(The Exalted Flower of This Royal Garden)

Prince Khurram's mansion,
Near Pushkar Lake, Ajmere
29 March 1615
Early morning.

A joyous shout went up from ladies assembled around Arjumand Bano's bed. The slaves, attendants, and midwives raised their hands in obeisance, as Sati Un Nisa, the chief nurse lightly thumped the new born.

Pink, puckered and covered in umbilical fluid and blood, the child let out a loud wail. Attendants wiped the sweat off a smiling Arjumand's face as Sati Un Nisa approached the door with the child safely wrapped in soft silk.

Prince Khurram, forbidden by Chugatai code to see the face of a newborn before its sixth day, made no move as he saw the silver door opening. Sati un Nisa, well versed in *Tibith* form of medication and an excellent midwife, stuck her head out, and with due salutations, announced, 'The heavens have smiled, Your Highness... a prince, Most Fortunate and Sun Adorning, is born!'

Prince Khurram fell to his knees; eyes raised in gratitude as he said, *'Ya Shukr-Allah!'*

At a signal from the senior eunuch, the pair of trumpeters standing in the courtyard raised their trumpets and blew a long victory spell. Immediately, the drummers in the naubatkhana played a celebratory roll and then picked up a fast, joyous cadence.

Drummers and musicians across the city of Ajmere joined in the festive notes coming from prince Khurram's mansion, and quickly the rejoicings reached the royal fort.

Emperor Jahangir, making his first entry of the day in his *Tuzk-i-Jahangiri,* wrote with great serendipity—*Gul awwalin gulistan shahi!*

***

Baradari,
Daulat Bagh gardens,
Ajmere.
04 January 1616.
8.00 p.m.

'Your Majesty, please forgive my intransigence, but I would like to desist from partaking of wine.'

'Why, Khurram? Are you not man enough to drink a goblet of this fine, liberating, commiserating wine?'

Khurram flinched at the words, and his eyes swung towards the Empress. The slur on his masculinity was an unkind cut.

Nurjahan noticed the prince's disquiet and tried to make light of it, 'Your Majesty, prince Khurram is your bravest and most worthy son. What glamour will a glass of wine hold for him— one, who has brought Mewar to its knees? You have been unkind, my lord, in your words.'

The emperor ignored her, and addressed Khurram again, his voice thick with drunken inequity, 'Khurram, if you have sired these three children of yours, then drink up!' He watched Khurram extend his hand for a goblet, and exhorted 'Chamberlain, give a tumbler to the glorious prince and fill mine with the goodness of Samarkand and a pinch of hashish!'

As prince Khurram warily brought the gold tumbler to his lips, his eyes remained fixed on the gloating face of his father. 'I am more of a man than you ever shall be, Padshah Ghazi!' reflected Khurram wordlessly, 'and maybe, the revelation should begin from tonight itself?' his eyes glittered as they took in the beatific form of his step mother.

Their eyes met.

***

Bedchamber, Baradari
Daulat Bagh, Ajmere.
Same night.
A few minutes past midnight.

Khurram entered the rectangular chamber which was separated by a formal sitting room from the emperor's bedroom, and served as an ancillary chamber.

In the darkened room, he could make out the shapely figure of Nurjahan standing by the filigreed window, her arms raised and touching the upper frame of the trellis. The soft fragrance of her favourite itr floated on the night breeze wafting in.

Khurram coughed softly. She stood still, her curvaceous figure seductively outlined in the gentle moonlight, and the curve of her buttocks clearly visible in the diaphanous gown. Her long hair, black and wavy with auburn flecks, fell to her waist in perfumed cascades.

He came and stood right behind her. His pelvis lightly pressed against her hips. She shivered slightly and pressed back, her hands reaching behind to rest on his thighs. Khurram pressed closer, his arms encircling her waist and coming to rest on the loose sash which held her gown together.

Nuzzling her perfumed tresses, his voice was a whisper, 'His Majesty?'

'His Majesty sleeps in the embrace of opium and wine.'

'Oh, Empress, how I have longed for thee!' Khurram's voice was heavy with desire, as he moved his hands to cup her full, rounded breasts. The nipples, turgid and swollen, pressed into his palms and he slipped his hands inside, gently tweaking them between his thumb and forefinger.

Nurjahan sighed pleasurably as prince Khurram caressed and kneaded her breasts. She could feel his hardened member pressing between her buttocks and slid her hands back to hold him. At her touch, Khurram stiffened and his fingers roughly squashed her rock-hard nipples.

With a gasp, she turned around and taking his hand, led him to a silver diwan.

Almost an hour later as they lay entwined, drenched in sweat, the emperor's favourite begum slid her fingers across Khurram's broad chest and lightly scratched his nipples, causing Khurram to fling himself upon her.

As he looked at her beautiful face, the half open luscious lips and grey eyes smoky with lust, it kindled his desire once more. He could feel his penis hardening between her thighs.

Nurjahan circled her arms around his waist and let her hands wander over his taut buttocks. 'Never knew you carried such a strong flame for me, Khurram!'

'I have always desired you, but feared being thrashed,' smiled Khurram.

She laughed throatily, 'Who would dare to lay a hand on prince Khurram, the future *Wali Ahad?*'

Prince Khurram smiled wickedly, 'Well, Empress, the emperor's harem is sacrosanct. Our revered emperor was also soundly thrashed once by Shah Baba's Tatar and Georgian female guards as he made a clandestine visit to Akbar Padshah's harem. He would have been killed in the furore, but thankfully, someone recognized him just in time.'

'Oh, Khurram, the stories you make! Do you know, many times I have thought of you, especially after His Majesty's illness last year.'

Khurram raised his eyebrow.

Nurjahan clarified, 'His Majesty has become weak with his continuous ingestion of alcohol, opium and hashish. His sexual prowess has also diminished, and several times I have heard the harem servants' gossip about your prolonged lovemaking with Arjumand and other begums. There are rumours that you sometimes make love through the night with several women?'

'Hmm...' she continued, 'I can well believe the rumours now!' She opened her thighs to let his erect penis enter her once again.

Khurram just lay still, his penis deep inside her, and queried 'Empress, I thought you loved the emperor dearly?'

'Dearly, yes. But I love the power and regality of my position even more.' She sought his lips, 'Come now, why waste time on trivial talk?' She clutched his buttocks and pushed against his erection.

Khurram raised himself on his elbows and gave a slow, deep thrust. 'Empress, I shall forfeit my life if I am ever caught. I need you to protect me, and espouse my cause to the emperor. As I shall be ever faithful to your safety and majesty.'

'But, of course, my darling prince!' exclaimed Nurjahan. 'We are both ruthless, ambitious, and totally unscrupulous... in fact, made for each other!'

A panting, smiling Mehrunnisa looked up and a shiver ran down her spine. Even while coupling like animals there was a hard, ruthless and unforgiving glint in the prince's eyes. He could prove to be her salvation. Or, destruction.

She locked her thighs behind his back and arched her breasts against his powerful, glistening chest, 'Don't ever worry, Khurram. I shall always speak for you.'

She moaned in pleasure as Khurram started penetrating her with deep, hard strokes. Dawn was still a few hours away.

The emperor slept soundly with just a light shawl covering him. The Ajmere winters were nothing compared to the chill of Agra.

***

Many such nights were spent as Nurjahan introduced Khurram to the pleasures of pure, lascivious sex, thoroughly enjoying the vigorous love making by the young prince.

Prince Khurram also stoked the sexual fire of the empress, and funnelled her thoughts to a more powerful royal position and unfettered power.

***

Hunting Lodge,
Three kos from Ajmere.
27 June 1616.
Just before *Asr Namaz*. 3.35 p.m.

'You have to believe in me, my darling Mehrunnisa! Your position and influence shall not be compromised... in fact, as the Dowager Empress, I shall ensure that...'

'Dowager Empress?'

Prince Khurram drew her closer, 'For the sanctity of our marriage, we shall have to wait for a reasonable time, you know that.'

'Will the royal household and the Ulemas allow it? There could be widespread opposition to the notion of a prince marrying his step-mother.' Nurjahan remained perturbed.

Khurram kissed her nose, 'There has been royal precedent.' His voice was firm, 'Did not Akbar Padshah marry his *ataliq's* widow in Salima Sultana Begum, may peace be upon her? Wasn't Bairam Khan more of a father to Akbar Padshah than *Jannat Ashiyani* Humayun Padshah ever was?'

Nurjahan's voice was churlish as she thought out loud, 'You definitely gain, Khurram, but I could be marginalised, if things don't work out the way we have planned.'

'You shall be my *Begum Padshah!* You know very well that if the emperor really loved you so much, he would have made you the Begum Padshah, it is well over four years since your marriage. Why is it that the insignificant, no-good Saliha Bano Begum continues as Padshah Begum?'

Nurjahan remained silent and pensive.

After a slight pause, he continued 'We just have to play our cards right. You have managed to get the emperor's approval to remove Pervez from Deccan, and sent to Allahabad. My appointment as Subedar of Deccan has also been confirmed, thanks to you. With this appointment, I shall beget a vast army, and the powerful garrison of Deccan. Most of the influential generals will also be under my command—and I shall be the natural successor should the emperor die.'

Peevishly, she retorted 'Natural successors would be Khusrau and Pervez. You are third in line.'

Khurram laughed aloud, 'One is blind, the other a wine sodden coward!'

'Have you thought about Arjumand, Khurram?'

'Honestly, no!' He kissed her lips, his hands roving across her flat stomach. 'She is heavy with her fourth pregnancy. She can wait...'

'Ya Allah! Four pregnancies in four years of marriage? Khurram, your penis shall be the death of her!'

'I hope so!' laughed Khurram.

***

That night, emperor Jahangir ordered the room of the recently deceased infant princess Hur-Al-Nisa to be walled up for ever.

He stayed for another week, consoling prince Khurram and a disconsolate Arjumand Bano over the loss of their first born.

Almost a week later, on 03 July 1616, prince Shah Shuja was born to Arjumand and Khurram.

Emperor Jahangir entrusted him to the care of a barren Nurjahan, just as Padshah Akbar had taken Khurram from him in 1592 and given to a childless Begum Ruqaiah Sultana.

The silent ceilings and furnishings of gold and silver marvelled at the Mughal's propensity to repeat History.

As Arjumand prepared herself for her fifth child, the ambitious duo of Khurram and Nurjahan examined and then discarded several theories of the emperor's assassination. It was thought prudent to take charge of Deccan first, and then eliminate the emperor.

* * *

Early July, 1616.
Ajmere Fort.
Royal Harem.

Prince Khurram had chosen his day well. The emperor had left on an early morning hunt for a man-eating tiger, and was not expected before nightfall.

The personal palace and royal harem were at a relaxed pace with the emperor away. Inexplicably, the *Malika-i-Jahan* had not accompanied the emperor, although Jahangir was an ardent admirer of Nurjahan's shooting skills.

Khurram sat in the high vaulted room with wet vetiver mats providing some respite from the grueling summer sun. Rains had been sparse, and the rocky terrain continued to blaze, offering little reflection of the monsoonal winds.

'It is urgent that prince Khusrau is relieved from the protective custody of Anup Rai Singh, and taken in our safekeeping.' There was an urgency to Khurram's words.

'It shall not be easy,' mused Nurjahan. 'The emperor still has a soft corner for his eldest son, faults and disloyalty notwithstanding.'

'His Majesty has put him in the custody of Rajputs, because his mother was a Kachhawa princess from Amber, and he is well secured.' Khurram leaned forward earnestly. 'Needless to mention, we cannot eliminate him as long as he stays under their protection.'

'I will see what I can do. What about Pervez?'

'Pervez is a coward,' scoffed Khurram, 'and he shall die like one. Drowned in a goblet of wine!'

'And the emperor?' Nurjahan's voice was subdued.

'Arsenic in his wine. Mercury in his opium. He shall melt from within.'

Nurjahan sighed, 'Oh, Khurram! Where is this leading us?'

***

Prince Pervez left Burhanpur for Allahabad on 10 July 1616, honouring the royal command. His plea to visit his father's threshold was refused by Malika-i-Jahan.

The unknown, hidden sexual trysts between a favoured prince and a ruling Empress was only seven months old, but it was destined to weaken the very foundations of the Mughal empire. The destructive virus of fratricide and regicide had been irrevocably sown.

* * *

CHAPTER 26

PIRUZI KAZEB VE TAZYINI

(The False and Decorative Victory)

Diwan-e-Khas,
Ajmere Fort
17 July 1616.
8.00 a.m.

Anup Rai Singh Dalan stood proudly, his long turban resplendent in mustard with burgundy weaves, set off with a cummerbund of matching hues.

Emperor Jahangir studied him intently, his mind wracked by the evident, growing closeness between his begum Nurjahan and prince Khurram. Word had reached him through his trusted eunuchs–even though much was left unsaid. He detested his own frailty, and in moments of soberness worried about the future possibilities. This summon of Anup Rai Singh was a result of his recent fears.

Emperor Jahangir's voice was weary, 'Step closer, Anup Rai, and listen very closely to what I have to say.'

'I have great faith in you, Anup Rai, which is why I have entrusted prince Khusrau to your care.'

'I am honoured, Your Majesty.'

Jahangir nodded. 'There are reports, and I also have a nagging feeling, that prince Khusrau's life is in danger. There could be vested interests which may try to wrest prince Khusrau from you, for which you must be prepared to defend.' Jahangir could not bring himself to take the names of Begum Nurjahan and prince Khurram.

'Your Majesty, prince Khusrau will never be harmed under my protection. I am a Bargurjar, descended from the ancient *Suryavanshi* rajputs. My men and I will protect prince Khusrau with our lives, so help me *Bhawani!*'

'I expect nothing less from you, Anup Rai. The title of Singh Dalan is a testimony to your bravery, and I shall never forget how you vanquished the tiger single-handedly in that forest hunt of 1611. Now go, and do your duty.'

* * *

Mansion of Anup Rai Singh Dalan,
Near Pushkar, Ajmere.
15 August 1616.
Close to midnight.

There was a clatter of hooves as about a hundred horsemen rode up to the gates. To shield themselves from the incessant drizzle since early evening, the men were draped in shawls and sheepskins.

Before they could knock, several archers appeared on the arrow slits of the stone wall. The leading horse neighed and shied as a long torch burst into flame.

The riders at the back of the posse could see more archers and musketeers appear on the roofs and crenelations of the mansion. A gruff voice challenged from behind the wall.

'Who comes at this hour? State your purpose.'

One of the lead riders, wearing a sequined cloak, answered 'I am Abu'l Hasan Asaf Khan, Vakil of the emperor. Open up.'

'State your purpose, Sire?'

'It is not for you, sentry. Open the gates, and let your master speak to me.'

'You shall have to wait where you are, Sire. I shall inform my master.'

A few minutes later, the small aperture in the huge iron gate opened, and the face of Anup Rai appeared. He peered at the rain drenched visage of Asaf Khan, and enquired 'What brings you here at this late hour, my lord? No drums have sounded from the royal fort to proclaim an emergency?'

'I am sent here by His Majesty to collect prince Khusrau and escort him to the royal palace. Here, read this.'

The Rajput chief took the proffered parchment. His face turned grey.

Wiping his rain smirched face with the ends of his turban, his voice held firm, 'I accept this royal warrant as a humble servant of His Majesty, but I cannot hand over the prince. The custody of the prince was given to me personally by His Majesty, and I shall deliver prince Khusrau directly to His Imperial Self.'

Asaf Khan's voice was stern, 'The Imperial Order is very clear, Anup Rai. Prince Khusrau is to be handed over to me forthwith.'

'The order does not carry the word 'forthwith.' Therefore, I assume that the matter can wait until daybreak, when I shall meet the emperor personally and deliver prince Khusrau. I bid you goodnight, Sir!' Anup Rai closed the iron aperture.

***

Early the next morning, Anup Rai Singh Dalan sought an audience with the emperor.

Having listened in detail to Rai's narration of last night's events, Jahangir observed drily, 'You did well to refuse Asaf Khan. You shall heed no one, and shall continue to protect the prince as a Rajput loyal. Your diligence and fealty will not go unrecorded, Anup Rai.'

As Anup Rai cantered out of Ajmere fort with five hundred of his followers in battle gear, prince Khurram and Asaf Khan winced at their failure. Begum Nurjahan remained morose and silent.

***

Imperial Chambers,
Ajmere Fort,
30 September 1616.
9.35 p.m.

A tired and inebriated emperor Jahangir leaned back on the bolsters, enjoying the musical performance by Ulfat Jahan, a current favourite with the emperor.

Begum Nurjahan sat on the emperor's right with golden platters piled high with roast meat and fowl, kept warm by a simmering bed of coals underneath the salver. Fruits, spiced and garnished with ginger, lime, and chilli pepper honey were presented with silver foiled mini skewers.

Jahangir waved the concubine away who had been delicately kneading his frozen shoulder, and turned towards Nurjahan.

'Begum, one more glass of wine please, from your divine fingers!' slurred Jahangir.

'Your Majesty, I think you have had enough for the day.'

'No, I think not, begum. The night has just begun.' His voice turned cold.

'You know that excessive wine is not good for you, Your Majesty. You always tend to fall sick, and *Hakim* Gilani has also warned you to abstain.' She looked at the narrowed eyes of the emperor, and tried to placate him 'I only have your good health and happiness in mind...'

Jahangir exploded, spewing slivers of food and saliva on an astounded Nurjahan, 'You wicked woman! Did you have my happiness in mind when you forbade my son Pervez from visiting me? Did you? Did you?' Illusions of a naked Nurjahan in the embrace of a robust Khurram further escalated his fury.

Nurjahan spat back, 'What utter nonsense! I will not have you talk to me this way.' She started to rise.

Jahangir caught her by the arm, and pulled her down.

'I will talk to you any which way I want! I am the emperor!' shouted Jahangir, his eyes bulging and cheeks flushed with inebriated rage.

'You are behaving like a drunkard!' exclaimed Nurjahan, shaking her arm free.

'You bitch!' bellowed Jahangir, as he slapped her hard. The music and the singing stopped.

Nurjahan reeled from the blow, and seemed almost to faint. Then, with a frenzied scream she flew at the emperor, pinning him underneath, slapping and scratching his face.

Jahangir, stupefied by this sudden assault, took a few blows and scratches on his face and chest, and then catching her by her neck, wrestled her underneath. Holding her by her hair, he gave a few resounding slaps on her face, drawing blood from her lips.

The slaves and eunuchs stood stricken with fear, and some of them started crying.

Nurjahan hurt and humiliated beyond reason, raised her knee and kicked the emperor hard in the testicles. Jahangir groaned and collapsed on her, choking her with his elbow.

All at once a mighty wail went up from the musicians as they started breaking their instruments and tearing their own clothes. The eunuchs and the attendants also joined the lamentations, with the Tatar harem guards rushing in.

Bleeding from a cut under his right eye, and clutching his genitals, the emperor was lifted off the Malika-i-Jahan. Coughing and cupping her stinging cheeks, Nurjahan scraped off the few strands of hair snatched from the emperor's beard, and was led weeping and staggering to her bedchamber.

* * *

Misery and bedlam reigned supreme in the palace as Begum Nurjahan refused to come out of her room. She refused all contact with the emperor, and remained incommunicado.

The emperor was sick with excessive ingestion of wine and opium, and continued to haunt the imperial seraglio for a possible reunion. All his entreaties were repulsed with disdainful silence.

After more than a fortnight of cajoling and intervention by her father, Mirza Ghiyas Beg Itmaduddaulah and her brother, Abu'l Hasan Asaf Khan, a compromise was reached.

One afternoon in the royal garden, as the sun traveled due West in late October, Begum Nurjahan stood screened behind a small *morpankhi* tree, facing north, with just the golden toes visible of her brocaded footwear. The emperor approached from the west, and with the sun behind him, his shadow fell across the brocaded toes of the queen, seeking forgiveness.

Two days later, on 27 October 1616, a more sinister form of absolution was carried out.

The emperor was forced to order Anup Rai Singh Dalan to hand over custody of prince Khusrau to the begum's brother, Asaf Khan.

Now, the emperor and his eldest son were in the custody of queen Nurjahan; prince Khurram was in her embrace, and prince Pervez was too far away, drunk and inconsequential.

The rule of Nurjahan was truly underway.

* * *

Ajmere Fort,
10 November 1616.
4 p.m.

The forecourt still echoed with the cries of *'Shah Sultan Khurram Zindabad'* and *'Manzil Mubarak!'*

Just a few minutes ago, as prince Khurram attired in a silver tunic encrusted with pearls and diamonds stood before the emperor, a sword won by the late Akbar Padshah in his first victory over Ahmednagar in 1598 was girded on the prince's waist.

Bejewelled robes, daggers, a gold caparisoned elephant and horse were all presented as gifts by the emperor.

With his hands on the prince's shoulders, Jahangir made a momentous announcement never made before in the annals of Mughal history.

'Khurram, my beloved son, go forth and wage war on the conniving Deccanis, and rub their treacherous heads into the black soil of Deccan. The slave, Malik Ambar, must be shown his place and the false bravado which surrounds him must be shattered. You carry the finest of Timurid blood in you, and your sword is heavy with righteous intent. Recover what has been lost, and let the Mughal flag rule supreme once more.' He paused for a brief moment.

'And, for all your endeavours, from today henceforth, you shall be known as Shah Sultan Khurram!'

Prince Khurram and the Court were dumbstruck. Never before had any prince been honoured thus. Recovering, prince Khurram bowed low and kissed his sword.

Moments later, the voice of Mir Tozak boomed over the assembly, 'Shah Sultan Khurram Zindabad!'

Begum Nurjahan stood beside the emperor as columns upon columns of cavalry rode out behind prince Khurram's gilded carriage. For the first time again, a prince departing to war was in a four–horse carriage and not riding the customary war horse or elephant.

Her thoughts went back to their last meeting a few days ago. She recalled his words, 'Empress, you must urge the emperor to shift to Mandu. It is a lightly defended fort, and now with prince Khusrau in our custody, we can think about eliminating the emperor.'

She looked at emperor Jahangir standing next to her, gloating in having sent his incestuous son away, and a shiver ran up her spine.

***

Shahi Qila,
Burhanpur Fort,
06 March 1617.
7.25 p.m.

Shah Khurram was looking intently at the mock display in clay of the Ahmednagar and Bijapur forts. Khane Khana Abdul Rahim stepped forward and drew several lines criss-crossing each other between the two forts.

'Your Royal Highness,' explained Khane Khana, 'These are the major defensive positions of Malik Ambar.'

Khurram reacted sharply, 'But I believe that they indulge in guerilla tactics, and do not hold permanent positions in the field?'

'That is true, Your Highness, but these Ahemediyas work in tandem with the Bijapuris. Malik Ambar sends out a war party of about three thousand horses to draw us out, and as we reach, the Bijapuris who are waiting in the forests of Sindagi, ambush us from the rear, and are explicitly focused on damaging and looting our supply wagons.'

'And, we let this happen every time?' The prince's voice was incredulous.

'We have tried providing rearguard echelons,' volunteered Afzal Khan. 'But somehow, in the heat of battle, the lines are breached.'

Khurram gazed silently at the mock battle terrain for several long moments, before speaking. 'Let us try another tack this time... I propose to lure Ibrahim Adil Shah with overtures of diplomacy and amnesty for his past transgressions. I shall promise him the benefactory hand of our emperor on his shoulder and the might of the Mughals at his back. To hasten his acquiescence, we shall show him the destructive power of our army, too. With Bijapur neutralised, we shall decimate Malik Ambar and seize Ahmednagar.'

There was a chorus of assent as Shah Khurram continued, 'Afzal Khan and Raja Bikramajit, you shall proceed forthwith to Ibrahim Adil Shah and Malik Ambar respectively. You shall convey a simple message—we can offer peace if they agree to pay tributes to our emperor and return our lost territories, or' he clenched his fist 'they can test us in battle!'

***

Prince Khurram ensured his envoys were noticed. Afzal Khan and Raja Bikramajit both presented themselves with several thousand liveried cavalry riding behind them, resplendent in their red and silver tunics and shimmering lances. The forward ranks were interspersed with Mughal flags in green with the golden couchant lion.

The capitulation of Bijapur was immediate. Ibrahim Adil Shah himself waited on the prince and deposited a vassal's tribute of rupees fifteen lacs. Malik Ambar, his right flank exposed by the surrender of Adil Shah, had no recourse but to accept defeat. He immediately withdrew his garrison from Balaghat which he had recently wrested from the Mughals, and also ceded the keys of Ahmednagar fort and other strongholds of Khandesh and Berar.

* * *

With the formal conclusion of the Deccan Treaty, Shah Khurram immediately dispatched Sayyed Abdullah Barha to convey the victorious news to the emperor. At Mandu, he was accosted by Nurjahan first, who conveyed the news to a drunk emperor, and immediately received a jagir worth Rs. Two lacs as a purveyor of good tidings. Sayyed Abdullah Khan, ravaged by battle wounds and exhausted by the adrenaline-charged rush of over seventy kos, was sent to recuperate in the *Shutur Khana!*

A few days later, another envoy of Shah Khurram was received at the imperial headquarters. The emperor was beside himself with joy as he learnt that Afzal Khan and Ray Rayan were escorting ambassadors of Ibrahim Adil Shah bearing costly gifts and priceless jewels.

Shah Khurram in a far-reaching gesture requested emperor Jahangir to honour Adil Shah as a 'farzand' of the Mughal family. Delighted, the emperor wrote with his own hand in the grandiloquent Shahi Farmaan:

"Thou'st become, at Shah Khurram's request,
Renowned in the world as my son!"

* * *

Exulting in his victory, Shah Khurram appointed Khane Khana Abdul Rahim as the Subedar of Khandesh, Berar and Ahmednagar, and his elder son, Shahnawaz Khan was made the *Faujdar* of Deccan.

Shah Khurram made one critical mistake.

On 2 September 1617, he married Izz-Ul-Nisa begum, the eldest daughter of Shahnawaz Khan, without the emperor's permission.

His allegedly beloved wife, Arjumand, had just given birth to their daughter, Roshanara, on the same day and was unavailable to participate in the festivities.

***

Sir Thomas Roe, who had endeared himself to emperor Jahangir with his robust drinking and presentation of miniature paintings, was entitled as 'Inglis Khan.'

Inglis Khan in a letter to his counterpart at Constantinople wrote caustically of prince Khurram's much lauded victory in Deccan, 'the Deccan Kings have been persuaded to part with a few rotten castles that may pretend a shadow of yielding somewhat. In truth, not an inch has been gained by the famed Khurram in this false and decorative victory—only, the emperor has been bribed!'

***

Mandu Fort,
Mandu.

On 11 October 1617, a victorious Shah Khurram was received by all the royal ladies and court grandees one stage outside the city gates.

At the auspicious hour, he climbed the steps of *Jahaz Mahal*, the elongated ship-like palace inside Mandu fort, and marched the long aisle towards the throne, stopping every few paces to make the customary obeisance to the emperor.

Emperor Jahangir, overcome with emotion, jumped to his feet and rushed forward to embrace his worthy son.

In a booming voice, and breaking protocol, the emperor himself announced 'From this day onwards, Shah Sultan Khurram shall henceforth be known as *Shah Jahan*—King of the World!'

Deep within Nurjahan, the nascent flame of insecurity and fear became stronger.

* * *

CHAPTER 27

ESTEKHANNPEHEI POOSIDEHYE YEK PADISHAH FASAD

(The Rotten Bones of a Rotten King)

Northern Periphery,
Mandu Fort,
21 October 1617
11 a.m.

Emperor Jahangir stood rooted to the spot, as Tash Beg Qorchi, the *Mir Arz,* narrated the story of Mandu's infamous ruler, Nasiruddin Shah, standing by his grave.

'Your Majesty, Nasiruddin Shah who lies buried in this grave here,' he indicated the simple grave with an arched headstone, 'was not only a regicidal son, but was so hot tempered that he spent most of his time in the tank here to cool off.'

'To cool off?' asked prince Khurram incredulously.

'Yes, Your Highness. Nasiruddin was addicted to mercury, and was reviled far and wide for his nasty temper. Many hours would he spend in this tank here, intoxicated with mercury and wine. In fact, this tank's water had turned combustible because of the heat radiated by him, and came to be known as the *Kapur* or Camphor tank!'

A hail of incredulous comments followed. Jahangir gazed at the tomb with squinted eyes.

'His ascension to the throne is also a story of shame,' continued Tash Beg. 'His father Ghiyasuddin Khilji was a voluptuary, hedonistic ruler who kept a harem of fifteen thousand women for his pleasure. The Jahaz Mahal was built only for this purpose.' He indicated the ship-like palace in the distance, 'He had let it be known that he was content with his kingdom and would wage no war, but would enjoy his remaining years in peace and pleasure. The neighbouring kingdoms also kept their peace with him, and he ruled for thirty-one years from 1469 to 1500 AD, immersed in the pleasures of wine and flesh.

'His son, Nasiruddin, spent most of his time planning his father's demise by various poisons, but each time was unsuccessful because of an amulet worn by Ghiyasuddin. Frustrated, he took to mercury and wine.'

'The ungrateful wretch!' exclaimed Jahangir, and struck the grave with his sword.

Tash Beg concurred, 'Scoundrel he was, Majesty. Now, as Ghiyasuddin turned eighty, Nasiruddin tried once more with a very potent venom. This time, Ghiyasuddin knowing fully well his murderous son's intentions, took the proffered cup of poison, and having thrown off his protective amulet, drank it. In a few minutes he fell dead.'

Something, somewhere cut deep inside Jahangir. Maybe, it brought back his own memories of having poisoned his father emperor Akbar, and his revolt to usurp the throne. Muttering expletives, he stepped forward and kicked the grave.

Jahangir glared at the forlorn grave with a covering of light moss on it, and spat upon it.

'This wretched scum has no place here,' he kicked the grave again. He thought for a moment, and then turning to prince Shahjahan and his retinue, commanded 'Destroy this grave and have the rotten bones of this rotten king flung into the Narmada. Let them be carried into the ocean and be lost forever!'

***

That night as Arjumand walked in the fruit orchard with prince Shahjahan, she pointed towards the marble mausoleum of Hoshang Shah in the distance, and spoke wistfully.

'Your Highness, look at the beautiful mausoleum of Hoshang Shah.'

Shahjahan looked at the marbled structure, its dome made luminous by moonlight. 'It is very beautiful, Arjumand, but it is only a tomb.'

Arjumand sighed and put her head against his arm, 'When I am gone, my darling lord, build me a mausoleum as beautiful as this.'

Shahjahan stopped abruptly, and took her face in his hands 'What morbid talk is this?' There was surprise and indignation in his eyes.

Arjumand's words were prophetic 'Somehow, my Lord, I am not feeling good after Roshanara's birth. As if something evil has entered our lives.' She nuzzled his arm.

Shahjahan tried to ignore the implied barb, for it was on that same day he had married Izz-Ul-Nisa, the beautiful daughter of Shahnawaz Khan.

'All will be well, Arjumand. And, if it soothes your soul, I promise to make a palace more beautiful, lustrous, and larger than this for us to reside in.'

'Promise?'

'Promise.'

Shahjahan was already thinking ahead of commandeering the palace of Raja Bhau Singh of Amer upon their return to Agra. It really was a striking building in red sandstone, along the curve of the Jumna. A little marble cladding would make it beautiful, he thought.

* * *

The Royal Fort,
Ahmedabad.
14 May 1618.
9 p.m.

The royal court had reached Ahmedabad in March after a leisurely march through Khambhat, and was now comfortably ensconced in the Ahmedabad fort.

Emperor Jahangir was weakened by the long, meandering march through dusty vales and hollows of Gujarat, and this harsh summer month was wearing him down.

Reclining on the bolster, he motioned for the musicians to play and signalled for his wine cup to be refilled.

'You have had your six cups of wine, Majesty. It does not do you any good.' Nurjahan deftly removed the wine cup.

'I live for a glass of wine, a morsel of roast meat, and a glance of my beloved! Deprive me not, my fair maiden, for my happiness resides in you. Now, come on, just one cup from your saintly hands!' implored Jahangir.

Nurjahan smiled and shook her head as she resignedly filled his wine cup from the golden flask, tipping the medicinal vial into it.

It really is a sin to poison this endearing, impotent husband, she thought.

***

Shahjahan's royal suite,
Ahmedabad fort,
19 May 1618.
11.30 p.m.

Arjumand's chief attendant, Sati-Ul-Nisa tip-toed up to the huge silver bed and whispered through the fine gossamer netting, 'Your Highness, they are at it again.'

'Where?' enquired a sleepy begum.

'In one of the rest rooms adjacent to the royal library in the west wing, mistress.'

Arjumand slipped out of the ornate bed, and pulling a long cloak over her thin muslin gown, followed her chief maid.

They walked swiftly past the long corridor, waving guards away, and turned left towards the library.

The library seemed unlighted, and the thick curtains were drawn. Surprisingly, there were no guards stationed there, and

Sati Ul Nisa tried to open the door gently. It was locked from the inside.

Sati led the way, past the large vaulted room of the library into the ante room.

Arjumand froze as she heard the primal sounds of coupling, and pulled Sati back. Wiping the perspiration on her brow with a corner of her sleeve, she steeled herself and stepped inside.

Sprawled on the gold embroidered divan was Malika-i-Jahan with her smooth alabaster thighs locked around the waist of prince Shahjahan, who was embedded deep inside her, clutching her buttocks.

A sharp cry emanated from Nurjahan's throat as she tried to push Khurram away. Arjumand, delirious with shame and anger, rushed forward and threw herself upon the prince, biting and scratching.

In one mighty heave, Khurram threw her into a corner and towered over her, his naked form terrifying. Sati Un Nisa, fearing for her life, lowered her eyes and moved back a few steps.

Khurram grasped a quivering, crying Arjumand and roughly pulled her to her feet. Thrusting his face close to hers, he rasped 'One more squeal, and I will squeeze the life out of you,' he moved his thumb against her jugular.

Hissing with anger, Arjumand tried to reach down and squeeze his testicles, but his thumb hardened against her neck.

From the corner of her eye, she could see Nurjahan hurriedly putting on her clothes. She spat at her, 'You dancing whore! You stay the fuck away from my family, or I will...' Her words ended in a choked whimper.

In a minute, Nurjahan rushed out of the room, and Shahjahan relaxed his grip on her throat. She thumped her fists on his bare chest and let out a wail.

Immediately, his palm clamped around her mouth, and he spoke low in her ears, 'Scream, and I shall break your neck. Do you understand?'

Numbed and terrified, she nodded.

'Good. I will slowly release my grip,' his hold slackened, but his voice remained hard. 'We can go back to the pretence of our normal life, and someday, maybe, I will explain myself.'

Arjumand stifled a cry and sank to the floor.

'You!' Shahjahan beckoned the trembling Sati Un Nisa. 'Take your mistress to her bedchamber. And remember, one word out of you, and not only you but your brother Taliba and his two lovely daughters on whom you wager your life, will be trampled by elephants. Beyond repair!

'Do you understand?' Shahjahan's words were dripping with venom.

***

Arjumand Bano woke up with a bruised throat and a heart thirsting for blood.

Nurjahan took an early bath, and scrubbed herself many times over. However, the stains would remain, covered by royal pageantry and the spurious words of deceiving court chroniclers.

***

The Royal Quarters,
Ahmedabad Fort,
31 August 1618
11 a.m.

Hakim Ali Qadir stood by prince Shahjahan's side, a worried look on his face. On the other side of the bed stood a heavily pregnant Arjumand Bano and her four-year-old daughter, Jahanara, holding her mother's hand. A few steps away, a three-year-old prince Dara Shukoh looked on, his eyes strangely solemn for his age.

The extended tour of Gujarat had not been entirely joyous for the royal entourage. Both emperor Jahangir and prince Shahjahan had been afflicted with high fever and dysentery over the last few weeks. The physicians were perplexed with the sudden onset of this malady in the emperor, and had attributed it to the heat and dust of May.

A month later, on 14 June, prince Khurram Shahjahan had also fallen violently sick with fever and dysentery—the palace was beset with gloom.

Hakim Ali Qadir had grave misgivings—the symptoms were clearly of poisoning, and one evening as both the prince and the emperor lay sheathed in sweat and semi delirious, the venerable Hakim spoke.

'Your Majesty,' he addressed Begum Nurjahan, 'I am afraid the symptoms are of poisoning.'

The begum's face paled 'Are you sure, Hakim Qadir?'

The hakim looked up, his aged face creased with worry lines. 'Yes, Your Majesty. The signs are of slow poisoning affecting the intestinal and colon tract. There can be no doubt about this.'

Hakim S'adr, who had just arrived from Persia, concurred. 'What the learned Hakim Qadir says is correct. Slow poison either by way of food or *khillat*.'

Syed Abdullah Barha, a childhood friend of the emperor and one of the chief military commanders spoke, his voice taut, 'We shall change the guards immediately, and imprison the staff of the royal kitchen.'

The queen raised her hand, 'Do not jump to conclusions, gentlemen. The emperor changes his clothes twice or thrice a day, so no garment is on him for more than a few hours. As you can see, not enough time for the poison to work on him. And, for the food, I shall instruct the *Mir Bakawal* that the emperor's food shall now be prepared under my supervision.'

Hakim Ali Qadir shook his head, as he focused on the present. The royal court was to leave for Agra the day after, and prince Shahjahan was certainly not in a condition to undertake the journey. However, the emperor's mind was made up, and the Court *would* depart on 2 September.

'What is your diagnosis, Hakim Ali?' queried Arjumand Bano. 'You have been attending to him for more than two months now.'

'What can I say, Your Highness?' His eyes clouded with concern, he repeated softly 'What can I say, when the emperor and the *Wali Ahad* have both been poisoned?'

There was the glitter of guilty tears in Arjumand's eyes.

The hakim turned to Mir Bakshi, 'The prince is in no condition to travel on an elephant. Please arrange for him to be carried comfortably in a palanquin.'

* * *

That night, princess Arjumand Bano came and sat by the prince's side after a very long absence.

She looked at the sunken cheeks and frail frame of a once proud Shehzade, and for the first time felt a streak of remorse. Maybe, she was too hasty in her act of poisoning Khurram? Tears flowed as she touched her bulging stomach—this child deserved a father!

***

CHAPTER 28

'SHEERT SHEEZADEH AZ GHAM VE ANDOOH O BARKHAHOD KHAST'

('The Shehzade's Fame Will Arise from His Sorrows')

The Meadows of Dohad,
¼ Kos from the Imperial Camp,
03 November 1618.
11.24 a.m.

Having left Ahmedabad exactly two months ago, the royal train had marched almost fifty kos and had reached the village of Dohad on the border of Gujarat and Malwa, just as winter had breached the autumnal spell. The royal camp was stretched to the east of the village, protected by a large crescent lake on its rear and both flanks, and by the village in front.

The emperor and prince Shahjahan had both regained their health, Allah be praised, and were now riding together over the vast lands of winter crop.

Khwaish Bux, the troop commander, approached the emperor, 'Your Majesty, the people gathered there.' He gestured towards the large knot of people, 'they have assembled to kiss the stirrup of Your Imperial Majesty and His Royal Highness.'

As the emperor rode to their midst, men, women and children, young and old, threw themselves on the ground chanting *'Padharo, Padshah Salamat!'*

'Rise, O Soldiers of the Plough, Rise!' Jahangir's voice was cordial and soft.

As the people scrambled to their feet, a few bold ones rushed to kiss the stirrup, when from amongst the throng rose a voice, shrill and quavering.

'O, Emperor of the World, listen to this old woman, for the stars speak through me!'

Jahangir wheeled his horse around. Dressed in a colourful patchwork costume, there stood an old lady, bent and crippled.

'A minute to spare, my lord? My name is Nalini, and I am blessed by the Gods to foretell the future. I read the brows of men of fortune—many have been warned, and many have benefitted.' She shuffled forward on her staff.

'If you must read the brows, then read it for our Most Fortunate Shahzada here,' Jahangir indicated to prince Shahjahan.

The old woman peered intently at the prince's forehead, and raising her palms skyward, went into a trance. Her face, lined with creases, turned almost red as she opened her eyes.

Her words, unadorned, spilled out, 'I speak with the Celestial Stars as my witness, O' Protector of the Poor! The prince here shall bring eternal fame to this dynasty through his deeds—but remember, O' King Of Kings, that the Shehzade's fame will arise out of his sorrows!

'The prince who travels with you in the princess' womb, shall hold the Destiny of our Shahzade in his final years. The Charming Prince...' She gestured towards Khurram, '...shall have four sons, who will be known for their play with swords.'

'Alas!' she moaned, her face grimacing, 'Their War for the throne will destroy the *Mughaliya Sultanat,* and...' She pointed towards the royal camp far away, '...the prince born tomorrow shall not only decide the Fate of his father in his evening years, but shall also be the cause of his brothers...'

The old woman shuddered and fell, her words unsaid.

For a few moments there was complete silence, then emperor Jahangir chortled 'Oh, the devious minds of ancient women! Damn thee to hell!' He kicked his horse forward.

Prince Khurram Shahjahan, his face waxen, galloped after his father.

As the Royal Standard receded into the distance, the old woman squatted on her haunches, pulling her silver hair, chanting in a quivering monotone 'The end will begin with this child's first breath; the end will begin with this child's first breath; the end will begin....'

* * *

Arjumand Bano's Royal Tent,
Dohad,
04 November 1618
9 p.m.

Hakim Asadullah, a physician of the royal court who had helped deliver several high-born babies, came out smiling. Hands still wet from the parturition, he made the full, formal kornish to an anxiously waiting prince.

'Allah be praised! The empire is blessed with a fair prince, healthy and lustrous!'

For once, there was no spontaneous exultation from a delighted father, or presentation of a jewel.

'What was the exact hour, Hakim Asadullah?'

'Your Highness, the prince was born exactly twenty-four *gharis* past *mugreeb*.'

Prince Khurram nodded and turned to a eunuch standing by, 'Let the emperor be informed of the prince's birth.'

Arjumand looked exhausted, but smiled as she saw prince Khurram sitting anxiously by her side.

'How do you feel, Arjumand?'

'Happy and relaxed, my lord.' Her eyes closed, then reopened after a few moments. 'How is the baby? I hear no music or rejoicing... is everything alright?' She tried to get up.

'Yes, yes, everything is fine, the baby sleeps. The drums were beaten, and festivities will begin from tomorrow,' Khurram assured her.

Arjumand tried to turn towards Khurram, and held onto his hand as he leant forward to assist her. Settled, she peered intently at him.

'My Lord?'

'Yes?'

'I am extremely sorry for the pain I have caused you these past few months.' She strained to sit up, but Khurram eased her down.

'Your Highness, I carry oceans of love for you, ever since I was twelve years old...'

'So do I, my beloved Arjumand.' Khurram clasped her hand between his own.

Tears spilled out as she brought his hand to her lips, 'I lost my senses, Sire, when I saw you that night with Malika-i-Jahan,' she blurted.

Khurram shook his head. What could the sentries do when the poisoning hand was within?

He looked at the pale, kohl smeared eyes of his begum and wondered if he could love her again? Trust her again?

Muddled, prince Shahjahan rose, his voice sombre 'Rest easy now, Arjumand. I shall see the prince with the rising sun tomorrow.'

Arjumand stared at the prince's retreating back. His indifference and reclusion frightened her. Was it possible that her efforts to poison him had reached his ears? Why had he said that he would see the newborn prince tomorrow, when Mughal traditions forbade it before the sixth day?

***

Emperor Jahangir named the new born as 'Aurangzeb.'

At the same time, he ordered for the old woman to be whipped once, who had uttered such unfortunate rubbish for *prince Aurangzeb—The Decorator of Throne!* She must be cured of her perversions and black tongue.

Nalini took the whiplash and blasphemed again.

'This newborn is the viper who will empty the nest!' she screamed.

The *Darogha* exceeded the emperor's command and whipped her twice more, till she fell unconscious.

* * *

That night there was a huge commotion in the camp as courtiers and royals ran outside to witness a comet streaking across the night sky.

A few moments later, a streak of gold seemed to separate from the comet and streaked towards the camp, turning red as it neared.

People fell over each other in their haste to escape, and emperor Jahangir also lost his golden slippers in the stampede.

A few moments later there was a loud crash in a forest west of the encampment, and riders brought news that a small particle of the comet had fallen about a *kos* from the camp, and had furrowed a crater almost a *bigha* in circumference.

All the astronomers and astrologers spoke with a single voice:

A comet streaking from West to East was a very unfortunate omen.

* * *

The day after.

Arjumand Bano begum lay on the black basalt slab, her body glistening with the perfumed mix of tangerine and lavender oil, considered so essential during the postpartum phase.

Her Chief Attendant, Sati Un Nisa, gently rolled the flesh of her midriff to erase the freckled lines of childbirth, and remarked casually 'It is a good effort, Your Highness, to have put the past behind you and to forgive the transgressions of our Most Revered Lord, Shahjahan.'

Arjumand smiled faintly, 'Forgiving is never easy, but once done, brings immeasurable peace. I was in no mood to forgive or relent, Sati, as you well know. When I asked you to mix that *Tibbi Unani* poison in his favourite mutton saffron *korma,* I was bent on exacting my revenge, but I felt so petty and wretched when I saw His Highness writhing in fever and being reduced to being carried in a litter!

'I also had a dream, Sati, wherein an old fakir wearing a large green turban with a heron's plume admonished me. His exact words were, "One sin cannot be erased with another sin. Your sins are grave because you have decided to exact revenge with your own hands. It is not your call, but Allah's prerogative to provide Justice. Death is His servant, not yours."

The begum shivered slightly, recollecting the fakir's words, "Much sufferance is writ in your husband's Fate, born out of thy womb, Begum. Hence, add not to his woes, but be the pillar which he so desperately needs."

Tears welled out of her eyes as she rolled on her side, 'I was shaken, Sati, and awed by the power which Destiny wields over us. I decided then and there, that I shall be his sanctum from all troubles, his harbour in troubled storms. If I have borne his misfortune in my womb, then I shall be with him till my last breath, answerable for my sin.'

'Oh, Your Highness!' implored Sati Un Nisa, 'Allah's Benevolent Hand shall always shield thee and Our Revered Prince.'

* * *

The royal court reached Fatehpur Sikri on 11 January 1619, after more than five and a half years on the move, and was advised to stay there till the bubonic plague subsided at Agra.

On 18 April 1619, emperor Jahangir's Rajput queen and Shah Khurram Shahjahan's mother, Manmati Bai of Jodhpur, or simply Jodh Bai, sought her eternal home.

The next day, on 19 April, the royal court entered Agra Fort.

Prince Khurram Shahjahan went into the prescribed mourning of forty-one days, while Begum Arjumand supervised the recitation of holy verses and feeding of the indigent during this period.

Prince Shahjahan often repented his bad luck in not being with his mother in her last days, especially since he was quartered barely an hour's ride away.

***

It was time also for empress Nurjahan to exercise her right as the Padshah Begum. Much water had flown since her marriage seven years ago, and much of the scandals and detritus lay buried under the plinth of royal threats and executions.

Nurjahan ordered the poisoning of the current Padshah Begum Saliha Bano. She had outlived her utility.

It was time for her to go.

***

The intervening months of summer and spring were utilized by Nurjahan Begum in first trying to ensnare prince Shahjahan into marrying her daughter Ladlii Begum, but it was a half-hearted attempt as she knew it would be very difficult to wean Khurram away from Arjumand and his own band of wanton ladies who were adept at sexual crafts. Ladlii would have been perceived as a frigid and unremarkable bride for the brilliant, exuberant prince Shahjahan.

Nurjahan also realised that Shahjahan was too ambitious and wily a prince to be dragged into an alliance, where his own desires and career would be subservient to the Empress and her family. The emperor was also noncommittal on the subject—it would be unwise to bring the family of Itmaduddaulah into such imperial prominence.

With his polite but firm refusal, Shahjahan cemented Nurjajan's suspicion. She could no longer bank upon Khurram.

Her eyes turned towards the eldest son, Khusrau.

To tempt him, he was offered freedom and was also released from his imprisonment on 5 November 1619.

Khusrau's refusal was equally unequivocal: he would not take a second wife, but would spend his life with his first wife, daughter of Mirza Aziz Koka. His reasoning was simple and absolute—she had stayed with him through his years of trials, tribulations, and eventual blinding, and he would not forsake her for another, even if she came bundled with freedom.

His first (and only) wife, Beti Begum, implored him with heartrending entreaties to embrace another wife and Freedom, but prince Khusrau did not waver.

He was again imprisoned and banished to his cell.

The dice now fell in prince Shahryar's favour, as the imperial court wound its way to Kashmere.

* * *

CHAPTER 29

DEKAN – DIG MORGBAR

(Deccan – The Murderous Cauldron)

The Royal Pavilion,
Shalimar Bagh, Srinagar.
02 August 1620.
10.30 a.m.

Over the last few weeks, several reports had been received from the ring of spies in the Deccan, warning of a joint incursion on Burhanpur fort by the inimical kingdoms of Bijapur, Ahmednagar, and Golconda.

It was time for the emperor to crush the impending attack.

A large canopy, embroidered with gold and silver threads was drawn over one of the terraces where Empress Nurjahan sat, dispensing with the empire's business.

With the mysterious death of Saliha Bano Begum on 10th June this year, the much-coveted position of Padshah Begum had finally come to her. The emperor was also at rest now, having been able to provide this one regal position which had eluded his beloved Nurjahan for so long.

Nurjahan was content; she was enjoying her new found power and had slackened her hold on the emperor's drinking habits. In fact, some of the close attendants and eunuchs had wordlessly observed that Nurjahan was covertly encouraging the emperor to drink more.

The emperor was drunk.

Nurjahan ruled more.

Empress Nurjahan had assessed the gravity of the Deccan imbroglio much better than the emperor. With her innate intelligence she knew that the Mughals could not suffer the Deccan from slipping away; it would incite the middle order unruly kingdoms of Malwa, Khandesh, and Bundelkhand to revolt, and a demoralised, reduced Imperial army would be unable to hold it together.

To provide immediate relief, a two thousand strong light cavalry was rushed from Agra to Burhanpur via Mandu to uphold the morale of the Imperial troops, and to assure that a mighty army was following in its wake.

On the 10 December 1620, it was decided that the Deccan Sultanates needed the whip wielding hand of Shehzade Khurram Shahajahan, and nothing less would do.

Supremely aware of the incursive politics at the royal court and harem, Khurram had no wish to be so far away from the royal court, especially when the emperor was not in good health, and prince Khusrau in such close proximity to the throne. Prince Khurram was only too aware that there were many in the court, especially Rajputs, who would definitely like to see Khusrau on the throne—even as per Laws of Primogeniture.

Prince Khurram Shahjahan, politely but firmly requested that prince Khusrau be remanded to his custody for the Deccan campaign.

Emperor Jahangir, impotent in the haze of wine and opium had no option but to agree, even though his conscience counselled against it.

Padshah Begum had no such qualms—she was getting rid of two heirs presumptive with one stroke. Her power, and the fortune of her future son-in-law, Shahryar, would be secure with these two princes so far away, and embroiled in the murderous cauldron of Deccan.

The other royal ladies of the harem went into mourning, lamenting the certain death of prince Khusrau in the coming months. For two days and nights, the kitchen fires were not stoked nor any lamps lit in the harem.

* * *

On 13 January 1621, emperor Jahangir watched prince Khurram Shahjahan riding away on a caparisoned elephant, at the head of an 18,000 strong army.

Prince Khusrau in chains and fetters, followed on a curtained elephant, surrounded by the troops of Khurram's loyal chief, Abdullah Khan.

Tears flowed from the emperor's eyes.

He was destined never to see his two sons again.

* * *

Diwan-e-Khas,
Shahi Qila, Burhanpur.
04 April, 1621.
07.40 p.m.

The central lobby with its large windows was awash with light as several dozen tapers burned from the wall mountings, and two huge silver candelabras shone brightly at both ends of the long table. The prince had insisted that the war council be held today, his tiredness of three months of constant travel be damned.

Prince Shahjahan stood with his arms akimbo, studying the enormous parchment spread before him. His senior commanders and Abdur Rahim Khane Khana had already briefed him about the various concentrations of the Deccani forces.

'The blade of the sword must be seen,' murmured Shahjahan. His eyes again swept over the spread map, and focusing on the citadel of Bijapur, he drew a line with his forefinger over to Golconda. For almost a minute, his finger traced and retraced the collusive line between these two kingdoms. At last, he turned to his field commanders.

'As I said, the blade of the sword must be seen. The Deccan rulers, fighting out of their own homes and citadels feel that they are at an advantage. We must turn that perceived notion into their disadvantage. We must take the fight to them and run a war of devastation.' His eyes gleamed, as his voice became firmer, 'We shall make them watch their houses and fields being burned, their women being raped and pulled behind wagons to be sold, their children being castrated, their old being weighed with stone and dumped in the Tapti.'

Abdullah Khan could contain himself no longer. He rubbed his hands in glee 'A brilliant strategy, Your Highness. A man is weakest when he is fighting at the threshold of his home!'

'Right! We must strike now, without wasting time. Khane Khana,' the prince turned towards the old general, 'I shall divide the army into five divisions, independently commanded by Raja Vikramaditya, Darab Khan, Abdullah Khan, Khwaja Abu'l Hasan and Raja Bhima.'

The five chiefs stiffened, eyes aglimmer. 'These five divisions shall move forward against Malik Ambar at Golconda, in a wide pincer movement, while Khane Khana will send word to the other two states, reminding them of their earlier treaty which they have violated.' Khurram picked up a long wooden pointer and scratched at the site of Golconda citadel till there was a rent there.

'Against Malik Ambar's troops numbering sixty thousand, you have five divisions of thirty thousand each.' He continued to scratch at the torn Golconda site, 'You shall endeavour to finish this menace once and for all. Bijapur and Ahmednagar shall surrender with a few harsh words.'

***

Just about a week later, two contingents of imperial troops escorting their envoys stood at the gates of Bijapur and Ahmednagar. The Shahi Farmaan being read out was identical.

'You have brought great dishonour to your name and your flag by the flagrant violation of the Treaty signed by you accepting suzerainty under the Mughal Sultanat.

You have also not remitted the annual tribute to His Imperial Majesty for the last three years, which may be done immediately, or punitive action will follow.

You are also advised to follow the path of righteousness and friendship; else we can cripple your lands and personally destroy you.'

Adil Shah of Bijapur and Qutub Ul Mulk of Ahmednagar readily succumbed and made peace.

Malik Ambar with his Nizam Shah overlord was forced to flee from Golconda after a series of defeats, and took shelter in the Daulatabad fort. As the imperial troops razed the neighbouring town of Khidki, Malik Ambar finally capitulated, sending word to Raja Vikramaditya for peace terms.

Shahjahan was harsh in his victory. An unprecedented war reparation of rupees fifty lacs was imposed, which left the three Deccan allies arguing bitterly amongst themselves as to who would bear the larger share. All Mughal territories were restored and a fifteen-mile wide 'Buffer Zone' was created on the southern borders, along which no Deccani soldier could come.

In just six weeks of relentless battles, the Deccan threat had been neutralised.

***

The Shahi Hammam,
Badshahi Qila, Burhanpur.
29 August 1621
11.30 a.m.

Prince Shahjahan sat on the broad triangular step of the *hammam,* brooding and silent.

Begum Arjumand tried to be her usual gay self, but she was concerned. The prince had not been his usual robust, energetic self this last month, ever since news had come that Ladlii Begum had been married to prince Shahryar.

'My Lord, I have been watching you these past few weeks,' she said as she waded across, 'and have found you pensive and sad...'

Khurram raised his eyes, taking in her exquisite naked form. 'Arjumand, these are worrisome moments for me.'

He took her hand and bade her sit on his thighs.

She wrapped her arms around him, pressing her breast against his hard chest. 'There is nothing that can harm you.' She sniffed his neck, 'See, I can smell apples on you!'

Shahjahan sighed, smiling wanly 'Climates change, sweetheart, so does Fortune. Both are unpredictable.'

Arjumand lifted his bearded chin, her eyes questioning 'Khurram, my beloved. Is it Ladlii's marriage which is bothering you?'

Khurram nodded wearily, adding 'Not just her wedding, Arjumand, but all the scheming and murky politics which is behind this.' He absently removed a rose petal stuck on her arm. 'The Empress is now working overtime to dislodge the succession process. With Khusrau and me stuck in the Deccan, Pervez at Allahabad and the emperor in poor health, she is well poised to place Shahryar on the Mughal throne, should the need arise.'

She stared into his eyes, troubled 'But, it shall not be so easy, my lord. The nobles fully know your capabilities and that you are the emperor's favoured successor. She can't possibly do it on her own.'

Khurram's frown deepened 'True, Arjumand, but she has also poisoned the emperor against me—and poisoned effectively! For my victory in the Deccan for a second time, which not even my revered Shah Baba had been able to achieve, what have I received? A single ruby!' He shook his head.

'Your Highness! That ruby is one of its kind... who else can boast of being rewarded with a ruby that once adorned the hand of the Great Taimur Lang's grandson?'

Khurram drew her closer. 'You are kind and gentle, begum. The Mughal court is a cesspool of intrigue, betrayal, and opportunism.'

'Wait, let me write to my father about your apprehensions. After all, my grandfather is the Vizier and my father the emperor's Right Hand!'

Khurram smiled, but his words were gloomy, 'You will know with Time, dear, that Power is the only surviving relationship. Everything else wanes in front of it. But, do not worry. I shall find a way around this.'

***

A few weeks later.
Near Asirgarh Fort, Deccan.

Prince Khurram put a steadying hand on his stallion's neck, guiding the horse expertly down the steep, stony path from the Asirgarh fort. Fidai Khan, riding ahead, was issuing constant expletives under his breath as his horse skittered from one rock to another.

Brushing a small branch aside, Shahjahan turned to his loyal attendant of many years, Saif Khan Barha, and said 'I think it is time Ghulam Reza Bahadur was sent for.'

***

The crypts of Burhanpur Fort,
26 February 1622.
10.40 p.m.

Prince Khusrau sat with his back to the wall, with the Holy Quran spread on its marble stand. As with every night, prince Khusrau would trace his fingers over the gold filigreed pages, invoking Allah's blessings upon this world, which his sightless eyes could not see.

His wife, Beti Begum, had retired about an hour ago, after ensuring prince Khusrau's favourite dish of mutton cooked with lentils had been served to him just as he liked it. A maid, an ewer bearer, and an attendant had been allowed to him, who had also been escorted out of the prisoner's cell about an hour ago.

Prince Khusrau busied himself with the rosary, and later sought his way to the cell's door to fasten the slim chain in its hook.

It was close to midnight when discreet knocks were heard.

Khusrau looked up in surprise, 'Who is it?'

'Ghulam Reza Bahadur, Your Highness.'

'What work do you have with me?'

'Highness, I carry robes of honour from the emperor as well as a Shahi Farmaan for your release.'

Prince Khusrau shuddered at this unexpected peril, but kept his voice calm, 'Who else is with you, Bahadur?'

'I am alone, Your Highness.'

'What devilry is this, Reza Bahadur?' shouted Khusrau, as his hands frantically searched for the copper mug kept nearby. 'Where is prince Khurram? And, where is Khane Khanan?'

'Prince Khurram Shahjahan and the Commander left for a hunting expedition this morning, Highness, and I am under the emperor's order to deliver these to you at the earliest, without fail.'

'You are a fool, Reza, to spin such yarns. Back off now, before you commit a grievous sin!'

'Your Highness, I am here with an imperial order. Please open the door.'

'Back off, Reza!' shouted Khusrau as his sightless eyes rolled dramatically in their sockets, and his hands scrabbled to find any utensil.

At a nod from Ghulam Reza, his two accomplices sprang and put their shoulders to the door. The flimsy chain gave way, and the three assassins rushed in.

Khusrau backed up against the wall, holding both his arms out for protection. The three murderers spread out, intent on pinning both his arms, as Ghulam Reza Bahadur looped a bow string across his palms and moved to come in behind the prince.

Khusrau's right knee touched against a copper table, and his hands instinctively reached out for the earthen pot of water kept on it. As two of the accomplices tried to bind his arms, Khusrau twisted from the hips and swung the earthen pot in a mighty upward arc, catching one of them flush on his right temple.

As the man crumpled and the other assassin held onto Khusrau's left arm, Reza got the opening he was looking for. He slid in behind prince Khusrau's unprotected back and looped the bow string around his neck.

Choking and gasping for breath, Khusrau tried to wrench the wire away, but Reza bore down grimly, hunching over the blind prince's body. He flexed his arms, crossing them behind the prince's neck for the wire to cut deeper.

Red in the face, and with his scarred eyes bulging out of their sockets, he tried to scream but only a feeble wheeze came out. He tried to twist his body to escape the punishing strangulation, but Reza swung to the other side and the bow string cut deeper.

Finally, prince Khusrau sank to his knees and keeled over. The other accomplice twisted Khusrau's arm behind his back and dug his knees into the prince's back.

Khusrau's tongue rolled out in a semi-circled pout, as the last of his breath came out in small gurgles. His eyes, scarred and accusing, hung grotesquely out of his pitted eyelids as his body became still.

Reza kept his hold for the next two minutes, slackening not a bit.

Five minutes later, having swept the earthen pot bits into a corner, they laid the dead prince upon his cot, and spread the thin shawl over him, turning his face towards the wall.

Dragging their unconscious accomplice with them, they nodded curtly to the sentries outside, who silently locked the door. One of them, an Afghan by birth, swore hideously at the treachery of it all, and finally spilt out his guilt, retching all over the stony floor.

* * *

Badshahi Qila,
Burhanpur.
27 February 1622.
8.22 a.m.

Prince Khurram Shahjahan thundered across the drawbridge, and swerved left towards the daftarkhana below which the dungeons were located, and where the body of the blind prince lay. The news of prince Khusrau's assassination had been delivered early in the morning at his hunting camp, and prince Khurram had immediately mounted to return.

High keening wails from the main palace on the right made him rein his white charger, *Sartaj,* and look up in puzzlement.

As the main body of Shahjahan's retinue galloped in, the wailing grew louder with several females covered in white shrouds appearing at the windows and balconies.

Disturbed, prince Khurram swung his horse around, and asked fiercely, 'Why is there lamentation in Mumtaz Mahal Begum's suite?'

The syces and attendants remained silent and knelt down in abject fear. Shajahan dismounted and ran up the stairs into the second-floor apartment of his queen.

As he turned into the main corridor leading into the royal suite, he stopped at the sight of many score white shrouded women thronging the aisle and the rooms ahead.

He hissed furiously at the *Mir-i-Saman* who had rushed after him, 'Who has ordered prince Khusrau's body to be brought up to my suite?'

Latfullah Begi made no sound, just bowed his head in sorrow. Enraged, Khurram strode inside his bedchamber, and froze.

Seated cross legged on the huge silver bed, Mumtaz held a small, still bundle in the crook of her arms. Tears flowed in silent cascades down her cheeks, with only small mewling sounds coming from her parted lips.

Khurram walked the few steps to the bed in a daze, his mind numbed as the wails of the gathered women rose to a crescendo.

Mumtaz pressed the infant closer to her bosom as Shahjahan prised the golden sheet away.

Shocked, he sank heavily onto the bed.

Cradled in Mumtaz's arm was their two-year-old son, Umeed Baksh. Dead.

* * *

That evening, two coffins left the royal precincts for the nearby cemetery.

Emperor Jahangir lost a son and a grandson.

Prince Khurram Shahjahan had his brother murdered, and lost a son to his sins.

* * *

The Royal Suite,
Badshahi Qila, Burhanpur.
Same night.

The attendants and harem guards posted on night duty outside the royal chambers were appalled and repulsed by the sounds of copulation coming from inside.

Khurram, his back and forehead beaded in sweat, was thrusting hard and fast between Mumtaz's spread thighs, even as Mumtaz, miserable and gasping, implored Khurram to go slower.

'Please, my lord, you are hurting me. Please!'

In response, Khurram tucked his elbows and lay full length over her, not for a second belaying his thrusting penis. She turned her tear-streaked face away as he attempted to kiss her.

'Oh, Khurram! What have you done?' she cried breathlessly, as he continued to pound inside her. 'The sin of murdering a blind prince will forever be a curse on us!' She started sobbing.

'We lost our little child today, an innocent, bright Umeed Baksh! Oh, whatever have you done, Khurram?' she was weeping openly now.

'Hush, Arjumand. I only did what I had to do for myself, for you and for our children!' He rolled off her, but stretched his arms to pin her breasts.

'Do you remember that night at Chavand when I had Mirza Aziz Koka imprisoned, and his little waif of an attendant, Wafa, spilled the beans on Mirza? Do you?' Khurram's voice had become harsh.

Mumtaz nodded as Khurram continued, 'That night Wafa showed me a letter written by Mirza Aziz Koka to Raja Mansingh, when Shah Baba was on his deathbed, suggesting that I should be killed as soon as I left Shah Baba's room. It clearly mentioned that with my murder, and emperor Salim Jahangir's assassination by the Rajput guards, nothing could prevent prince Khusrau from becoming the emperor.'

'Do you recall that Zia Ul Mulk Qazwani had run up the river barge on which emperor Salim Jahangir had arrived to pay his last respects to a dying emperor Akbar?'

Arjumand nodded, her eyes wide open in alarm.

'My refusal to leave Shah Baba's side till his last breath saved my life. It was his *rehmat* on me,' so saying, Khurram's tears spilled over. 'You should know, Arjumand, that Khusrau would have laughingly had me murdered, if he ever had a chance. I did what I did, to ensure our survival... our children's survival.'

Arjumand's voice was weak, 'But, we lost our Umeed Baksh today, cursed by the soul of that sightless prince?'

Shahjahan kissed her lips, as he again entered her 'Children will be born, and children will die. We must ensure that our own survive.'

Cuming deep inside her, Shahjahan planted yet another seed within her womb.

The Timurids must survive.

***

The next day, prince Khurram Shahjahan had a Letter of Condolence drawn up for the royal court, in which it was clarified that prince Khusrau died because of *Kalanj*, or severe colic pains.

It was attested by all of the senior nobles attached to the Deccan Suba.

Over the next three days, almost seven hundred people were executed at Burhanpur for protesting against the suspected murder of a blind prince.

The avenging spirit of a sightless, innocent murdered prince was now to forever haunt the Badshahi Qila at Burhanpur.

***

CHAPTER 30

'BADVALAT'

('Be-Daulat!')

Diwan-e-Khas,
The fort, Koh-e-Maran,
Srinagar.
12 March 1622
10 a.m.

Emperor Jahangir sat on a wide silver chair, the sides bolstered by fluffy cushions of geese downing encased in turquoise silk. He tried coaxing the empress to pour him a cup of wine from the ruby encrusted decanter.

'My sweet beloved! Pour me a cup of this gracious wine so that I may drown in the goodness of your heart.'

Nurjahan could not help laughing at the guile of the emperor in chasing his wine.

Nurjahan extended her beautiful, slim arms and pushed the glass closer to his lips. Her voice was cheerful, 'Of course, Jahanpanah!'

She smiled as she picked up the two scrolls lying on the silver salver and addressed the emperor, 'What should be done about this, Majesty?'

Jahangir looked with contempt at the two scrolls, and replied wryly, 'You are intelligent enough to know the truth, Begum.' He pointed towards the more ornate of the two scrolls 'This imperial report from prince Khurram is a patchwork of lies.' He was silent for a few moments, before speaking again 'Poor Khusrau was murdered by his own... And I am to blame.' He looked reproachfully at Nurjahan, willing her to share the blame. She remained silent.

'The Deccan generals and court nobles have also sold their souls to the devil, to put their signatures on a document as disgraceful as this.' Lunging forward, he grabbed the royal scroll and flung it far away.

Eyes glistening with tears, he stretched his hands for the other smaller, simple scroll. 'Only Nuruddin Quli had the guts and loyalty to state the truth.' His voice broke as his tear dimmed eyes read the scathing indictment of prince Khurram's heinous fratricide.

Nurjahan eased closer to Jahangir's side as his frail shoulders shook and grief laden words tumbled out, 'My eldest was so delicate and pious, not a word out of him even when I had him blinded by pushing burning, searing iron rods into his eyes.' His words trailed into heavy sobs. 'Oh, Khusrau, my beloved son, I stand a sinner before you,' wailed the emperor as he lurched from his chair and fell onto his knees, hands clasped.

'The sinner is prince Khurram, Your Majesty, not you. To slay a blind, defenceless person who is in your protection is a sin which shall beget no absolution,' she tried to comfort the monarch.

'Khusrau was his elder brother, Begum!' The emperor's grief was unremitting.

'Allah shall find no mercy for Khurram, Majesty. And he should find none from you either.' Her words were like a command.

Nurjahan signalled for the eunuchs and the attendants to draw the screens and leave the room. She took her silken handkerchief and carefully poured some of the fine Persian wine kept by the bedside. Drawing the kerchief across the emperor's lips and nostrils, she stroked his forehead with her other palm, trying to straighten the furrows.

'Your Majesty!' she whispered, 'prince Khurram needs to be dealt with. He has to redeem his fealty to your royal threshold. Surrounded by a vast army and grovelling nobles, he has forgotten his place in Your Majesty's court.'

A tired Jahangir asked wearily, 'What do you suggest, Begum?'

'Sire, send him on the Kandahar campaign. Reduce his stranglehold on the Deccan dominions. Take away his army divisions and call his senior commanders to wait upon you at the royal court.' Her words became harsher, 'Let him show his bravery on the battlefield, and not on manacled, blind prisoners of faith!'

'So be it!' murmured Jahangir, as he turned on his side and buried his face into the silk sheathed thighs of Nurjahan.

***

The Upper Forecourts,
Riverside, Burhanpur Fort,
27 March 1622
Early morning.

Prince Khurram Shahjahan lay on his back enjoying the first rays of a rising sun. Having returned late at night from a forward post inspection, he let the attendants rub perfumed almond and lavender oil on his legs and shoulders to draw away the pain.

Khurram asked for a bolster to be put under his head, and then addressed the waiting waqia navees, 'Write carefully.'

'My Most Illustrious Father,
Jewel of the Timurids and The Caliph of Justice,

To thy stirrup of magnificence doth I send my greetings from your Suba of Burhanpur!

I have received your Farmaan of 13th instant and most humbly accept your commandment to proceed to Multan, as the staging point for the Kandahar campaign. In compliance, my tent equipage is already being loaded for onward transport.

Protector Of the Poor and The Most Resplendent Padshah Ghazi, your accusing words with regard to prince Khusrau's death has numbed my senses, and has spun a web of despondency around me.

Your anger stems from the malicious lies and reports possibly being sent to you by the malcontents and garbage of Deccan, probably insinuating some other deep, sinful reason to my pious brother's death rather than the pertinent cause of acute colic. The highest of Your Majesty's nobles have put their signatures on the official report sent by me, in testimony.

For all of my life I have served every command of yours with complete diligence and fealty. What confounds you now, O Mir-e-Adl, that you point to such grievous sins on my part?

With utmost deference and respect I draw your attention to the world's condemnation of you, when your name was dragged as the hand behind the poisoning of Shah Baba in 1591, even before I was born? Did not Shah Baba repose his faith in you?

King of Kings, remember the evening of 26 October 1605, the day after Shah Baba's death, when I gave that last letter of Shah Baba addressed to you? I am sure that you remember it was dictated by Arsh Ashiyani, but written by me in Turki. You may also recall Shah Baba's admonition that the contents of that letter should remain only between the three of us.

My Lord and Sire, these past seventeen years I have carried Shah Baba's accusation of you and Begum Salima Sultana (may Allah rest her soul) poisoning him, close to my chest. Never have I indicated this devastating truth to anyone, lest it taint the Majesty of Your Brow.

Illumined Emperor, do you also see a similarity in prince Khusrau's death and the demise of prince Khusrau's mother, The Most Revered Shah Begum, whom you had poisoned in the fort of Allahabad as you purportedly hunted tigers and cheetahs in the forests of Shankargarh?

If you feel that I am the instrument of prince Khusrau's death, then it may please Your Majesty to ascribe it to my hereditary traits, and forgive me.

As for your grievous insinuations regarding the dastardly attack on a blind, defenceless prisoner, may I remind Your Imperial Self of the brutal murder of Sheikh Abu'l Fazl commissioned by you in 1602, and executed by the coward Bir Singh Bundela? The Sheikh was a scribe, not a warrior. Even then, when urged to flee by Mirza Mohsin and Gadai Khan Afghan, the brave wordsmith preferred to fight believing in the creed of Akbar Padshah!

May I remind you also of the highly perverse murder of Sher Afghan by a posse of your thugs led by your bosom friend, the now deceased Sheikh Qutubuddin Chishti? For what purpose? Just to slake your thirst for the body of a woman!

Where dost thou stand, O Mighty King, belaboured by such filthy acts?

My words are only to reassure you, My Protector and Refuge, that I always have been, and shall forever be, your most obedient servant.

I shall embark on the Kandahar trail within the next few days, and fervently pray, that having let the dust of treachery be swept under, Your Majesty shall again favour this unfortunate son with Your Bejewelled Gaze.

While kissing the threshold of Your Imperial Majesty,

I remain,

Your obedient son and servant,
Shah Khurram Shahjahan.
Deccani Subedar.
27 March 1622.

* * *

A few hours later, the waqia navees mysteriously fell through a trapdoor near the central well, breaking his neck and skull.

* * *

Two weeks later, Emperor Nuruddin Mohammed Jahangir read the pernicious letter several times and, having torn it into small bits, took it to the lavatory and urinated all over it.

In his *Tuzuk-i-Jahangiri* he made a simple two-line insertion recording prince Khusrau's death, devoid of sorrow or remorse.

In hindsight, he ordered for Khusrau's dead body to be exhumed and brought back to the *Darul Hukumat* at Agra. What had been lost, must be retrieved.

Even if it was the maggot ridden bones and flesh of a blind, defenceless prince.

***

The Shahi Darbar,
Burhanpur Fort,
01 April 1622.
03.45 a.m.

The court astrologers had been checking and rechecking the planetary positions over the last one hour conforming to the astrologically auspicious time frame. Both the Hindu and the Muslim astrologers had opined that this period was good to proceed on the Kandahar campaign.

Prince Shahjahan looked keenly at the celebrated Pir Mir Faiz-Ul Buqa. The celebrated astrologer sat silent, his bundle of astrological charts wrapped in green muslin.

After a few minutes of pregnant silence, the Mir Tozak approached the learned sage, and quietly asked 'Your silence hangs heavy, Huzoor. Is there something that troubles you?'

The mystic raised his eyes, and addressed the prince in sombre tones, 'Your Highness...The Lord giveth, and the Lord taketh; mighty and unknown are his ways! My learned brothers have spoken, but my calculations are contrary.'

'Speak your mind, Learned Oracle. Allah speaks through each one of you.'

Mir Faiz-Ul Baqi inclined his head at the prince's command. He looked upwards, as if his gaze could streak through the vaulted dome and seek the stars above. For a few moments he closed his eyes.

'I see a great disaster awaits you, prince, if you leave now and proceed beyond Mandu. Your major planets are in an inverted triangle, proclaiming great pain and sorrow for you, maybe even the loss of your life in a conspiracy inspired by the royal throne. The inverted triangle signifies the lost throne, buried forever.

'The stars evidence the creation of jealous tempests and scorching ambitions up North. It would do well to stay at Mandu till Jupiter and Saturn come to occupy vantage positions in the Eastern hemisphere. Thereafter, the clouds of blood shall lift, and you shall march to your Destiny.'

Prince Khurram nodded, and silently handed over a small purse of gold coins for Mir Baqi. The sage had articulated much of his concerns, and they conformed to Khurram's own uneasiness over the Kandahar campaign.

His mind was made up.

'We shall depart the day after for Mandu.'

***

The *Naubatkhana*,
Main Gate, Qila Mandu,
18 April 1622
4 p.m.

The musicians playing the welcome tune and the citadel guards gathered at the main gate, watched the royal procession of prince Khurram Shahjahan's imperial army and retinue wind slowly up the tortuous serpentine route to the main fort.

However, the words of Mir Faiz-Ul Buqa kept resonating in Shahjahan's ears, and consequently, his mind was made up as he passed underneath the naubatkhana amidst a shower of rose petals—Kandahar could wait; first, his destiny must be secured.

That night, retiring to the imperial chambers after an early supper, he decided to discuss it with Arjumand.

The room felt snug and warm as several candles and *diyas* were flickering towards extinction, and the illumination had tapered to just a warm glow. The Narmada flowing to the south of the fort, sent a steady breeze through the well-spaced corridors and vaulted rooms.

Shahjahan played with Arjumand's perfumed forelock as she lay cradled against his chest. Warm and comfortable, her silent nap was broken by Khurram's soft words.

'Mumtaz, dearest, I have a nasty feeling about this urgent summons for Kandahar.'

She sleepily opened her eyes, 'I know Khurram. Everybody knows that this is a punishment for prince Khusrau's death.'

'No, Arjumand, this goes deeper than that. It is Padshah Begum's trap to draw me away from my stronghold of Deccan, and have me sent to the far north to tangle with the Persians who are well entrenched there and are kept supplied by their neighbouring territory of Khorasan.'

Khurram sidled up on his elbow, leaning against the wide bolster, 'Her ultimate aim is to see me dead, so that the *naushidaan* Shahryar can become the emperor, and her daughter, the Padshah Begum.'

'Hush, darling! Speak not such woeful words...'

'It is *the* reason, Arjumand, make no mistake.' His voice grew hard. 'I have thought much about it, and Mir Baqi has also presaged the negative aspects of an onward march, hence, I have decided to stay here till the rainy season gets over.'

'Will not the emperor be furious?'

'I will keep him occupied with certain demands which are relevant to this expedition. However, the queen's little cartel may not find it palatable enough to grant. It will give us the time needed to shore up our war plan and rest the army for the punishing battles ahead.'

'Killing Khusrau was not a good idea, my lord,' sighed Mumtaz.

'It was not an idea, Mumtaz. It was a necessity,' Khurram said tersely.

***

Diwan-e-Aam,
Koh-e-Maran, Srinagar.
15 May 1622
10.40 a.m.

Emperor Jahangir sat in state as prince Khurram Shahjahan's envoy, Mulla Shukrullah Shirazi presented the prince's letter to the

Crown. Sheikh Farid Bokhari officiating as Mir Arz read aloud the contents in his stentorian voice.

'In the service of

His Imperial Majesty Nuruddin Mohammed Salim Jahangir Padshah Ghazi,

Defender of the Faith and The Sun Resplendent Sovereign,

A thousand valorous taslims and zaminbos!

In compliance with your imperial command, I have entered the fortress of Mandu with a bulk of the imperial army, artillery and the elephant corps for the Kandahar campaign.

It is my duty to inform you that our onward movement towards Lahore, Multan, and Kandahar can be staged only after the monsoons are over; till then I propose to be garrisoned here.

Your Majesty will grant me this privilege as Raja Bhima with his troops is away collecting the annual tributes for your royal treasury from the states of Gondwana and Khandesh, and will return by June end. Thus, a major part of our loyal Rajput troops is unavailable at the moment.

It will also be impossible for me to ferry our heavy cannons over the slushy Malwa hills and the flooded basins of Narmada, Betwa, Chambal and Kane, during the monsoon months.

I also have a small request to make of thee, Jahanpanah!

May it please Your Majesty to allot the Suba of Punjab to the undersigned as it will ensure adequate provisioning during the battle campaign?

In the same vein, it is submitted that the fort of Ranthambhor should be made available for the womenfolk of my harem for their safety and upkeep, till I am engaged in resolving the Kandahar issue.

I am taking the liberty, My Lord and Protector, of staying at Mandu till the appearance of 'Suheil', the southern Pole Star indicating clearer weather.

Thereafter, I shall raise my banners for the conquest of Kandahar, and the rise of your Imperial Status!

Permit me to kiss the stirrup of obedience at your earliest grace!

Your dutiful son,
Shah Khurram Shahjahan,
Subedar, Deccan.

Camp: Mandu.
24 April 1622

The emperor gnashed his teeth and struck his fist on the silver arm of his throne. Eyes bulbous with rage, he erupted.

'This *Be-daulat* prince! Does his greed for money and power have no end?' he sputtered in rage.

'Do I have to suffer his impertinence and his astronomical demands?' His stuttering became more pronounced, as he leapt up from his throne and pounced upon the nearest mace bearer, knocking him down with an elbow across the temple.

Furious, he signalled for the Mir Arz to come closer. 'Write this down,' he commanded.

In a voice loud enough to be heard in the far corners of the pavilion, he dictated the Shahi Farmaan –

'We have received your parwan of 24th last, and are dismayed at your lack of cohesion with the imperial demands, and your foetid response to the critical issue of Kandahar.

It seems your greed and ambitions have taken over your senses and vows of fealty, and left you bereft of any princely qualities. You may continue to squander away your time in the confines of Mandu Fort, but note, that henceforth you are not welcome at the royal court, unless sent for.

You are again commanded to send the imperial commanders and troops immediately to wait upon me for the Kandahar conquest. You may continue to stay at Mandu or any other place of your choice in the Deccan.

You have shrunk enough in my vision to be consigned to the status of a 'Be-Daulat', and we disavow ourselves from you.

The dispatch of the imperial forces is urgent, the same to be confirmed to Mir Bakshi, and we bar you from appearing in my presence, till such time as your vows of allegiance and obedience once more rules your heart.

Issued under the Muhr Uzek of
Padshah Ghazi Nuruddin Mohammed Salim Jahangir
Camp: Kashmere, Koh-e-Maran.

15 May 1622.

* * *

The Mughal Gardens,
Jumna Riverfront, Agra
20 June 1622
11.20 a.m.

The cortege bearing the exhumed remains of prince Khusrau entered the city of Agra in a long procession of lamenting citizens and silent mendicants and fakirs.

The royal troops escorting the prince's body from Burhanpur had been amazed at the outpouring of grief from the citizens en-route. At places, where the body had rested on the journey, common people had thronged the resting site and had placed wreaths and flowers. Earthen lamps and incense sticks had been placed around the cortege, and populace had maintained night long vigils, as would befit a saint.

At several places, small shrines had sprung up overnight for the prince, and his corpse had taken on the mantle of a martyred saint. News of this was being periodically conveyed to empress Nurjahan at Kashmere.

As it reached near the Agra fort, the cortege was escorted to one of the freshly laid gardens on the Jumna riverfront for burial.

The very next day, on the 21 June 1622, the Persian forces of Shah Abbas finally captured the ancestral fortress of the Mughals at Kandahar.

When news of this reached the royal court, Nurjahan exclaimed, 'The curse follows the prince in death also! His life was a litany of woes, and even in death he blights the Kingdom and his father's winter years.'

Her next words were harsh and vindictive, 'Move his body to Allahabad where his mother lies. Born from an evil womb, let him return to it.'

In due course, the disinterred remains of a slaughtered prince reached Allahabad, and was laid to rest in a huge mausoleum built in the same garden where his mother, Shah Begum, was buried in May 1604. The garden-mausoleum came to be known as Khusrau Bagh.

Frustrated and disconsolate, an embittered Jahangir commanded that Shah Khurram Shahjahan should henceforth be addressed as Be-daulat, or, The Wretch!

***

In the ensuing months of monsoon, prince Shahryar was given command of the Kandahar campaign, and his status raised to 12000 Zat and 8000 sowars, and Mirza Rustam was assigned as his guardian.

Nurjahan, pursuing a policy of relentless retribution, persuaded the emperor to transfer the lucrative northern jagirs of prince Khurram to Shahryar.

The Be-daulat was peremptorily informed to choose jagirs in the Deccan.

The imperial inclination was now abundantly clear to Shahjahan 'Be-daulat' and the vacillating legions of Mughal nobles, who had a history of choosing flags to fight under, based on the wind beneath them!

***

CHAPTER 31

GUAWACPEHEI GHARGH DARK HON

(The Blood-Drenched Guavas)

The Shergarh Qila,
Dholpur,
02 September 1622
10 a.m.

The sentry commander marched into the Daftarkhana. Sharif-ul-Mulk, the Mughal fort commander, sat finalising the pay sheet for the royal garrison stationed here.

'Sire, the small Mughal contingent which had camped across the Chambal late last night, now seeks an audience with you.'

'How many men?'

'Huzoor, more or less a hundred. And, they are all armed.'

Sharif-ul-Mulk frowned, 'Rather large for a messenger posse.' After a moment's pause, he said 'Ahmed, tighten the security and assemble a large squad of your men in the outer courtyard.'

'*Jo* hukum!'

The fort commander watched apprehensively as several score horsemen rode in from the huge gates, and in direct violation of court protocol sat seated on their mounts. He glanced around and was satisfied to see that most of the fort's troopers had assembled around the forecourt. A few archers were peering down from the arrow loops in the upper quarters.

The lead mount, a burly officer with a trimmed beard and hawkish nose, flanked by the royal Mughal standard, asked loudly, 'Who is in charge here?'

Sharif-ul-Mulk answered calmly, 'I am. But first, tell me who are you all?'

The mounted officer kneed his horse forward and commanded loudly, 'I am Darab Khan Afghan, and I carry a *Shahi Parwana* from Shah Khurram Shahjahan to hand over this fort of Dholpur to our charge.' He thrust a rolled parchment towards the fort commander.

Sharif ignored the proffered parchment, and instead called out, 'This fort is the jagir of prince Shahryar and assigned to us for safe custody, by the Empress of Hindustan under her royal seal.'

Darab Khan leaned down from the saddle and again shoved the scroll towards Sharif-ul-Mulk, adding threateningly, 'We carry prince Shahjahan's *hukmnama* to reclaim this fort in his name. Faujdar, please do not make this unnecessarily hard for yourself. Handover the fort keys in the name of Shah Khurram Shahjahan, and all will be well.'

Sharif scoffed, 'Show me a Royal Warrant to this effect, and I shall honourably do so.'

Darab Khan guffawed and wheeled his horse in a circle. 'The weakling prince's faithful wants to see our Royal Warrant!' he chortled violently, and pushing the parchment into his cummerbund, swiftly drew his sword. Immediately, swords were drawn on both sides, as Darab Khan's cavalry started wheeling their steeds in a threatening manoeuvre.

Sharif tried to play down the moment, 'Darab Khan, your acts are treasonable, and documents spurious. His Highness, prince Khurram would never condone such disobedience of His Majesty's commands. Back off, or we shall be forced to use arms against you and your men.'

In response, Darab kneed his horse wickedly, and the steed surged forward. Leaning to his left, Darab hit the ducking Sharif a glancing blow with the broad blade of his sword, drawing blood from his right eye. In seconds, the armed riders were besieged by the charging soldiers of the Imperial Army.

A reeling Sharif-ul-Mulk with a half torn right eye, inspired his men with a rousing battle cry *'Fateh ya maut!'* and the foot soldiers rushed forth cleaving with their swords at the riders and also at the shanks of the horses to disable them. Archers, strung across the roof, were shooting carefully, picking their targets from the swirling mass of fighting men.

Darab Khan, mounted, dishevelled and shouting like a madman, was plunging into the thick of the grappling, slaying crowd and hacking away with demonic fury at the imperial soldiers. The other cavalry troops were also mercilessly cutting down the royal troops and trying to force their way towards the colonnaded chambers, from where stairs led to the upper chambers and the roof.

Darab Khan's horse reared, and he caught sight of an injured Sharif-ul-Mulk being ushered towards the main palace, surrounded by a detail of imperial guards. Letting out a martial whoop, Darab

Khan spurred his horse towards the retreating Faujdar. A few of his cavalry galloped after him.

Darab Khan suddenly reined his horse causing it to rear, and let its hooves smash the forehead and chest of the closest soldiers. They collapsed with broken skulls and crushed ribs, while Darab and his fellow riders surrounded the helpless Sharif, keeping his bodyguards at bay.

'Yo, *Faujdar!'* Darab placed the point of his sword on top of Sharif's skull, 'I have no enmity with you. Just obey the royal command of prince Khurram, and I shall spare the lives of you and your men. If you continue to resist,' he moved the sword point, cleaving the scalp with a fine cut 'I shall quarter and string you up on the main gate. Now, what say you?'

Sharif-ul-Mulk staggered to his feet, face covered with little rivulets of blood, and took in the situation around him. Most of the imperial soldiers still standing had already laid down their arms, and were being herded into a far corner of the forecourt. He waved wearily at the archers atop the roof, signalling them to come down. He turned to Darab Khan, and holding his eye hanging from its socket, spoke low.

'The fort is yours, Darab Khan. You came dressed in sheep's clothing, waving the imperial flag. If you had come to wage war and capture the fort, you should have raised battle pennants and fought like brave soldiers, rather than come in as deceiving rats.' He spat a gob of bloody phlegm in contempt.

Darab Khan derisively snorted and with his blood smeared hands smoothed his hair. With a wicked smile, he lanced the sash of Sharif's cummerbund causing it to fall to the ground, along with the huge ring with three large keys of copper.

He pointed towards the keys, and mocked Sharif, 'Be glad that it is only your *patta* which I have cut. Next time, it will be your trouser strings. Now, pick up the fort keys and give them to me.'

Sharif picked up the keys and flung it at the mocking Afghan.

Darab caught the keys, and laughed derisively 'It is only right that you should throw the keys at me. Just like you threw away the fort without a fight. Now,' he turned towards his adjutant 'Put them in the dungeons till I decide what to do with them.'

***

Khuldabad,
Allahabad.
15 September 1622
11 a.m.

The exhumed body of prince Khusrau, kept in a sandalwood coffin and wrapped in perfumed shrouds of muslin to quell the stench of decayed flesh, was slowly lowered into the three-metre deep grave.

As the nobles, mullahs and prominent people of Allahabad sprinkled mud in the final ritual of farewell, the sonorous words of the *Salat-al-Janaza* floated in the vaulted hall of the new mausoleum, under construction.

The tomb of prince Khusrau's mother, Shah Begum, lay to the west, and the whole compound was surrounded by high walls and four major gates. Inside were groves of guavas and a large pond.

Within the hour, the grave had been filled, and a marble slab with Quranic inscriptions was placed over it.

In a final gesture, the green and gold embroidered turban, as well as the prince's personal Quran was placed over it. A sheet of woven roses was reverentially laid on top.

The much slighted and accursed prince had finally come to rest close to his mother.

For many nights thereafter, loud keening wails were heard from the compound now known as Khusrau Bagh. The imperial soldiers on sentry duty shivered as they recounted these ghostly laments of mother and son for years to come.

***

Royal chambers,
Shahi Qila, Mandu.
26 November 1622
10.43 p.m.

A sweating, crying Mumtaz Mahal strained to push the child out, even as her personal physician, Sati ul-Nisa and other midwifery attendants exhorted her to push harder.

Sati un-Nisa held Mumtaz's sweating palms and whispered in her ears, 'Just heave once more, my royal princess, the head is almost out.'

Straining every muscle in her groin and pelvis, she heaved upwards. 'Yes, Yes,' cajoled Sati, 'the head is almost out... yes, we have it!' Supporting the newborn's tiny head, she flexed her palms and the little body slid out.

A shout of jubilation went up, '*Meherba!* Meherba! *A prince is born to the Luminous Queen!*'

The newborn let out a loud wail and its tiny hands flailed upwards trying to reach for its neck. Suddenly, its head rolled sideways and all movements ceased.

That night, amidst the soft lamentations in the imperial harem, Mumtaz Mahal could not ignore the hushed whispers of her attendants and eunuchs. The infant prince had been born exactly nine months to the date and time of prince Khusrau's murder. Inexplicably, he carried a livid scar on his neck reflective of harsh strangulation.

For a few days, even prince Khurram Shahjahan was rattled by this unfortunate event and complained of headaches and stomach cramps. The female Tatar guards assigned for night sentry duties, witnessed another spectacle.

For several nights, Khurram knelt by his bedside and beseeched forgiveness from Khusrau. Each time, the sobbing and the pleading were clearly audible to the harem guards.

But Khusrau had had enough. His spirit was to torment Khurram and the fort of Burhanpūr for eternity.

***

The Imperial Camp,
Sarai Lashkar Khan, Near Ludhiana.
10 December 1622.
4.15 p.m.

Emperor Jahangir, hurrying back from Lahore to Agra, was looking at the revenue accounts from the jagir of Hissar, when the Hada sentry commander entered and waited for permission to speak. After a few minutes, Jahangir looked up.

'Your Majesty, messengers have arrived from the garrison at Allahabad. There is also the *Darogha-i-Dak* waiting outside with an urgent message from Khandesh.'

'Send the Darogha first.'

The Master of Posts entered and prostrated himself on the carpet, a rolled parchment in hand.

'Rise!' commanded Jahangir.

The officer lay stretched and refused to look up. His words, muffled by the thick carpet, were ominous. 'Alampanah! May my life be spared, for I am just a conveyor of reports and mail!'

'Speak up, you miserable fool!' The emperor's words were harsh, but riddled with anxiety.

The post officer almost groveled, 'Alampanah! There is a report from the Khufiya Navees which confirms that prince Khurram Shahjahan is acquiring a large army to march upon Agra.'

'That Be-daulat!' roared Jahangir. 'He dares to defy me! After all that I have done for him, the favours and honour bestowed? I will teach this wretch a lesson he will never forget!'

Sputtering with rage, he commanded the Mir Bakshi, 'Withdraw all the *jagirs* of Be-daulat and assign them to prince Shahryar. Also, send word to prince Pervez at Allahabad by fast horse to march immediately for Agra with all troops under his command.'

He signalled for the quivering *Darogha-i-Dak* to be dismissed.

A few moments later, three dusty and weary messengers of prince Pervez from Allahabad were escorted in.

Performing the customary obeisance, they extended the sealed leather parchment box to the closest attendant.

The Mir Arz unrolled the parchment, and read.

'Padshah Ghazi, Zille-Illahi,
Lord of this Universe and Beyond,
Hukumat-i-Hind Zindabad!

May thy Imperial Self be constantly affectionate on this son of thee, who prostrates himself at your Auspicious Feet and your Threshold of Good Fortune!

I am delighted to report that your Suba at Allahabad is prospering in the shadow of your magnificent reign, with peace and tranquillity prevailing everywhere. The harvest has been good, and tax collections have surpassed last year's collection.

There is just one niggling worry—the famed guavas of the garden where Her Ladyship Shah Begum is buried, and where my revered elder brother, prince Khusrau has been recently laid to rest, have blood stains within them. Not one, or two, but all guavas now carry these blood stains inside as well as on the outer skin. I am sending ten seers picked randomly for your verification.

There are ominous discussions in the Suba that the blood of an innocent, anguished, martyred Khusrau has infected the guavas as a grim reminder of the atrocities committed on him.

The guavas definitely seem blood drenched.'

Vexed, emperor Jahangir stopped the oration and gestured for the guavas.

The green skin of the guavas definitely had red spots scattered on them. With the tip of his ruby encrusted dagger, Jahangir sliced it open.

The flesh and the core inside were speckled liberally with red bloodstains.

* * *

Inexplicably, the famed guavas of Allahabad's Khusrau Bagh were forever to carry the bloodstained marks within them.

Even to this day...

***

CHAPTER 32

'ZIRA KHIANT BA O CPEHMARAH MISHOD!'

('For Treachery Marches with Him!')

Vaulted Hall of Asharfi Mahal,
Mandu Fort.
02 January 1623.
08.15 a.m.

Shah Khurram Shahjahan stood with his back to the decorated wall, his eyes scanning the assembled generals for their show of support or dissent.

An ageing Abdur Rahim Khane Khana, a world-weary traveller of more than sixty-seven winters, could easily predict the words to follow now. Was he not with Akbar in 1602, when the current emperor Jahangir had raised a similar banner of revolt against his father, the mighty Akbar?

The unfolding scenario seemed to be an orchestrated repetition of the past. The old soldier-commander could very well recite the forthcoming words—and action.

'The forcible and unfair withdrawal of my princely estates, and their subsequent assignment to that *nashudani,* prince Shahryar, is a revocation of all that is great and desirable in the Timurids. It is an abrogation of Arsh Ashiyani's mighty triumphs and majestic reign, where he carved out an enormous and steadfast empire from the fragile threads bequeathed by his revered father... are we to stand in impotent complicity and see this great empire wither in the greed and guile of an empress, who is willing to consign this mightiest of empires to an untested weakling of a prince, to ensure her own continuity?' Shahjahan's words were cutting.

'Are we to stand, and decay?' roared Khurram, at the commanders' silence.

'No!' shouted the commanders.

'Which way lies Victory?' thundered Shahjahan.

'To Agra! To arms!' was the explosive response.

'The spirit of Arsh Ashiyani resides in Agra, the *Darul Hukumat!* We must march to Agra first and liberate the anguished spirit of a mighty warrior from the clutches of an evil empress.' Khurram's words were ablaze with patriotic fervour.

The assembled commanders stomped their feet and unsheathed their swords. Rebellion had been declared.

Only Khane Khana stood silently, ruminating. Must History repeat itself?

* * *

The Fort ramparts,
Agra Fort.
18 February 1623.
7.50 a.m.

Emperor Jahangir's trusted eunuch and fort commander, Aitbar Khan, stared gloomily at the rebel troops assembled towards the open areas of the Jumna River bank and royal preserves. This was the third day of siege, and today, the rebel artillery had been ominously moved closer.

Prince Khurram sat on his caparisoned war elephant, *Hukum*, surrounded by a squadron of Mewar's cavalry in their signature *kesariya* turbans and glittering lances. Behind him stretched several formations of infantry, horses and heavy artillery.

Aitbar Khan stood at one of the crenelations towards the left of the *Lahori Darwaza*, with Rehmat Khan, the chief cannoneer beside him.

'Rehmat Khan, I think the time has come to move our heavy cannons on to the battlements.' Aitbar surveyed the rebel formation, then advised 'Move the small cannons to the front of the machicolations, and depress them to fire at an acute downward angle, should the rebels attack. Please remember, Rehmat, the first shot must be a warning shot on the elephant line.'

'Sire, what about prince Khurram on his elephant?'

Aitbar looked towards the mounted prince, and had an instinctive feeling of being watched from behind the *howdah's* screen.

'He is still the *Wali Ahad*, Rehmat. Spare him the cannon shot. I will ask the *Teerandazs* to riddle him with arrows—at least, his face would be discernible for burial.'

Almost an hour later, as the gates remained steadfastly closed, Khurram gave the order to attack.

Trumpeting loudly, a brace of elephants approached pulling a very heavy log behind them. As they came to within a hundred metres of the main gate, a detachment of about forty burly Afghans, Turks, and Rajputs sidled under the enormous log and started running towards the main gate, over the semi-permanent drawbridge spread on the moat.

'Hold your fire,' commanded Aitbar Khan.

The ramming party threw themselves along with the log on to the massive gates, but the wooden gates girded by iron bands held.

'Now!' shouted Aitbar, and a volley of arrows rained down on the leading rebel echelons. From atop the crenellations and loops in the forward battlements, soldiers started pouring burning oil and rocks on to the stranded ramming party, who immediately dropped their battering ram and ran back. Many fell to arrows and musket shots.

Rehmat signalled for the huge cast iron cannon *Kala Badal* to fire. As the master cannoneer primed and lit the fuse, the enormous cannon fired and rocked back on its wheels. A few more cannons ranged across the fort battlements fired into the rebels, forcing them to retreat. Far amongst the elephants, the cannonade wreaked devastation as several elephants fell with shattered legs or shrapnel in their bellies and trunks.

Khurram Shahjahan looked pensively at the silent, barricaded doors of the main gate, and a flood of remorse and guilt swept over him. How could he order his own heavy cannons to return fire upon a fort which had remained the favoured abode of his revered grandfather. How many summer nights and winter mornings had he spent inspecting these same battlements with *Shah Baba?* His eyes were drawn to the Mughal flag on the prime bastion, and his eyes misted over.

He would not drop cannon shells and burning arrows on his own home.

Commanding his *mahout* to turn around, he desultorily lifted a hand to signal retreat.

Aitbar Khan watched the retreating elephant of prince Shah Khurram Shahjahan with a lump in his throat. The Timurid fealty had ruled at last—the rebel army was turning back without firing a shot!

He could not restrain himself, and shouted, *'Shah Khurram Zindabad!'*

Astonished, the imperial troops as well as the retreating rebels echoed the cry again and again.

From the royal howdah, a hand clad in golden armour came out and waved a brief farewell.

***

Meanwhile, Shah Khurram Shahjahan loitered in the vicinity of Fatehpur Sikri and Gwalior, loathe to return to Mandu empty handed.

On 22 March 1623, Emperor Jahangir detached four divisions of cavalry numbering 7000 horses each, under his most able commanders Abdullah Khan Firoz Jung, Lashkar Khan, Fidai Khan, and Asaf Khan to engage prince Khurram at the earliest.

Shahjahan, camping in the vicinity of Mathura, drew his troops together, preparing for battle.

***

The Battle of Bilochpur,
Near Agra.
28 March 1623.
09.30 a.m.

The battle had been raging for the last thirty minutes with both sides resorting to an avalanche of arrows and artillery fire.

The Mughal vanguard was headed by Abdullah Khan Firoz Jung, and the flanks were led by Lashkar Khan and Asaf Khan. The reserve was under the charge of Fidai Khan, who waited a small distance away with his reserve cavalry and infantry.

Shahjahan mounted on his war elephant, Hukum, watched the unfolding battle from atop a small atoll. Hukum, who had been fed on an unusually large dose of opium mixed with his sugarcane and rice this morning, trumpeted frequently and stomped his foot aggressively.

A few minutes later, Raja Vikramaitya signalled for the *harawals* to move forward. As the vanguard marched forward in a blare of trumpets and war drums, the *Kol* or Central Reserve under Saif Khan Barha raised their banners and moved in to fill the gap.

Suddenly, at a signal from Raja Vikramaditya, the front of prince Khurram's echelons parted, and Abdullah Firoz Jung made a swift charge with his ten thousand cavalries straight down the human tunnel, riding right through the formations until he reached the rear of the columns, where he wheeled right to form up with the rebels Left Reserve.

The Mughal commanders were stunned by this treacherous desertion of a valued commander and his ten thousand troops. It was a pre-planned, well-orchestrated desertion.

The battle seemed doomed.

Far in the distance, Shahjahan's smile was wide as he observed this desertion of the Mughal's main commander with his entire troops.

Fidai Khan raced ahead with his reserve forces to bridge the large gap left by Abdullah Khan's treachery. Lashkar Khan and Asaf Khan reined in their horses and tried to marshal their troops into a tight fighting formation.

When the lumbering elephants of Shahjahan's army were less than five hundred yards away, the imperial cavalry charged with bellowing calls of 'Allahu Akbar!' The two armies met in a thunderous, murderous clash of human and animal flesh, of leather and steel. The war elephants high on opium were shrieking and using their metal clad trunks as great destructive booms, flinging men and horses in all directions.

Raja Vikramaditya chose this moment to turn his elephant around. Instantly, there was a sharp cry of pain from the Raja's howdah and then his inert body toppled over the side. A stray bullet from a royal musketeer had pierced his forehead.

For a second it seemed as if the battle froze in time, but the next second was again suffused with the sounds of clashing arms and crying souls.

The battle waged for the next four hours with fluctuating success. However, with the ebb of time the Rajput troops seemed to lose their zeal to fight, grieving at the loss of their Raja.

By early afternoon, the rebel troops were retreating in disarray, and Shahjahan, goaded by his personal bodyguards and Khane Khana, ordered his elephant to be turned around.

Hukum, with his golden howdah and Shahjahan's personal war pennant flying from near his tail, lumbered his way back to the war camp, swaying and leaving little mountains of intestinal debris to mark the debacle.

From the war camp, Shahjahan moved rapidly towards the safety of Mandu, via Rajasthan.

* * *

A week later, when the news of Abdullah Khan's treachery reached emperor Jahangir, he held his head in his hands, and used only one expletive:

'Lanat-ullah!'

* * *

Shahjahan's Camp,
Beawar, 52 *kos* before Udaipur.
10 April 1623
1 p.m. Just after *Zuhr Namaz.*

Prince Khurram Shahjahan wedged the bolster under his arms, and continued to play with the large ruby on his fingers. Arjumand sat by his side, lightly caressing the soles of his feet. Aurangzeb played with a toy cannon by her side

Shahjahan had been unnaturally quiet and reflective on the retreat, seldom meeting his commanders or troops, spending most of his hours in solitude. The focus had been on reaching the relative safety of the Mewar kingdom, where his old friend Raja Karan Singh ruled.

The sentry commander's voice broke the summer afternoon silence.

Shahjahan glanced up wearily. 'What is it, *Yatishbegi?*'

'Your Highness, there is an old sage from Ajmere. He insists that he carries an important message from the Holy Shrine of Hazrat Chishti.'

Shahjahan thought for a moment, then said 'Send him in.'

The screen opened and an old man with long, curly hair and a green turban entered. On his right shoulder he carried a folded blanket, and a wooden staff in hand.

Khurram and the old man stared at each other for long moments. His eyes seemed to have a peculiar glint as they fixed on Shahjahan and then slowly swivelled towards the five-year-old Aurangzeb. Bending slightly, he performed three slow salutations and resettled the blanket on his shoulders.

'My name is Ghulam Jilani Sufiyaan and I carry a message for you.'

Khurram signalled for a rug to be spread for the mendicant, but the Sufi waved it.

His eyes glinting in the summer warmth, he fixed them on Khurram. 'Listen carefully, O Prince, for the name of your ancestors now depends on you. Let go of the doubts which burden you, for they will drag you down.' He pointed towards Aurangzeb, and muttered with slow emphasis, 'Beware of this child, for Treachery marches with him!'

Arjumand looked at Shahjahan in alarm, as the Sufi continued.

'There is the Will of Allah which adorns the Cosmic process—the sun rises and sets, flowers bloom and birds fly, humans procreate only to wither away and die, but the Cosmos does not stop. It answers to the Divine Call and continues to function day after day, for aeons together!

That is Faith. Without Faith there is nothing. Nothing.' He spread his hands for emphasis.

'All Life manifests itself in Faith. It is Faith by which empires are built, deserts crossed and mountains conquered. You are young, Shah Khurram, and your Destiny is to be forged. Mark my words, O Prince, for you shall be tested on the furnace of grief and abject surrender. Lustre is attained not by caresses of silk and muslin, but by the hazardous heat of the forger's furnace, which you must remember when the searing pain seems unbearable.

'Have faith in your Destiny, have faith in yourself, and above all, have faith in God, for no one can destroy a man with faith, not even God, because God *is* Faith!'

As the Sufi abruptly turned to leave, Shahjahan scrambled to offer a purse.

The dervish waved it away. 'I have done my duty. An old man with snow white hair, yellow sunken cheeks, wrinkled brow and a staff in his hand bade me in my dream to convey to you the virtues of faith. My work is done, and I must go.'

He raised his hand in benediction, 'Remember me, child, for I will come again when you are seated on the throne at Agra. Till then, may Allah protect you!'

* * *

CHAPTER 33

SHKAST VE PIRUZI – DOGHALVEYAYE JEDAYINAPAZIR

(Defeat and Victory – The Inseparable Twins)

The Palace of Baz Bahadur,
Mandu Fort.
17 August 1623
11 a.m.

Weary from the long march after the defeat at Bilochpur, travelling through inhospitable and dry terrain of Mewar in the scorching heat of a Rajasthani summer, the miserable prince and his wife Arjumand had spent a few weeks resting in the cool environs of the Gul Mahal set as an island in the midst of Lake Pichola.

With the onset of monsoon in mid-July, prince Khurram had marched from Udaipur to reach the relative safety of Mandu, escaping the pursuing army of prince Pervez and Mahabat Khan.

While crossing the Narmada, a few skirmishes took place with the advance scouts of the imperial army, in which the rebel troops were soundly thrashed. Unfortunately, Rustam Khan, one of the main generals in Shahjahan's army took advantage of the confusion, and joined the imperial troops.

That same night, the artillery of the rebels which was trailing the troops, turned around as darkness fell and trundled back to join prince Pervez's army.

Next morning, when Shahjahan was informed of *Mir-i-Aatish* Barqandaz Khan's defection, he ran out of the tent to see for himself. The artillery positions at the rear wore a desolate look with almost all of his heavy and medium artillery pieces missing. Just a few light cannons, drawn by mules, remained. Shattered, prince Khurram moaned in disbelief and slowly sank to his knees in the slushy field.

Rushing pell mell towards the safety offered by Mandu, Shahjahan and his entourage had just entered the citadel this morning and petrified by the unrelenting chase of prince Pervez and Mahabat Khan, Shahjahan embarked on a deathly, evil plan.

Shahjahan strolled around the Rewa Kund with the ageing Khane Khanan Abdur Rahim, deep in conversation.

Prince Khurram turned around and asked with deep worry lines threading his forehead, 'Khane Khanan, will you be my Hand in this? I ask thee not for my own favours, but in the name of Arsh Ashiyani who would not have let the empire sink in the hands of a wily, ambitious seductress working assiduously to unravel this great empire.'

Khane Khanan lowered his eyes as Khurram spoke again. 'If you feel that what I ask of you is against the interests of the Timurids, then refuse me. If not, then the long march of Babur, the sufferings of Humayun and the tireless work of Shah Akbar would not have been in vain.'

The loyal and veteran general glanced up. His words were firm 'My life is tied to the honour and preservation of the Timurids. As a fatherless child, I was brought up by Arsh Ashiyani as one of his own. What you ask of me will forever taint me with the brush of shame and treachery, but it is a price I am willing to pay. Your honour is my honour; your grief, my own.'

Delighted, Khurram took his palm in his own hand. 'Many a ruse we shall have to play, O Valorous Chief, for the current regime rules by proxy, seduction and misrepresentation.' His smile turned wicked, 'We shall best them at their own!'

They turned at the clatter of hooves. Round the bend of the Rupmati Palace rode a soldier, huddled over the horse's neck. Reining the horse in a shower of mud and pebbles, he flung himself from the saddle and rushed towards the prince.

Panting, his salutations forgotten, the words tumbled out, 'Your Highness, they are coming! They have come!' his mud caked sleeves pointed to the east.

'Easy, boy. Who has come?' Khane Khanan had moved between the rider and the prince.

'*Huzoor*, the Shahi Lashkar has come. They are just a few miles beyond the Narmada, and their advance troops are foraging the nearby villages for supplies.' His eyes were wide with fear.

'You have done well, Sepoy. Get some rest.' The man hobbled away.

Shahjahan's voice was bleak, 'We must leave immediately.'

***

The next morning on 18 August 1623, an embittered, tired and hounded Shahjahan rode out of Mandu with his family, retinue, and troops to find refuge in his old haunt of Burhanpur fort.

However, he did not forget to carry the one million rupees lying at the Mandu Treasury, brought by his faithful servant Salih from Gujarat. Similarly, Kunhar Das, brother of Raja Bikramjit and current Qiladar of Ahmedabad rushed to Khurram's aid, carrying a sword belt worth rupees two lakhs.

Pensive, Khurram looked skywards and thanked Allah for these small mercies.

***

Having been informed that the Burhanpur fort had been taken by a small detachment of Imperialists, Khurram turned towards the impregnable fort of Asirgarh.

It was time now for the cunning and diabolical ruse to be put in action.

***

War camp of Shahjahan,
Two stages from Asirgarh, Deccan.
28 August 1623.
8.22 p.m.

An unarmed, dishevelled Khane Khana Abdur Rahim was roughly pushed in front of prince Khurram.

Shahjahan, crimson with fury, extended a parchment and roared, 'What treachery is this, Khane Khana? Have you no shame?'

Abdur Rahim kept quiet, head bowed. Shahjahan shouted again, 'Read thou this note of betrayal, and tell this court of your miserable deceit.'

Abdur Rahim slowly took out a black scarf from his tunic and wrapped it around his neck, but this silent admission of guilt did not assuage Khurram's temper.

'Read!' he shouted again.

'A hundred eyes watch me, Mahabat Khan, or I would have deserted this camp and joined the illustrious brigade of the Imperials under Shehzade Pervez,' Khane Khana stopped, but was urged to read on with an impatient flick of Khurram's finger.

'I am waiting for an opportune time to rush over to your side, and my eldest son Darab Khan, has also shown his keenness to work once more under the emperor's flag. The rebels are in poor spirits and everyday there are hundreds who are leaving the camp. It is only a matter of time before prince Khurram also succumbs to the destruction of his grand plans.

I might crossover this moonless night; please inform your ferry commanders to expect some deserters over the coming nights.'

Khane Khanan dropped the parchment on the floor and prostrated himself.

Shahjahan exercised prudency in these disturbed climes. His sentencing was short and without rancour.

'You have served the Timurid empire over many decades, and senility does set in when a person passes over sixty winters. So must be the case with you. I am inclined to take a lenient view and will not have you executed, but will hold you in captivity along with your son.'

He turned to the guards 'Take him away.'

***

A few days later, an ecstatic prince Pervez told Mahabat Khan, 'The cracks have begun, Mahabat Khan. One of the strongest pillars of Khurram's army lies shackled with his son!'

***

Central forecourt, Asar Masjid,
Asirgarh Fort,
30 August 1623.
07.30 a.m.

Prince Khurram had led his victorious column inside the Asirgarh fort exactly at ten minutes past seven in the morning, and now stood in the huge central forecourt near the black-stoned Asar Masjid, with his personal bodyguards ranged around him.

Shahjahan watched bleakly as the Mughal fort commander Hissamuddin Khan walked by the side of his horse, followed by his wives, children and a few trusted servants. None of them were permitted to mount in the prince's presence.

Yesterday, as Shahjahan's army had reached the western approach and started climbing the serpentine road, Hassimuddin unnerved at the array of 800 elephants, ten thousand swords and fifteen thousand cavalries of Shahjahan, sent a personal emissary with an offer to surrender the fort. His only request was to be promised a safe passage for himself and his family.

Elated at his first victory, Shahjahan nevertheless kept a stoic façade.

A few nights later, the field commanders assembled in the vaulted hall which served as a temporary hall of audience. Shahjahan's vision was very clear.

'Brave Kings and loyal commanders, let my words first record the tremendous debt of gratitude which I owe to you. You have bled for me, and all of you have lost your close friends and family in the battles that we have been forced to fight. Men of your lands have laid their lives to test the edges of trickery and greed!

'We had a few setbacks in the early stages and retreated. Think of it as the recoil of a dangerous, humongous cannon. It recoils a few feet as it fires; its crash of destruction is heard a few seconds later. We fired; we recoiled; we destroyed!'

His eyes raked the room. 'We have made the first dent in the Mughal shield. This seemingly impregnable fort of Asirgarh fell with only a show of our flags. We shall inflict some more dents.'

'The time to flee is now gone. We will no longer be running like a frightened hare, but shall streak like the hounds to rend imperial bastions and scatter Mughaliya pride. Our purpose is not to mock the imperial banner, but to eliminate the ingrates and the unworthy who lust for the throne, lured by the sorcery of a devil woman.

'Bab-e-Deccan is ours, now we must vanquish the other Mughal Subas of Odisha, Bengal, Bihar and Allahabad, before we set our sights on Agra.' Shahjahan waited for the customary war cries to erupt, instead, there arose a question.

Abdullah Khan's query was pertinent, 'Your Highness, to reach any of the above Subas, we will have to cross Bijapur and Golconda, hence, our first battles will be fought there.'

'No, Abdullah Khan. If we fight them, we shall remain entwined in the Deccan, dissipating our energy and resources. We shall also rake up old enmities which is the last thing we need with the Imperialists breathing down our necks. The Adilshahs and the Qutubshahs shall only be too happy to align with the emperor's forces against us. We shall be doomed.'

He stared at the expectant faces around him. 'We have been assured of safe passage through their territories towards Odisha.'

There were a few heartening smiles at last.

'But first, I must write the next chapter of this play.'

* * *

Camp of Prince Pervez,
Narmada river bank.
02 September 1623.
7 a.m.

Prince Pervez looked with interest at the sealed parchment which bore the unmistakable fine Persian script of Shahjahan. A smile spread across his face as he read the contents.

'Respected brother,

You will grant me the liberty of baring my heart out to you—as Allah is my witness, you can be assured that I carry not the slightest shadow of animosity against our Revered Father and Emperor (may he live long!), but am against that evil circle of false men and women in high circles who surround him. They have just one aim—self-aggrandisement!

It is unfortunate that my protest took the form of an armed rebellion, because my loyalty to the emperor is complete, and I am willing to forfeit my life in his name. As his representative, I repose the same trust and fealty unto you.

I wish to surrender and request that my unworthy acts be pardoned with the same high-minded consideration for which the emperor is known far and wide as the Mir-e-Adl. You carry the same Timurid blood and I am assured that your voice will rise high in seeking clemency for me. Peace with Honour is my aim, all other considerations are secondary.

I await your reply anxiously.
Your loving brother, Khurram.'

'Mahabat, there is regret in the prince's missive. And unconditional surrender.'

'Yes, Your Highness, however, his words have to be backed by deeds. I think it would be prudent to ask him to release Khane Khanan immediately—it does not become a grand courtier to be shackled thus. Also, ask prince Khurram to send Khane Khanan to negotiate for surrender, the current envoy is unfit to handle such a delicate matter.'

'Excellent, Mahabat Khan,' beamed Pervez. He turned to the *Waqia Navees* and dictated an affectionate, cordial reply assuring Shahjahan of the emperor's pardon. It also stipulated that Khurram should stay where he was and send Khane Khanan to negotiate in lieu of Rao Ratan Hada, who was deemed too inexperienced.

***

Prince Khurram's harem.
Camp, near Burhanpur.
03 September 1623.
7.30 p.m.

Prince Khurram Shahjahan knelt in front of a silent Khane Khanan, as begum Arjumand watched the whole scene with sadness. It grieved her to see her proud prince on his knees, begging for relief.

Shahjahan's words were quiet and dignified. 'You embark on this journey a free man, a brave soldier and a great statesman. My honour, and that of my innocent wife and children is in your hands. Your words raised in my favour shall not go unheeded at the Court, for you have always served as the Emperor's Hand.

Place your hand on this Holy Quran and promise that you will never betray me.'

Khane Khanan slowly put his palm on the Holy Quran and whispered, 'I shall never betray you, my Royal Prince.'

Khurram rose and took both of the general's gnarled hands in his own, 'May Allah protect you and your endeavours!'

* * *

That night the camp was agog with camp attendants and harem eunuchs enacting the scene of a kneeling Khurram, begging forgiveness and favours from Abdur Rahim Khane Khanan.

Dejected and saddened at the plight of their prince, several hundred soldiers deserted over the next few days. Few could convince themselves to fight for a prince who grovelled on his knees.

Khane Khanan crossed over the Narmada with a small band of his soldiers, and was met by Mahabat Khan who escorted him to prince Pervez's presence.

Khane Khanan lost no time in throwing himself at the prince's feet and confirming his allegiance to emperor Nuruddin Jahangir.

***

Almost a week later, on the 10th of September, 1623, the rebel war camp shorn of its unnecessary baggage of nonessential humans and articles, unfurled its banners and sped through the lands of Bijapur and Golconda with its remaining eight hundred elephants and fifteen thousand troops.

The Adilshahis of Bijapur made no effort to contain the speeding army of Shahjahan, despite royal requests to engage the rebel troops. After all, prince Khurram still commanded a massive army and elephant corps!

Mohammed Qutub Shah of Golconda responded warmly to the prince's appeal and gave him seventeen lakhs of rupees to defray expenses.

This largesse from an earlier enemy paved the way for Shah Khurram's conquest of Odisha, Bengal and Bihar, who surrendered without a dignified fight.

As Khane Khanan was to so eloquently write in his journal—*'the symbols of Victory and Defeat are but inseparable twins; both a mirage, none permanent!'*

***

The dispirited Ahmed Beg Khan, Governor of Odisha, eventually fled to join his uncle Ibrahim Khan at Dacca.

Soon after, prince Khurram captured Burdwan after a fierce battle, and as Ibrahim Khan marched out of Dacca with a huge imperial army, the two forces met at Rajmahal where the royal troops were defeated and Ibrahim Khan killed in a gruesome hand to hand scuffle with Abdullah Khan.

Dorab Khan was made Subedar of Bengal, and prince Shahjahan veered westward to wrest Bihar from imperial control. Raja Bhima made a lightning charge, and the Patna fort surrendered meekly.

Now, Odisha, Bengal and Bihar were firmly under Shahjahan's control.

Jubilant and reckless after these string of victories, prince Khurram set his sights on capturing Allahabad and Oudh.

The Allahabad campaign was handed over to Abdullah Khan while Darya Khan Afghan was given Oudh to capture.

With these two seats of power under his belt, Shah Khurram Shahjahan dreamt of striking for the jugular—the *Darul Hukumat* at Agra!

The victorious prince lurched forward towards Allahabad, drunk on his recent successes. They were forced to halt near Rohtas Fort as news came of Mahabat Khan and prince Pervez doubling back to blockade the Agra route.

Prince Shahjahan was quick to turn this obstacle into an opportunity. He prepared to attack Rohtas Fort, considered as impregnable as Asirgarh.

Intimidated by Shahjahan's recent string of victories, the Qiledar Sayyed Mubarak sent a missive of surrender imploring prince Khurram 'to neither wield the sword nor the spears.' He came down personally to hand over the fort keys to Shahjahan. He was drafted into the rebel forces with his garrison and the fort put in charge of an old faithful.

Around the middle of March, 1624, Abdullah Khan and Raja Bhima marched towards Allahabad, while Shahjahan took to his flotilla of river boats recently acquired from the Bengal campaign, and sailed up the Ganges to Chausaghat, near Jaunpur.

Abdullah Khan besieged Allahabad fort while setting up his war camp at Jhusi, across the river Ganges, while Raja Bhima positioned his troops five *kos* behind him.

Abdullah Khan's biggest mistake was relying on his new found love for river boats. Instead of setting up a siege around the fort on three sides (as the fourth side faced the confluence of river Jumna and Ganges), he ensconced himself on the opposite bank and used his flotilla to ferry his men across.

Abdullah Khan rammed the fort gates for seven days to no avail. The main fort cannons were sited more on the land exposed sides and could not be made to bear on the boats, however, the lighter cannons started shelling from the third day and claimed some sinkings.

Finally, on the eighth day, as the troops of Abdullah Khan started disembarking on the riverbank, Rustam Khan led a fearsome charge slashing, maiming and killing the unprepared troops. The Imperialists pushed the rebel troops back into the swirling waters of the Ganges, now made more virulent by the combined waters of the tempestuous Jumna. Many were drowned or swept away as the buglers sounded a hasty retreat.

The military contingents of Raja Bhima and Abdullah Khan both retreated to the forests of Kampet, where Shahjahan waited.

* * *

The massive armies of prince Pervez and Mahabat Khan, numbering around fifty thousand, had reached Allahabad fort by early May, 1624. As per sovereign directives received from Empress Nurjahan, they lost no time in crossing the Ganges in pursuit of the rebels.

***

Battle of The Tons,
Near Kampet.
01 June 1624.
07.40 a.m.

Shahjahan rode his horse in tight circles amidst the silent ranks of troops. In spite of being requested, cajoled and pleaded to mount his war elephant as was the custom, Shahjahan insisted on riding his charger *Ghazni* into battle.

His plumed helmet and armour glistened in the morning sun, as he wheeled his horse around. Half standing in the stirrups, he addressed his troops.

'Yo, *Lashkar!* The hour has arrived when courage beckons the brave!' He pointed his sword towards the Mughal army in battle array, far in the distance. 'They are forty thousand as you well know, and we are twelve thousand, but let not the numbers overwhelm you. Numbers are just numbers, and battles are won by hearts of steel and the unyielding sword.'

'Allahu Akbar!' roared the legions.

Khurram rode a few paces to the left. 'Jannat Ashiyani Babur won Hindustan with a handful of soldiers who marched with him from Ferghana. They won it with courage and fortitude and they taunted Death.'

'Allahu Akbar!' roared the troops again.

***

Far away, a grim prince Pervez ordered Mahabat Khan, 'They seem to be preparing for a full- scale battle even with their numerical disadvantage. Send messengers to call forth the ten thousand reserve troops to join the battle now. Merge them into the Left Vanguard.'

Mahabat Khan knew exactly what he would do with the additional forces when the time came.

***

Prince Khurram spurred his horse into a gallop across the front of his leading ranks, his voice hoarse with shouting, 'The battle will not be over till the last Mughal has been slain. This war is for us, and for our release from the tyranny of a conniving court!'

He raised his sword, his voice sharp. 'Death or Glory!' he roared.

'Fateh! Fateh!' thundered the twelve thousand.

With a blare of trumpets, the army rolled forward in a menacing wave. Almost three hundred war elephants lumbered forward from the right and left flanks in a converging arc. This was Khurram's innovation as he had argued that the traditional straight skirmish line of elephants right in front of the massed troops always invited cannon fire, and took a heavy toll of these behemoths as they practically had no room to manoeuvre, and literally plodded head on into devastating cannon fire.

The Imperial army also moved forward in a hesitant spurt, its long front meandering as some squadrons of cavalry galloped ahead while others moved forward in a slow canter.

The sections of archers riding on five hundred elephants at prince Shahjahan's rear, let forth a fusillade of arrows on the advancing Mughal cavalry, killing dozens instantly.

With Raja Bhima holding the Left Van and Abdullah Khan on the Right Van, Shahjahan, commanding the central *harawals* exhorted his cavalry to hold formation and move forward in a tight phalanx.

In a few moments, the earth shook as men, steel and animals clashed in a geyser of rage and ravaged blood. Bodies fell, limbs flew and animals shrieked as steel met steel and humanity broke.

Mahabat Khan riding atop his elephant could see the ten thousand reserve cavalry storming in from the west. He sent a rider rushing to intercept the reserve cavalry and give them fresh orders.

Raja Bhima with his three thousand Rajput braves was forcing his way into the Imperial Right flank. Suddenly, he realised that his left flank was completely exposed as the flanking elephants had already lumbered forward and were trying to wreak havoc amongst the Mughal infantry.

Mahabat signalled for a messenger and asked him to ride immediately to prince Pervez and convey a message. 'Tell him,' commanded Mahabat, 'that as per our decided strategy of yesterday, the full ten thousand reserve has been ordered to engage Raja Bhima. Now, go!'

Raja Bhima saw the mass of enemy cavalry rushing in from the unprotected side and immediately turned his horse around to face them. His five hundred Rajput clansmen who formed his personal bodyguard swung around with him.

The imperial cavalry descended upon them like a swarm of locusts. The Rajputs outnumbered twenty to one, surged into the enemy cavalry with blood curdling cries of 'Jai Bhawani!'

Wielding swords with demonical strength, they cut and hacked till the hordes finally overwhelmed them by sheer numbers, and they started falling. Raja Bhima, caught in a vortex of a dozen imperial soldiers continued to hack with his sword even as he received several wounds from lances and swords.

Prince Khurram, informed of the attack on Raja Bhima immediately rode towards the Left flank with his three thousand cavalries. Rao Rattan Hada and Shujaat Khan with their contingents rushed ahead, but were still a few moments too late.

In the struggling milieu, a lance flew through the air and pierced the neck of Raja Bhima, severing his jugular. With a fountain of blood gushing from his torn throat, the valiant Rajput slowly toppled from his horse and lay still.

Shahjahan arrived just as Raja Bhima was pierced. Slaying, hacking he forced his way through the battling soldiers and reached Raja Bhima. For long moments, Shahjahan sat motionless, aghast at the sudden demise of his closest friend and bravest general. As tears rolled down his cheeks, his horse *Ghazni* neighed in terrible pain and sank on its forelegs.

Shahjahan was nearly unseated and quickly jumped aside. The horse kept neighing and rolled over on its side, legs thrashing. Jutting out from his left eye was the shaft of a long arrow.

Bewildered and nonplussed, Shahjahan stood transfixed by the sight of his slain ally. The imperial troops were coming closer, when suddenly out of the chaos emerged Abdullah Khan on his black charger.

Jumping down, he pulled Shahjahan by the hand and literally manhandled him up into the saddle. Several of Shahjahan's bodyguard ranged themselves around him and used their shields to deflect arrows and spears.

Commandeering another horse, Abdullah Khan galloped after a weeping Shahjahan.

The surviving Rajputs of Mewar, retrieved the body of their slain prince and left the battlefield. They had no reason to fight now.

***

Decimated, a desperate and forlorn Khurram Shahjahan limped slowly back to Rohtas Fort, his army and dreams in tatters.

***

CHAPTER 34

GEROGAN SARNOSHT

(Hostage to Fate)

On the 8th of October, 1624, princess Arjumand Bano gave birth to her eleventh child, prince Murad Baksh.

Fortified by the emboldening prophecy of astrologer Jagannath Rai 'that the newborn prince shall bring good luck to the Mughals, and especially to his father,' Khurram set out to retrieve his treasure and stashed weaponry from Jahangirnagar in Bengal. From the royal family, only the two princes, Dara Shukoh and Aurangzeb accompanied him, as also Begum Arjumand. The others, including the infant Murad Baksh with his wet nurse, were left behind in the comparative safety of Rohtas Fort.

Retracing his path back to the Deccan via Bengal and Odisha, Khurram reached Ahmednagar where he was received warmly by the Nizam Shahi general, Malik Ambar. Putting aside their blood vendetta of a few years back, they joined hands to oust the Mughals from Khurram's old haunt of Burhanpur Fort.

For many months, Khurram besieged the Burhanpur fort but was unable to dislodge Rao Rattan and his garrisoned troops.

There were heavy casualties on both sides, till Khurram realised that it was the wily Deccani general's brilliant strategy to engage Mughals against Mughals and decimate each other.

Late in December of 1625, Khurram decided to lift the siege of Burhanpur and withdrew to Rohangarh.

***

A few months earlier, empress Nurjahan alarmed now by the growing closeness of prince Pervez and Mahabat Khan, and insecure of her own future, contrived to deal another vicious blow.

With the emperor's inebriated consent, she ordered the transfer of Mahabat Khan from Deccan to the far-off Suba of Bengal.

Sometimes, a venomous snake can bite its own tail!

This decision would come to haunt her time and again in the coming years.

***

The Royal Pavilion,
Rohangarh.
06 January 1626.
09.35 a.m.

'Your Highness, Abdullah Khan Firoz Jung seeks your audience.'

Shahjahan nodded.

'Abdullah! What has happened to you?' cried an astonished Shahjahan.

Abdullah Khan dressed in a white ungarnished cloak, and with the green turban of a Sufi mystic wound around his head, bowed low and performed the kornish.

Keeping his eyes lowered, he explained 'Your Royal Highness! This loyal follower of yours, now seeks to be in the service of his Allah.'

'Why this sudden change, Abdullah?' Khurram could not keep the incredulity out of his voice.

'My Liege Lord, these past many months I have been thinking about the futility of my endeavours. I have sought worldly gains which shall not accompany me when I am lowered to my grave. They will not even accompany me on my last journey—what shall walk with me are my good deeds and piety.'

Shahjahan was struck dumb with this new incarnation of a cruel, merciless, and murderous general.

Abdullah looked up, his voice firm 'Your Highness, I would like to take leave of Your Most High and Illustrious Presence, and spend my remaining years in the garb of a dervish.'

'What can I say, my friend?' Shahjahan was utterly at a loss for words.

'Fare thee well is enough for me, Your Highness.'

'Then, fare thee well, my loyal friend.'

Without looking up, Abdullah Khan performed the obeisance and walked backwards, his unshod feet making no sound on the flag stones.

Choking with tears, Shahjahan retired to his chambers, profoundly bewildered.

***

Rohangarh.
24 January 1626.
8.30 p.m.

Arjumand Begum watched with trepidation as Khurram sat with a quill and a parchment on the low divan. For almost two hours he had sat, quill in hand, but had been unable to write more than a few lines.

'My beloved Khurram...May I ask something?'

'Yes.'

'Are you sure of what you are doing? You know that there will be no turning back once this reaches the royal court?'

Shahjahan spun around to face her, his face gaunt and eyes a hollow shell. His words were just as melancholic.

'Turn back to where, Arjumand? The past is just a dream now, of riches, happiness and power gone by. Our present is this—friendless and penniless, dependent on the largesse of those kings who once prostrated in front of me!'

Arjumand could bear it no more. She came and sat beside him, clutching his bony fingers.

'Khurram, my love, forget not that you are still Shah Khurram Shahjahan, the most adept of the lineage and the future of this empire. This is just...'

'Enough, Arjumand!' Khurram interrupted her rudely. 'You know what my father calls me now? Be-daulat! The Wretched One! This is what I am now, and this is what I will remain. Be-daulat!'

Extracting his hand, he began writing.

'In the service of Padshah-i-Hind,
Caliph Of the Faith and Ornament Of the Throne,
Nuruddin Mohammed Salim Jahangir Padshah Ghazi.

Revered father and my Sovereign Emperor,

Unto thine eyes do I render my apologies, and unto thy feet do I repose my Life.

This unworthy son of yours, once your Hand in all matters, lies broken and penniless in exile.

This mind of mine sullied by improper greed, and my body tarnished by my rebellious acts, will wallow in the dust of eternal shame.

I raised my arm against an emperor and father who had nothing but endless love for his unworthy son; Forgetting the comfort of your arm, I sought to wrest happiness away from those very arms!

May Allah rescind that day when I left your illustrious shadow at Lahore and departed for this hellish cauldron of Deccan. If I could travel back in time, revered father, I would unravel every second and plant myself in your arms once again.

But Time has marched on, and I see myself on the brink of familial and financial penury. Because of my mutinous hands, my children have been deprived of their grandfather's love. Murad Baksh is now sixteen months old and toddles around saying, 'Abba, Abba!'

I have made up my mind, Shahenshah-i-Hind, to divest myself of worldly matters and don the garb of a dervish. Give me your permission and blessings to proceed to Mecca and spend my remaining days in the service of Allah, begging forgiveness for my inglorious acts.

I entrust Arjumand and my children unto your care, as also my other begums and attendants who have remained loyal to my despicable self.

I know they shall receive the same glorious love and care which you bestowed upon us.

I know I have offended the Malika-i-Riyasat also, and offer my deepest apologies for all the hurt I have caused to you and the empress.

I await thy permission to don the cowl of a mendicant and proceed to Mecca...

I know you will find it in your heart to forgive this undutiful and wretched son once again.

May your life be long and reign, glorious!

Shahenshah Zindabad!

Your unfortunate son,
Khurram Be-daulat.
24 Januray 1626.

* * *

Rohangarh,
02 March, 1626.
2.15 p.m.

Shahjahan galloped out of the small fort with a small retinue. The news had just reached him that a special messenger had arrived from the royal court carrying a Shahi Farmaan.

The royal messengers had dismounted and stood by their horses. Shahjahan reined in his horse and quickly slid off the saddle.

The senior messenger stepped and extended a sealed satchel with red wax. The stamp of the *Muhr Uzek* was prominently displayed on the front.

Shah Khurram Shahjahan prostrated himself and then with a great show of reverence took the royal scroll and brought it to his forehead thrice, each time kissing it reverentially.

Finally, he unrolled the scroll and quickly read it.

'I accept.'

***

A week later, an eleven-year-old Dara Shukoh and an eight-year-old Aurangzeb were sent as hostages to the imperial court at Lahore. Accompanying them were a handful of attendants and chests of precious jewellery.

At the same time, the forts of Asirgarh and Rohtasgarh were surrendered to Mughal commanders, and came under imperial rule.

Shahjahan, Arjumand, and their remaining children had no place to go. They retired to a small mansion in Nasik.

However, in emperor Jahangir's eyes, Shahjahan still remained a Be-daulat.

Some cuts were too deep to heal.

***

CHAPTER 35

KHIANT DAR JOHALAM

(Treason on the Jhelum)

The Royal Camp,
Right bank of river Jhelum,
22 March 1626.
09.40 a.m.

Mahabat Khan stood at the camp entrance, awaiting permission to call upon the emperor who was now on his way to Kabul from Lahore.

In early January, Mahabat Khan had marched from his Suba of Bengal having emptied the treasury and with nearly a hundred intimidating war elephants seized from Bengal.

Ever since his dismissal from the Deccan, he had been seething with humiliation at the cavalier manner in which his services had been relegated to the shadows. The use-and-throw policy of empress Nurjahan and her crafty brother, Asaf Khan, had gone a bit too far this time, and Mahabat Khan was now determined to salvage his honour, whatever be the cost.

En route, he had recruited several thousand Rajputs from near Ranthambhor and now led a substantial contingent of more than five thousand Rajputs and almost a thousand Afghans.

He was surprised to see Gajpat Khan, Superintendent of the Elephant Stables approaching him.

Abandoning due protocol, the stable keeper addressed the veteran general, 'Mahabat Khan, the emperor does not wish to receive you till you have settled your accounts with all the complainants and handed over the elephants to me.'

Mahabat's eyes blazed with anger. 'This was conveyed directly by the emperor to you?'

Gajpat Khan thought of saying yes, but the fury in the general's eyes restrained him. 'No. The message was given by Asaf Khan.'

'I thought so,' replied Mahabat Khan and wheeled his horse around.

'My Lord Khan,' sneered the Elephant Keeper, 'hand over the Bengal herd to me. For what purpose do you keep elephants when the boat of your life has sunk?'

Mahabat Khan snapped at last. Leaning down, he caught the Elephant Keeper by the scruff of his neck and shook him like a duster.

'One more word out of you, Gajpat Khan, and I will bury my sword in your rectum!'

* * *

The same evening, Nurjahan and Asaf Khan received the report from *Filkhana* Keeper, exaggerated in its violence.

The next morning, on 23 March, Asaf Khan, apprehensive of a reprisal from Mahabat Khan crossed the Jhelum to the other bank taking a majority of the troops and imperial treasure with him. In violation of military protocol, he also took the *Qurkhana* with him, leaving the emperor dangerously unguarded and without the imperial armoury.

A skeleton guard of only two hundred troops remained in the royal camp.

***

Emperor's Royal Camp,
Right bank of river Jhelum.
24 March 1626.
8.15 a.m.

Motamid Khan, the Mir Tozak came out of the ante room upon hearing raised voices outside the tent.

He immediately drew his sword as he saw Mahabat Khan pushing aside the lone sentry, and walking towards the imperial state rooms. Following him were about one hundred Rajputs carrying swords and spears, and leading a horse.

Motamid Khan rushed to intercept, 'Enough, Mahabat Khan! There is no room here for more discourtesy. Stop right here and end your disgraceful behaviour.'

'I need to speak to His Majesty!'

'Stay here. I shall apprise him of your presence.'

Mahabat brusquely pushed him aside, but Motamid Khan held onto him. Mahabat Khan kicked at the door of the emperor's private chamber and a few of his followers started hacking at the makeshift walls.

Mahabat Khan prostrated himself before the emperor and kissed the ground.

'My Emperor and Sovereign Lord, this servant has been forced to take up arms only to save his honour. My honour, integrity and decades of loyal service to Your Majesty has been consigned to flames of infamy by the wily, scheming Asaf Khan.

'If I have taken up arms today, it is only to salvage my honour. If you feel that I have erred grievously, then I throw myself at your feet... have me executed, but save my honour!'

Jahangir's face was red with anger at this unprecedented insult. His hand went to the hilt of his sword, when Mir Mansur Badakshi whispered in Turqi, 'This is not the time, Your Majesty. Bear it with fortitude, and wait for *Allah* to deliver a day of retribution when this faithless fellow shall fall under Your Shadow. Strike then.'

Mahabat, who could not understand Turqi, confronted Mir Mansur. 'What have you whispered in the emperor's ears?'

Mir Mansur looked coldly at the offending general, 'I just told him, that in spite of your transgressions, it is his duty as the *Mir-i-Adl* to hear your grievances.'

Mahabat Khan turned to the emperor and requested, 'Your Majesty, please accompany me to my camp. I do not wish to bathe your royal camp in innocent blood, hence, I request you to mount my horse and proceed, as if going for your usual ride. I wish to avoid violence.'

Jahangir's hand again flew to his sword, but Mir Mansur quietly laid a restraining hand on the emperor's.

Jahangir spoke for the first time, his words cold 'I will only mount my own steed. Get my horse,' he ordered.

Mounting his own stallion and surrounded by Mahabat's renegade Rajput troops, Jahangir rode out. Mahabat, in a feigned act of servility walked with the horse's bridle in his hand, head bowed.

Having gone two arrow flights, Mahabat again turned to Jahangir, 'Your Majesty, it is imperative that the people see you in good fettle—it will save a lot of bloodshed, hence, please mount the elephant.'

The emperor dismounted and climbed upon the elephant. Mahabat's most trusted Rajput lieutenant sat in front of the howdah, while two more Rajputs with drawn swords sat behind him.

Muqarrab Khan, a trusted physician of the emperor pushed his way and tried to climb up. Immediately, he was hit on the forehead by a Rajput's mace.

Blood flowing heavily from his wound, he implored Mahabat Khan, 'Mahabat, you know I am his physician. He needs me at this juncture. Please allow me to travel with him.'

At Mahabat's nod, he was pulled up onto the howdah, and Ghulam Raza Bahadur, the emperor's wine cup bearer, also scampered up the trailing ropes to sit in the crowded howdah.

Mahabat smiled in tolerant familiarity as he saw the wine flask and bejewelled wine cup being carried by Ghulam Raza Bahadur. This would definitely keep the emperor in good humour!

The procession had hardly covered half a kos when Gajpat Khan lumbered up to the emperor's elephant riding a female elephant from the royal stables. While he rode the elephant as a *mahout* would, his adolescent son sat at the back.

Mahabat knew that some of the *khasa* elephants were extremely fast, and could easily outrun normal elephants. Suspicious of a rescue attempt, he ordered his soldiers to kill father and son.

Further on, Jahangir saw a huge congregation of soldiers manning both ends of the bridge. As they came near, a Rajput chief rode out.

'Hiren Singh, hold the bridge at all costs. No one is to cross from either side. Keep two thousand soldiers here, and send the remaining three thousand to man the local ferries and shallow fords. Burn the boats, if necessary.'

The Rajput chief saluted Mahabat with his riding crop and galloped away. A short while later, the procession reached Mahabat's camp where emperor Jahangir was escorted to the general's personal tent.

A few minutes later, an agitated Mahabat Khan entered the tent.

'Your Majesty, you shall have to mount again.'

'What nonsense is this, Mahabat?' asked Jahangir angrily.

'The inconvenience is regretted deeply, Your Majesty. But, ride you must!'

They rode back to the royal camp, where Mahabat with a few of his trusted followers rushed into the empress' tent, only to find it empty. Next, he rushed into prince Shahryar's tent, but that too was empty.

Furious, he caught hold of Chhaju, a young grandson of Shujaat Khan, and in his chagrined state, beheaded him with one swipe of his sword.

He sent an officer to enquire at the bridge if anyone had crossed over in the last one hour. The rider returned shortly.

'Sire, the commander says no one except two eunuchs and a midwife with a small child have crossed over. They have turned back all others.'

Mahabat let out an expletive. The empress was truly a sorceress!

'Burn the damned bridge. The witch has escaped.'

That night, the emperor stayed in his own camp, guarded by over a thousand Rajputs.

***

The Mughal Camp,
Across the Jhelum.
Same evening.
7 p.m.

Empress Nurjahan was red with fury. All the nobles and troop commanders had been summoned, and they now stood like whipped rabbits in front of a furious queen.

She turned to her brother Asaf Khan, 'Are you completely out of your mind, Asaf Khan, to carry the entire troops with you leaving the emperor poorly guarded?'

'I thought since the treasure was being transferred...'

'What use are your few chests of gold and silver, when your emperor is in danger? I see cowardice in you, Asaf Khan, and make no further excuses or I shall forget our family ties and be compelled to execute you for treason!'

There was pin drop silence in the tent. Abu Taleb, the teenage son of Asaf Khan started shivering with fear.

Roused, she berated the assembled nobles in very harsh words. 'Just look at yourselves' she swung her arms around, 'the pride of

Mughaliya Sultanat! Look what your stupidity and carelessness has brought upon the empire... the emperor in chains!'

'Shame be upon all of you for letting your emperor down like this. You stand accused in front of God and man for your careless, negligent handling of the emperor's safety. Generations will laugh at you,' She raged, 'unless you can repair the damage done. Immediately!'

Eyes red with anger and unwept tears, her scathing words echoed, 'Does your shame spur you into doing something? Or, will you just stand here like miserable eunuchs?'

'To arms! To horse!' cried Fidai Khan, drawing his sword.

'To horse, right now!' shouted the chiefs.

'No!' commanded Nurjahan. 'They will be expecting us tonight. We shall attack early tomorrow morning. Draw up plans, Khwaja Abul Hasan.'

'And, you, Fidai Khan. You create a diversion tonight. Take a small party and keep them occupied.'

***

Close to midnight, Fidai Khan with several small squadrons of cavalry kept harassing the rebel troops all night long, feinting attacks from different points on the river bank.

***

Banks of the Jhelum,
25 March 1626.
5 a.m.

Empress Nurjahan led the charge sitting atop her elephant *Buland Hausla*, a behemoth of gigantic proportions. As on most battle occasions, there were two mahouts for any eventuality, and three archers sat behind the empress.

On her lap, she carried her fifteen months old granddaughter, Meher Afroze, and a nursing maid sat opposite her. The entire howdah was encircled by a two feet high metal screen to offer some protection.

From the left bank, the Imperialists waded into the quick flowing waters of Jhelum, and faced immediate difficulties. Ghazi, the Chief Boatman, had erroneously chosen a fording place which had several deep pools and severe undercurrents.

While several horses and infantry were swept away, a major part of the imperial forces did make it to the right bank, where Mahabat's renegade troops stood in battle array. Cunningly, Mahabat had placed his elephants right in front as an effective bulwark against any rapid charges of the enemy.

Asaf Khan and Abul Hasan had found a shallow path to cross, but as they reached mid river, their own troops in front were spiked, lanced and charged at by Mahabat's elephants, pushing them unceremoniously back into the river. Caught in the middle of the disarrayed retreat, their horses recoiled at the swirling wash of fleeing men, horses and elephants, and turned back, snorting and champing at their bits. Weighed down by sodden harness, saddles and accoutrements, the horses barely made it back to the muddy shores.

Motamid Khan, Iradat Khan and a few nobles had stopped in the middle of the river, at a shallow spot and were watching the confused scramble of horses and men in either direction, devoid of any goal.

Jawahar Khan, a trusted eunuch of Nurjahan swam up to Motamid Khan and said, 'The Padshah Begum wants to know if this is the time for delay and procrastination? Strike boldly forward, so that with your resolute advance the enemy may be put to flight.'

Without a word, the field commanders plunged headlong into deeper waters.

Empress Nurjahan's war tusker *Buland Hausla* was treading forward with measured steps in the swirling waters and was more than halfway across, when the Rajputs on the opposite bank identified it as the imperial tusker and sent a fusillade of arrows its way.

Several of the arrows bounced off the iron guards on the elephant's head and trunk, though one pierced his long, flapping ear and swung there like a wind vane.

To everyone's horror, a terrible shriek was heard from the imperial howdah. A terrified Nurjahan had flung herself on top of Shahryar's wailing daughter as an arrow embedded itself into her tiny arm. The three archers were galvanized into action, and crowded into the howdah to form a human shield around the empress. Her maid, in an act of supreme bravado, stood up and showed herself. Immediately, a flight of arrows pierced her bosom and abdomen.

Nurjahan gasped as she saw her maid topple off the seat, and another archer being pierced by an arrow on his jaw. Before she could decide, she felt the huge beast turning and slipping in the heavy current.

Having noticed the empress' distress, Khwaja Abul Hassan urged his horse across the river to her aid, but soon the horse floundered in a deep cleft and went under. Khwaja Abul was also dragged down as his foot caught in the stirrup, and the horse rolled over, caught in the terrible undercurrent.

A few nerve-wracking minutes later, Khwaja's head popped out, clinging to an unharnessed saddle. Several hands pulled him to safety.

Almost eight hundred metres downstream, Fidai Khan with over two hundred of his followers had managed to cross over, and galloped to the royal camp, where they met stiff resistance from the thousand odd Rajputs guarding the kidnapped emperor.

As his followers engaged the rebel soldiers, Fidai Khan with a few close and brave soldiers rushed towards the tent where the emperor was being kept. A strong body of Mahabat's men came out to confront the loyalists, and in the ensuing melee, Fidai Khan shot several arrows into the royal tent, relying on happenstance to slay the Rajput rebels inside.

Emperor Jahangir's face lit up as he heard the fight raging outside. If his troops had reached till here, there was hope yet!

Next moment, as Fidai Khan's arrows fell perilously close to him, and his Sword Keeper Mukhlis Khan jumped in front of him to shield him with his body, a seething emperor exploded.

'Devil take the madman shooting arrows at us!'

Hearing the tumult inside the royal tent, the Rajputs intensified their fight and killed Sayyed Muzaffar and Wazir Beg. The heavily outnumbered Mughal soldiers had to flee the camp and cross the river once again to safety.

With the empress' elephant in retreat, whatever little fight was left in the Mughals vanished.

Hustling, jostling, punching, the Mughal soldiers turned tail and fled. Many were drowned and swept away by the unforgiving Jhelum. Many more lay wounded and dead on the slushy river banks.

Only Motamid Khan and a few chiefs fought on from the Mughal side of the river, keeping the pursuing Rajputs at bay.

Asaf Khan with his son, Abu Taleb, and about two hundred followers immediately set course for Attock fort, to save himself in his jagir.

Fidai Khan fled to Rohtas to be with his sons.

Khwaja Abul Hasan joined Mahabat Khan and swore allegiance to him. He also tried to influence Irdadat Khan and Motamid Khan to change sides.

Meher Afroze, the infant daughter of Shahryar survived, although the scar on her arm stayed forever.

The common soldiers sat silently, nursing their wounds and burying their dead.

***

That same night, empress Nurjahan surrendered to Mahabat Khan with her retinue, and was permitted to join the emperor.

***

CHAPTER 36

SHAH NAYABATI

(The Proxy Emperor)

The Royal Camp,
Jhelum.
30 March 1626.
10.15 p.m.

Emperor Jahangir, for once, had much to teach his beloved Nurjahan. The events of the past one week had somehow invoked the emperor's interest in governance once again, and his eyes had a merry glint.

'My beloved Begum, there is nothing funnier than playing the little rabbit with a snorting Bull! Look at Mahabát, that silly fellow... he thinks he has us under his control, and struts around like a proxy emperor!'

Wide eyed, Nurjahan implored him 'But, Your Majesty, he does hold us captive, and in a way controls us?'

'No, Mehrun...nobody can control the majesty of the Timurids. We can enact subservience to serve a cause, but not for long. You are missing the point here. It is we who are controlling him.'

She looked perplexed.

'Let me explain,' Jahangir said. He picked up his wine cup and swirled the contents.

'You see the wine here, Mehrun? Everybody thinks that I am having twenty cups of wine a day, and am completely sozzled, unable to rule, and led by a wicked, cunning Empress.' He gave a short laugh.

'Nothing could be further from the truth, dearest. Khidmat Parast Khan prepares a special concoction for me using a few squirts of Persian wine and a pint of pomegranate juice mixed with Bitter Gourd extracts to give it the pungency of wine and opium. I have been having this since the day of my capture, and no one is the wiser for it.' A mischievous smile played on his lips.

'Oh, Salim, you are back to your earlier wicked ways!' Nurjahan clung to him.

'Hey! We cannot be seen to be too happy. We are prisoners here, remember?'

'True!' She started weeping in mock misery.

Jahangir turned serious. 'Listen, sweetheart. We have to gain Mahabat's trust by deceiving him.'

'Not us, my lord, just you,' interjected Nurjahan. 'Mahabat Khan is too smart to believe that I will ever trust him, the poisonous snake!'

'Yes, you have a point there. Fine, let me gain his confidence. The drama begins tomorrow.'

Nurjahan sought his lips, 'Just don't get too carried away in your role, Your Majesty!'

Jahangir cupped her breasts and rolled on top of her.

***

The next morning, Jahangir had the chess board spread as Mahabat arrived for his daily visit.

Accepting the general's salutations, Jahangir invited him for a game of chess.

Fifteen minutes into the game, Jahangir moved his horse two and a half paces. 'You know, Mahabat? I am quite enjoying this compulsory vacation.' He looked up, his smile in place.

'Your Majesty, please believe me, I mean you no harm. Whatever I have done is only to uphold my honour and save my life.'

'What has upset you so, Mahabat? If you had a grievance, you should have brought it to me. Our friendship goes back to our childhood, or have you forgotten?'

Mahabat's eyes welled with tears, 'How can I forget our childhood, Your Majesty? I was your shadow in thick and thin.'

'Then what prompted you to insult me like this?'

Mahabat dropped to his knees, 'Your Majesty, the Begum Sahiba and her rogue of a brother, Asaf Khan, are mortal enemies of mine. They not only wish me dead, but hope to disrobe me of my honour and integrity. It would not have come to this pass, Majesty, had they not summoned my son in law, Barkhurdar Khan to court at Lahore, and had him beaten with shoes and maces in full court. And the reason? That I had forgotten to seek your imperial permission for this marriage!'

'Was it not a violation of protocol by you, Mahabat Khan?' The emperor's voice was tetchy.

'It was an unforgivable omission on my part, Majesty, for which I should have been punished. Now, I stand puny and weak in my daughter's eyes, in Barkhurdar's eyes.'

His eyes glinted with malice, 'Now, I have redeemed that insult.'

'Listen, I now do believe that great injustice has been done to you by the empress and her cowardly brother. Nor have I forgotten your loyalty when I was a young prince, shunted by my father.' He beckoned Mahabat closer and whispered, 'Catch hold of Rai Govardhan Surajdhwaj, the Chief Steward of Her Majesty. He knows where all the absconding nobles have hidden their wealth in this camp. I will command him to help you.'

Mahabat looked questioningly at the emperor whose countenance only reflected innocence and pity.

His mind ruined by the possibilities of an easy treasure hunt, he lost the game in a few quick moves.

Over the next two days, he recovered almost a million rupees in gold and silver, aided by Rai Govardhan Surajdhwaj.

***

Forest tract near the river Jhelum.
05 April 1626.
6 a.m.

Nurjahan reined in her horse, and nudged it towards a shallow pool where small clusters of Narcissus grew in wild abandon.

She spoke loudly for the escorting troops of Mahabat Khan to hear her clearly, 'Look at these *Gulaab* growing in such wilderness!'

'Yes, Your Majesty... they are the harbingers of Spring.'

She lowered her head and gritted her teeth, 'Rai Govardhan, are you completely demented? Why did you indicate all the hidden treasures to that thief, Mahabat Khan?'

Rai Govardhan Surajdhwaj was taken aback by her sudden vehemence. 'It was at the direct bidding of the emperor himself, Your Majesty.'

She shook her head in dismay. 'You are a disgrace to your position in the court. Don't you know the emperor magnifies everything? You should have exercised your own intellect, *Munshi*. Now, this thief will use our money to hurt us...' Her voice was jaded as she spoke again, 'I will have to reconsider your post as my munshi once this disgraceful drama is over.'

She kicked her horse into a gallop, leaving her sixty-four-year-old munshi, anguished and hurt.

He cast his eyes to the sky, accusingly. God was a witness to all that he had done for this woman, and this was the cavalier manner in which he was being repaid?

The April sky remained unconcerned.

***

Within a week, the royal camp was en route to its previous destination of Kabul, with the emperor and empress in Mahabat's protective custody.

The two thousand Ahadis of the emperor's personal bodyguard were permitted to follow the camp at a distance of one stage.

Dara Shukoh had found a new playmate in Askaran Rai, a ten-year-old Kayastha scholar of Sanskrit and Persian, whose tales of Ramayana and Mahabaharat fascinated Dara with facets of syncretic beliefs. Aurangzeb, on the other hand, preferred to spend time with hard core Moslem clerics of Islam.

At the same time, Mahabat sent a sizable army under his son, Behroze, to attack the fort at Attock and make prisoners of Asaf Khan and his son, Abu Taleb.

Behroze was also instructed not to kill Asaf Khan or his son, but only to make them prisoners. Mahabat did not want to incite the royals to violence, especially as he was just a nomadic emperor with no capital or fort to call his own.

Asaf Khan in his emaciated state at the under provisioned Attock fort could see the futility of braving a battle, and asked for guarantee of amnesty for the lives of his son and his own.

Being assured of their lives being spared, Asaf Khan surrendered Attock fort and prepared to live a life very different from his earlier one.

Worse was yet to come.

***

Royal Camp outside Attock Fort,
10 April 1626.
11 a.m.

The sentries at the gate withdrew the spiked barriers as Mahabat Khan rode in with Abul Hasan and his son Abu' Taleb walking behind him, tethered to another horse.

That night in a tent far away from the royal enclosure, Asaf Khan and his twenty-six-year-old son, Abu Taleb, were brought in just after dinner.

Mahabat Khan sat on a silver chair, a whip lying close by.

Asaf Khan's bravado had increased in the last few hours, safe in the knowledge that empress Nurjahan was in the near vicinity.

He stood defiantly, shackled but erect, gazing at Mahabat with his heavy-lidded eyes.

'So, Asaf Khan! You ran away like a timid mouse, did you?' Mahabat's words were coated with loathing.

Asaf Khan looked away.

'Oh, the mice roars like a lion only when the empress is around?' taunted the general.

'Mahabat, the empress has dozens like you in her employ, who kiss the ground she walks on,' sneered Asaf. 'Don't let the circumstance fool you into preening yourself like a king.'

Something snapped inside Mahabat Khan. In two quick strides he was in front of Asaf Khan, and with a deft movement removed his leather slippers. Infuriated beyond reason, he thrashed the manacled Asaf Khan with his slippers and as Abu Taleb tried to grab Mahabat's hand, he hit him with slippers too, and felled him with an armour shod elbow to the temple.

Calming down a few moments later, he left the tent, but his cold words lingered, 'What has happened just now, stays in the tent. You talk about this to anyone, just anyone, and I shall not only relieve you of your heads, but,' he pointed towards Abu Taleb, 'I shall bring your beautiful wife to my harem, and give her the son she so desires.'

He looked at their faces, pale with suppressed fury and humiliation.

'Understood?'

Asaf Khan started retching with loathing.

***

The royal train slowly wound its way towards Kabul, with the emperor frequently indulging in his passion for hunting and *qamargahs*. To a lay person, it resembled a normal imperial procession with all its pageantry and articles in place. To a trained eye, the sequestered emperor and his subdued paraphernalia would have been evident.

The domination and ubiquitous presence of Rajput cavalry and soldiers was complete, with the imperial Ahadis reduced to a demoralised, satellite force.

Jahangir, to gain Mahabat's confidence and to relax his vigil, invited him frequently for evening entertainment and games of chess. Frequently, he spoke about their shared past during his governorship of Allahabad or of the trying times during the succession period, lauding him all the time for his loyal and faithful service.

During a game of chess, Jahangir spoke nonchalantly, 'Mahabat, if I were you, I would be extra careful.'

'Why, Your Majesty?' He did not take his eyes off the board.

'Because, Farzand, you did something nasty to my worthless brother-in-law, Asaf Khan, and to his equally worthless son.'

Mahabat looked up in surprise.

'Don't be surprised, Mahabat. Asaf mentioned everything to Begum Mallika of what transpired that night. My purpose in warning you is because Abu Taleb's wife, whom you threatened to impregnate, has publicly vowed to shoot you with her musket at the first opportunity.'

The old general sat back, his brows furrowed.

'Also, Mahabat, the empress does not carry favourable thoughts for you. I hear she has selected some roughnecks from the Ahadis to create a disturbance when you are passing by, and then have you murdered in the stampede.'

'Majesty, thank you for your support. I was waiting for the Empress to do something like this... I just knew that she would not be sitting idly.' He got up quickly and performed the kornish.

'Majesty, thank you once again for covering my back!'

A beaming Jahangir waved him away.

Sure enough, a few days later a spear was thrown at Mahabat Khan as he entered a defile in the surrounding forest, missing him by a few inches.

***

Emperor Jahangir entered Kabul on the 27 June 1626, and under Mahabat Khan's instructions, threw silver and copper coins to the welcoming crowd on the streets.

In the same week, Shahjahan, having been informed of Mahabat Khan's treachery, left Nasik with his remaining eight hundred troops, and moved towards Thatta in Sindh, ostensibly to release his father from the clutches of Mahabat Khan. He was hopeful of raising an army from the recruiting fields of Rajasthan.

***

Kabul,
Mid July, 1626.

Monsoon set in rather late, and the scrubland of Afghanistan started showing some flora, especially over the steppes and the vast, stretching meadows.

The plains next to Shahrara Bagh were green with new grass, and the royal camp was suffused with treacherous forays—each comfortable and blooming in their chosen role.

Nurjahan had been drumming up local support as well as exhorting the imperial commanders and troops to punish the treacherous 'idol worshippers' who had so blatantly usurped the emperor's throne, and who 'now prance around like peacocks with their false plumage.'

'Crows with stolen peacock feathers will never be able to dance, and shall remain crows!' The earthy wisdom delivered in Shamsher Beg's coarse Pakhtun had brought many a smile to the royal's tent.

The Rajput cavalry, inflated with their new found status, decided to acquire the *Shahi Maidan* reserved for the emperor's use, to graze their own horses. A group of Ahadis rode up and remonstrated with them, and soon words came to blows, and then murderous assault with swords and daggers.

The Ahadis, much fewer in number, lost a dozen men and retired to their camp. That evening, Nurjahan listened to their woes and feigning helplessness, asked them to petition Mahabat Khan.

Next morning, Mahabat Khan listened casually to their complaint and promised to look into it. He returned to his tent exulting in the perceived degradation to which he had brought the emperor, and the supremacy of his own force.

Over the next few days, the Ahadis waited for some semblance of punishment to the quarrelsome Rajput troops, but nothing happened.

However, the imperial camp was hard at work.

For the next one week, all muslim clerics and chiefs were secretly exhorting their followers to avenge the infidel's claim on the throne, and free their emperor.

* * *

Deh-i-Murad Khani,
Northern Suburb of Kabul,
27 July 1626.
3.15 p.m.

The imperial troops waited patiently behind houses and gullies of this small hamlet, awaiting the return of a large contingent of Rajput cavalry which had gone for a training exercise in the rugged terrain.

This time, the Ahadis were fully prepared to punish the preening Rajputs for their insolence and temerity in kidnapping the emperor. The bloody altercation of a few days back also simmered within their hearts, and revenge was the current flavour.

Presently, the clatter of a thousand hooves could be heard as the Rajputs rode back along the old Bala Hissar route into the city.

Shujaat Khan, whose teenage nephew Chhaju had been killed by Mahabat was in charge of the ambush. He waited for the cavalry to enter the narrow lanes and defiles within the hamlet, and then fired a musket signalling the beginning of the attack.

Hundreds of Mughal cavalries emerged from both ends of the hamlet, completely hemming in the Rajputs, and matchlocks sited on the narrow lanes started firing into the terrified Rajputs.

Archers and topchis handling miniature metal cannons, hiding behind windows and roof ledges, started shooting into the confused, swirling mass of Mahabat's men.

The rebels, tired after a day's training and most of their ammunition expended, just had swords and lances to defend themselves. The horses, crushed and wheeling in the confined lanes, were careening into each other and rearing with fright.

Sujjan Singh, a Rajput chief, was hit by a musket shot from close range and fell off his horse. Immediately, two young men emerged from a doorway and pulled him inside by his legs. A few moments later, his severed head was thrown into the street only to be squashed by the hooves of a frightened horse.

The massacre carried on unabated for almost twenty-five minutes, till the vanguard of the Rajput troops in a petrified rush broke through the Ahadi echelons. Maimed and beaten, they streamed towards the safety of Mahabat's camp.

An hour later, Mahabat Khan entered the hamlet with a large force. The houses remained shut, and bodies lay everywhere.

An eerie silence prevailed, and some sinister foreboding made Mahabat Khan return to his camp. Late at night, the muster roll showed almost eight hundred Rajputs killed or missing. For Mahabat, the writing was now on the wall.

Over the next two weeks, almost five hundred more Rajputs went missing as the local Kabulis and Hazara tribesmen gleefully abducted them and sold them in the slave markets over the Hindukush.

The remaining Rajput soldiers were unwilling to stay here any longer.

A peremptory order was given to march back towards the safety of Lahore, and on 22 August, 1626, the abducted emperor marched for Lahore.

Empress Nurjahan sent her own secret missives to her loyal commanders, as well as a stern reprimand to Be-daulat Shahjahan to immediately return to Nasik.

Upon receiving the empress' note, there was much rejoicing at Lahore as the nobles prepared to welcome the emperor back. Hoshiar Khan, her trusted eunuch, raised an army of three thousand and rode forward to receive her at the Punjab-Kashmere border.

***

Bank of River Jhelum,
12 September 1626.
Early evening.

The royal procession had reached almost the same place, where six months ago the emperor had been kidnapped by Mahabat Khan.

As per plan, emperor Jahangir sent a Farmaan to Mahabat Khan in his own hand that he wished to review his troops the next morning, and that he should remove his men to a day's march ahead, to avoid any unpleasant incident.

Mahabat understood the significance of the royal command. Not only had he lost more than half his army, but also the respect of his men for loitering around for six months with an emperor in tow, without achieving anything.

Dejected and forlorn, he crossed the Jhelum with his troops and marched through the night, desirous of putting as much distance as he could between the two armies. He knew that neither the emperor nor the empress would leave any stone unturned to execute him, and that pursuit would begin with the new dawn.

To forestall any immediate punitive action, he was careful enough to take Asaf Khan, Abu Taleb and the late prince Daniyal's sons Tahmuras and Hoshang as hostages. As an added surety, he also took Lashkari, son of Mukhlis Khan to dampen his ardour for any foolish, precipitate action.

The next morning, 13 September 1626, saw the fourth Mughal emperor, Nuruddin Mohammed Salim Jahangir again as a free man, hardly a few furlongs away from where he had lost it six months ago.

***

Issued with dire threats of extreme chastisement by empress Nurjahan, Mahabat Khan set free his hostages spread over several weeks, even as he continued to flee towards Thatta.

His mind was made up. He must align himself with the rebel Be-daulat to escape the wretched woman's fury.

***

On 22 September 1626, the aged Abdur Rahim Khane Khana sent his trusted bodyguard, Fahim, carrying a terse letter for prince Shajahan, shorn of honorifics.

'Shah Khurram Shahjahan,
A thousand Salaams and Taslims!

The matter which you had entrusted to me that August night at Mandu fort, shall now mature.

It has taken three years because I could not find the right person to administer the medicine.

A few weeks back, a dancer from Benares who has been with me for more than seven years (I had taken her in when she was orphaned) was found trustworthy enough for the task in hand, and she was sent to prince Pervez as a gift from me.

I have received a short missive that she is administering the medicine frequently now.

You should receive some blue kerchief news from Burhanpur soon.

History will judge me as a habitual turncoat and disloyal courtier, but you know better. I have always done what was right by the Mughal empire. I was your 'Ataliq', and hence, your Guardian for all times.

Remember, whenever your life is in peril, seek the help of the young Guru Hargovind. You shall be pleasantly surprised... The matter is too sensitive and critical to be put on paper.

I am getting on in years, and may not survive the ongoing campaign.

With all my blessings for the royal throne, which you so richly deserve!

Obedient Servant of Sultanat Mughaliya,
Khane Khana Abdul Rahim.'

***

Twenty seven days later, on the 28th of October, 1626, prince Pervez died at Burhanpur of suspected severe colic and stomach cramps. The deadly ruse and evil machinations of Shahjahan and Khane Khanan Abdur Raheem had done its work. Prince Pervez was dead!

***

A small posse of prince Pervez's personal attendants rode swiftly to Lahore with blue kerchiefs tied to their arms.

Almost a month later, as they presented themselves at the royal court, a soft moan escaped emperor Jahangir's lips.

The Deccan attendants stood with heads bowed. No words were needed. The Blue kerchiefs said it all.

The emperor fell violently sick the same day with a severe asthmatic attack, including high fever with acute pain in the bones.

The empire was beginning to unravel.

***

Far away, in the plains near Dilli, an event of enormous historical importance was being played out.

Guru Hargovind's Camp,
A few kos outside of Dilli,
27 March 1626.
11 a.m.

Sant Hargovind looked at the missive from Khane Khanan Abdul Raheem with immense astonishment. He would have taken the contents to be a ruse or a prank had it not been accompanied by a massive escort of nearly a thousand burly Mughal cavalrymen.

Bewildered, he read the parchment again and then studied the gentle cavalry officer standing before him.

The saint chose his words carefully, 'Brother, the learned Khane Khanan has entrusted me with a treasure that is bigger than Imagination itself! I do not know if I can provide the shelter that you so richly deserve, or the comforts that you are used to? Our faiths and way of life are different...'

The cavalry officer interrupted with a smile, 'Your Holiness, pardon my interruption, but, if I may use your own words? Have you not taught us that faiths are just different paths to the Supreme One? You have called me "brother"; I shall try and live up to your trust and credo.'

Seeing the pensive look on Guru Hargovind's face, he spoke again, 'You will not find us wanting, Sire. My comrades and I, will do all that you command.'

The saint looked up sharply as the soldier drew closer and whispered, 'I have no one else, and no other place to go, Sire.'

'Then so be it! Welcome to our fold, brother,' the sage's voice was resolute. 'Let me send a note to Khane Khanan confirming your station here.'

'Respected Sire, Khane Khanan has specially requested that no further communication be done, considering the sensitivity of it. Whom do we trust? With your permission, I shall send two of my sowars to his jagir at Kannauj with a short missive. It will then be sent to him at Deccan with his household news.

'When I left him, I lost the only father I knew.' There was grief in the officer's voice.

Guru Hargovind rose and embraced him. 'We are your family now. I am your father, friend and brother! You shall henceforth be known as Sardar Bhana Singh.'

***

CHAPTER 37

'PARCHAM EMPERATORI RA BARAFFRASHTAN'

('Furl the Imperial Flag!')

In early March, 1627, emperor Jahangir was beset with a severe attack of asthma leading to acute respiratory problems, and the *hukmas* suggested another return to Kashmere to escape the stifling heat of the plains.

Accordingly, the royal court again turned to Kashmere in the middle of March.

Upon reaching Srinagar, prince Shahryar was suddenly infected with Fox's Disease and all the hair on his face and body fell off, including his beard, moustache, eyebrows, and eyelashes. His hideous appearance was a cause of repugnance in the delicate Mughal court, and Nurjahan ordered him to go back to Lahore.

The emperor spent several months recuperating in the cool embrace of Kashmere, but this time his health fluctuated wildly. The old malaise of stomach cramps and low appetite surfaced again.

The emperor became weak, but still, Nurjahan did not forget to relentlessly hunt Mahabat Khan, and a large force under Ani Rai

Singh Dalan and Sipahsalar Khan foraged the routes for Mahabat Khan.

Though they could not catch Mahabat Khan, they came across a convoy carrying Mahabat Khan's treasure from Bengal. The accompanying troops hid themselves in a *serai* and barricaded it, but the imperial troops burnt down the *serai* and plundered the plunder!

Lonely, destitute, and bereft of allies, Mahabat Khan 'The Terrible', was forced to consider an alliance with prince Shahjahan, whom he had so devastatingly pursued and hunted in the recent past.

Mahabat sent a letter seeking forgiveness and promising his allegiance to prince Khurram Shahjahan at Junair, through a trusted adherent.

Khurram received the missive in late August and immediately raised his hands in supplication to Allah. With foes becoming allies, the road to the throne seemed comfortable.

In his own hand, Shahjahan sent a very reassuring letter to the brave veteran commander, promising him full amnesty and a place of high honour in his court, as befitted a celebrated general of the Realm.

Reassured, Mahabat Khan marched forth for Junair via Rajpipla with his cavalry of two thousand.

* * *

Srinagar Fort,
Hari Parbat, Srinagar.
15 September 1627.
11 a.m.

Padshah Begum Nurjahan heard the Khufiya Navees' report with great consternation.

It had never crossed her mind that two avowed enemies, who had sworn to decimate each other, would so easily forget their past enmity and form an alliance.

She ordered Mir Arz to send a strongly worded Farmaan to Nizam Shah at Ahmed Nagar and compel him to put prince Khurram Shahjahan under house arrest at Junair.

On the 08 October 1627, the royal decree reached Ahmed Nagar and its ruler Burhan Nizam Shah III received it at the palace gates with due obeisance and show of honour.

The cryptic words read inside the royal chamber had a vicious touch to it.

Hail Burhan Shah,

The Majesty of the Sultanate Mughaliya wishes eternal prosperity and harmony to your rule.

It has come to our notice that the renegade old general Mahabat Khan, who has turned his face of infamy to the Royal Hand that raised and nurtured him, is on his way from the deserts of Pokhran to Junair, where the ostracised prince Khurram 'Be-daulat' resides.

The merger of two evils will beget a bigger evil, therefore, you are charged to put prince Khurram 'Be-daulat' under house arrest with a heavy contingent of Nizam Shahi troops. Mahabat Khan's movements should also be restricted, if possible.

This matter is expressly charged to you, hence, please ensure that there are no lapses at your end, or we shall be forced to carry reprisals to the extremities.

Hukumat Padshah Begum Nurjahan
15 September 1627.

* * *

Habshi Mahal
Mansion of late Malik Ambar,
Junair.
10 October 1627.
12.30 p.m.

Burhan Nizam Shah III watched as a feeble Shahjahan was helped to his feet by his chief eunuch. Even while offering the *zuhr namaaz*, the prince's weakness was quite evident, and at times his body shook as he bent to touch the ground with his forehead.

They walked slowly towards the forecourt, where the Nizam Shah's retinue waited.

He turned to prince Khurram, 'Your Highness, I hope you understand that the house arrest is being done at the empress' command? I have no enmity with you...'

Prince Khurram took his hand in his own, 'You don't have to say anything, Burhan Shah. I have always cherished your friendship, and am grateful to you for permitting me to stay in this lovely mansion left behind by the late Malik Ambar, revered Vizier of your kingdom.'

'In a way it is better, prince Khurram, that I am tasked with ensuring your imprisonment, where you will feel the elasticity of our long association. It would be much worse if an imperial contingent were to be sent by the empress.'

'Allah has been most kind, my friend. Go in peace!'

'And peace be unto you too, brother!'

About five hundred cavalries of the Nizam Shahi troops surrounded the mansion, and barricaded the exits. The orders were clear—prince Shahjahan was not to be harassed in any way, just his movements outside the mansion were to be curtailed.

***

Before starting the long march again for Lahore, the emperor expressed his desire to hunt once again. Consequently, a hunt was organised for the next day.

***

Bairamkala,
Royal Hunting Ground.
21 October 1627.
11.30 a.m.

Emperor Jahangir rested his matchlock on the lip of a well and waited for the animals to be driven forward by the troops and local people engaged in beating drums, plates and spoons to force the animals towards the emperor.

A lone foot soldier running along the edge of a precipice chasing a deer, lost his footing in panic at the sharp report of the emperor's matchlock, and tumbled over the precipice. The deer, too, injured by the emperor's shot, spun and fell into the depths below.

Jahangir was aghast at the mishap.

Horrified, he lurched to his feet and started running towards the edge. He had hardly run a few yards, when he fell foaming at the mouth and gasping for breath.

As the stewards and soldiers lifted him, his panic-stricken eyes were rolling and small wails were coming, 'I have killed that man, I have killed him! Ya Allah, what have I done? I have killed him!' the sobbing got louder.

That night, time and again the emperor got up from deep sleep, his words slurred but eyes wide with fright, 'the Angel of Death had come for me, but my poor soldier gave his life instead!'

The hakims were worried. Their medicines to sedate the harried emperor seemed to be affecting his cognitive abilities, for Jahangir seemed to be in delirium.

The next morning, a disconsolate emperor called for the dead soldier's mother, who was a part of the field kitchen staff, and gave her a hundred gold coins.

He turned his imploring eyes to his beloved Nurjahan, 'Take me home, Mehrun. Just take me home.'

The royal entourage immediately set forth for Lahore once again.

* * *

The next day, on 22 October 1627, in the far-off dusty land of Junair, the much-feared veteran commander Mahabat Khan entered the city with his two thousand battle hardened Rajput cavalry, and immediately swore allegiance to Shah Khurram Shahjahan.

Bound by shackles of a solemn pledge made to Burhan Shah, the newly infused Mughal ranks did not try to overpower the small Nizam Shahi contingent holding prince Khurram Shahjahan hostage.

***

The Imperial Tent,
Rajauri,
Safar 17, 1037 (28 October 1627).
5 a.m.

Asaf Khan, Fidai Khan, Baqar Khan and others stood around the emperor's bed with bated breath. The prognosis had not been good, and the hakims had already given up, fingering rosaries instead of preparing medicines with their mortar and pestles.

The emperor's eyes were closed, and breathing, laboured. Empress Nurjahan sat by his side, his hand in hers, with her beautiful face set in grieving repose.

Almost ten minutes later, the emperor opened his eyes and beckoned Asaf Khan close to him.

'Fetch me my Holy Qoran, Asaf Khan,' he whispered feebly.

Asaf Khan touched the Holy Qoran to the emperor's forehead. Jahangir whispered again.

'Where is my Dawar Baksh?'

'Here, Jahanpanah!' Dawar Baksh's voice was heavy with grief.

'My dear *Bulaqi,*' Jahangir addressed him by his nickname, 'I have done much wrong to your father and prince Khusrau in my life.' A stray tear rolled down the gaunt cheeks of the dying emperor. 'He was my eldest, and my most beloved, but Destiny drove us apart.' His voice grew faint.

He beckoned Dawar Baksh closer, his voice a hoarse whisper 'I shall try and make good my mistakes, Bulaqi!'

'Don't worry, Jahanpanah. Please get well first.' Prince Dawar Baksh struggled to keep his voice even.

Jahangir shook his head, 'There is not much time left, Bulaqi.'

'Asaf Khan!' cried a tired emperor.

'Your Majesty?'

'Put your hand on the Holy Qoran, and the other on your thigh, and give me your solemn vow, all of you standing here, that prince Dawar Baksh will succeed me as the next Padshah.' His voice almost died.

'I promise, Alampanah! I promise.'

'Good. Now let me rest.'

***

Five hours to noon, the royal procession commenced its journey to Bhimbar, with an eye to reaching Lahore in the shortest possible time.

As they neared Basghar Fort in the foothills, the emperor gave a soft sob and then was still.

Empress Nurjahan screamed. The palanquin was set down and the buglers called the 'Halt.'

A few minutes later, Asaf Khan conferred with the hakims and then instructed the sentry commander.

'Furl the imperial flag. The emperor is no more.'

* * *

CHAPTER 38

MOLKEY RONEMAYI KARD

(The Empress Unveiled)

Bhairon Ka Sthan,
Irchha, One kos west of Walled City,
Lahore.
15 November 1627.
11.25 p.m.

Pundit Ramadeen sat with his back to the cold wall, the sheaf of royal parchments angled to catch the light of the flickering candles. He squinted his eyes, the fine Persian script seeming to blur with the strain.

He read a few lines, then looked up, his old wrinkled face a maelstrom of emotions.

He shuffled the sheets, and peered intently at the flowing hand... it had been so long...

22 October 1627 (11 Safar, 1037)

'The Most Holy Pundit Ramadeen Saheb Janab,

Please extend the honour of accepting a thousand 'taslims' from a daughter of your house!

Thirty winters have passed since I left your doorstep that April morn in 1597, and so much has happened since. At times, I feel as if my heart and Firdaus are still there at the shrine, safe and happy!

I am writing today because darkness again seems to envelop my being, and my future seems consigned to helplessness and despair! The emperor has been grievously ill these past few years, but today, it seems as if Death has become his constant companion... While His Majesty was shooting a deer, a soldier fell off the precipice, for which the emperor blames himself. He insists that he can see the Angel of Death!

When in despair, one turns to their own, hence, my hurried missive to you.

Before I forget! Sire, I am enclosing a Shahi Farmaan carrying the emperor's right palm impression, commanding eternal imperial protection to this shrine of Shree Bhairav. I took the impression, even as he lay insensate, and am happy that as his demise draws near, he will depart having issued an auspicious Royal Decree, if it be his last!

Now, for my story:

You are aware that I was forced to leave the temple and hide in the old Walled City because of Baqar Khan and Mazhar burning down the Shahi Qila during the Navroz celebrations of that year? I found refuge at Laal Haveli near Morchi Darwaza.

As Providence would have it, a close companion of Shehzade Salim saw me in the market, and for a few brief months I was blissfully united with him. Somehow, emperor Akbar got an inkling of our clandestine meetings and regular door to door checking was initiated. We had no option but to relocate.

There were rumours that the old sentry there, Moti, betrayed our secret trysts to a harem eunuch, and it reached the emperor!

For a few months we stayed at the hamlet of Gulyana, near the village of Gujar Khan, till that wretched night of 02 February 1599, when the royal troops took us captive.

And then, on the 18 February 1599, that cursed, ill-omened day, Firdaus was taken away from me. Forever.'

The next few words were a bit smudged, and Pundit Ramadeen moved his thumb over them as if to wipe away her tears.

For the world, I was bricked alive that night in the abandoned garden of Qayamat Khan, four kos south of the Walled City, but the truth is otherwise, revered elder.

The dark skinned and bony Vizier, Sheikh Abu'l Fazl Ibn Allami, found some vestiges of mercy in his heart, and for the first and only time in his life, flouted the emperor's orders. He decided to spare my life!

I was brought to the isolated garden and was kept in the shack meant for the guard commander Mubarak Sarwani and Hamid Gul Afghani. As per the directives of the Vizier, I was hidden in a large travelling trunk, and a Christian girl, Grace, I think was her name, was substituted in my place. She had been abducted the night before from her hut, which was quite far from habitation as she had been ostracised by her relatives for converting to Christianity.

You will remember that the Shahi Qila was completely ruined in the great fire of 1597? The senior Moslem clerics blamed it on emperor Akbar's tolerant attitude of permitting a Church to be built in Lahore, which attracted Allah's ire in retribution, and thence, the great fire. We know it was not Allah's vengeance but the avenging hand of our Baqar Khan and Mazhar!

Anyway, this girl, Grace, was heavily drugged and clothed with the veiled cloak which I was supposed to wear. The heavy gold 'serpench' which Shehzade Salim had gifted to me, was prominently affixed to her chest.

Senseless and blabbering, she was dragged before Sheikh Abu'l Fazl and the Sadr-i-Sudur Bakhtaruddin Khan who were sent to witness and report my burial. The Sheikh managed it such that with a fleeting glance of the dishevelled, senseless woman, she was dragged to be bricked alive in their presence.

The Sheikh also had the heavy serpench given to the Sadr-i-Sudur as the final evidence of 'my enwalling'. The religious head, thus, himself became a witness to my death and burial, never to raise a suspecting finger again.

I spent the night there at the sentry shack, and before dawn rode out dressed as a Mughal sowar with Afghan Mubarak Sarwani to the tiny hamlet of Niaz Baig. There, I was handed over to a tribe of women performers, and over the next two months danced and sang my way to Mathura, near Agra.

I was there for hardly a week, when Rai Govardhan Surajdhwaj, a Kayastha from the neighbouring hamlet of Govardhan came and took me to his house, at Sheikh Abu'l Fazl's express orders.

Almost a year later, I received a short letter from the Sheikh enquiring about my wellbeing. He also mentioned that he could not carry the perfidy of hiding his dishonesty from the emperor, and therefore, covertly conveyed to him that I had been spared, but Firdaus, who was a spitting image of prince Khurram had been executed, as he was a threat to the Timurid throne. He communicated that the emperor was resigned to this fact now, and bore no malice. Maybe, age and wisdom had mellowed him?

Much later, when I moved into the royal quarters as the twenty fifth wife of emperor Salim Jahangir, he showed me the last letter which Arsh Ashiyani Akbar had written to him, just hours before his death. I have read that letter so many times that the words are more or less etched in my mind. He wrote, and I quote, ***"History will remember me as the cruel emperor who had Anarkali walled up, but, know this, son, cruelty was not my speciality. I always nurtured love, never buried it. Believe what you may...Only time will tell!"***

Emperor Jahangir was fond of telling me that before we were reunited in 1606, he always used to speculate on these mystifying words from the dead emperor!

Do you know, Sire, that emperor Jahangir wept like a child when I told him about Sheikh Abu'l Fazl's role in saving me from enwalling that night? He cried, he lamented, and he struck his forehead with his armour-clad wrists berating himself for having the old Sheikh killed near Gwalior by the Bundela roughneck, Bir Singh Deo.

Sire, how I wish that my life had been taken and my precious child, Firdaus' life spared!

History played on, and I continued to lead a semi secluded life in the Kayastha's household. In due course, my benefactor was raised to a high mansab, and now works as my munshi.

After my reunion with emperor Salim Jahangir at Lahore in 1606, events happened at a dramatically fast pace.

To defray the focus from our unfolding romance, Salim Jahangir married Saliha Bano Begum in 1608 and immediately made her the Padshah Begum. But, Sire, if truth be told, his Rajput queen Jagat Gosain (mother of prince Khurram Shahjahan) deserved it more... The emperor said, much later, that it was to keep the Moslem clerics and nobility happy!

The emperor's childhood friend and milk brother, Khubu Qutubuddin Chishti, was made a partner in crime, and sent to Bengal as the Subedar, and I was also sent with him. Close to Bengal, we separated, and Khubu Chishti rode on to Burdwan while I was kept in a small camp in the nearby forests of Damin-i-Koh.

In an orchestrated fight, Mehrunnisa's husband, Sher Afghan, was killed as was Khubu Chishti. At the emperor's order, Sher Afghan's widow Mehrunnisa and infant daughter, Ladlii, were forcibly abducted by the imperial troops and taken back to Agra.

Enroute, as the contingent rested at Burdwan, Mehrunnisa was kept at the house of Haider Malik to complete the ritual of forty days mourning.

I remember that day so well! It was Friday, the 06th of April (9- Dhu-al-Hijja 1015), when we reached the outskirts of the city, early in the morning. I was taken to the house of Ashq Jolaha, a close confidant of Haider Malik, and secured in a room.

Late at night (it must have been past midnight), I was escorted to the house of Malik Ambar and put in a room which was part of his zenanakhana, but completely secluded. I was left with an infant girl of about eighteen months and the lingering perfume of a dead woman.

Early next morning, several maids and attendants were brought into my presence, and I was introduced as Mehrunnisa, the widow of Sher Afghan, and the little girl as Ladlii, my daughter from Sher Afghan. These servants had been sent by Her Highness, Begum Salima Sultana and were implicitly loyal to her.

That day I realised how far my beloved Salim would go to have me by his side. To my discomfort, I also realised how callous he could be of human life in his quest for personal gratification!

The days passed peacefully, with little Ladlii being kept in a semi sedated state with low doses of opium mixed in her food. I think those early days of sedation squashed her vigour and gaiety forever. She has lived her life with me, silent and unhappy at her existence.

On the 15 May 1607, we resumed our march towards Agra, under escort of Islam Khan. Initially, it was difficult to be another woman, and a mother to another's child, but my seclusion and enforced silence gave me enough time to grow into my role.

Around the middle of June, we were about to cross the Ganges into Patna, when near the small hamlet of Shahpur Mircha we met the famed mystic, Pir Shahbaz Hamadan who assured me that I was travelling on a journey of great munificence, and that I would be the Empress! He also mentioned that I was protected by Pirs and Fakirs, which immediately reminded me of the pious fakir at the Three Domed Mosque of Kalanaur, way back in 1596. He had blessed me that my fame as Anarkali will live on for centuries.

Who will believe that from a Kashmiri concubine, Nadira alias Anarkali, I would become the Queen Empress Nurjahan?

The actual testing times were yet to come!

As we crossed the Ganges and settled into the caravanserai at Patna, a group of Uzbeg assassins were sent by Mohammed Shareif, son of Itmaduddaulah, and the elder brother of Mehrunnisa. In these past three months, news had somehow reached them that their Mehrunnisa had been slain, and secretly buried, and they wanted revenge.

By Allah's Will, I was saved that night.

At Agra, the whole family of Mirza Ghiyas Beg Itmaduddaulah was in murderous rebellion, and I can't blame them! Who would tolerate their daughter being murdered like this?

The emperor took harsh steps. Khurram's engagement to Arjumand was deemed void by royal command.

The evil deceit and enormity of its vulgarity went even further...

To bring Khurram under his complete command and to lure him with the possibility of a future marriage to Arjumand, my love obsessed Salim forced him to conjure up a conspiracy of an assassination attempt by prince Khusrau and his supporters. The detritus of this farcical conspiracy was massive; prince Khusrau blinded, Itmaduddaulah imprisoned, his son Shareif, and nephew Nuruddin, executed. All of them innocent of the crime that never happened!

Also executed were prince Khurram's diwan, Khwaja Wais and his sister-in-law, Andaz Bano, as innocent victims of this murderous drama. I did develop a soft corner for my step son Khurram, and found solace in his arms as the emperor continued to be faithful to his golden cup of wine and opium.

Ghiyas Beg's family was then threatened with further punishment, including extermination. Next, they were bribed with the dreams of high mansab, power, and immense wealth. The temptation was too much, and they relented.

A dead daughter was of no use; the trappings of power and money were welcome.

However, I was never welcome at their house, and I, too, preferred it that way.

In a few years, the addiction of money and power beyond calculation, made them the staunchest pillars of my reign.

Their animosity conquered, the emperor still took his time in solemnising the marriage, which happened four years later on 25 March 1611. The emperor kept silent and no official recordings were made in his Tuzuk-e-Jahangiri. Our marriage was mentioned in a terse noting, three years later in 1614, for the first time! The emperor's excuse was always the same—he did not wish to endanger my life or my reputation with public attention.

His words were—'Graze in peace; Only donkeys bray!'

Prince Khurram, as the emperor's devoted son and privy to such confidential acts, reaped the maximum benefits with unprecedented mansabs and titles. No prince, ever, had been titled as Shah or Shahjahan before their reginal coronation! For him, I can say that he truly deserved what he got!

As we started meeting clandestinely in Salima Sultana's royal apartment, the emperor, often in his inebriated state, would call me 'Zehrun'... my actual name before I became Nadira urf Anarkali. To quell the harem gossip, I forced emperor Salim to have a mausoleum built at Lahore, for the persona of Anarkali to lie buried forever.

In my place were buried the disinterred decaying bones of that innocent Christian girl, Grace!

I think I am the only person in this world to be an Empress, while I supposedly lie buried in my mausoleum at Lahore!

Maybe, someone in the future will question the emperor's deafening silence and reticence on a matter so precious to him; maybe someone, someday, will question the abrupt decay and meteoric rise of Ghiyas Beg's family, within a matter of months?

What will history record?

That Anarkali lies buried in Lahore, while she actually ruled as Nurjahan?

Or, that Mehrunnisa, widow of Sher Afghan ruled as empress Nurjahan, while she actually lies buried and decomposed in some paddy field of Bengal?

Or, most fittingly, was it all just a figment of some storyteller's imagination?

The emperor may be dead before this letter reaches you, and I may also be archived in a grave or a prison cell...

So, this is my untold story, Pundit Ramadeen.

The rest is recorded history!

Empress Nurjahan,
Padshah Begum
Sultanat-e-Mughaliya Al-Hind.

Royal Camp: Bairamkala.
22 October 1627.

***

Bhairavi, the younger daughter of Pundit Ramadeen, born mute, gathered the sheaf of papers which seemed to have troubled her beloved father. She marvelled at the fine flowing script bounded by green and gilt edges—it was definitely worth copying.

For the next several days, Bhairavi spent much of her time painstakingly emulating every curve, slant and dot of the empress' missive.

***

Who was to know that many centuries later, this reproduction of an empress' letter, would be the only surviving proof of a secret so astonishing, that it would turn History on its head?

History itself would refuse to believe its own pages!

***

EPILOGUE

'BAR MAZAAR-e-MAA GHAREEBAN...'

('On the Grave of this Poor Stranger...')

The Tomb of Nurjahan,
Shahdara Bagh, Lahore.
06 October 2017
11 a.m.

I stand in front of the two marble cenotaphs in the centre of the huge vaulted room.

There is enough light, even on a wintry Lahore morning when the sun plays truant amongst the clouds, to keep the square sanctum well illuminated. Nurjahan was afraid of the dark, and her sensibilities have been taken care of.

The two graves are almost identical. Nurjahan and her daughter Ladlii Begum lie in silent repose these last four hundred years. Almost.

I wonder at the simplicity and pathos of it—an empress whose identity is now suspect, still giving her imperial protection to an orphaned Ladlii!

Both the graves are nearly identical, with the slate carved on top to indicate a lady of repute. They are placed on a raised square podium.

There are no markings to indicate their identity, and I stand in silent dilemma. To my left, or my right, where lies the enigmatic empress Nurjahan? Or, is it really the prodigal Anarkali playing out her last part in a drama which is centuries old?

A gentle tap on my shoulder, and I turn around.

'What are you looking at so intently, Janab? The marble will melt with your gaze!'

I smile at the toothless old man, whose rheumy eyes are glinting with mirth.

'I know, Chacha. I have travelled from very far, and just thought of spending a few more minutes here,' I reply sheepishly.

'Oh, you are from India?' His sentence is both a statement and a question. 'Yes, your tone is different. Gentler. More *Lakhnavi*.' He becomes more animated now.

'Come, I will show you something.' He takes me by the arm and leads me outside.

As we come out of the central arch, he calls out to a guard sitting under a tamarind tree, and then speaks to me, 'You were wasting your time there, Janab. Those marble slabs are kept there only for cosmetic purposes. She lies below.'

He signals the guard to open the sliding rectangular iron sheet which covers the raised platform just outside the central arch. A small ordinary lock secures such a massive secret!

The guard pushes the iron sheet on its railings, revealing steep, narrow steps descending into a dark pit. Switching on my mobile flash, I follow the old man down the rough narrow steps. There is a wicked curve on the last four steps.

We enter a narrow tunnel, unlighted, which slopes into a central vault. As we near the vault, there is a very low stone doorway, and just before that, my ancient guide stops.

'You see this opening now all bricked up?' He points to my right. 'It leads to Jahangir's tomb. And there,' he points to another walled up opening on the opposite side, 'that leads to Sheikhpura, where the *Hiran Minar* is.'

'Come,' he leads me into the central vault, ducking underneath the low doorway.

He points to a piece of cemented floor, marked with an old chain on iron posts.

'She is buried here.'

I look at the unremarkable unmarked floor, and feel a little disappointed. I was hoping for a statelier accommodation for this magnificent Mughal empress.

'Before that she actually hung from there!'

The words jolt me—I look up in complete bewilderment. I just see two hooks dangling from the plain ceiling, and a crude line sketch of a supposed coffin.

He smiles at my utter incredulity of it all.

'Yes, Sir,' he explains happily. 'Her coffin was hung on chains from the ceiling as she always maintained that she was afraid of being buried in a grave.'

'Then what happened? Why was she buried then?'

'Oh, the Sikhs plundered this tomb during their rule. They threw her bones for the dogs and the wolves. There is nothing buried here. Just nostalgia and stories.'

My head was spinning, but I still asked, 'And what about her daughter, Ladlii Begum, whose grave is by her side upstairs?'

'Oh, that's another hoax! She lies buried at Agra, with her grandfather Itmaduddaulah. Why would she lie with a woman who was the reason for her mother's murder?' He quickly turns and walks away into the underground vaults.

I almost stumble and fall. *Who is this man?*

I turn quickly, and my head bangs against a protruding cornice. Stunned in the dark crypt, I wait for a few minutes.

I rush forward to catch up with him in the uneven, dangerous dark confines of the maze, but he is nowhere to be seen.

Finally, I see a square patch of sunshine in one of the alleys of the crypt and reach the winding steps once again.

As I step out, I stub my toe against a large stone. I look down and see a piece of pink paper carefully placed underneath.

The words are in a fine script ~

'Bar Mazaar-e-Maa Ghareeban
Nay Chiraagh-e- Nay Gulaal;
Nay Par-e-Parwaana Sozad
Nay Sada-e-Aie Bulbuley!'

I again search for the old man to no avail, and finally accost the guard.

The guard reveals nothing—just that the old man appears infrequently every year and sits in the shade of the trees, in silence and solitude, bothering no one.

'Is he an old guide? He seemed to know so much.' I persist.

'Maybe. All we know is that one of his ancestors, Jawahir Khan, was a favourite eunuch of empress Nurjahan.'

'Really? Do you know where he lives?'

He shrugs his shoulders. 'Try the Shah Allami area, most of the eunuchs stay there.'

I look at the paper again, and the meaning becomes clear.

'On the grave of this poor stranger,
There are no candles, no flowers;
Neither any moth's wings are burnt,
Nor do any nightingales sing here!'

***

One woman. An Empress. A Seductress.
Unforgettable, even centuries later!

***

HISTORICAL NOTES

Chapter 1: Prologue — The Lahore Chronicles

Anarkali's mausoleum is actually located at the Lower Mall, Lahore. The whole campus, once the walled garden-mausoleum of a buried enigma, has been converted into the Records Office of the Civil Secretariat, Lahore.

In between the centuries, it was also used as a Church and as the residence of a French Gunnery Officer.

The white sarcophagus still remains, and the inscriptions are very much there.

The ancient temple of Bhairon Ka Sthan at Ichhra, on the outskirts of Lahore, still stands. It really seems to be protected by a Shahi Farmaan.

Lahore continues to be a city of ancient lores, bustling ghosts and royal secrets so many, that it simply boggles your mind!

* * *

Chapter 2 — Silent Were The Birds

It is a matter of recorded fact that for a few years, the Agra Fort was haunted by spirits which were said to be of Akbar's dead children—Fatima Bano, Hassan and Hussain. The ensuing scare was so much that Akbar and his entire court had to relocate to Fatehpur Sikri.

Their spirits are still said to cavort near Babur's Baoli in Agra Fort, and at Akbar's tomb at Sikandra.

It is recorded in the *Tuzuk-e-Jahangiri* that Sheikh Hussain Jami had predicted one hundred days prior to the Coronation, that Jahangir would be enthroned on the 04th of November, 1605. Twelve edicts were proclaimed by emperor Jahangir on his Ascension Day.

It is also a fact that Shah Beg Khan Arghun compared the nobles of Jahangir's court to his pubic hair!

* * *

Chapter 3 — The 13th Decree:

It is an unfortunate fact that emperor Jahangir did reward the murderous Bir Singh Bundela with increased *mansab* and a fief.

A young prince Khurram found this totally loathsome, and vowed to decimate the Bundelas, which he was to ensure during his reign.

* * *

Chapter 4 — The Vizier's Villainous *Nishan:*

It is a matter of historical records that Sheikh Abu'l Fazl was warned by a forest hermit on the 11th of August, 1602, on a forest tract near Antara, District Gwalior.

The very next day, 12th August, he was ambushed and slain by the murderous Bundela chief, Bir Singh Bundela.

It is also true that Raja Birbal had to leave for the Swat Valley campaign, having won the wager against Sheikh Abu'l Fazl, on the roll of a dice in the emperor's presence. He was never to return and his body was never found.

The famous bard, Baiju Bawra, did live in the relevant age and roamed the forests of Bundelkhand in a semi demented state after his adopted son, Gopal, left for Kashmere without even informing Baiju. It is quite possible that Baiju Bawra did meet the ill fated Abu'l Fazl Sheikh Allami on 11th August, 1602, in the forested area of Antara, Bundelkhand.

It is a well hidden fact, but strongly advocated issue about emperor Salim Jahangir not being emperor Akbar's son.

The story has been told in different ways, but, at least three historians have pointed out this fact: H G Keene, E.W. Smith, Syed Mohammed Lateef and P.N. Oak.

As you stand facing Hazrat Salim Chishti's *dargah* at Fatehpur Sikri, there *is a small grave with a marble slab and a stone railing running around it, denoting a royal infant's burial.*

History is deep!

* * *

Chapter 5 — The Salt Of Remorse:

Akbar's promiscuity in his early years is well known. His intimate familiarity with Sheikh Salim Chishti's family is also recorded, and was much resented by his sons and nephews.

Hazrat Salim Chishti did have a son who was Akbar's namesake—Badruddin!

It was Badruddin's new born son who is supposed to have replaced Akbar's still born child as prince Salim (emperor Jahangir), affectionately called *Sheikhu* by his doting father.

It is also true that none of Akbar's children survived, after he had his regent Bairam Khan exiled, and then killed in 1561. The spirits of these firstborns—Fatima, Hassan and Hussain were reported to have played havoc in the Agra Fort, forcing the emperor to move to Fatehpur Sikri.

It was only after the divine intervention of Hazrat Salim Chishti that Akbar's children survived.

Raja Birbal may have been privy to some very private secrets, as it was only his residence which was permitted to be built within the royal enclave of Fatehpur Sikri, lending credence to my spin of prince Salim being a replaced child of the Chishti Family.

It is also glaringly evident how sons of the Chishti clan smothered key posts in large numbers. At the time of Akbar's death in 1605, the *mansabs* allotted to Sheikh Chishti's family was only 3200 *Zats*, which rocketed to 12,500 *Zats* in the very next year under Salim Jahangir's reign (1606).

Interestingly, with the entry of Nurjahan in 1611 and her gradual climb to power and Jahangir's own somnolence and opiated indifference, the Chishtis were again reduced to a mere

5000 *Zats* by 1619. Nurjahan, alias Anarkali, really felt no need to cuddle the unexplainable affection of Jahangir for this family.

She had no inkling of 'the river of milk' which flowed between Salim Jahangir and the Chishti clan.

* * *

Chapter 6 — The Silenced Minstrel:

Prince Khurram did meet Arjumand Bano within the palace at Agra Fort, and it was love at first sight!

Baiju Bawra was not executed, but died sometime between 1610-1612 at Chanderi, Bundelkhand.

Prince Khusrau was promised a lac of rupees and the mansion of Munis Khan by emperor Jahangir, who later reneged on his promises and threw Khusrau under house arrest.

* * *

Chapter 7 — Sheath not your sword, Khusrau!:

Mirza Raja Man Singh of Amer was the maternal uncle of prince Khusrau, and tried to escape to Bengal after Akbar's death, to avoid persecution by Jahangir for his part in instigating Mughal nobles to put Khusrau on the throne.

Jahangir is believed to have his chief Rajput queen, Manbhawati Bai (titled Shah Begum by Akbar) and the mother of prince Khusrau, poisoned at Allahabad Fort. Her clan, the Kachhawa Rajputs, had neither forgotten nor forgiven Jahangir for this heinous crime. Raja Man Singh did incite Khusrau to revolt against his father, Jahangir.

* * *

Chapter 8 — For Kingship knows no Kinship:

Prince Khusrau did abscond from the Agra Fort on 06th April, 1606, ostensibly to visit his grandfather, Akbar's grave at Sikandra.

The route depicted is exactly the same as followed by the fleeing prince.

Emperor Jahangir did send Sheikh Bukhari in pursuit with a large force at midnight, and himself followed in close pursuit at daybreak.

Jahangir had explicitly commanded that no mercy was to be shown to the rebel prince.

Prince Khusrau was joined by about four hundred Badakshis near Mathura, and the confrontation with Dilawar Khan and Abdur Rahim, did happen. Rupees One lac in silver coins of the Mughal Treasury was confiscated by prince Khusrau.

* * *

Chapter 9 — The Princely Seeker:

The fugitive prince Khusrau did seek shelter with Guru Arjan Dev at Tarn Taran. He was gifted with five thousand rupees by the seer and the vermilion caste mark was put on his forehead by the revered sage.

Khusrau did lay siege to the Shahi Qila, Lahore, but was repulsed. He was soundly defeated by the Imperial troops in the Battle of Bhaironwal on 24th April, 1606, and fled with his remaining soldiers.

* * *

Chapter 10 — 'Thou hast wronged me, Chenab!':

Prince Khusrau, after losing at Bhaironwal, fled towards the ferry at Shahpur. His boat got wedged in a sandbank near Gujrewala, where he was captured midstream.

On the 01st of May, 1606, he was presented before his father, Jahangir, at Mirza Kamran's Baradari, near Lahore. He was forced to sit on an elephant, with an eunuch, Reza Bahadur Khan sitting behind him with a drawn sword, and was paraded through a two mile stretch, on either side of which were impaled his followers on wooden spikes. That horrendous scene, and their pitiful cries were to paint his visage for his remaining years.

It was the same eunuch, Reza Bahadur Khan, who assassinated him in early 1622 at Burhanpur Fort.

Abdur Rahim was packed inside the carcass of a donkey, and Hussain Beg inside the hide of an ox, and paraded through Lahore. Rahim survived; Hussain Beg perished.

* * *

Chapter 11 — The cry of the raven:

Guru Arjan Dev was subjected to the most painful of tortures but he never lost his equanimity. Though, he was put in a sand pit allegedly at Jahangir's order, however, Jahangir tried to wash away his guilt by saying that Murtaza Khan exceeded his brief.

Guru Arjan Dev did sent the fruit of a 'bel' and five copper coins to his son, Hargovind, appointing him as the sixth Guru. Bhai Baba Budha Singh did anoint Guru Hargovind as wished by Guru Arjan Dev.

Guru Arjan Dev, with his skin and scalp hanging in simmering streaks walked into the river Ravi, never to be seen again.

* * *

Chapter 12 — *'Degh! Tegh! Fateh!'*

Sant Hargovind, just eleven years old at the time of his anointment, did gird two swords—*Miri and Piri*—one for the Temporal world and the other for the Spiritual world.

His rousing battle cry definitely was *'Degh! Tegh! Fateh!'*

It is now the motto of Sikh Light Infantry in the Indian Army.

* * *

Chapter 13 — The Birth Of Delusions:

If we follow the logical footprint of a disguised Anarkali after her farcical enwalling, the probable meeting place would have to be Lahore, and away from the Shahi Qila. Most probably, Kamran's riverside Baradari, where she had spent many happy days in 1597.

Khubu Chishti (Qutubuddin Chishti) the 'milk brother' of emperor Jahangir was made the Governor of Bengal, and tasked with the murder of Sher Afghan (Ali Quli Khan Istalju). In the fracas, both Khubu Chishti and Sher Afghan were killed.

Sher Afghan's wife, Mehrunnisa, was escorted back to Agra and put under Begum Salima Sultana.

It is quite often referred to that Nurjahan was actually Anarkali, masked by an emperor's decorated history written by compromised court historians. Well known historians, fearful of toppling the apple cart of 'accepted' history, prefer to remain silent.

The gruesome murder of Mehrunnisa, Sher Afghan's widow, and her replacement by an imperial substitute (Anarkali) is an absolutely possible historical secret.

Khwaja Wais Beg was the *Vakil* of prince Khurram. Andaz was a beautiful attendant of Jahangir's harem in recorded history.

On the 02nd of October, 1606, Qutubuddin did depart for Bengal with a sizeable force.

* * *

Chapter 14 — The Dancing Wraiths:

The incident of *'Be-Qaid Fakirs'* and emperor Jahangir is historically correct. Jahangir ate, sang and then wept with them is also correct.

Prince Khurram and Arjumand Bano were engaged on the 28th of March, 1607.

* * *

Chapter 15 — 'With Iron In Our Veins...':

Shah Abbas of Persia did try to take the Kandahar fort surreptitiously by involving the Governor of Heart, Hosayn Khan Shamlu.

It is recorded history that a naked Mughal fort commander, Shah Beg Khan Arghun, danced on the fort ramparts, taunting the Persian archers. He was commonly known as *Chaar Lazeez Khor,* or someone who loved the four things—Cannabis, wine, poshtu and opium!

The Persians withdrew, scared by the mad Mughal commander and his garrison.

After raising Khurram's *mansab* to 8,000 *Zat/* 5000 *Sowars,* and attending his engagement on 28th March, 1607, emperor Jahangir did depart for Kabul on the 30th of March.

* * *

Chapter 16 — The River Of Milk Is Gone Forever:

The slaying of Sher Afghan and Qutubuddin Chishti closely follows the historical event as it must have happened. Almost all the characters, and their roles, are historically correct.

Qamar Sultan was the younger brother of Sher Afghan, and Ladlii was the infant daughter of Sher Afghan and Mehrunnisa.

Mehrunnisa was actually kept for three days in the house of Ashq Jolaha and then spent the customary forty days mourning in the house of Malik Haider. (Ref: Tarikh-i-Kashmir).

It is very possible that Mehrunnisa was murdered during this forty three days period and replaced by Anarkali.

Malik Haider had a special place in the hearts of Jahangir and Nurjahan (Anarkali), as his ancestral village in Kashmir was renamed as Nurpur.

It is also a historical fact that Mehrunnisa/Anarkali stopped at the hermitage of the revered mystic Shahbaz Hamadan at Shahpur Mircha, who foretold her future as an Empress.

Qamar Sultan disappeared from the pages of History.

* * *

Chapter 17 — Shrieks From The Abyss Of Darkness:

The marriage alliance of prince Khurram with Itmadudullah's grand daughter, Arjumand, was used as a bait to get his family into an 'acceptance mode' regarding the identity of Anarkali as Mehrunnisa.

Several historians and courtiers were of the opinion that Jahangir's assassination plot ascribed to prince Khusrau, was just a ploy to blind him and make him permanently unfit for the throne.

It was with the active connivance of father and son; emperor Jahangir and prince Khurram.

It also gave them a chance to show the might of the empire to Itmadudullah's family and make them tow the imperial narrative that it was Mehrunnisa who came back, and Anarkali never ever mentioned. Mirza Ghiyas Beg Itmadudullah was put under house arrest, and his son and nephew, executed.

However, a few historians have conjectured that Nurjahan was indeed Anarkali. (Ref: article by Aamir Butt in The Nation, Pakistan, where it is mentioned that Jahangir kept Anarkali hidden at Kasur near Lahore, and gave her the name of Nurjahan after marrying her in 1611 AD).

Prince Khusrau was blinded by Mahabat Khan by having burning iron skewers passed through his eyes. It did happen on the banks of the river Surkhab.

* * *

Chapter 18 — The Burial Of A Beautiful Dream:

Mehrunnisa, *urf* Anarkali, was put in the service of the erstwhile queen, Begum Salima Sultana, and the harem did thrum with rumours about Mehrunnisa's identity.

The family of Mirza Ghiyas Beg Itmadudullah was alternately bribed and threatened to win their consent and acceptance of Anarkali as their slain daughter, Mehrunnisa.

* * *

Chapter 19 — Let The Storm Pass!:

The Sikh Guru Hargovind and the minstrel Baiju Bawra were imprisoned at Gwalior Fort roughly around the same period.

Some historians have reported covertly about Akbar's promiscuity, and his infamous tryst with a Rajputani princess who put a dagger to his throat is also a part of historical lore!

Queen Jagat Gosain was dark complexioned but with a voluptuous figure.

Jahangir did make his newly wedded wife, Saliha Bano Begum the new *Padshah Begum,* much to the astonishment and chagrin of the imperial harem.

Khwaja Wais beg and Andaz Bano did vanish. Mulla ShukrAllah became the new *Vakil* of prince Khurram.

Prince Khurram was actually tasked with building Anarkali's mausoleum, which he did from his own coffers.

* * *

Chapter 20 — 'Bury The Stubborn Bones!'

With the arrival of Mehrunnisa in the royal harem (1607), Jahangir's affections had strayed away from his other queens, which caused great resentment. Queen Jagat Gosain (Jodha Bai of Jodhpur) was known for her wit and sarcasm, and her Rathore clan of Jodhpur were not enamoured of emperor Jahangir. Their animosity was legendary.

Anarkali's mausoleum is actually a plain building with no high celebratory minarets.

If my twist of 'alternative history' is to be believed, then it would be the Christain girl, Grace's 'stubborn bones' that were buried in the mausoleum!

Prince Khurram's first bride was Hamida Bano, daughter of Mirza Muzaffar Hussain Safavi. In History, she was only known by her sobriquet—Kandahari Begum.

In 1610, a not so young scallawag by the name of Qutub with defective eyes, did masquerade as the blind prince Khusrau, and having raised a ragtag band of gullible followers, was able to capture the Patna fort. He was later driven out and executed.

On the 05th of September, 1610, three Mughal princes—Tahmuras, Hoshang and Baisanghar were forcibly converted to Christianity by emperor Jahangir to forever destroy their hopes of the Mughal throne. However, all three later recanted in 1614.

* * *

Chapter 21 — The Hem Of Freedom:

The sixth Sikh Guru Hargovind was granted freedom on 29th October, 1610, and 52 Indian princes did walk out with him, holding the hem of his specially made gargantuan cloak!

This day is still celebrated as *Bandi-Chor Diwas* by the Sikh community.

Prince Khurram married his first wife, Kandahari Begum (Hamida Bano) on the same day.

* * *

Chapter 22 — The Silent Bells Of Disgrace:

Emperor Jahangir and Mehrunnisa were married at Agra fort on 25th May, 1611. It was deliberately kept a low key affair, as Jahangir did not want to draw attention to this marriage, very strange for the Mughals.

Even stranger is the fact that Mehrunnisa/Nurjahan alias Anarkali find no mention in historical records till 1614, a full three years after their marriage! That too, in a terse one line sentence!

Arjumand had learnt by rote the *Quran Sharif* in this period, and thus, became a *hafiz*.

* * *

Chapter 23 — 'We are born to command by the force of our arms!'

Prince Khurram and Arjumand Bano were married on the 10th of May, 1612, almost a year after Jahangir's wedding with Mehrunnisa.

Khurram did leave for the Mewar campaign on the 26th of December, 1613, with a heavily pregnant Arjumand in tow.

The story of Rana Amar Singh being forced by the Salumbhra chief to fight the Mughals is true, in the fashion told.

Prince Khurram did hold in detention Khane Azam for his insolence and indifference to the Mewar war effort. He was sent back to Ajmere.

* * *

Chapter 24 — 'Mewar, for thee I bleed!'

The Mughal army under prince Khurram met the Mewar troops in a fierce battle at Chavand, 18 *kos* South of Udaipur. The loyal Bhils fought alongside the Mewaris in gruesome close combat. The Mughals were repulsed.

Khurram then declared a 'scorched earth policy' by burning crops, villages, livestock and poisoning wells.

To save the general populace from starvation and poisoning, Rana Amar Singh agreed to conditional subjugation and sent his son Karan Singh as a hostage to the Mughal Court.

In time, Kunwar Karan Singh (later Rana) became a close friend and ally of Shah Khurram Shahjahan.

* * *

Chapter 25 — The Exalted Flower Of This Royal Garden:

Prince Dara Shukoh was born on March 29th, 1615, at Ajmere.

Emperor Jahangir did taunt prince Khurram upon his abstinence from wine on the 04th of January, 1616, the eve of Khurram's twenty fourth birthday.

The incestuous relationship between prince Khurram and his stepmother, Nurjahan, is hinted upon by several historians, both Mughal and European.

By this time, emperor Jahangir had become weak due to opium and wine and lost his vigour. The ambition for power and lust for pleasures of the flesh brought Nurjahan and prince Khurram closer than societal norms permitted.

The Nurjahan Caucus comprising Nurjahan, prince Khurram, her father Itmaduddaulah and brother Asaf Khan were to influence Mughal politics for the next few years.

The coming months and years were a witness to the slow poisoning of an opium ridden emperor, and his declining health.

* * *

Chapter 26 — The False and Decorative Victory:

In the middle of August, 1616, prince Khurram and Asaf Khan with the active connivance of Begum Nurjahan did try to wrest prince Khusrau away from the protective custody of Anup Rai Singh Dalan, the brave warrior who had once felled a lion with a single blow to save emperor Jahangir. Anup Rai refused to give custody citing emperor's orders.

The wrestling and fisticuffs between emperor Jahangir and Nurjahan did happen in the manner depicted. It is recorded in many historical documents.

Prince Khurram was bestowed with the title of Shah Sultan Khurram on the 10th of November, 1616, before leaving for the Deccan campaign.

Shah Sultan Khurram did marry Izz-Ul-Nisa begum on the 02nd of September, 1617, and a daughter, Roshanara, was born to Mumtaz Mahal the same day. Both proved inauspicious for prince Khurram.

After his Deccan victory, which the English derided as 'false and decorative,' *Shah Sultan Khurram* was given the awe inspiring title of *Shahjahan*—on 11th October, 1617. This was unprecedented in Mughal history.

Prince Khurram Shahjahan's growing influence and power deeply unnerved Nurjahan, and this was the beginning of their rift.

* * *

Chapter 27 — The Rotten Bones Of A Rotten King:

Emperor Jahangir did kick and order the destruction of Nasiruddin Shah's grave, and commanded for the bones to be thrown into the Narmada.

Nasiruddin was an intemperate and nasty fellow who murdered his own father. He was addicted to mercury and used to spend many hours in the tank to cool off.

Mumtaz and prince Khurram Shahjahan did find the white marble tomb of Hoshang Shah at Mandu to be marvelous, and an inspiration for a similar mausoleum. Maybe, the Taj Mahal? But, that's another story!

Incestuous sex between Nurjahan and her step son, Khurram Shahjahan, has already been explored before, and is historically indicated.

Mumtaz Mahal never really had any love lost for her paternal aunt, Nurjahan, and openly despised her. Maybe, she was Anarkali after all!

In 1618, both emperor Jahangir and prince Khurram Shahjahan had fallen violently sick, and poisoning was discerned to be the cause.

* * *

Chapter 28 — 'The Shehzade's Fame Will Arise From His Sorrows!'

The prophesy by a village oracle, Nalini, about Aurangzeb's destructive effect on his father, Shahjahan, is chronicled in history. Refer—Aurangzeb, by Muni Lal.

On the night of Aurangzeb's birth, 04th November, 1618, a comet did fall near the royal camp. Jahangir had a sword fashioned out of the molten substances. Since the comet was streaking from west to east, it was considered to be highly inauspicious.

History proved it so.

Agra was consumed by plague in late 1618 and early 1619, and the royal entourage entered it only on 19th April, 1619.

Jodha Bai (queen Jagat Gosain), mother of prince Khurram Shahjahan had died just a day before, on 18th April, 1619.

Nurjahan did try to tempt the blind prince Khusrau, eldest son of Jahangir, into marrying her daughter, Ladlii, promising freedom to an incarcerated prince Khusrau. He refused.

* * *

Chapter 29 — Deccan - The Murderous Cauldron:

Saliha Bano Begum, Padshah Begum since 1608, and died under mysterious circumstances on 10th June, 1620. Thereafter, Nurjahan became the Padshah Begum.

The custody of prince Khusrau was given to prince Khurram Shahjahan at his insistence, and they left for Deccan on 13th January, 1621.

Emperor Jahangir was destined never to see his two sons again.

Sher Afghan and Nurjahan's daughter, Ladlii, did marry Shahryar, the younger brother of prince Khurram.

A blind and defenseless prince Khusrau was brutally murdered in his cell at Burhanpur fort on the night of 26th February, 1622. Ghulam Reza Bahadur was the assassin, and he was garroted to death. It was at the behest of prince Khurram.

It is also a historical fact that prince Khurram Shahjahan's two year old son, Umeed Baksh, died the same night.

Such is Divine Justice.

The spirit of a blind prince Khusrau still roams the Burhanpur fort, colliding with ancient walls and falling down stony steps, as he flees in blind abandon from his murderers.

* * *

Chapter 30 — 'BE-DAULAT!'

Nobody at the royal court, including emperor Jahangir believed the spurious report sent by prince Shahjahan, implying that Khusrau had died because of severe Colitis.

To break Shahjahan's stranglehold on the Deccan, and to weaken and punish him, he was ordered to proceed to Kandahar on the war campaign.

The Moslem sage Mir Faiz- Ul Baqi did warn prince Khurram Shahjahan not to proceed beyond Mandu.

For his intransigence, and ambitious demands, prince Khurram Shahjahan was called 'Be-Daulat' or 'The Wretch' by emperor Jahangir. Till his death in October, 1627, emperor Jahangir always referred to Khurram as 'Be-Daulat!'

The body of prince Khusrau was exhumed from Burhanpur and buried beside his mother at Khusrau Bagh, Allahabad. It is just across the city side of Allahabad Railway Junction.

* * *

Chapter 31 — The Blood Drenched Guavas:

The fracas between troops of prince Shahryar and prince Khurram Shahjahan did take place at Dholpur, and Shahryar's garrison commander Sharif-Ul-Mulk was severely injured amongst others. The Dholpur fort was taken over by prince Khurram's troops led by Darab Khan.

It is also a strange and supernatural fact that a prince was born to Shahjahan and Mumtaz Mahal on 26th November, 1622, *exactly* nine months after prince Khusrau's murder. It lived for just a few minutes.

This event sent shock waves throughout the royal retinue at Mandu, and the specter of a doomed prince Khusrau was to haunt Mumtaz Mahal and prince Shahjahan forever.

It is a fact that even today, four centuries hence, the famed guavas of Khusrau Bagh at Allahabad, where prince Khusrau lies buried, carry blood stained flecks on their inside.

Believe it or not!

* * *

Chapter 32 — For Treachery Marches With Him!

The rebellion of prince Khurram Shahjahan against his father and emperor, Jahangir, started in January 1623 from Mandu fort.

Prince Khurram actually did lay siege to the Agra fort and then retreated without attacking, stung by a sense of remorse at the prospect of destroying a fort which held so many happy memories for him. His magnanimity was much lauded even by the besieged defenders.

In the Battle Of Bilochpur, the Mughal commander, Abdullah Firoz Jung did desert the imperial army and joined the rebel army of prince Khurram with his ten thousand troops. However, prince Khurram was defeated.

While fleeing to Mewar to be in the protection of Rana Karan Singh, his childhood friend, he was visited by the mystic Ghulam Jilani Sufiyaan, who did tell him to believe in his Destiny, and that he had been commanded in his dream by an old sage to convey this message to prince Khurram.

* * *

Chapter 33 — Defeat & Victory - The Inseparable Twins:

On the 18th of August, 1623, prince Khurram Shahjahan had to flee from Mandu fort, fearing a siege by the Imperial Army.

Khane Khanan Abdur Rahim was punished for writing a treasonable letter and was imprisoned.

Prince Khurram did write to the pursuing prince Pervez, seeking forgiveness from the emperor for his rebellion, and Khane Khanan was sent to the imperial war camp, where he immediately deserted prince Khurram and joined the royal army under prince Pervez.

The diabolical ruse is my own spin of how history might have played out behind the scenes. Many historians have hinted that prince Pervez was poisoned by an insider planted by prince Khurram.

Prince Khurram won Odisha, Bihar and Bengal in quick succession, but was soundly defeated at the Battle Of The Tons, near Allahabad on 01st June, 1624.

Defeated, derelict and forlorn, prince Khurram limped back to the safety of Rohtas fort, Bihar.

* * *

Chapter 34 — Hostage To Fate:

Emboldened once again, prince Khurram marched towards Deccan and laid siege to Burhanpur fort in mid 1625. He was unable to dislodge the Imperial army and after heavy casualties on both sides, decided to lift the siege, and moved to Rohangarh.

Around this time, Empress Nurjahan made a critical mistake by removing Mahabat Khan from Deccan and posting him to Bengal.

From the fort of Rohangarh, a dejected and weary prince Shahajahan wrote a *parwana* to the emperor seeking unconditional surrender and forgiveness.

Emperor Jahangir accepted his surrender and ordered him to vacate the fort of Rohangarh and retire to a small mansion near Nasik.

Princes Dara Shukoh (11 years old) and Aurangzeb (08 years old)were sent to the royal court as hostages. Shah Shuja was already with the empress since his infancy. Only the toddler, prince Murad Baksh, was left with Mumtaz Mahal and prince Shahjahan.

The rout was complete.

* * *

Chapter 35 — Treason On The Jhelum:

Emperor Jahangir was kidnapped from the banks of the Jhelum on 24th March, 1626, by the Mughal general Mahabat Khan, who was a childhood friend of the emperor. However, Mahabat Khan had a deep loathing for Nurjahan and held her responsible for his days in the fringes of the Grand Empire. It is true that he was not given a raise in his *mansab* for over twelve years, though he was the bravest and the most able of all generals. The final straw was the beating of his son in law, Barkhurdar Khan, in the royal court with shoes and sticks for a minor lapse, which was not even his fault.

The kidnapping and the failed rescue attempt by Nurjahan are culled from historical records and closely follows the event as it would have happened four hundred years ago.

* * *

Chapter 36 — The Proxy Emperor

With a little prodding from emperor Jahangir and the veiled connivance of Nurjahan, Mahabat Khan was able to recover almost a million rupees worth of gold and jewelry, with the help of the Empress' *munshi*, Rai Govardhan Surajdhwaj.

It is a mystery why Mahabat Khan meandered for six months in the north west provinces with an emperor and empress in tow?

During this period, both empress Nurjahan and Mahabat Khan tried to have each other assassinated, unsuccessfully.

All this while, Nurjahan was assiduously sending missives to Mughal garrisons to come and free their emperor.

The beginning of the end was really the fight between Mahabat's troops and royal cavalry over some pasture land. Later, there was a full scale attack by the royal cavalry on Mahabat's troops, killing more than 800 of his men.

This effectively ended the kidnapping of emperor Jahangir as Mahabat Khan continued to flee towards Thatta.

On 28th October, 1626, exactly one year before emperor Jahangir's death, prince Pervez
died at Burhanpur of severe Colitis. The actual cause was poisoning, and several historians have alluded to prince Khurram Shahajahan being the culprit.

* * *

Chapter 37 — Furl The Imperial Flag:

Prince Shahryar was indeed struck with Fox's Disease, a form of leprosy, and lost all the hair on his body, almost like a peeled onion.

Prince Khurram welcomed Mahabat Khan into his fold at Junair, forgiving his deadly trespasses of the past. They became close allies thereafter.

Prince Khurram was put under house arrest at Junair by Burhan Nizam Shah III under directives from empress Nurjahan. He was given the mansion of Malik Ambar, which is even today known as 'Habshi Mahal.' I have been to this ruined mansion, which is hardly four kilometres away from the Shivneri fort in Junair.

Jahangir did accidentally kill a soldier while hunting for deer on 21st October, 1627, and it seemed to cast a death spell on him.

He died a week later.

Some historians have given a very vivid description of Jahangir's dying moments, and have corroborated the fact that it was his dying wish to have prince Dawar Baksh (Khusrau's eldest son) succeed him on the throne—his penance for all the atrocities committed on prince Khusrau.

* * *

Chapter 38 — The Empress Unveiled:

Several historians have nudged around the fact that Nurjahan was actually Anarkali.

Emperor Jahangir's utter silence on this matter in his *Tuzuk-i-Jahangiri* is again mystifying, especially since he recorded even the most trivial of observations. How could a matter of such import be neglected, unless there was a malignant reason?

The sacred temple of Bhairon Ka Sthan at Ichhra, Lahore, does seem to be protected by a Royal Warrant. Even today, it stands unmolested while most of the temples have been demolished in Pakistan.

This chapter is my way of reconstructing History as it may have happened four hundred years ago.

Much of it would have been true if recorded accurately by the *khufiya navees* of that era.

Maybe, I have walked you down the hidden chapters of History?

* * *

Chapter 39 — Epilogue - 'On The Grave Of This Poor Stranger...'

The tomb of Nurjahan at Shahdara Bagh, Lahore, is exactly as described.

She died a lonely widow, exiled to the fringes of the Realm, where she tended to the destitutes and to her fading memories of an imperial past.

Jawahir, her favourite eunuch and attendant, was privy to all her secrets, but, that's another story!

The epitaph in four lines of Persian accurately sums up her parting sentiments.

"On the grave of this poor stranger,
There are no candles, no flowers;
Neither any moth's wings are burnt,
Nor do any nightingales sing here!"

*****

GLOSSARY

1. Aalim – Learned Moslem priests
2. Aameen – Amen
3. Aasi – Criminal
4. Aghori – Hindu ascetic
5. Ahadis – Royal guards
6. Alampanah – Refuge of the Universe
7. Allahu Akbar – Allah is great!
8. Androoni Sheher – Walled City of Lahore
9. Argajah – Fragrance favoured by Mughals
10. Arrack – Opiate
11. Arsh Ashiyani – Residing in Heaven
12. Asir Namaaz – Late afternoon namaaz
13. Atagha – Guardian
14. Ba-adab Ba - Mulaizah, Hoshiar – The call to be respectful
15. Bagicha – Garden
16. Bandooqchis – Matchlock men
17. Baradari – Building open on all sides
18. Barangars – Right wing of army
19. Barasingha – 12 horned deer
20. Barchis – Spears
21. Behroopiya – Indian folk artists who impersonate in different forms

22. Bewafai – Treachery
23. Bishtis – Water bearers
24. Burj – Tower
25. Chaar Taslim – Form of obeisance
26. Charbagh – Four square gardens
27. Charpoy – String bed
28. Cheetah – Indian Leopard
29. Chogah – Male outer wear, loosely worn
30. Daftarkhana – Office
31. Dak – Post
32. Dak Chowki – Mail Post/ Also for relay horses
33. Dams – Monetary units (40 dams made one rupee)
34. Daroghas – Inspectors
35. Dastarkhwan – Feast
36. Dharma – Religion
37. Diwan-e-Khas – Hall of Private Audience
38. Diwan-e-Aam – Hall of Public Audience
39. Diyas – Small earthen lamps
40. Djinns – Ghosts, spirits
41. Emperor Echebar – Emperor Akbar
42. Faateha-e-Janaza – Funeral Prayers
43. Fakir – Moslem ascetic
44. Farman-i-Sabtis – A form of Imperial Order
45. Farzand – Son
46. Fath-ul-Mulk – Humayun's sword: Victor of the Realm
47. Faujdar – Head of a Garrison
48. Firangis – Foreigners
49. Firmaan – Imperial Request
50. Gurj – Mace
51. Hakim – Physician

52. Hamam – Royal Bath
53. Harkaras – Drum beaters during hunting
54. Hathi Paer – Elephant's Walk (P ath in Shahi Qila, Lahore)
55. Haveli – Mansion
56. Hijri – Moslem Year
57. Howdahs – Seat on an elephant's back
58. Hulqa – Inferior Elephant
59. Huzoor – Sire
60. Illahi – Year set by Akbar
61. Janab-e-Auliya – A form of respectful address
62. Jaranghars – Left wing of army
63. Jharokhas – Protruding balconies
64. Jharshahi – Five coloured flag, also known as "Panchrangi."
65. Jinsi Muamalaat – Matters of sex
66. Khadims – Servants, attendants
67. Khamagami – Greetings in rajasthani
68. Khasa cadre – Elite cadre
69. Khidmatgaars – attendants
70. Khutba – The prayers read proclaiming Emperor's rule
71. Khwajasera – Chief Eunuch
72. Koh-e-Ilm – Mountain of Knowledge
73. Kornish – Form of obeisance
74. Kos – 3.66 kms
75. Kutub Khana – Library
76. Langurs – Indian monkeys
77. Magreeb Namaz – Evening prayers
78. Mahouts – Elephant drivers
79. Makhdum-ul-Mulk – High Priest
80. Malechh – Unclean person
81. Mansabdars – Nobles

82. Markhor Goat – Goat of enormous size; now extinct
83. Masha-Allah – Praise to Allah
84. Mir Arz – Chief of plaints
85. Mir Bahri – Admiral of the fleet
86. Mir Bakarwal – Head of the Kitchen
87. Mir Bakshi – Head of Army and war material
88. Mir Kutub – Chief Librarian
89. Mir Manzil – Master of Road Journeys
90. Mir Saman – Chief of Imperial Furniture and Estate
91. Mir Tozak – Chief of Protocol
92. Mohurs – Gold coins
93. MuhrUzek – The Royal Seal
94. Muns – 1 Mun =40 kilos
95. Mureed – Disciple
96. Mushrif – Clerk
97. Naggara-i-Shadiyana – Drums of Celebrations
98. Naggaras – War drums
99. Naubatkhana – Portal above the main gate for musicians
100. Nilgai – Blue Bull
101. Nishaan – Imperial Letter/ Royal Order
102. Padshah Ghazi – Emperor
103. Panchrangi – Five Coloured
104. Panjari – Sailor
105. Parvankhs – Royal Orders
106. Peregrims Cave' – Traveller Beware!
107. Pethas – Famous sugary sweets of Agra
108. Poshtu – Drink made of Opium
109. Qaba – Cloak like attire for men
110. Qamargah – Form of hunting
111. Qarawal Baigi – Chief of Hunt

112. Qarawals – Skirmishers
113. Qol – Centre of the army
114. Qorchis – Royal attendants normally of Persian origin
115. Qubbedar – Persian conical head wear
116. Sadr-i-Sudur – Head of Religion
117. Sahiban-i-Ihtemam – Mace bearers tasked with path clearance
118. Salat-al-Janaza – Funeral prayers
119. Sehr – Dawn
120. Serpench – Aigrette
121. Shahajida – Male outer wear
122. ShahiFirmaans – Royal Orders
123. ShahiKotwal – Chief of Police
124. ShahiQur – Emperor's personal arms bearer
125. Shama-i-Kafuri – Lamps almost 3 yards high and with multiple wicks
126. ShastKhatt – Male outer attire
127. Shi' ar-o-ture-yi-Chugatai – Code of Chugatais
128. Shikargah – Hunting lodge
129. Shikaris - Hunters
130. Sowars – Horse riders, cavalry
131. Suba – Province
132. Subedar – Governor of a province (Suba)
133. Sultanat Mughaliya – Padshah Ghazi, Zillu' Illah, Imam -i-Adil- Empire of the Mughals, Emperor, Shadow of God and Chief Justice
134. Syce – Horse attendant
135. Takhliya – Dismiss
136. Tapancha – Reserve Elephant
137. Tarahs – Reserves of the troop

138. Taslim – Form of obeisance
139. Tasliq-i-Qar – Guard of Honour
140. Tir-Andaz – Archers
141. Topchis – Cannoneers
142. Toshkhana – Treasury
143. Tribeni – Confluence of 3 rivers - Ganga, Jumna, and mythical Saraswati at Allahabad (Illahabas)
144. Ulemas – Moslem Priests
145. Umeras – Nobles
146. Ustaad – Master, expert
147. Vakil – Senior representative
148. Waqia Navees – writer; recorder of facts
149. Zamindoz – form of obeisance by the upturned palms on the floor
150. Zat – Rank
151. Zenankhana – Harem
152. Zille' Illahi – Shadow of God
153. Zuhr Namaz – Namaz at noon

BIBLIOGRAPHY

THE JHELUM BETRAYAL

1. The Emperor Akbar – Ferdinand Augustus, Count de Noir
2. The Relics of the Lesser Mughals – P.K. Dutta
3. Ain-i-Akbari – Abu'l Fazl Allami; translated by Blochman
4. History of Jahangir – Beni Prasad
5. The Mughal Throne – Abraham Eraly
6. Nobility under Akbar and Jahangir – Afzal Husain
7. Tabakat-i-Akbari – Nizamuddin Ahmad Bakhshi
8. The Great Mughals and their India – Dirk Colliers
9. The Mughal Empire – J.F. Richards
10. History of Mughal India – Satish Chandra
11. The Central Structure of the Mughal India – Ibn Hasan
12. The Great Mughals – Bamber Gascoigne
13. Muntakhab Ut Tawarikh – Al' Badauni; Vol. 1,2 and 3
14. Jahangir's India – Paelseart
15. Akbar – Rahul Sanskritayan
16. Maathir-Ul-Umara – Vol. 1 and 2 – Nawab Shams Ud Daula Shah Nawaz Khan
17. Mughal Durbar ke Sarkar – in 5 volumes – originally written by Abdur Razzak Khwafi.

18. The History Of Jahangir – Francis Gladwin
19. Tezkereh Al Vakiat – by Jouhar Khan, ewer bearer of Emperor Humayun
20. The Jahangirnama – By Thackston
21. Shahjahanama – Munshi Devi Prasad
22. Muntakhab Al Lubab – Mohammed Hashim Khafi Khan
23. Diary of a Moghul Princess – Jahanara Begum – Daughter of Emperor Shahjahan

The above list is not exhaustive.

DURBAR-E-MUSANNIS
(About The Author)

Nniraj Srivastava hails from an illustrious family of eye surgeons (three generations!) but decided to deviate into Management to seek 'Ophthalmic relief' from studies. Being a direct descendant of Diwan Rai Gurbuksh Singhji, Diwan to the erstwhile Maharajah Chet Singh of Benares, the author revels in the majesty of royal courts, and all things martial, ceremonial and ludicrous! He blames his past life connections for his inherent interest in the Mughals, and why his narrative has so much plausible fiction in it—voices from the past?

Nniraj has a Master's in Business Administration from University Of Allahabad, and a Doctorate in Management from the University of Canterbury, England. He is also a Member of the Royal Society Of Literature, England.

Nniraj Srivastava is an All India University Boxer, accomplished bathroom singer and an intrepid yodeler. He is a versatile writer, who can write across all genres. He is a much sought after Motivational Speaker on Effective Communication, Leadership, and Lost History.